By the same author

A Very Civil War
Out of the Shadows
The Widow
The House on the Hill
Three Sisters

Dark Lantern

CAROLINE ELKINGTON

Copyright © 2020 Caroline Elkington
All rights reserved
www.carolineelkington.net

To Mum, for giving me an obsessive but dashed expensive love of reading, The Scarlet Pimpernel, Leslie Howard and Robert Donat, and imbuing me with all things mythical, mystical and legendary by osmosis.

To Dad, for being my pre-internet Search Engine, a born romantic and indefatigable cheerleader.

I miss you both every day.

To all the much-put-upon editors, test-readers and loud-squealers in the family — you know who you are. (No, not you Lyds.) And Cousin Simon for his invaluable ophthalmic guidance.

To those "children" I didn't manage to browbeat/coax/bribe into being bookish — I'd like to say I'm sorry for letting you down. (Yes, you Lyds.)

And, to cricket — for just being you.

I started writing Dark Lantern at 23 for Tess and Isobel and finally finished it some forty years later just after Mum and Dad left in 2019 — it was a rampart, a moat, a portcullis.

One

This was, without doubt, the worst day of my life. I thought it couldn't possibly get any worse.

I was mistaken.

Ice-cold rain slithered down my neck. A bullying gust of wind tugged at the hood of my cloak, lashing wet hair across my numb face. The parson's cassock billowed and flapped about his spidery legs and the wind whipped his words away, clawing angrily at the Bible in his hands and ripping the pages.

The gravediggers, with very little consideration for the grieving family, hastily lowered the coffin into the freshly dug pit, keen to get the job done as speedily as possible. My fists clenched nervously inside a thoroughly sodden fur muff and I cursed my fashionable shoes which were proving to be entirely woefully inadequate against the ferocious November squall.

Reverend Nathanial Pender nodded to my cousin Miles who, taking his cue, scraped a handful of soil from the mound beside the grave and dutifully threw it after the coffin. The wind had other ideas, snatching the dirt and hurling it back over the huddled mourners.

A gleeful snort of laughter from Cousin Lucius was clearly audible above the roar of the wind.

My aunt, Lady Louisa Polgrey, glared at him before stealing a glance at the sky above the storm-lashed church. I knew just what she was thinking and given the ridiculously theatrical setting, I could hardly find it in my heart to blame her.

Finally, the service was wisely curtailed by the parson and the grateful few turned away with deep gratitude, heads bowed, not in sorrow, but in order to keep the rain out of their faces. Like a straggle of depressed crows, they made their way along the path to their waiting carriages.

Reverend Pender smiled bleakly at me through the slanting rain and tried to usher me away with him. But I couldn't leave. Mutely, I shook my head and signalled for him to go on without me. He cast me a concerned look but turned away and tottered back towards the church, leaning hard into the wind, his duties performed, his conscience assuaged.

The carriages rattled away down the rough track to Maker Heights and Polgrey Hall.

Watching them go, I wondered what conversations the occupants would be having now they were out of earshot. With a fatalistic sigh I turned back to the grave where the gravediggers were shovelling earth like demented moles. They would not wait around unnecessarily in such bleak weather, keen to get back to their warm hearths or the local tavern.

I stepped a little closer to the edge of the gaping mouth in the earth, the smell of it raw, like freshly cut meat.

My mind seemed paralysed, overwhelmed by the events of the last few days, unable to grasp the information needed to make sense of this unfamiliar life I had returned to.

Something made me look up.

Standing beneath the spreading boughs of an old yew tree, merging with the encroaching shadows, I could just make out a figure.

Assuming him to be another gravedigger I apologised to him. He didn't move or respond. He continued to stare past me towards the grave. Thinking the noise of the storm may have drowned out my words so I tried again, a little louder.

"I'm so sorry to have kept you waiting in the rain but I'm leaving now."

He seemed to shake himself out of his preoccupation and became aware of me for the first time, "Thank you, Miss Pentreath. I have no intention of lingering either."

I realised my mistake — he was no gravedigger or local labourer.

"I thought you were here to help. Did you know — ?" I glanced back at the grave.

"Your mother? She was — " he trailed off.

I wasn't quite sure what to say. "A force of nature?" I stepped a little closer, curious to see this stranger's face. A stranger who had apparently known my mother well enough to attend her funeral. I thought I'd heard a slight musical lilt to his voice, a stranger from across the Irish Sea I guessed.

"Vida was certainly like no other." He used my mother's Christian name with ease.

I blinked at him through the rain, "We haven't met before, I'm almost certain. Are you local, sir?"

He shook his head, "Far from it. Your father and I had occasion to work together in the past. You are unmistakably a Pentreath."

"I'm sorry, should I know you?"

To my surprise, he laughed, a melancholy sound. "Indeed, you should not," he said. Then, he glanced up at the dark rolling clouds, "Let us retreat to the church porch, Miss Pentreath, where at least it will be dry." He took my arm, even though I had shown no sign of assenting, and guided me firmly across the graveyard towards the church. The porch was lit by the fitful, sombre light from the parson's hurricane lantern. As we dashed for cover, I had to wonder why this man wished to prolong our conversation in such disagreeable circumstances.

Reverend Pender appeared to be about to leave but he paused as we entered the porch. I shook out my heavy skirts and pushed bedraggled curls back under my hood before glancing up at the two men.

The parson's expression showed dismay and disapproval and had he not been a man of the cloth I would have said I'd seen a glimmer of hatred marring his usually placid face.

"Martha! What can you be thinking? Abroad on a night like this and with no chaperone? I will escort you home at once. Your family will be most anxious if you tarry too long in this filthy weather. Come, let us make haste and take the last carriage. Jenkyns has been awaiting these two hours or more and must be impatient for his supper."

"Reverend Pender, you are all goodness. I thank you but if you could just give me a moment. This gentleman says he was acquainted with my parents." I turned to the silent man in the dancing shadows. "Sir? Was there something you wished to say to me?"

The stranger stole a sidelong glance at the parson. "I was only going to offer my condolences, Miss Pentreath and suggest that if you were in need of anything, I feel honour-bound to proffer my assistance."

"Honour-bound?" I exclaimed, stiffening. "Why, I thank you, sir, for your gracious offer but I have no need to rely upon a complete stranger's reluctant generosity. My family will provide any support I may require without the need for any obligation. I shall be residing with my aunt at Polgrey Hall where I believe I shall be tolerably happy."

He said nothing for a moment as he studied my rain-drenched face.

"You truly believe you'll be happy there?"

"But of course I will!" Even to my own ears I sounded unconvinced.

"In that case, I shall leave you in Reverend Pender's care and bid you good night." A curt bow and he was striding away into the storm.

I heard the parson sigh, "Most unsuitable, Martha, indeed, *most* unsuitable. Your aunt would be scandalised if she knew you had been in that man's company! We will not mention it. I feel partly responsible. No, we shall say nothing to Lady Polgrey. If she found out you'd been anywhere near Captain Cavanagh she'd have my guts for garters!"

And he continued in similar tedious vein as we hastened through the nearly horizontal rain to the last carriage, clambered in and grumbled away down the track, the wind hammering loudly on the roof of the vehicle, causing it to rock so violently that we had to cling on to the leather straps for our own safety.

A memory came to me as I nodded absent-mindedly at the garrulous parson: an elegant, sun-filled withdrawing room in Bristol, a little knot of smiling, chattering friends, fans a'flutter, ostrich feathers gracefully trembling, someone playing a sprightly tune upon the spinet — Only a week ago, everything had been so different, so hopeful.

* * *

As we approached Polgrey Hall I could feel the old unwelcome apprehension returning to remind me that my confidence in declaring to Captain Cavanagh that all was well was nothing but misplaced bravado.

The old house looked bleak and unwelcoming, its cold, grey walls filled me with dread. The Hall was a hotchpotch of various and incongruous architectural styles ranging from the earliest parts, which had been laid down in medieval times, to the more recent addition of the north-west tower which had been added some time in the seventeenth century. The sizeable grounds, once much admired, although presently neglected, sloped down a gentle incline towards a wide swathe of woodland and far beyond, the estuary. From the preposterous tower and the west-facing windows one could watch the sun setting over the Channel. However, in this kind of tempestuous weather most present and previous occupants must have wished their predecessor had thought to select a more sheltered spot to lay the first foundation stones.

Jenkyns helped me down from the carriage and thoughtfully lent me an arm up the sweep of steps to the front door. A portal of immense proportions, constructed from planks wider than me, its main duty to intimidate anyone foolish enough to believe they might find a warm welcome behind its forbidding facade.

Jenkyns lifted the heavy iron latch and swung the door open with some difficulty as not only was it tremendously heavy but the wind was still buffeting us as though we were nothing but delicate fern fronds. I took a deep steadying breath as he stood aside and let me cross the threshold of my new home, knowing full well that my aunt would be secretly gratified to see that I looked the part of the bedraggled poor relation.

The crowning glory of the whole beautiful fiasco of a house was the Great Hall, its plaster and wood ceiling, oak-panelled walls, minstrel's gallery, elaborately tiled floor, immense stone fireplace and carved screens all from bygone eras when such a room would hold gatherings of several hundred guests with plenty of space. The furniture, from several disparate centuries, was mostly heavily ornate and impossible to move, some pieces being nearly two hundred years old and were decidedly worm-eaten in places.

A fire was burning brightly in the hearth and my relations, arguing with equal ferocity, were gathered around it drinking mulled wine. My uncle's pack of dogs lolled on the shabby Persian rug before the flames, their limbs twitching as they chased imaginary rabbits in the woods; two Irish wolfhounds, an ancient cocker spaniel, a foxhound and a small scruffy creature of indeterminate origin.

The spaniel, always a crotchety beast, sensing a possible threat, opened one eye and seeing me loitering in the shadows, growled menacingly and then gave a sharp warning bark. The other dogs took no notice, but the sudden noise cut short the humans' argument abruptly.

For an all-too brief moment there was unpromising silence as they observed the unwanted intruder shivering from cold and weariness on the edge of their privileged lives. I was aware that the rain was dripping from my black skirts onto the ancient tiles, making a small puddle where I stood motionless.

Aunt Louisa rose majestically, her expression making the weather outside appear infinitely more hospitable, "You've certainly taken your time. We've been waiting this half an hour for you to return. We've been discussing your future and trying to decide what to do for the best."

I swallowed nervously. I seemed to have a lump in my throat which was preventing speech. I was about to be ambushed. I had been secretly dreading a hostile reception, knowing that it was inevitable. I could see from their faces that I had been right to expect that Aunt Louisa would do her worst. Uncle Joshua gave me a weak smile without quite meeting my eye, then busied himself choosing another log for the fire.

Cousin Lucius looked down his beaky nose at me as though I was something caught beneath his boot heel. "You look like a drowned rat," he remarked, tapping his nails irritably against the spiralled stem of his glass.

I fumbled with the ties of my cloak with fingers so numbed with cold that the knot just became more tangled. Had I had anywhere else to go at that moment I would have turned and disappeared into the night without regret. But this was all the family I had left.

They continued to stare at me with a mixture of animosity, embarrassment, and disinterest. Cousin Rowena hid a satisfied smile behind a slender, useless hand while her younger brother, Harry, gazed vacantly into the leaping flames; I could expect no help from either quarter.

I felt completely drained, hollowed out, and emotionless, as though I was watching a performance on stage from a great distance. At this moment insensibility was far preferable to the tide of raw feelings which was only just being kept at bay by a barricade of pure stupefaction.

At the far end of the Great Hall, beyond a screen, a door opened. I felt a surge of relief as Cousin Miles strode purposefully into the room. Almost immediately his wonderfully familiar bright eyes took in the awkward situation and he let out a string of unseemly oaths. I braced myself.

"The devil take you Lucius and may you all rot in Hell! How dare you treat one of your own like a plague-ridden outcast!" He glared furiously at the silent gathering. "I would have expected better of *you* Harry, at the very least. You miserable coward." His young brother hung his head and stammered incoherently but Miles, took no notice. In full flow he crossed the hall and deftly freed me from my cloak, flinging it, along with my rain-soaked muff, onto a nearby wooden settle.

He then almost dragged me to the hearth, slapped a glass of mulled wine into my frozen hand and pushed me unceremoniously into a high-backed armchair. I had never seen him seething with so much pent-up rage and was dismayed to be the cause of such an exhibition.

Aunt Louisa's once-handsome face was marred by open and very obvious hostility directed entirely at me. It had frequently occurred to me that she might have had good reason to be envious of her beautiful and much-courted younger sister but until that moment I never appreciated the depth of her enmity nor had I fully comprehended that when she looked at me, she suffered a renewal of those long-suppressed feelings. The fact that I favoured my plain-featured father did nothing to alter her twisted view.

She turned her burning gaze upon her unfortunate spouse, "Will you say *naught* to defend us from such incivility, sir?"

Uncle Joshua spluttered and looked wildly about for assistance of any kind and when none was forthcoming could only shake his head forlornly, reminding me of an elderly donkey.

"Sir, I will not be subjected to this kind of behaviour in my own home. Is it not enough that Vida has constantly shamed us in the eyes of the world? Are we now to have a constant reminder of that dishonour?"

Humiliation and anger stained my cheeks and I stared at the floor, reluctant to argue.

"'Tis no more Martha's fault than ours. Children cannot be held to account for the actions of their parents," said Miles pointedly.

"When we are all being made to suffer for Vida's sins you may not be so eager to take her part," snapped Aunt Louisa. "When all the skeletons in our cupboard are discovered, taken out and given a good rattle, what then my impetuous son? What then?"

"Don't be so dramatic, Mother. Reverend Pender is the only one who knows why Uncle Ralph left and he will keep his own counsel of that I can assure you."

"Of course, I had forgot. He had a weakness for Vida himself, did he not?" said Rowena spitefully.

"Aunt Vida was kind to me," muttered Harry unexpectedly and everyone turned to stare in astonishment at him.

"I *beg* your pardon, Harry?" said my aunt in menacing tones and my poor young cousin blenched in terror and took refuge in silence once more.

"Oh, for God's sake Harry!" groaned Miles. "Speak up for once in your life."

"Oughtn't to have said anythin' at all," mumbled Harry with a fearful glance at his mother.

Miles gave a crack of angry laughter and I wondered how he had managed to retain his sanity growing up in this loveless environment. He had always been an affectionate boy and must have been sorely tried at times by his constantly warring relations. It had always puzzled me that he should have stayed in the family home for so long, but it wasn't hard to understand the reason now; it was as though a veil had been lifted. Harry. Poor defenceless, faint-hearted Harry. Miles stayed to stand guard over his brother and, in so doing, it seems had sacrificed his own chance at happiness.

Of all my cousins I felt closest to Miles. As children we had given one another unquestioning affection and support, discovering at an early age that we shared the same sense of humour and adventure and this had bound us together in adversity. His strength of character always came as a surprise to people who didn't know him well, his slight frame and cheerful disposition giving no clue to his inner might. A youthful face, gentle brown eyes and thatch of almost-white, blonde hair concealed hidden resources. He and Harry, both so fair, looked very much like their father in everything except height; while Lucius and Rowena favoured their mother, both raven-haired and tall, with the same sharp features. Miles and Harry could have passed for Dutch and Lucius and Rowena, Italian. They made an eye-catching foursome. Beside them I was a sparrow amongst goldfinches.

"We're all tired. Perhaps we should continue this discussion in the morning when we might be more rational," suggested Miles wearily.

"I have already made my decision," snapped his mother. "As Martha's father saw fit to shut Wild Court and dismiss the servants, we will be expected by everyone of any distinction in the district to take her in ourselves. Of course, 'tis our Christian duty to do so. However, I don't think anyone would deem it unreasonable to expect her to make a contribution to her upkeep. These are costly times, and we don't have money to burn. There are six of us in this house — and good servants are thin on the ground. I have no doubt that Mrs Talbot will be glad of the help."

Miles, who had been listening to this with increasing impatience, refused to meet my pleading gaze. "Not *unreasonable*? Do you jest, Mother? You can't possibly believe that people will applaud you for forcing your only niece into servitude! I think it is the maddest thing I have ever heard. You've surely lost your reason. Father, have you nothing to say on the matter?"

Uncle Joshua stood before the fireplace gazing into the flames with his usual distracted air. On first acquaintance he appeared to be a man of diminished intellect, his untidy aspect, unsteady gait and confused speech seeming to indicate a thoroughly confused mind. Aunt Louisa ruled both house and family with undisputed authority, seldom even acknowledging her husband's presence or taking into consideration his preferences and he had long since given up concerning himself with trifling household matters preferring to channel his energy into his menagerie of creatures, his unruly pack of dogs and stable of mettlesome thoroughbreds. Most days he could be found shambling about the estate amidst a hurly-burly of baying, muddied hounds, his wig askew and spiked with twigs and dry leaves, pockets brimful with carrots, apples, and sugar, and a faraway expression in his eyes. Most people were convinced that he was a little unbalanced although they politely labelled him an eccentric. He was, in fact, a man of very simple tastes, who, finding himself in an inescapably awkward position had, at some point, decided to take an easier route. To avoid an uncomfortable life, he severed all connection with reality, leaving behind the mere husk of a man. He had turned in on himself so completely that only his precious animals were allowed to intrude upon his self-inflicted solitude. His wife despised him, she felt cheated; having chosen a landed, titled gentleman to further her ambitions, she found that he had no desire at all to become a man of influence and belatedly she discovered she had wed a man with little social standing, no aspirations, and an apparently impaired understanding. It had devastated her.

She found herself tied inextricably to a social non-entity but after a brief period of mourning for what might have been, she turned the situation to her advantage becoming a ruthless manipulator and scheming social climber, who would stop at nothing to achieve her objectives.

"Father?" said Miles urgently.

Uncle Joshua turned to look at his son. "Beautiful woman, Vida. Sad business. Not at all the thing, y'know. D'you think this waistcoat too gaudy?" He absentmindedly stroked the black and silver embroidery stretched beyond its limits across his large paunch.

Miles made a sound of total despair and punched the back of my chair.

"Miles, I'll be just fine. Don't worry," I murmured.

"God knows what your mother and father would say if they had witnessed this fiasco!"

"I have made my decision and there's an end to it," announced Aunt Louisa in tones reserved for wayward servants.

Lucius, who had been observing the proceedings with cold indifference, rose slowly, his whole demeanour one of extreme boredom. "Well, I must say, although this has all been *vastly* entertaining, it's been a long day and I find one *can* have too much of a good thing."

Throughout our childhood Lucius and I had never seen eye to eye. He had always shown a marked dislike for me and to be frank, I had never much cared for him. He was distant and acerbic and seemed to find his younger relatives a harum-scarum bunch not worthy of his valuable consideration. Miles and I didn't care in the slightest because we had always had our own agenda and would never have sought his approval. I felt sure he would be quietly satisfied if my life at Polgrey Hall was unbearably uncomfortable as long as it didn't inconvenience him in any way.

He sauntered from the room without another word. Miles sighed with a mixture of frustration and relief.

Rowena, having relished my discomfort, could barely conceal her delight any longer, "Mama, 'tis most inconvenient sharing your lady's maid. Could not Martha take over her duties for me? You did promise me you would engage a new one when Bessie left to wed."

"I don't think that would be a good idea at all. Martha has no experience in dressing hair or any of the other skills your maid would require. 'Twould make more sense to seek a suitable local girl with the essential abilities. Do you not agree?" asked her mother tenderly.

"No. I do not," replied Rowena testily. Aunt Louis silenced her with a frown and looked at me.

"You will report to Mrs Talbot in the morning. She will find a place for you. And there will be no mention of your mother if you wish to stay under my roof, do you understand?"

As she knew, I had no other choice, so I agreed.

Having been dismissed, I threw Miles a speaking glance and made my way to the chamber I had been allocated at the back of the house; realising a little late that I had raced, without thought, up the main staircase, an unforgivable error for a servant.

Slamming the door behind me, I threw myself onto the threadbare ottoman at the end of my bed. It was hardly time to retire for the night and I realised that I hadn't eaten since that morning. I was ravenously hungry but did not dare make enquiries about a meal. Nobody had mentioned supper. My bedchamber was cold and smelt strongly of mildew and mice;

no-one had thought to light a fire for me and with a rueful sigh I supposed this was the treatment I was to expect in the future. I realised I must contemplate my prospects. I had considered at great length the possibility of returning to Bristol to stay, perhaps permanently, with my father's friends, Lady Sarah and Sir Aubrey Finch but however many times they professed to love me, I didn't think that being a perpetual houseguest was the ideal solution. Although anything was preferable to the present arrangement, I had no desire to become a burden to those I held in highest esteem.

A gentle rapping on my door awoke me from my unhappy but resigned brooding. Thankfully, it was Miles and by the way he crept into the room, I gathered he was on an unauthorised visit. The candle he carried threw eerie shadows across his face.

"Are you all right? I thought you might be hungry. Look, I've brought you something to eat. Not much. Just what I could conceal in my pockets without being rumbled." He delved into the inner recesses of his coat and brought forth a parcel wrapped in a neckerchief. I took it gratefully and found within its linen folds a slice of meat pie, some cheese and pickles, a lump of gingerbread and a rather squashed slice of quince tart. It looked like a Royal Feast to me and as my stomach grumbled, I fell upon the food with unladylike gusto.

Miles grinned. "I knew you'd at least be glad to see your supper, if not me!"

"Idiot." I said, fondly. "You'll never know what a welcome sight you are," I told him with some difficulty as my mouth was full of wonderful meat pie. "I've been sitting here feeling like a leper."

"Good God, Martha! You know if there was anything I could do to change Mother's mind, I would do it! Vida's death seems to have entirely unhinged her." He took an impatient turn about the small room, his face grimly pale in the feeble candlelight. "Sometimes, I truly cannot believe she's my mother. Don't worry though, I shall endeavour to find a solution to this intolerable business. I'll think of some way out. For both of us."

"I'd rather you didn't vex Aunt Louisa. It's bad enough that I'm in her bad books without you being persecuted for aiding and abetting me. I'm glad you're here though."

I nibbled at the last fragment of pie then wrapped up the remainder of my impromptu supper in the neckerchief and hid it away in the bottom of the cedar chest where I kept my belongings, hoping the mice wouldn't find it. Miles gave me a warm hug and then went off probably to tell Harry that he was a dolt.

I took a drink from the pitcher of water on the side table; it was a little stale, but I was beyond caring. Having washed my hands and face in the remainder, I changed into my nightclothes, climbed into the unwelcoming bed, and blew out the candle.

Waiting for sleep, my head filled with every tormenting memory and countless impractical plans for escape.

It was still raining.

* * *

I have no idea what time it was when I suddenly awoke. It was dark and I had left the curtains slightly open so that the moon, its cold blue light piercing the narrow gap, woke me. Reluctantly, I pushed back the bedcovers and tiptoed across the freezing floorboards to the window. Peering out between the curtains I saw that the rainclouds had finally gone leaving an almost clear sky of deepest inky blue. A last rag of bright cloud trailed lazily across the shining face of the moon and something, a slight movement perhaps, caught my attention in the stable yard below. I drew back into the concealing darkness of my room and watched with sleepy interest, thinking it might be a fox on the prowl. I stood there for maybe half a minute but seeing no further activity I reached up to draw the curtains. At that moment a figure emerged from the pitch-black shadows, pausing briefly to listen before vanishing into the stable block.

I would have thought little of it had the figure been less furtive. But the hair on the back of my neck prickled and I waited. Then, a few moments later, in the distance, the muffled sound of horse's hooves.

I closed the curtains and jumped back into bed. In my highly emotional state, the scene took on a sinister slant. Shivering, I tried to make sense of it but was doomed to another sleepless hour while my skittish imagination played mischievous tricks upon me.

Eventually sleep claimed me but senseless, frightening dreams made sure that I didn't sleep well.

I opened my eyes in that unsettling moment just before dawn when the darkness seems even more impenetrable. I was wondering if the dreams had woken me when I heard the distinct sounds of someone moving stealthily, along the corridor outside my room. I froze, holding my breath. Listening. Who on earth was moving about at this hour? It was too early for the servants. I was unable to resist the impulse to satisfy my curiosity, sliding silently from the now warm sheets to ease open the door a crack.

I peeked cautiously though the gap to see Miles stepping softly along the corridor still wearing his greatcoat and boots.

Miles. Dear, kind Cousin Miles. Could he have been the suspicious figure in the stable yard? What had he been up to? Surely he wasn't the kind of fellow to be finding sport with unsuitable tavern wenches, or wasting his money cockfighting? It just wasn't the Miles I knew.

There had to be a more reasonable explanation and I determined to discover the answer.

Two

The morning following my mother's funeral was, at least, cloudless, the storm having blown through, leaving the air clean and everything looking as sharp as a new pin. A lively breeze from the sea teased the uppermost branches and flecked the distant water with spindrift. Seagulls mewed plaintively as they soared, slicing through the air like ivory blades. It was the kind of brisk, invigorating day that would, in normal circumstances, have enticed me to walk along the coastal path towards Kingsand but instead I had to face a much-altered life and an uncertain future.

I pulled on a practical, brown woollen gown, without the fashionable but hampering hoops, anticipating that I would need to wear something I wouldn't mind getting stained. There was, of course, the small matter of mourning clothes to consider. My aunt had stipulated that black should, of course, be worn to the church to satisfy any gossiping locals who might see us but thereafter second mourning would be sufficient for close family and the household staff. It was patently obvious that the idea of being forced to wear black when it didn't suit her was just not going to work for Aunt Louisa. Convention be damned! She insisted that grey, lilac, or puce would be perfectly acceptable, and black arm bands for the gentlemen.

I did the best I could with my hair, twisting it into a high knot and securing it with a chestnut brown ribbon; it looked a little severe, but I quickly discovered that tending one's own hair required very long arms, several hands, and the patience of a saint.

With a feeling of quaking dread, I raced down the back stairs, having concluded that as I was expected to do servant's work, I had better become accustomed to behaving like one and conduct myself accordingly right from the start. The grand staircase was now out of bounds.

I arrived at the kitchen door breathless and not at all sure what to expect. I could hear the sounds of activity already and taking a deep breath I entered this frighteningly unfamiliar world. I was greeted by the delicious aromas of boiled ham and coffee and the earthy sweet scent of peat smoke.

The kitchens were up to date by most provincial standards, having been extensively modernised when my aunt took over the running of the household. There were two fireplaces and a stone sink into which water could be pumped from outside, a clockwork spit, and shelves and racks laden with pots and pans of shining bronze and brass. Bunches of dried herbs, hams, and strings of onions hung from the beams and two wooden trestle tables in the middle of the main room were scrubbed and ready for the day's work.

Meggie Inch, the kitchen maid, already busily about her chores, was the cheeriest of souls, with merry eyes and shiny pink cheeks. She lived nearby with her widower fisherman father and came in daily to work. I guessed she was about fifteen now, although she had gone into service at twelve, starting at Polgrey Hall as a scullery maid. Even though I had known her for most of her life, I had never had occasion to talk to her at any great length - she had always been too busy to spare the time. And here I stood, on the edge of her territory, wondering what she would think of the new arrangements and wishing I had taken the trouble to get to know her better before this uncomfortable predicament we found ourselves in.

We smiled warily at each other while I tried to think of something helpful to say.

Meggie pushed a stray lock of hair back under her cap, "We was all terrible sorry 'bout Mistress Pentreath. We be sad for'ee, Miss Martha."

"Thank you, Meggie," I replied, glad of the unexpected sympathy and the first truly welcoming smile since returning to Devon. "Has Lady Polgrey had time to tell everyone about — about my situation?"

Meggie looked embarrassed, "Well, we've not been told 'zaccly, but we knows just the same."

"It seems such an imposition — but unfortunately I have no say in the matter. I don't want to be in the way. I want to make myself useful, but I've never had the opportunity to work in a kitchen before — I'll need a great deal of guidance, I'm afraid."

"Oh, don't'ee worry thee'sen 'bout that, Miss Martha, I'll be right happy to learn'ee."

"I'd be so grateful. I'm only permitted to remain here on the condition I earn my keep. I don't doubt that at first I shall be more of a liability but I'm willing to learn. Are you preparing breakfast? Is there anything I can do to help?"

I watched anxiously as Meggie deliberated, a perplexed frown furrowing her brow. She bit her lip, completely at a loss, knowing full well that there was plenty to be done but not at all sure that it was her place to instruct me.

"It's all right. I don't mind."

She nodded decisively. "Well, if it suits'ee, I shain't grumble. You'm a mite too genteel I'm afeared. But if them's Lady Polgrey's wishes, then so be it. Mrs Talbot is like to throw a fit but 'er bark's worse than 'er bite," she said with a grin. "An' Sir Joshua?"

"My uncle has agreed the plan. In his own way," I said a trifle stiffly, hating for anyone to see just how little my relations thought of me. Meggie made disapproving noises and I tried to reassure her, but she just shrugged her plump shoulders and pulled a face, "I'm sure'ee knows best, Miss Martha."

"I'm not at all sure that I do but I shall do my very best. And, please, do you think you could call me Martha, I would much prefer it."

"If'ee thinks it be fittin', I'd be right glad to."

* * *

Relieved beyond measure to find that Meggie bore no resentment towards me, I found that I was able to discuss the chores that lay ahead with something like enthusiasm.

Meggie had already tended the fire which stayed in all night, stirring the embers and banking it up with more peat and then she showed me how to light the other one and I felt a disproportionate sense of pride in this humdrum achievement as the fire sprang into life. But before I had time to become complacent, Meggie was moving swiftly to the next task. It soon dawned on me that the appearance of a simple meal in the dining room was akin to watching a swan's effortless progress across a lake oblivious to the furiously paddling feet beneath the water.

In the not-so-distant past I had spared shamefully little thought for those instrumental in keeping the household running smoothly. I had, like many people, taken the unseen, unappreciated army of helpers entirely for granted. I would not do so again.

After overcoming my initial hesitancy, I began, rather to my surprise, to enjoy working alongside Meggie, who often sang as she toiled. When the hearthstone was hot enough, I swept it clear of ash and grit and set the bread dough she had made upon it, covered it with an iron pot and piled burning peat over the whole. Although there was a perfectly good brick oven for baking, both Meggie and Mrs Talbot were agreed that the traditional method made a tastier loaf. We then set a pail of water beside the fire to heat and while Meggie fetched butter and milk from the dairy, I sat on a low stool and roasted the precious coffee beans on the fire shovel. Next, she taught me how to make the chocolate for my aunt's first drink of the day. Having pounded the cocoa nibs and stewed them, we then boiled them in creamy milk and added eggs to thicken the mixture. Meggie poured it into a stone serving jug and put it beside the fire to keep warm.

John Pezzack arrived in a bit of a flurry, still pulling on his footman's coat and adjusting his wig. He greeted me with a sleepy smile, accepting my presence with complete composure. Meggie made tea from dried blackcurrant leaves and woodruff and under instruction I pounded the roasted coffee beans and made coffee.

It was half past eight as I sliced up the warm, freshly baked bread and a few minutes later Meggie wiped her forehead with a floury hand and beamed at me. "There now. We can have a bit t'ate dreckly."

I was savouring a slice of Meggie's bread and a dish of the blackcurrant tea when the door crashed open and the housekeeper swept majestically into the kitchen like a galleon in full sail. Here was the woman who was virtually in charge of running the entire house. Even though I had barely exchanged more than a few words with her over the years, she filled me with consternation. One could not help being intimidated by tales of her magnificence and legendary short temper. Every member of the household, family and staff, were in awe of her. She stood no nonsense from even the most elevated personage; I had even seen Aunt Louisa give in to her wishes and quailed at the unedifying prospect of having to explain the extraordinary position I found myself in.

Anne Talbot was a striking looking woman, somewhat on the masculine side; she was tall with a man's stance and stride and possessed of a pair of fiercely intelligent eyes, a positive mouth, and square jawline. She looked as though it would be an impossibility for her to utter a tentative word.

I stood rooted to the spot, my mouth opened to speak, to offer an apology, an explanation, but she silenced me by raising a large hand, rather like a Roman Emperor quelling a rabble. "Don't say a *word*. Am I to understand that they expect me to take on an inexperienced member of staff just before Christmas? With no warning? They must be *deranged*. And one who is still wet behind the ears!"

My heart sank even further into my sensible shoes. My fingers pleated my dress. "I beg your pardon, Mrs Talbot, but I was only told myself last night. I'm very willing to help wherever I can if you think you can find a place for me."

Mrs Talbot's mouth tightened into a thin, disapproving line. "Well, isn't that pretty! Work needs doing." She reached out and took my hand in hers. "Soft, white hands seen no housework. You won't last a day. I shall speak with Lady Polgrey."

"Please, Mrs Talbot, I beg you! Don't go to my aunt. If I fail at this — I have nowhere else to go." We were within walking distance of my old home, Wild Court, but until I was sure that Miles had not got himself tangled up in some situation he couldn't handle, I wanted to stay close to keep an eye on him.

Mrs Talbot shook her head. "It's highly irregular. You don't look very strong. You'd be worse than useless."

"Let me but try! I'm stronger than I look," I persisted, sensing a slight change in her viewpoint. She seemed to be sizing me up, weighing up the advantages against the disadvantages. "I *cannot* return to live at Wild Court by myself; my aunt holds the key and would not allow it."

The housekeeper twitched her white linen apron into place, "You've just buried your mother and your father… well, who knows? Seems to me that your aunt is a mite too eager to keep you quiet. I don't doubt she thought I wouldn't stand for this sort of nonsense. But I'm damned if I'll be used as a pawn in her schemes. She'll not make a fool of Anne Talbot!"

I felt a surge of hope.

She gave me a speculative glance, "As long as you don't expect to be waited on hand and foot, I expect we'll deal well enough. Though…" and here she paused for effect, "I won't be putting up with rattling tongues, understand?"

I nodded fervently, supposing she meant that if a few candles or a bottle of port went astray, it would be prudent to turn a blind eye. I was so delighted not to be thrown out that I would have agreed to anything she demanded.

She then went on to list my duties which seemed interminable. My future, bleak and lonely, . Is this all there is, I wondered, and for a moment contemplated immediate and undignified flight before sternly reminding myself that I was honour-bound to Polgrey Hall and those living beneath its mossy roof. I had set myself the task of discovering the truth behind those missing eighteen months when I had been away from my family, living in Bristol with the Finches.

Anne Talbot, I soon discovered, was a complex woman, who could not abide fools and who had no doubt that she was right in everything. The small army of servants, whilst appearing to fear her, were unstinting in their loyalty. While I worked in the kitchen, I was never to hear a bad word said against her. I felt bound to try to explain the finer details of my peculiar circumstances, but she stopped me in my tracks before I could finish, remarking in sepulchral tones, "Truth will out, and justice be done."

When asked what she meant, she told me gruffly not to heed her. I was wise enough not to press her further.

* * *

I had just started scraping clean a large, blackened cooking pot when John, the footman, came running in saying that Aunt Louisa wanted to see me immediately. I untied my greasy apron and quickly tidied my hair. As I hurried from the kitchen, I intercepted John's pitying glance which did nothing at all for my confidence but nonetheless I marched forth into the Lion's Den.

Aunt Louisa was alone in the old dining room, a depressing place at the best of times with its dark panelling, ancient mouldering tapestries, and overpoweringly musty smell. The table was already set for dinner; five places had been arranged, the silver and porcelain bright in the subdued morning light. She was sitting at the head of the table sipping coffee from a fluted cup. For a brief moment she reminded me of my mother; her morning gown of dark grey silk still covered by a gossamer wrapper, in a shade of deep rose not mentioned in the list of colours acceptable for second mourning. One might have thought her rather beautiful had it not been for her expression which brought to mind a poisonous snake I had once seen in a travelling show.

She didn't ask me to sit down so I hovered anxiously near the door ready to dart out if necessary.

"I observe that there is no place set for you at the dinner table. I have sent for John to rectify this oversight immediately. It is my express wish that everything will appear as it should. I will not tolerate any gossip about how we conduct ourselves. Servants talk. We will therefore, for appearances, all dine together from now on. You will also take breakfast with us in the Breakfast Room."

"Will not that make things awkward with the staff, Aunt Louisa?" I asked.

She put the cup back into its saucer with something of a snap. "What do I care for that? I am not interested in what *servants* think! You must realise that your future here depends entirely upon unquestioning obedience. Now that you are without immediate family, with no one to take the burden of responsibility for you, it has fallen upon us to provide for you until, that is, we can find a suitable position for you elsewhere."

"I'm not completely alone." I said defiantly.

"Oh? And how do you reason that?"

"My father. He'll come back for me. I know he will." If there was one thing certain in my upside-down life, this was it. Somewhere, deep down, was the conviction that whatever had happened, whatever might happen, my father would return to me and take me away with him.

"Your *father*?" she scoffed. "That pathetic excuse for a man? He won't come back. He was a coward and a failure as a husband and father. He couldn't face the truth. He deserted his dying wife and abandoned his only child. What a fine upstanding specimen!" She pushed her chair back and rose menacingly to her feet, "Your mother could have married for wealth and title but chose instead to marry for…*love*." She spat the word out as though it were an obscenity.

Reaching behind me, I groped for the door latch, but my fingers found nothing. Then, as suddenly as her anger had flared, it seemed to drain away, leaving her strangely subdued, her eyes dull and lifeless.

"I have an errand for you. After breakfast you will walk into the village and collect some items I have ordered from the lacemaker. And, I have a letter to be delivered to Lady Anstey at the Manor. You will wait for a reply."

"Yes, Aunt." I said feigning obedience and wondering why on earth she didn't send John to deliver the letter.

* * *

Breakfast proved to be an extremely uncomfortable time even though Miles, once again in his role of peacemaker, did his utmost to alleviate the tension by sitting between me and Lucius and carrying on a steady flow of inconsequential conversation with anyone who would listen. I kept my eyes firmly fixed upon my empty plate in the forlorn hope that I would somehow escape notice.

Lucius was regarding me from glittering eyes. I felt like a fat wood mouse cornered by Moses, the yard cat. I carefully studied the unappreciated and untasted bread and preserve before me. Miles managed to give my cold hand a surreptitious squeeze under the table, the thoughtful gesture of support imbuing me with a little courage but a glance at my aunt's face utterly destroyed any false confidence I may have been harbouring.

John had served breakfast in silence and then retired to stand like a statue at the back of the room, his eyes focused on the far wall but ears alert for anything interesting to share with the other servants.

After a prolonged and uneasy lull in the conversation, my aunt suddenly addressed her youngest son, startling him out of his usual wool-gathering daze.

"Harry! What have you got to say for yourself?"

Harry dropped his knife with a loud clatter and turned an alarming shade of grey. "I haven't — I didn't — " he floundered, nerves visibly shredded.

"Stop gabbling like a fool in Bedlam! You've obviously been misbehaving — I can see it in your face. Have you and Miles been gambling again?"

Harry slid his brother a desperate glance but Miles, who was somehow managing to remain outwardly calm, reassured him with a slight smile. "You know very well, Mama, that Harry and I have been breaking in father's new colt, *Nonpareil*. We have most certainly not had any time for gambling or other such agreeable pursuits."

A brazen lie. I tensed, knowing just how foolhardy it was to try to hoodwink Aunt Louisa. Remembering past times when he had lied to protect me from the wrath of various incensed adults, I recognised a certain blankness behind his usually expressive eyes. I knew with certainty that they had been indulging in some kind of mischief.

Harry fidgeted, staring helplessly at Miles, distressed at having failed his brother under the first volley of fire from the enemy lines. He suddenly brightened with dawning comprehension, "Yes, indeed! Training the new colt, that's what we were about! A fine animal to be sure." Miles shot him a look I at once recognised as a warning. But I knew Harry and it would take more than fiercely lowered brows to silence him once in full spate. So, taking my life in my hands, I reached out for the pitcher of hot chocolate and seemingly in my haste, knocked it flying across the table, leaving a dark brown river on the once immaculate tablecloth. I had a brief glimpse of Miles reproving Harry in a fierce undertone before John quickly inserted himself between us and began mopping and Aunt Louisa started shouting.

"Look, what you've one, you clumsy creature! Disgraceful. Get out of my sight!"

I needed no further encouragement. I ran.

* * *

Mrs Talbot and Meggie were still hard at work preparing various foods for the day's consumption but they both looked up in surprise at my hurried and undignified entrance into the kitchen.

"I take it that your audience with Lady Polgrey was not a success?" Mrs Talbot wiped her hands on her apron. "You'd better sit down before you keel over."

My knees suddenly felt very weak, so I slumped gratefully into the nearest chair. The previous few days had obviously taken a far greater toll on me than I had realised.

"'Tis no more than I expected," said the housekeeper, "Did I not say she'd be set upon and they'd make her regret ever having come back to Devon?"

Meggie nodded, "Aye, that be what'ee said, all right. 'Ee said, if they don't set on 'er and make 'er sorry she came back, my name's not Anne Talbot," she beamed, "Which it is."

Mrs Talbot handed me a dish of sweetly scented herb tea, "Drink this… 'twill soothe your nerves. Let me give you some advice, Miss Martha. Bide thy time and do just as they say. Don't give them cause to notice you and don't ask questions and maybe you'll get by."

I sipped my tea and mournfully considered all the warnings careering my way. It seemed that everything I did, or didn't do, brought a whole new cluster of dire predictions. Everybody seemed to need me to be the soul of discretion, a quality my father had possessed in abundance but which I would not have counted amongst one of my attributes. Discretion in all things seemed to be my licence to stay at Polgrey Hall. I thanked Providence that I, at the very least, had his ability to contain anger and frustration, to face the displeasure of others with a show of impassivity. It was, I supposed, a form of defence against an unforgiving world and its unbridled emotions.

Looking back with clear sight I could see that an unfortunate lack of prudence had been an aspect of my mother's character I had hitherto failed to acknowledge. I remembered how my father had often seemed distressed by her unguarded behaviour; she had been inclined to gamble recklessly at the tables, squandering a small fortune on the turn of a card; and win or lose, she would gaily laugh, immediately forgetting any losses. Or if she had the good fortune to win every so often, those winnings were never long in her reticule. I had heard my father admonish her for courting financial ruin, but his disapproval would be smoothed away with a kiss and a devastating smile.

Remembering my aunt's instructions, I asked for directions to the lacemaker's cottage.

Mrs Talbot exchanged a speaking glance with Meggie. "Ah, that would be the *new* lacemaker, I expect." She pursed her lips, "Katherine Fry died last spring. Of the brain fever, so they say. I think it was more likely the drink. Still, she was ninety, if she was a day. This new girl came, when was it Meggie? Last July, I believe. Moved into that terrible old place on the edge of the village. Roof almost falling in. Water in the well gone sour." Another glance at Meggie. "Water's fine now though," she said with obvious satisfaction. "Course, we know *why*," she added, and Meggie shuddered from a mixture of nameless horror and sheer delight.

"I don't understand. What is so strange about that? It sounds very fortunate to me." I asked them.

"Fortunate, indeed, Miss Martha, fortunate indeed," uttered the housekeeper portentously. "But never you mind now, it's no concern of yours. You'd best be off. There's bad weather coming, you mark my words. Do you want the cart brought round?"

"No, thank you, I think I shall walk. I could do with the air."

"A fine idea. I'll send John for coin enough to pay for the lace. You'll need your warmest cloak and some stout boots."

By the time John had returned with a small drawstring purse containing a sample of the lace that Aunt Louisa required and a few coins, I had found my cloak and it was almost midday.

I pulled up my hood against the biting wind and set off briskly. The dainty boots Lady Sarah had bought for me in Bristol were more suitable for perambulating about a well-paved town than navigating the muddy and rutted lane below the Hall, but they did possess a pair of very beautiful silver buckles which had pleased me greatly. I was glad to be free of the house and everyone in it but being unused to strenuous exertion of any kind, I found the first part of the walk extremely hard with the wind in my face and the mud so deep it threatened to swallow my darling little boots whole. My skirt and petticoats were soon sodden and sticking to my legs and it was a struggle to keep my cloak on, the wind tugged at it so greedily.

The lane turned into a track then dwindled into little more than a path for sheep. When I reached the hills overlooking Cawsand Bay I stopped to catch my breath and savour this brief moment of freedom. I could see right out over the wrinkled pewter sea towards where Eddystone Lighthouse guarded the coast.

Moving along smartly some half a mile off the shoreline was a lugger leaning a fair way into the breeze, her sails filled to capacity. I turned away to follow the path across Minadew Brakes and up Blackendown Hill which rose above the twin villages of Cawsand and Kingsand. As I turned down the hill towards Kingsand I caught sight of unusually dainty hoof prints on the bank, in the shelter of a stunted windblown tree. Too small to have been made by horses and definitely not deer, I briefly wondered what had made them. My attention, however, was not long held because I was determined to race through my onerous task so that I would have a little time to spare before returning to the Hall. I planned to walk along the beach and look for shells.

When I found the lacemaker's cottage it was even worse than I could have imagined; a tiny, tumbledown place built from fieldstone and old rotting timbers. It was thickly cloaked in ivy that was in the process of engulfing it entirely. It looked dark and neglected. It was isolated, pushed beyond the boundary of the village as though the occupant could not be tolerated by its grand neighbours. I approached it with caution, Mrs Talbot's words fresh in my ears. I knocked and waited.

I had no idea what I'd been expecting but I'd never imagined the lacemaker to be anything like the vision who opened the door to me. I introduced myself and explained my mission.

She invited me to step inside, her voice as surprising as her looks.

She introduced herself as Eleanor Fairchild in a pleasingly musical voice.

"What a perfectly lovely name." I told her, thinking how well it suited her. She reminded me of a snowdrop, frail and fine-boned with large limpid blue eyes and a mouth of child-like sweetness. I showed her the lace sample and watched curiously as she sorted through various bundles looking for a length to match. Eventually she found what she was looking for and spread it out on the table for me to examine. The work was exquisite, as intricate and delicate as frost caught on a cobweb. I had never seen its like and told her so. It was hard to imagine it having been fashioned by a mortal's hand. I studied her face again and decided there was a chance she had faerie blood in her veins. No wonder Meggie and Mrs Talbot were beguiled by the whispered rumours.

I folded up the lace. "This seems to be an exact match. My aunt will be delighted, I am sure." Eleanor Fairchild's face lit up with a smile that was like the sun coming out in the sparse, dismal little room. "I understand from our housekeeper that you haven't been here for very long. Do you like the village?", I asked conversationally.

She turned her head away quickly but not before I had seen the look in her eyes. "Benjamin, my brother, is in the Navy. He wants me to stay here until he returns. He's due back in a few weeks. He'll want to go back to London, I expect."

I noticed that she hadn't said anything about the village but decided not to press her on the matter. "London? I've never been to London," I said, intrigued. "I've heard it's a wonderful place, full of poets and writers and philosophers. You are very fortunate to have lived there."

"It may be wonderful, if you are wealthy but it's also a heartless city if you are poor and without friends. The streets are unspeakably filthy and it's not safe to walk even when accompanied. There are pickpockets and cutthroats and all kinds of ne'er-do-wells. I was so relieved when Ben said I was to join him here. I thought it would be different."

"You disappoint me! My mother adored London. She would much rather have lived there than here where nothing ever happens. She told me stories of how the streets sparkled like diamonds and the inhabitants were all so sweetly perfumed. The theatres and the opera and the ballet. The fashionable soirées and balls. She made it sound heavenly."

"I think it depends who you are and where you live. For the poor it is a desperate place to be. I thought I would find a new life in the country but in many ways it's just the same." She closed her eyes as though to block out a distasteful memory.

"In what ways?"

She smiled sadly, "It's all the fault of the well in my garden. They think I cast a spell on it to make the water drinkable again. Nonsensical, of course, there was nothing wrong with it in the first place. Now they're saying I'm a witch. I don't even *look* like a witch, do I?"

"It's quite absurd." I agreed, ashamed that I too had been thinking along the same lines. "Do they make your life very difficult?"

"I can bear it. They dare not go too far for fear of my brother - he has quite a reputation locally. And they still buy my lace, so at least I can afford to feed myself and keep this —," a wry smile, "roof over my head. As long as I keep to myself, they leave me alone."

"But why do you stay if you're so unhappy here? Your brother surely would not wish you to be so wretched."

"I have a reason," she said quietly.

"If you could tell me, perhaps I might be able to help?" I realised too late how presumptuous it was to assume I would be able to offer assistance when I was trapped in a nightmare of my own. I felt strangely drawn to her and could see that she was very much alone in the world and vulnerable. I wondered what her brother could be thinking, leaving her to fend for herself, when it was obvious, she needed to be guarded and cherished. "I don't mean to pry especially on such short acquaintance, but I can't help feeling we're in the same boat."

She smiled gently as though she didn't think our situations could be at all alike but was willing to humour me.

"Yes, I think I know what you mean. I heard of your sad loss. I saw your mother once — she rode by one day last spring. I'll never forget the way she looked, in her scarlet riding habit - she smiled at me and I couldn't believe anyone could be that beautiful. You must miss her very much."

I couldn't reply; my throat had contracted as though gripped by an unseen hand. I could see her as clearly as if she stood before me, resplendent in that outrageous riding habit, which my father had secretly hated, a jaunty tricorne perched on her raven's wing hair, a secret smile on her deeply red lips and not a care in the world. She could have been in the room with us, her fragrance filled the air, and I could hear her wonderful laughter; my skin prickled with gooseflesh and I shivered.

"Miss Pentreath? I'm sorry, perhaps I shouldn't have mentioned — "

"No, 'tis nothing. Truly." I rubbed my eyes to rid them of the ghosts and schooled my face into a smile. "You see, no one talks about her. It's as though she's just disappeared, and only I remember her as she really was. My aunt… hated her. And you just conjured up such a potent image of her I could have almost reached out and touched her. She was here with us." I looked around as though I might still find her in the shadows but there was nothing but a few items of simple, roughly hewn furniture and the trappings of lacemaking. I suddenly felt her loss so painfully that it was like a blow to the body. Eleanor Fairchild reached out and laid a sympathetic hand on my arm. Again, I found a smile from somewhere, "It's not real to me yet. I just need some time to assimilate — I'm sorry, I really must be on my way, I have yet to call at the Manor. How much for the lace, please?"

She mentioned a sum I considered too paltry, but I nevertheless counted out the coins and placed them on the table amongst the tools of her trade: the lacemaker's pillow, the threads and bobbins made from sheep's trotters and the pins of fish bone.

She came with me to the door. "If you are ever this way again, I would be pleased if you would call in, Miss Pentreath, " she said in a rush.

"Oh, how lovely!" I replied, delighted, "Please call me Martha. I feel sure we are destined to become firm friends."

"I do too — Martha."

"'Til we meet again." And I set off for The Manor feeling far more carefree.

Before I had crested the headland, Eleanor's evocation of my mother began to press down on me anew.

Three

I dashed through the outskirts of the village seeing neither houses nor those people who remembered me and called out a greeting. I was running from the vivid image of my mother that had become trapped in my head and couldn't understand why I should be so afraid of that radiant vision when I should have welcomed it. By the time I reached the gates to The Manor, I was gasping for breath and my knees were shaking.

"For heaven's sake Martha Pentreath, pull yourself together," I berated myself. I deliberately turned my thoughts to the task ahead and thinking of Lady Anstey drove all else from my head.

Amelia Marchant had only recently become the wife of the elderly and extremely wealthy Lord Henry Anstey, his first wife having died two years before in an unfortunate and uncharacteristically careless hunting accident. Miss Marchant, a close friend of the Anstey family for many years, had been conveniently on hand to give comfort and make herself indispensable. It was felt by the local gossips that, for the sake of common decency, the second marriage had come a little too hard on the heels of the first. The interloper was considered in general to be a "flighty piece". The present Lady Anstey was an intimate friend of my aunt's, and I had the uncomfortable thought that when they put their heads together it usually bode ill for some poor soul and I surmised that the letter I carried would probably contain mischief of one sort or another. I hoped grimly that it wasn't about me. The audacious idea of somehow losing the letter only lasted long enough for me to imagine the wrath this might incur.

I recalled meeting Lady Anstey, when she was just plain Amelia Marchant, at a summer ball when I, wearing my first real ballgown of jade green silk and feeling quite pleased with myself, overheard her talking about me in a derogatory fashion to her companions. Even now I couldn't think about it without my cheeks burning. I never told anyone, hoping that one day, I would be able to forget the sound of their unkind laughter as they compared my homely appearance to that of my effortlessly glamorous mother. As I continued on leaden feet, I fervently hoped no one would be at home.

Through the high, arched gates up the long, imposing driveway to the front of the newly built Manor house, which had so outraged the district. It was built in the new classical style, symmetrical and very modern and, had it been anyone else's home, I would have let myself admire the understated elegance, the graceful proportions, but as it was, I was unable to appreciate its finer points as I considered which of the many entrances I should approach. A discreet enquiry at the kitchen door or a full-frontal attack? A surge of bravado decided me on the latter course — after all I was bearing a missive from my Aunt, not delivering goods to the kitchen. I pulled the bell and listened to its muffled announcement deep within the house.

The vastly superior footman who opened the door was quick to let me know that Lady Anstey never accepted unexpected visits from unknown persons as his eyes lingered on my clothes. And that muddied servants should apply themselves to the *rear* of the house. I assured him as politely as I could that I had a letter to deliver to Lady Anstey and that there was not the remotest chance that I would hand such an important and personal missive over to a mere footman.

He sniffed balefully but I could see my resoluteness had made an impression. While I still had the upper hand, I demanded to be allowed to enter so that I could surrender the letter to someone in authority.

He quivered slightly but let me pass. I didn't have long to wait until the butler marched into view. He, however, proved even more uncooperative than the affronted footman. He didn't seem to understand that although I had refused to give the letter to the footman, I was perfectly content to trust it to an imposing personage such as himself. He would not hear of it and refused point-blank to take the letter from me. I became quite exasperated, but he was unbending, so I was forced to give in, albeit rather ungracefully. He guided me up the sweeping staircase, along a beautifully decorated corridor, at the end of which was a large withdrawing room. The butler opened the door and announced me in booming accents. I wanted to shush him.

"Miss — Pentreath, m'lady."

"Miss *who*, Biddick?" demanded a petulant voice that I recognised as Lady Anstey.

I stepped into the room, feeling like I was a fly stupidly steering a direct course towards a spider's web.

It was an elegant spider's web, furnished in the latest fashion, painted and gilded, with velvet curtains and an embroidered carpet. Lady Anstey, the very picture of style and grace in pink and white, was ensconced on a pale grey settee in the centre of the room. She brought to mind a porcelain shepherdess, with a face of almost angel-like sweetness and an abundance of glinting corn-gold curls. Her silk morning gown was, I considered primly, rather vulgar, every inch of it trimmed with silver bows and waterfalls of lace. Her décolletage was alarmingly revealing, and I quickly averted my eyes to look about me with a kind of terrified fascination and saw, to my horror, the others in the room.

Beside the fireplace stood someone I immediately dismissed as being not worth of my attention — a ridiculous popinjay. A slave to the very worst of fashion's outlandish designs. His painted face little more than a mask beneath an elaborate white wig; his coat of lilac satin heavily embellished with embroidered flowers and sporting lace in such quantity it would have left Eleanor Fairchild agog. A half-witted, mutton-headed fool. He took a pinch of snuff from an ornately enamelled box, sneezed twice and wafted a lace-edged handkerchief across his face.

On the other side of the room, a man and a woman sat together on the window seat. The man, who was turned away from me, twisted around to view me from his one good eye, which was such a pale blue, it looked like ice; the other eye was hidden by a grey silk eyepatch. I had an unsettling image of him as a small boy, glassy-eyed and still-faced, pulling the wings from hapless butterflies. I shuddered inwardly, hoping our paths would never cross again.

His companion, a stout woman, of late middle age, with orange hair and a crabbed and painted face was picking sweetmeats from a long-stemmed glass dish. Her eyes were so dark they were almost black as though she were under the influence of some kind of opiate.

For a moment there was silence, then the Vision in Lilac raised his quizzing glass and surveyed me disdainfully.

"'Melia, m'treasure, had no notion you was providin' entertainment for us this afternoon! How very rusticated it is. Let me hazard a guess! No, don't tell me! This is vastly entertainin'! It's a songbird, ain't it?" He made patterns in the air with his quizzing glass. "On the other hand, of course, it could be a dancer. Need to see an ankle to be really certain, y'know."

With flaming cheeks, I ignored his remarks and addressed Lady Anstey who was enjoying the repartee, "I apologise for intruding, m'lady but Lady Polgrey instructed me to deliver this letter to you."

She imperiously beckoned me towards her, snatched the letter from my hand and tore it open. As she read it, I retreated while she made little grunts of satisfaction and amusement, nodding and smiling to herself, evidently gratified by the contents. At one point she glanced up at me and actually snorted with laughter. I stuck my chin in the air and stared out of the window affecting what I hoped was an air of deep and unruffled serenity. I was disconcerted when the Vision moved away from the fireplace where he'd been posturing and came to stand just in front of me, his eyeglass raised to examine me in detail.

"Been thinkin', Amelia, my love. She ain't no dancer. Too plump by half. No, almost sure of it. Must be a linnet." He prodded my arm with his eyeglass. "Are you goin' to sing for us then? Demme if I couldn't do with my spirits bein' raised. Country livin' ain't for the faint-hearted, eh?"

I felt sure I must be scarlet from head to toe. I could feel their merciless eyes upon me like pins sticking into my skin.

The red head laughed, "Why, Sir Montagu, she can barely talk let alone sing!"

There was a murmur of amusement and Sir Montagu prodded me again. "What d'you say to that, then?"

A sudden wave of fury swamped me, and my head came back up with a jerk; I glared, meeting his eye for the first time, and suffered a jolt of surprise when I discovered I was being viewed with what appeared to be thoughtful amusement. I must have stared for rather too long for he raised a painted eyebrow and aped my transfixed expression.

"Faith," he said archly, "I do believe there's a smidgeon of hawk in this little songbird."

The redhead roared with unseemly laughter, "No, Monty, 'tis surely just a sparrow. So dull and brown. Have you ever seen anything so provincial, so *lacklustre?*"

"Oh, do be quiet, Hester! How am I expected to think clearly with all this commotion?" Lady Anstey had been attempting to pen a response to the letter which she now waved in the air to restore order. To my surprise and relief, they fell silent and Sir Montagu returned to his place before the fire and resumed his pose. The woman called Hester helped herself to another comfit and noisily devoured it.

The man with the eyepatch had said nothing during this exchange but I couldn't help feeling he had been watching us with the kind of undisguised interest that chilled me. Of all those in the room, he was the one I disliked most, even though he hadn't said a word.

At last, Lady Anstey finished her reply with a flourish and rising from the couch she opened a bureau and found paper to fold it in and sealing wax. She dripped wax onto the paper and pressed her seal into it with a sigh of satisfaction. She held out the letter to me so that I was forced to cross the room again to receive it.

"You will not be tempted to read this, will you?" she asked in menacing tones.

"No, of *course* not, m'lady." I replied, in a tone that made me bite my lip.

"La! The little songbird is vexed!", cried Sir Montagu, waving his handkerchief in the air and looking quite absurd. I gave him a look of utter contempt, thanked her ladyship, performed an exaggerated and clumsy curtsy and, clinging desperately to my dignity, hastened from the room. Their raucous laughter followed me as I sped down the stairs and let myself out of the front door.

* * *

The beach at Sandways called so enticingly to me that I ignored the warning voices in my head and took the detour down the hill towards the familiar rocky shoreline. I'll just stay a moment, I told myself. I made my way along the cliff path towards Warn Sandway, a favourite beach of my father's and not very far from Polgrey Hall. I knew I could reach the beach with very little effort. It was exhilarating being up there above the purple and grey sea; I felt as though the salty wildness of the place would make me clean again after my encounter with Lady Anstey and her repulsive cohorts. Even though the landscape was clad in drab winter colours, there was still something which was a soothing balm to my subdued spirits. I could taste the sea salt on my lips and felt the brisk wind tightening my face.

I battled along against the churlish headwind and had to hold on hard to my cloak. Aware of the dangers, I was careful not to lose my footing, slowly easing my way down between the rocks. I hadn't been there for nigh on two years and, filled with childish excitement, I slipped and slithered, eager to get to the water's edge. I clambered over the dark rocks careless of the cost to my clothes and shoes and jumped onto the sand with a triumphant and most unladylike squeal of delight. Despite the cold wind coming in from the sea, I kicked off my shoes and rid myself of my stockings, thrilling to the feel of the coarse, wet sand between my toes. I kilted up my skirts, revealing a pair of unexceptional, sturdy legs and ran down to the water.

I lost track of how long I spent dancing along in the shallows, my feet and legs bright pink from the cold. I collected a few shells and inspected the flotsam and jetsam bobbing in the foaming waves. I found all manner of creatures amongst the rocks and pestered the tiny green crabs which hid in the crevices and under the seaweed. Immersed in the memories of childhood I was oblivious to the deepening shadows. Idyllic times spent with my father, Miles and Harry, and sometimes even Rowena, before she lost her childish enthusiasm and fell under the malevolent and corruptive influence of her mother. All other thoughts were blotted from my mind and I paid no heed to the darkening sky.

A gull let out a particularly piercing cry just above my head, as it swooped down from the top of the low cliff. I looked up and to my dismay saw that the light had faded dramatically. I sprang to my feet, snatched up my shoes and stockings and ran. Across the black, slippery rocks I scrambled, finding it almost impossible to find a purchase in my bare feet. In my haste I dropped a shoe and had to stop to retrieve it from where it had become wedged in a crevice in the rocks. It took me several minutes to prise it out and by the time I had, I was weeping with rage and frustration, furious that I had allowed myself to be lulled into thinking I had all the time in the world for dallying on the beach, dreaming the time away like a little girl with nothing better to do.

I had nearly reached the base of the shallow cliff, when my right foot slipped down a split in the rock and my ankle twisted sharply. For a moment the pain was so agonising I was afraid

I was going to faint. I fell heavily to my knees and was unable to do more than remain on all fours for several minutes until the waves of nausea abated. Another few minutes passed before I could bring myself to try to move at all. Eventually, I was able to raise myself into a position where I could pull my injured foot free, easing it out of its narrow prison. I closed my eyes against the pain. I was shivering with cold, my hands numb and the tips of my fingers turning white. The wind was heavy with sea spray now and I knew I'd have to attempt to stand before very long because my clothes were already damp, and the shivering was getting worse. I tried to lever myself up onto my haunches, but each time was forced to give up because the pain took my breath away. I don't remember how long it took before I finally managed it. It started to drizzle as I crawled slowly over the rocks like a broken crab.

I knew that my prolonged absence would have been noticed but had no illusions that they would send anyone to search for me; they'd just think I'd been detained at the Anstey's.

After I'd dragged myself closer to the cliff, I heaved myself up onto a flat rock to have a rest. I wondered if there was an easier way to get to the top or if there was any point in calling for help. My ankle was swelling, and I knew I'd never be able to squeeze my shoe back on. The drizzle turned rapidly to rain and the sky was overcast with leaden clouds. I couldn't think clearly anymore, my tears mingling with the rain on my frozen cheeks. I had just come to the conclusion that I might never leave that place alive when someone spoke.

"Feeling sorry for yourself?"

Startled, I looked around. Standing beside me, his back to the wind, was the dark-haired Irishman I'd spoken to after my mother's funeral. I stared helplessly up at him, unable to make sense of his sudden and unexpected appearance. Something stirred uneasily at the back of my pain-filled mind.

"You've picked some oddly inclement weather to sit and admire the view," he said, the sea-mist swirling about his dark head. I was still struggling with my tired and uncooperative brain. I sniffed miserably, wishing I could think of something to say that would make sense. His face was as colourless as the mist, like the ghostly victim of a shipwreck with seaweed for hair, his cloak swirling as if swept by the currents —

"Damnation!" I heard him exclaim from far, far away. "What madness is this?"

And then everything became hazy as the sea mist filled my head and I fainted for the first time in my life.

* * *

Light returned slowly to my comfortable, comatose world, seeping into the darkest corners so gradually, that it was like dawn breaking inside my head. I became aware of pain. A dull, throbbing ache. It took me a few moments to work out that it came from my right ankle. There were other aches, but I wasn't able to pinpoint them exactly.

Progressively, I became aware of other sensations; of a softness beneath my sluggish limbs, an unpleasant smell in the air and a peculiar rocking motion as though I were in a cradle. It was such an unfamiliar combination that I made a concerted effort to surface from the gloom.

As I forced my eyes open, I quickly realised it would have been wiser to have remained insensible in the blackness, for the pain and the peculiar smell and the rocking motion all combined forces and I was overcome with nausea. I groaned feebly and raised a trembling hand to my mouth.

From somewhere nearby a young voice exclaimed, "Aha! Look, Cap'n! She's woke up! An' what's more she's goin' to cast up 'er accounts."

Someone laughed quietly, a none too pleasing sound, although I couldn't fathom why it discomfited me. "I believe you're right, Jeckie. You'd best give me a hand. With your overabundance of sisters, I'm sure you'll prove far more capable than I at ministering to the wretched creature."

"Oh, yus, Cap'n, them's allus bein' sick. That's girls fer you," he added, with a measure of brotherly affection.

"Stop your damned chattering and fetch that bowl and be quick about it! She's about to disgrace herself." An earthenware bowl was brought just in time. It was some while later when I heard Jeckie say, "Y'know, Cap'n, she may *nivver* get 'er sea-legs. Some doesn't. She might be sick *every* bloomin' day. Fancy *that*."

"I'd much rather not, thank you. And I'm loath to disappoint you but she'll not be staying long enough for us to find out whether she'd make a sailor or not. I think she probably hit her head on the rocks which would explain her being so — peculiar. However, while she's here, she'll have the very best of nursemaids in you, you young scoundrel," replied the other, in a voice which seemed to strike a chord in my fuddled brain.

I sensed someone leaning over me and cautiously opened my eyes again. A face floated into view; it was blurry around the edges, but I knew I'd never seen it before. It belonged to someone young, with high cheekbones and taut sallow skin. I guessed him to be about twelve or thirteen. He wore his dark blonde hair tied back into a sailor's pigtail, his ears stuck out like jug handles and his teeth were very crooked, one at the front was chipped. He was grinning.

"Are you goin' to be sick again, Missus, 'cos if you are, I'd like fair warnin'." He looked away, "Can't stand it meself… 'ad enough of it at 'ome."

"I do assure you that I am now quite well, thank you. I apologise for any inconvenience I may have caused by being so —indisposed," I said, my voice little more than a croak.

"D'you 'ear that, Cap'n? I think she's gone an' swallowed a bloomin' book! I'm damned if I can understan' a flamin' word of it. Anuvver toff. Just what we needs! She ought'a learn to talk so's folk can understan' what she says."

"Am I on a boat?" I asked the garrulous boy and he cackled loudly and turned to his companion.

"Is she on a boat! Makes you wonder dunnit!" He looked back at me. "Course you're on a boat. Cap'n found you while we wus searchin' the cliffs fer… anyway, 'e brought you aboard an' we bin lookin' after you while you wus…"

"Jeckie!" interrupted the Captain coldly. "That's more than enough. Spare me any more of your prattle."

The boy looked disappointed then shot me a quick grin. "It wus 'orrible," he muttered. I turned my head, and another face was there. I caught by breath.

"You!" Consciousness flooded back and I made a clumsy attempt to sit up. The object of my disquiet put out a hand and without apparent effort held me back against the improvised sailcloth pillow. "I'd be inclined to remain still, if I were you. You don't want to — er —upset yourself again."

The light in the pokey little cabin, if one could call it that, was poor but I couldn't mistake the brogue. The Irishman. "I don't understand. What are you doing here?"

"It be 'is rig you be on, Missus," said Jeckie puffing out his skinny chest with pride.

"His rig? I don't understand."

"There's really nothing to understand," said the Irishman. I looked from him to Jeckie, who in turn was watching his captain, his wide mouth clamped firmly shut, as though to barricade an avalanche of words. His bright eyes were alive with untold secrets. He was longing to boast - I could see it in his mischievous face.

"Who — *what* are you?" I demanded hoarsely.

The Irishman sketched a slightly ironic bow, the ghost of a smile playing on his lips. "Liam Cavanagh. Irish by birth, adventurer by nature. Jack-of-all-trades but, at present, madam, pirate and smuggler." The man was utterly shameless. I wasn't so much scandalised by his appalling occupation as by his brazen disclosure. To just state that he was a murderous brigand as though he was admitting to being a parson or a clerk! Outrageous.

Jeckie crowed with boyish delight. "'E's the most afeared on all the high seas, ain't that so, Cap'n? They don't call 'im the Sea Wolf for nothin', y'know."

"Jeckie," admonished the smuggler captain. "I'll thank you to keep a hold on that clacking tongue of yours. I won't tell you again."

I struggled to find words to express my feelings. "Pirates and smugglers? Mighty pretty words for murderers and traitors. You betray your country for personal gain. You should be ashamed but instead you parade your occupation as though it should be commended. 'Tis unbelievable."

He seemed about to say something then paused, gave me a look I didn't understand and turning away, ordered Jeckie back on deck.

"Oh ho!" said Jeckie, wagging a bony finger, "Takin' h'umbrage, are we?" He moved quickly out of his captain's range, "Smugglers we be, like it or not. Pay no mind to petticoats, them's all the same; they'd make us all parsons if they 'ad their way!" And having had the final word he ducked out of the door as though anticipating a sharp clout from his beloved captain and I heard him running lightly out onto the deck.

There followed a strained silence in the cramped and dingy cabin while I fought the urge to berate my rescuer further.

"I want to go home," I managed eventually. He didn't respond but continued to regard me thoughtfully. I stirred restlessly, "I *said*, I want to go home now, *Captain* Cavanagh. My family will be anxious about me."

"Will they?" he murmured, as though he thought it highly unlikely.

"They'll probably be searching for me already." I told him as crossly as I could, given my doubts.

"You could be right," he agreed. But I knew the truth. It wouldn't bother them, in the slightest, if I disappeared for ever, leaving no trace. Miles was the only one who might send out a search party, but he was preoccupied at the moment with his own problems. I sank back in despair.

Then a thought suddenly occurred to me, "The housekeeper will send someone to look for me. They'll have missed me in the kitchens."

A shutter came down across his face and it became as cold and blank as moorland mist. "No-one will look for you," he said, and his words overwhelmed me.

"I want to go home," I said quietly.

"You consider Polgrey Hall to be your home?"

I couldn't answer him. The pale, indistinct face seemed suspended over me like the moon. He was right, of course. The Hall could never be home to me because my aunt would never allow me to make it so. I would always be the poor relation to be kept in my place and made to feel unwelcome and beholden. I couldn't help thinking of Wild Court, longing to return there, even though all there would be to greet me would be empty, dusty rooms and cold ashes in the hearth. It was impossible to believe that I would never live there or be happy there again. The house was a part of me. Wild Court was my home. No other place, however grand, could ever take its place in my heart.

The hateful Liam Cavanagh was looking at me with hawk-like interest, as though he were expecting me to act in a way that was entirely familiar to him. As though he knew *exactly* how I would react. His shadowed face showed no sympathy, only an expression of such detachment that I felt a stab of fear.

"You can be taken back to the Hall whenever you feel up to the journey," he said, lifting the corner of the large frock coat covering me and briefly examining my injured ankle. I'd have withdrawn it from his probing touch, but it was too painful to move. "I believe it to be twisted, I can feel no broken bone. I will bind it tightly so that it is supported. Take care not to use it too much and it'll be good as new in a week or so. No doubt you'll be subjected to quite an inquisition when you get back; you'd better have a plausible story ready to explain away your little adventure. On no account are you to mention my part in it, do you understand?" He sounded distinctly threatening which I recklessly chose to ignore.

"I don't see why I should lie for you." I said sullenly.

His eyes narrowed and I could see why he was called the Sea Wolf. "If you should say so much as a word, you'll not have time to regret your folly."

"Are you threatening to — kill me?"

"Only if you give me cause."

"Oh, of course, I had forgot! You've murdered countless innocents during your villainous career, one more would make no odds."

"None at all."

"Well, I suppose you'd better get on with it because when I leave here, I shall not rest until you're hanged for the murdering blackguard you are!"

"Brave words, indeed, Miss Pentreath, but I think you'll find your silence will buy security for your loved ones. Most beneficial to *everyone's* health. Consider, if you will, your cousin Harry — "

I swallowed fearfully. "Harry? You wouldn't harm him! He's just a boy. He's no threat to you." My palms were slippery with sudden sweat and my stomach twisted into a terrified knot.

"There you are," said Captain Cavanagh silkily, "You begin to see my point." He moved a little closer. "'Tis not only you who will suffer should you decide not to heed my warning. Do you understand me now?" The Irish brogue was pronounced as he issued the threat.

I managed a curt nod, not trusting my voice and thought if only I had a knife or a pistol, I would cheerfully kill him.

"I was certain I could convince you."

"Arrogant brute!" I hissed. "I hate you — "

He reached out and flicked my chin just as though I were merely a headstrong child. "You may not look much like your mother but there are times when you sound uncommonly like her, y'know."

No one had ever compared me with my mother except unfavourably; I wondered what he could possibly mean but dared not ask. It also struck me forcibly that I didn't like the comparison.

"You haven't asked why you're on my boat, which in the circumstances is very restrained of you. Are you not at all curious?"

I shrugged, pretending disinterest, but he just smiled as though he could read my thoughts.

"You're on an old fishing lugger we use on occasion for retrieving cargo. It's inconspicuous. It doesn't look fast enough to be in any self-respecting smuggler's employ but is, in fact, as fleet as a greyhound. It was moored off Hooe Lake Point while I was ashore exploring possible hiding places," he told me candidly. "It's been especially adapted, of course."

"Don't tell me! I don't want to know," I exclaimed, clapping my hands over my ears. "I want nothing to do with you and your foul trade."

"I thought you had a burning desire to see me hang. You'll need evidence for that. Anyway, I found you sitting on a rock, like a land-bound mermaid and then you fainted."

"I did *not* faint. I passed out. It's not at all the same thing!"

"Fair enough. As you probably know there's not much around Sandways, so I rowed you out here, which was far easier than trudging for miles with your inert body over my shoulder. And, of course, I hardly wish to broadcast my presence and have every damned Dragoon for miles breathing down my neck. "It's stopped raining now. If you're feeling up to it, one of my men will escort you safely home."

"I don't want to be any trouble," I said.

"Bit late for that," he replied grimly and before I could say anything else, he abruptly left the cabin, leaving me to wonder what I had said.

Four

Later that evening a burly, bow-legged sailor, who introduced himself as Colquite, helped me up on deck, where I discovered the source of the unpleasant, all pervading smell: the day's catch was stowed in baskets about the deck. I was surprised to see evidence of honest toil on a boat used for smuggling but Jeckie, who had reappeared to watch my departure, explained that one would, of course, expect to find fish upon a fishing boat. So, the fish were there in case the Excise Officers took an interest in the boat.

There was no sign of the captain. Jeckie held a lantern while I was lowered, as if a crate of fish, into a small rowing boat, where I perched daintily on the damp seat and clung to the sides, as the silent Colquite took up the oars. Jeckie handed me the lantern and wished me luck and then Colquite heaved on the oars and we pulled away into the darkness.

"'Hoy there!" shouted Jeckie from the stern of the lugger, "If she turns green, Colly, throw 'er overboard an' row for y'r life!" Colquite grunted and the sound of Jeckie gleefully splitting his sides echoed over the water.

On reaching land, my companion skilfully manoeuvred the boat into the shallows just below Maker Church, where there was an easily negotiable beach and then hauled it up onto the sand with ease born of a lifetime of hard seafaring. He carried me ashore by the light of the lantern I was helpfully holding aloft and stood me carefully upon the sand and then without a word disappeared into the starless night. Presuming that he wouldn't just desert me in the middle of nowhere, I propped myself against the little boat and waited patiently for his return. It was a strange sensation being so completely alone, trapped in a tiny pool of yellow light, like a moth, with just the sound of the surf and the steady thump of my heart. I didn't have to wait for very long. He reappeared leading two sturdy ponies. With a sigh of resignation, I allowed myself to be assisted aboard one of the tiny beasts and was then led like an inexperienced child up the gentle slope towards Maker. I managed to cling on during the bumpy journey despite several attempts by the sorely tried pony to unseat me. It suddenly occurred to me that the small hoof prints I'd seen earlier on the cliff top must be those of the ponies used by smugglers.

On my instruction Colquite escorted me straight to the front entrance of the Hall. With his help, I dismounted and hopped awkwardly to the door where I thanked him for his assistance and bade him farewell.

Colquite remained unmoved, folding his arms resolutely across his broad chest.

"I'll be all right now, Mr Colquite," I said.

"Cap'n said I was to be sure you was treated right. To wait until I'd seen you *"welcomed back into the bosom of y'r devoted family"*, with me own eyes," said the sailor gruffly.

"I can assure you there is no point in your waiting because the likelihood is that Hell will freeze over before they do any such thing!"

"Cap'n said…"

"Captain Cavanagh may be master of all he surveys at sea, but he holds no sway over me or my life. He really should just mind his own business."

"I don't like it, Miss. He don't give orders lightly."

"Then don't tell him. Say you saw me safely home and leave it at that."

"Lie to the Cap'n! I couldn't never do that."

Goodness, I thought, he's actually shocked I would suggest lying to a *smuggler*. I almost laughed out loud. To be considered lawless by a seasoned criminal like Colquite was quite a compliment.

"All right let me put it this way… if my aunt were to find me in the hall in the company of — and I have no wish to offend but — a bearded outlaw with an earring and a cutlass, I believe it might make things a good deal worse than they already are. Do you see my dilemma?"

Colquite lovingly fondled the handle of the offending weapon which was tucked into his broad leather belt and looked thoughtful. "As long as you're sure, then. Though, if you'd like me to stay around for a while — just in case — "

"All right, if it makes you feel better that would be quite comforting."

He happily led the ponies off into the night, to hide in the bushes, I supposed.

The Great Hall was mercifully empty and for a moment there was complete silence. I breathed a sigh of relief to find myself safely back and wondered what to do. Then John raced helter-skelter into the room.

"Miss Martha! I thought I heard somethin'! I hoped it was'ee." He spoke quietly, distress plainly etched on his usually impassive face.

I was very aware that I must cut an alarming figure, my clothes dirty and crumpled and my hair hanging in salty tangles about my shoulders. "Is it really bad, John? Am I in for a scolding?"

He glanced warily over his shoulder, "T'ain't really my place, Miss — but — there's been a real rumpus this afternoon. All manner of commotion. When she found'ee was still not returned, ee'd have thought there'd been a *murder*! Her Ladyship said'ee was no better'n a tavern wench, if ee'll pardon me for saying so. She had the whole place searched, top to bottom, then when you still wasn't found, she said ee'd run off just like y'r father — sorry, Miss. She called'ee a viper in her bosom, or some such thing, which made Meggie cry and Master Miles jumped to 'is feet, knocking his chair right over and said, in a terrible voice, "*The only serpent in this house is the one I must call Mother.*" Well, we was right pleased he spoke up. Mrs Talbot even said'ee may have been set upon by footpads an' be lyin' in a ditch but Lady Polgrey told 'er not to be so fanciful. Master Miles said he was goin' out to look for'ee and he stormed out and slammed the door like'ee wished Lady Polgrey's head had been in it!"

I couldn't help it, I had to choke back a slightly hysterical laugh. "What happened then?"

"Well, I don't like to say, Miss," he said, averting his eyes.

"It's all right. I won't mind. Whatever it is. I must know how things stand." I smiled encouragingly.

"She said 'ee'd run off with some man and that it was no more than she'd expect, considering what your mother had done. I'm so sorry, Miss."

I gasped. "My mother? What did she mean? I don't understand."

"Nor did we, Miss," admitted John sadly.

"Where is my aunt at the moment?"

"In the library, I think."

I considered my situation for a moment. "John, did not, Nell, your mother I mean work as lady's maid at Wild Court? Yes? I thought as much. This is a delicate matter. I can trust you to be discreet?"

"More'n happy to help."

I found paper, quill and ink and quickly penned a note to Eleanor Fairchild presuming on a friendship forged barely twelve hours ago. "Would you make sure this is delivered to the lacemaker, Miss Fairchild? It's extremely urgent and no one must know."

John folded the paper and tucked it carefully away inside his coat. "I'll see to it, don't'ee worry."

Then, trying to calm the hammering in my chest, I limped off to the morning room.

* * *

I knocked on the door and didn't wait for an answer, letting myself in before I lost courage.

She was seated at the bureau in the bay window, writing. All the candles were lit, giving the room a deceptively warm and welcoming glow.

"Aunt Louisa, I am returned and am so very sorry that I was delayed so long."

She turned slowly to face me.

"'Twould have been better for you had you stayed away," she announced grimly. "Where have you been and where is the reply from Lady Anstey?"

I took out the rather damp and dog-eared letter and crumpled packet of lace, from where I had wedged them into my bodice, and put them on a small silver tray on a nearby table.

"There, all safe and sound. Mission accomplished." I sounded far too flippant. "On the way back from the Manor I remembered that I had left your purse at the lacemaker's and had to turn back to recover it. As I approached her cottage, I stumbled and turned my ankle badly. I had no choice but to remain with Miss Fairchild until transport could be arranged. She was most obliging, providing me with a hot drink and a place at her hearth, while I waited. She really couldn't have been more considerate. She was able to beg a ride for me from the miller's son."

Aunt Louisa was watching me closely. I tried to appear contrite and truthful but couldn't help swallowing guiltily as I waited for the inevitable outburst.

"If I find this is a fabrication — " she warned, "there will be hell to pay."

"You may ask Miss Fairchild to corroborate if you doubt my word." I crossed my fingers under my cloak.

"I will do just that, and if I find you have further besmirched our good name, I will deal with you myself."

More innuendo and sly remarks. It was more than I could bear after such a trying day. Something exploded inside me. "I think it is time, Aunt, that you stopped prevaricating and told me precisely what Mama is supposed to have done!"

Of all the reactions I could have anticipated, this slow, destructive smile was the least expected. I had learnt not to trust her vacillating moods and waited for the axe to fall.

"Your mother was never able to control her base desires even after she married Ralph. She was always destined to bring shame upon us. It made no odds that I warned her time and time again; she always went her own way just to spite me. She was ever the same as a child, wilful and shameless. I do not comprehend how your father tolerated her improper behaviour. Of course, 'tis what drove him away in the end, he could suffer it no longer.

I felt years of resentment welling up like flood water and knew there would be no holding the words back and that if I didn't want to be thrown out into the night, I had to remove myself before things veered out of control. I hobbled as quickly as I could to the door, probably leaving Aunt Louisa glaring after me though I didn't look back. I had to stay at Polgrey Hall, whatever the cost, if I was hoping to keep Miles and Harry safe and vindicate my father. I had to hold my tongue when I would much rather have spoken my mind.

"If you are to remain here under my roof, you had better learn to curb your hoydenish ways," snapped my aunt, as a parting shot.

I ignored her and closed the door behind me.

* * *

I limped and hopped my way to the kitchen where Mrs Talbot and Meggie were waiting impatiently. John had passed on the news of my return before taking my message to Eleanor Fairchild. The housekeeper strode across the room and propelled me into the nearest chair. She asked no questions, her lips compressed into a furious downturned horseshoe. Meggie had made me a hot posset from thickened milk, cloves and sugar and I gratefully sipped it while Mrs Talbot tended to my injury. She unwrapped the makeshift bandage the smuggler had strapped around my ankle and bound it with a poultice of moss, tutting crossly all the while.

I was unsure whether Mrs Talbot's disapproval was directed at me or her employer, or both and I was too exhausted to ask. I wondered if I should tell her about my unfortunate meeting with Captain Cavanagh but then thought it was probably best kept to myself and I couldn't help but think that if the housekeeper cared to know something, she'd probably know it before anyone else; she was that kind of woman.

I did feel obliged to apologise for being late knowing that even an inexperienced pair of hands like mine would still have been missed. I didn't want them to think I was the type of person to avoid their duties with the flimsiest of excuses. I put down my empty cup and tried to stand up, but a large hand pressed me back into the chair.

"'Tis very bruised and you looks like you could do with a good night's sleep. Meggie will fix you something to eat and then you can turn in for the night."

"That's kind of you but there must be chores still to do. Will the family be having their usual light supper? Perhaps, I could help prepare something for that?"

"Cold meats and such later on but there's no need for you to wait up. 'Tis very little work."

"I don't think I could sleep just yet. I could sit at the table and prepare the meats?" I pleaded. If I stayed up, I might get the chance to talk with Miles. I knew he would be extremely interested in my encounter with the smugglers.

Mrs Talbot gave in and allowed that I could remain for a while as long as I had a slice of goose pie to restore my stamina. I hadn't eaten anything since breakfast and was ravenous, so the goose pie was downed in a few unladylike minutes. In between bites I did what I could to help with the supper. I was slicing a side of beef when tears began to slide, almost unnoticed and certainly un-welcomed, down my cheeks.

I don't even know what started it but suspected a mixture of pain, alarm at my day's adventures, and pent-up grief. I continued chopping and slicing, unable to see what I was doing through the mist of tears and sniffing quietly. I wiped my eyes periodically with a greasy hand and tried to contain the embarrassing display lest I make a complete fool of myself. But it was like trying to hold back the ocean with a teaspoon.

I heard Meggie's muffled exclamation and then found myself enfolded in the housekeeper's muscular arms. I allowed her, because I really had no other choice, to rock me to and fro. I was hardly able to breathe but it was altogether a most soothing and almost forgotten sensation. She smelt of baking and rosemary and remembering my mother's cursory and expensively scented embraces, I was left wondering about the depth of her affection for me.

Was my memory of her as devoted mother or distant goddess? Which had been the real Vida? I recalled how, after I'd been tucked away into my bed, her gay laughter had drifted up from downstairs and I'd been lulled to sleep to the sweet sound of her playing the walnut spinet father had given her. She liked to play and sing for dinner guests and there was nothing I liked better than to lie in the dark imagining how she looked in her golden yellow evening gown; my father gazing at her with undisguised adoration. Looking back, I realised that I couldn't remember how she had looked at *him*.

When I finally emerged from Mrs Talbot's clutches, I was crushed but very much reassured by her unexpected reaction. She returned to her work without a word.

I arranged the meat on a dish and then with nothing else to do, I watched as the others added the finishing touches and carried the trays through to the Great Hall, where the family would have their light supper. I smothered a huge yawn and reluctantly admitted that I'd be better off in bed. Mrs Talbot told Meggie to give me a helping hand up to my bed chamber, which she did with her usual cheery efficiency.

I wanted to speak with Miles and even though it was late, and I was longing to close my eyes and forget the day's tribulations, I sat on the window seat, wrapped in the eiderdown and waited for them to finish supper and retire to bed.

* * *

I was still awake half an hour later when I heard Miles and Harry on their way to their rooms. I picked up my candle and hobbled as quickly as I could to open the door. The two boys were staggering along the corridor, Miles with his arm about Harry's shoulders, Harry singing a distinctly silly song.

"Miles! Miles, I need to talk to you," I called out as loudly as I dared.

Miles turned and grinned over his shoulder, "Give me a hand will you! Harry's three sheets to the wind and I can't do a thing with him."

I hobbled willingly to his aid, taking Harry's arm to guide him in the right direction.

"*Hey nonny no! Men are fool that wish to die*," sang Harry lustily. "*Is't not fine to dance and sing, when the bells of death do ring?*"

"Oh, do be quiet, Harry! You're behaving like a complete ass," said Miles, through affectionate laughter.

"*And sing hey nonny no!*" bellowed his brother cheerfully.

I met Miles's bright gaze over Harry's inebriated head. "He's lost his wig again," I chuckled.

"I know. The last I saw it, the dogs were tossing it in the air, convinced it was some kind of fuzzy vermin!" said Miles. "He's got through more wigs than those damned dogs have fleas. They must be strewn all over the county; hanging in bushes, lining bird's nests and frightening old ladies and horses."

"*Is't fine to swim in wine —* ", warbled Harry.

"I fear he's been in the tavern most of the day. Needless to say, Mother's none too pleased. For the love of God Harry! Stop that damned awful row — Martha, I'm sorry — "

"Don't be silly. You're right, Harry's singing is not one of his finest attributes. Let us confine him to his room and hope he's sober by morning."

We somehow managed to get Harry to his bedchamber although Miles had to practically carry him the last few feet because his legs gave way and he appeared to find something so wildly funny that he kept doubling over with helpless laughter, which meant it was quite a struggle to remove his coat and muddied boots.

In the end we had to tuck him into bed still partly dressed. Miles pulled the counterpane over his giggling brother and told him to be quiet. Harry beamed blearily at us over the edge of the cover. "*Men are fool to wish to die. Hey nonny no*," he intoned.

Miles sat down on the bed. "We need to talk, Harry", he said, desperately trying not to laugh. "Harry! I'm serious. Stop singing for a moment, will you?"

"I should wait until morning, he doesn't appear to be listening," I said, smothering unsuitable giggles.

"I know. It'll serve him right if he has an absolute stinker of a head in the morning. He's going to do this once too often and find himself in gaol or pressed into the Navy."

"Miles? I think I should tell you about what happened today." I confessed, suddenly reminded of the day's events.

He looked up keenly, "What have you been up to, cousin? I heard from Mother that you went missing for a while this afternoon. I was out for the day trying to persuade the labourers on the estate to do some work; Father doesn't seem interested any more, he's let it go to the dogs in the last few years and it's time someone did something about it before it's too late. Lucius doesn't give a damn, thinks it should be just left to run riot. Typical of him. Won't lift a finger unless there's something in it for him. I talked to the head keeper and it appears no wages have been paid for some time. I had thought the estate almost ran itself, but Father has dropped the reins. And, unless a great deal of money can be found pretty damned quickly, the stable hands, gardeners and gamekeepers will all leave, and I can't say I blame them. They cannot be expected to work for nothing. What am I to do?" he asked despondently.

"I had no idea things were so bad! Although, your mother did tell me she couldn't afford another mouth to feed, I'm afraid I didn't believe her."

"Mother has no clue of the depth of our debts. She still thinks it's all being taken care of. Lord knows how she'll react if I have to tell her the truth."

"What do you mean, *if* you have to tell her? Surely she'll have to know? She cannot believe your father is still capable of managing the estate?"

"She hasn't really faced up to the truth staring us all in the face; that Father is no longer able to manage anything but his animals. I'm going to do my utmost to keep the worst from her. I only hope that I can rectify things before she realises. I wish Uncle Ralph were here, he'd know what to do."

I nodded, wishing the same. My father had always been able to remain calm in a crisis. "What can be done?"

"The first thing is to convince the workers that they'll be paid in the not-too-distant future and then somehow I must raise the funds. I'm going to speak to Father's lawyers and try to reason with his creditors and if that doesn't work, I shall be forced to go cap in hand to our benefactor and hope they can suggest some scheme to bring us about."

"What if you can't raise the money, Miles? What then?"

"Then I'll have to tell Mother. I don't want to even think about it. But I'm sorry, Martha, you wanted to tell me something of your own? What kept you out so late? You're not in a fix again, are you?"

I looked into his troubled eyes and knew I couldn't burden him with thoughts of me falling into the hands of smugglers. He had enough to deal with as it was; it would serve no purpose to add to his worries.

"I had errands to run for your mother, a letter to deliver to Lady Anstey and lace to buy from Miss Fairchild in the village. It took quite a time as I had the misfortune to twist my ankle and had to wait with Miss Fairchild for suitable transport to be arranged." It was very nearly the truth, just not the whole truth.

"You should not be carting our intoxicated friend about, then." He gave me a sidelong glance I could only describe as sly. "And how did you find the new lacemaker? I understand she is considered to be something of an enchantress," he asked with a studied indifference so transparent that I couldn't help the urge to tease him a little.

"Miss Fairchild? Why, she seemed a very level-headed sort of girl and her lace is quite remarkable. I don't think I've ever seen the like. The quality of the workmanship, the delicacy of the tallies and picots, the purity…"

"Martha! I'm not interested in your opinions on her lace-making! As you are no doubt aware," he said crossly. "Did you not think she was the most exquisite creature you've ever seen?"

"She was certainly a very agreeable young woman," I said enjoying myself immensely, but I could no longer keep a straight face. "Oh, Miles, don't tell me you've fallen in love *again*?"

"Again? I've never been in love before," said my cousin sincerely.

"That's what you said the last time. Does the name Kitty Anstey ring any bells?"

"Oh, Kitty! I was never really in earnest, sweet though she is. My God, you have only to look at her stepmother to realise I could never tie myself to that family! That woman could curdle milk."

"So, you cast poor Kitty aside the very minute this new and mysterious beauty arrives upon the scene. You didn't used to be so careless with other people's affections. I think Kitty really loves you, Miles and believed her feelings were returned."

"I swear I did nought to encourage her. Doubtless she's transferred her regard elsewhere already. She is, after all, only seventeen and, like most chits her age, inclined to romantic notions."

"As I said — poor girl. I hope that you let her down gently. A sensitive girl like Kitty might be scarred for life by such a cruel blow. Rejection is hard to bear at any age but she's young and impressionable so it's quite likely to alter her outlook on life forever. Indeed, it is not unheard of for warm-hearted girls such as her, when crossed in love, to renounce men and romance altogether and enter a convent; there to waste away, pale and unloved, to expire broken-hearted — "

"No, no, you go too far, Martha! People don't actually die for love in this day and age. Only in melodramatic novels written by bitter spinsters."

"I'm not sure I agree with you, you know, there have been documented cases of people pining away entirely from unrequited love."

"Well, I've never heard of them," said Miles sceptically, "Come, on, Harry's sound asleep now. You'd better be off to bed to rest that ankle."

I agreed and after tucking the covers in around the gently snoring Harry, followed Miles from the room. He escorted me to my door. "I know there's no need to remind you that the problems with the estate are to be kept quiet for now. On no account must Mother suspect the truth or heads will start to roll," he drew a finger across his throat in a simple but effective gesture.

"Don't worry, I'll not say a word. If there's anything I can do to help you must let me know. You shouldn't have to bear the burden alone, it's not fair. I just can't see how you're going to raise the funds. It seems like an impossible task to me."

Miles smiled. "If our benefactor fails me, I have a contingency plan, but we shall wait and see." He reached out and briefly touched my cheek, "Never fear, I shall be careful. Goodnight and sleep well, dear coz," and he turned and disappeared down the dark corridor. I stood for a moment staring after him, the light from my candle casting eerie shadows on the walls. What kind of plan did he have? I was bothered by the veiled look in his usually candid eyes. It was so unlike the Miles I grew up alongside that the more I dwelt upon it the more uneasy I became.

Later, when I was on the edge of sleep, I silently prayed that he would find the strength to succeed without jeopardising his good character.

Five

Two days after my meeting with the smuggler captain, Liam Cavanagh, I was told there was to be a dinner party and I was summoned into Rowena's presence to dress her hair and help her prepare for the occasion. She was wearing a silk chemise covered by a lacy wrapper; embroidered white stockings encased her pretty legs and, on her feet, she wore dainty, high-heeled mules of embroidered kid. She was so beautiful, the kind of beauty that transfixed one and actually took one's breath away; dark almond-shaped eyes, slanting eyebrows and a curled, full mouth, inclined unfortunately to petulance, smoothly flawless skin like porcelain and a perfectly straight nose of an ideal length. I couldn't help a wave of envy, and a small wave of sorrow for the girl she had once been. She was now little more than a shadow of her overbearing mother.

I set about my task with some trepidation. Although I had been keenly aware of all the current fashions for dressing hair whilst in Bristol, I had never actually tried to recreate one myself and the prospect of having to make my debut on this particular head was daunting.

Rowena sat in front of the looking glass and handed me an ivory-backed brush. My hands were not as steady as I would have liked, and I wondered what would happen if I made a mistake. I brushed her long black hair until it shone, then teased it and curled it and pinned it into a pleasing shape, close to her head, leaving some glossy ringlets to curl artfully into the curve of her graceful neck. Afterwards, I tucked some small black silk bows into the curls above her ears and a tiny wisp of silver lace at the back, to fall over the nape of her neck. I limped back a pace to admire my handiwork and decided, with a wry smile, that I had quite missed my vocation; it looked most becoming. I held a small mirror for Rowena to see my creation and could tell she was well satisfied with the result even though she would never admit it.

I helped her into a rather muted gown of dark amber taffeta, which despite its restraint would never pass as traditional mourning dress. However, as the gathering was in private and Rowena was but a niece, I suspected it would pass muster. It was well known locally that Louisa and Vida had not exactly been close so in all probability allowances would be made accordingly. The boys were in black arm bands and black stocks and I wore brown when working as my black and grey gowns were of superior quality and not suitable for the kitchen or traipsing across Maker Heights.

I reluctantly powdered her lovely face with scented white ceruse and applied rouge to her cheeks although privately I felt it was a shame to cover up such natural beauty with obvious artifice. I carefully placed a heart shape patch beside her mouth and once she had been sprinkled liberally with Rose Water, her breath sweetened by a perfumed pastille and she had been armed with a painted fan and black kid gloves, she was finally ready to greet the guests, who were due to arrive at half past four.

As I made last minute adjustments to the lacing on her gown, which she had complained was too loose, Rowena asked if I was attending the party.

"Apparently so." I replied, pulling the laces around their hooks.

"As family or staff?" she enquired in a voice sweet as honey.

I concentrated hard on the back of her gown. "As family. I believe it's for appearance sake, nothing more." I was feeling very cynical for my age.

"Indeed?" she said, patting her hair complacently while admiring herself in the full-length looking glass. "Well, you had better be on your best behaviour. We don't want a scene like the other day. We have guests of great consequence coming tonight."

"Oh?" said I, feigning disinterest and tugging hard on the obstinate laces.

"Mother has invited Lord and Lady Anstey, of course and Kitty and Edmund. And there's Squire Tregallas and his pitiful little wife. I can't think why she's included them. He's such a crashing bore, seldom talks of anything but hunting and honestly, I think him quite mad at times. As for Letitia Tregallas, what a fright she is, touched in the attics, I'm certain of it. Oh, and those odd friends of the Ansteys who came down from London. *Such* queer folk. I believe she was on the stage, Hester Jarrett, that is, not at all the thing, I understand. I have no idea why Mama likes them so." Rowena chatted on, overcome with excitement and I kept quiet, glad to be given a clue to what the evening held for me. "Baron Rosenberg, her companion, is the famous duellist; they say he's never failed to kill his opponent and yet has still not been forced to flee the country. He must be very clever, with friends in all the highest circles. 'Tis rumoured his last mistress took poison, although" she continued, considerably put out, "they don't say why, of course. I'm quite sure it's something absolutely wicked. When he looks at me it makes me shiver," she added with undisguised delight. I had my own suspicions about the notorious Baron, whom, I had discovered from Miles, was the silent man with the eye patch I had seen at the Manor. It would be a while before I could forget his chilling demeanour, but I was wise enough not to share my feelings with Rowena as I had no wish to be tricked into an indiscretion I may later regret or accidentally encourage her in her fascination with the man.

"I should pity any poor female who might become involved with him," sighed my cousin wistfully and I had a moment's anxiety for her, which she quickly squashed with a rap of her fan across my knuckles, probably suddenly aware that she had rattled on for far too long. "Are you still not finished? Do hurry or I shall miss the first guests."

I gave the laces a final tug, tied them tightly and tucked the ends out of sight. Looking at her tiny, tortured waist, I marvelled that she could breathe at all. She turned away from the glass and there was no need to tell her that she looked positively radiant because there was no doubt she already knew.

She dismissed me with a wave of her fan. I made my way gingerly down to the kitchen wondering what Aunt Louisa had in store for me that evening. I could think of no logical reason for her to include me in this ordeal, apart from a desire to impress her guests with her boundless magnanimity.

In the kitchen I found a scene of complete and utter pandemonium, in the centre of which stood the commanding figure of Anne Talbot; all about, her maids, cooks, and the extra footmen hired for the occasion scurried to and fro like disturbed ants, intent on performing their allotted tasks come what may. Each face frowning with exertion and concentration as they arranged dishes here and added finishing touches there. The noise was deafening as they called for assistance, shouted at those who dared to hinder and bellowed for a clear path to the door. I'd never seen or heard anything like it. In the midst of this uproar Mrs Talbot, quietly but firmly in charge, kept the whole from descending into a common brawl. She was like the captain of a ship caught in the noise and destruction of a storm at sea; at any moment I expected to hear her cry, "Reef the man'sle! Batten down the hatches!"

Crowded onto the long, scrubbed trestle table were a growing number of mouth-watering dishes for the dinner party: goose pie, venison pastry, stargazey pies, shrimp, buttered crab, cheeses and various sweets, including my favourite, a cake made from eggs, cream, sugar, orange flower water and sweet Canary wine, and stuck all over with almond quills. The table was creaking beneath the weight of food.

Meggie staggered past bearing a huge dish of candied carrots and sweetbreads, closely followed by John with a tray laden with flagons of wine, saffron cakes and clouted cream.

Mrs Talbot beckoned me to her side. "Lady Polgrey expects you to help tonight but I reckon there's no need, it's all under control. 'Tis better if you goes and makes ready. 'Twould give you a head start, and you'll be needing all the help you can get if you don't want to disgrace your aunt." She regarded me solemnly, "Though it has occurred to me that Lady Polgrey would like nothing better than for you to let her down in front of her fine friends. She would look all the more saintly for taking you in"

I looked at her sharply, but she shooed me away. "Go on with you. There isn't much time to dress before dinner. 'Twould make her very happy for you to be late and dressed like a homeless orphan. Mind you don't give her the satisfaction."

* * *

I shut the heavy oak door on the bustle and mayhem and for a few blissful moments savoured the silent haven of my bedchamber. I leant with my back against the door. I just had to find a way through this. I rubbed my tired eyes with the heels of my hands. With a resigned sigh, I began my search for a gown to wear to the party. I'd been forced to abandon all my fashionable gowns when I'd left Bristol in such haste and there had been no time to arrange for them to be sent on to me or have others made. Apart from the dull brown work dress, I had brought with me three serviceable day dresses, all of them stylishly cut, but very plain, lacking the profusion of ribbons, tucks and ruffles which were deemed essential for the well-dressed woman of fashion. Two were in shades of grey, the other black - colours my mother had so disliked that she had insisted they should never be worn in her presence under any circumstances. None of them were suitable for evening wear. But I knew that hidden away in my press were several of my mother's gowns which had been brought from Wild Court and although I couldn't bring myself to wear one of her favourites because of the memories attached and the unsuitable colours and styles, I remembered that there was one which she had declared dull in the extreme before tossing it carelessly aside.

I unearthed it and pulled it from the press, stroking the fine charcoal grey silk and prayed it would fit. I managed to squeeze myself into it with something of a struggle being shorter and wider than my mother. It dragged a little on the ground and pinched uncomfortably around the waist, but its style suited my shape although the décolletage was a trifle too revealing for my taste. The bodice laced at the front, so I was just able to cope with the fitting of it. I dressed my hair simply, pinning it up and threading a narrow black ribbon through the disorderly coppery curls and looked in the glass at my reflection. The gown was, it was true, too long and too tight in places but would have to do.

Fortunately, the extra length hid the unseemly sparkle of my mother's silver kid mules, which were slightly too narrow and would no doubt leave me with blisters by the end of the evening.

I studied my reflection; pale and anxious, I looked as though I was trying to hide behind the ill-fitting gown. I couldn't help compare myself to its original owner who would have shone like a beacon in it, dazzling all who came into her orbit. My looks would certainly never be my fortune, I thought with a smile. Chin too rounded. Mouth too wide. Nose too long. And eyes, although undoubtedly my best feature, an unusual tawny gold. My father's eyes. Tiger's eyes which could gleam and twinkle when he laughed. He had laughed often once upon a time.

I rearranged the falls of dark lace at my elbows, straightened my spine and was ready to face whatever the evening had in store for me.

As I descended the stairs, I heard the first carriage draw up in front of the house.

*   *   *

I entered the Great Hall and saw John taking the ladies' cloaks and gloves. He looked up and gave me an encouraging smile. With a determined squaring of my shoulders and swish of my silk skirts I limped across the hall to where the family and guests were milling about exchanging pleasantries.

Aunt Louisa cast a gimlet eye over my appearance, and I was afraid for a moment she might burst a blood vessel, but she quickly reined in her displeasure and turned away.

Miles was there and came swiftly to my side, kissing my hand in a welcoming gesture. I inclined my head as calmly as I was able but allowed my fingers to cling to his for a reassuring moment.

"Cousin, how charming you look. That gown becomes your hair most delightfully," he said warmly and led me to a comfortable chair set well away from his mother.

The door opened and more guests were ushered in; Squire Tregallas and his wife, Letitia were awkwardly greeted by Sir Joshua, who seemed rather flustered. He looked to his wife for assistance but received no more than a dissatisfied frown. Poor Uncle Joshua, somehow without anyone really noticing or caring, he had slipped the chains of adulthood and taken refuge in a kind of second childhood. I pictured the man he had once been — a roistering, bellowing giant of a man, arrogant, and sure of his place in life's grand scheme. How had they allowed such a bluff and hearty fellow to become so diminished? I was sad for him and the confused child trapped in that great bear-like frame.

Introductions were made, greetings exchanged, condolences offered and then to my dismay I found myself hemmed in by the dreadful Hester Jarrett on one side and pitiful Letitia Tregallas on the other. The actress still clung desperately to the last remnants of her youth and beauty, grasping at them as they drifted away, as a drowning man might clutch at the slenderest of straws. The startling red hair was tonight dulled by powder and bedecked with several tall plumes, a tiny golden harp and strings of pearls; her face white, her cheeks excessively rouged and the thin mouth painted scarlet. Her faded eyes were heavily outlined, and her face peppered with a profusion of patches of every size and shape. Her embittered gaze lingered upon Rowena, who was looking enchantingly young and beautiful and in Hester Jarrett's eyes I read not only envy but ill-disguised malevolence. Rowena, unaware of the powerful enmity she was provoking, continued to flirt brazenly with the Baron. His mistress fanned herself furiously, the fan making little bony, snapping sounds as it came perilously close to breaking.

Letitia Tregallas perched quiet and pale on the edge of her seat, her wispy hair unfashionably dressed, her clothes relics from a bygone age, eyes downcast and still candle-white hands, clasped tightly in her lap. She reminded me of a half-starved nestling.

Her husband was standing with his back to the blazing fire holding forth on the reasons why the underclasses should not be provided with citrus fruit to prevent scurvy.

"Pri'thee tell me, sir, where is the point? Exactly so! I can answer meself well enough. There *is* no point! There! 'Tis the only solution. D'ye not agree? Over-crowding, no? That fool Scot with his outlandish ideas. Country gone to rack and ruin. D'ye not agree, sir?"

My uncle, who was on the receiving end of this asinine diatribe, and had been listening with growing alarm, cleared his throat, "My dear fellow — " he began, at a loss.

"Exactly so," interrupted the Squire in blustering tones. "Did I not say so? Knew you'd be at one with me! After all, a bit'o scurvy never did anyone any harm."

Uncle Joshua, sensing the close proximity of another unsound mind began to hum softly to himself and Miles, realising his father was floundering, proceeded to engage the Squire in lively conversation.

"'Pon my soul, 'tis most diverting, is it not?" said Hester Jarrett with a sly smile. If it were possible Letitia Tregallas became even smaller and paler than before, seeming to shrink into her chair and on impulse I reached out and laid a sympathetic hand on her frail arm. She jumped at my touch and cast a frightened glance at her husband, who although deeply engrossed in discussion with the long-suffering Miles, appeared also to be eerily aware of his wife's consternation. She drew away from me.

From the corner of my eye, I observed the Squire, who, like his unhappy wife, was sadly behind the times as far as fashion was concerned; he wore a soiled and bedraggled full-bottomed wig, dark brown overcoat with wide stiffened skirts, a brocade waistcoat and stained lace cravat. His breeches and buckled shoes were mud-spattered. The florid complexion with purple broken veins across his slab-like cheeks and swollen nose proclaimed him to be a heavy drinker; his lantern jaw and thick red neck were strangely at variance with his bloodless fingers.

His wife's hands twitched spasmodically where they hid amongst the folds of her drab skirts. "I beg of you, Miss Pentreath, do nothing to attract my husband's attention," she whispered so quietly I thought I'd imagined her words.

"I have no intention of so doing," I murmured. She didn't respond. "Mrs Tregallas?"

"There's nothing to be done. Nothing anyone can do." She cast a furtive glance across the room, "They'll all die," she breathed.

"*Who'll* die?" I asked in an urgent undertone.

"Every last one," she replied in a strangely matter-of-fact manner. Then she smiled; a haunted, slightly deranged smile. "Still, 'tis probably all for the best," she said wearily. "Dead men tell no tales."

I was surprised into uttering an audible exclamation which, fortunately was drowned in a sudden commotion as the door to the Great Hall was flung open and John, poker-faced, announced the arrival of the last guest.

Sir Montagu Fitzroy sauntered gracefully into the room, his yellow satin coat glittering with gold embroidery, every buckle and bow, every button and jewel, catching the light of the many candles. There was a perceptible moment of silence as he surveyed the guests.

"Egad!" he drawled, "Am I late?" and sketching an elegant bow, he raised his quizzing glass to his eye. "Abject apologies, my lady. Can't understand how it can have happened. *Never* late for important engagements." He waved a bejewelled hand at the astounded gathering. "'Tis monstrous unkind in you to stare so. Makes a fellow feel dashed awkward."

With the utmost reluctance the guests resumed their various conversations while Sir Montagu made his leisurely way across the room, an exotic butterfly looking for somewhere to settle. Unfortunately for me, he chose to seat himself slightly behind me, next to Hester Jarrett, which meant he was uncomfortably close. I hoped and prayed he wouldn't single me out for any more of his unwelcome comments. He and the actress exchanged pleasantries and he laughed in a rather nasty fashion at something she related to him *sotto voce;* their heads close together like whispering lovers.

I found the sight particularly distasteful and twisted around in my chair, deliberately turning my back on them. Letitia Tregallas sat motionless as though by making no movement she would escape notice. I pitied her but at the same time wished she was strong enough to stand up for herself. Had it just been madness talking or did the Squire's wife really believe people might be going to die? Somehow, I had to find a suitable moment to ask her.

"Zounds! Is that not our little brown linnet I spy over there?"

I looked up quickly to find Sir Montagu's quizzing glass gleaming in my direction. My stomach lurched and I looked around hopelessly for Miles. All eyes were upon us and I knew there was nothing Miles could do anyway.

"Odds fish though, 'tis a bird of a very different colour tonight. I suspect 'tis borrowed plumage. Could it be that this little bird is seeking a mate?" And he stared pointedly at Edmund Anstey, who was lounging in a wing chair bedside the fire, kicking his booted foot against the fender and looking bored. "Your pretty display is falling upon stony ground, I fear," he observed, his painted lips curving into a malicious smile.

"I think, sir, that what I choose to do is none of your business," I said clearly, heedless of the trouble I might be provoking.

"And, I think, Miss Pentreath, that you are very much mistaken," he replied.

"Why, Monty, what can you possibly mean? You dark horse! Do tell us!" demanded Hester Jarrett eagerly.

Sir Montagu polished his eyeglass with a silk and lace handkerchief, "Hester, *mon ange*, 'tis for me to know and you to find out. Otherwise, where is the fun?"

The actress laughed but I could tell she wasn't best pleased at being so obviously fobbed off. I could see the curiosity gnawing at her and wondered what kind of actress she could possibly be if she couldn't easily conceal her emotions.

That curiosity however was to remain unsatisfied for John chose that moment to announce the serving of dinner. I breathed a sigh of relief and as both family and guests filed from the room, I picked up my long skirts and slid quietly into the dimly lit antechamber between the Great Hall and the library, in order to avoid the crush. The heat of the fire and the strain of being in such exasperating company had left me with a dry throat and I was longing for a drink of plain water.

Alongside some flagons of wine and brandy on the sideboard, I found a pitcher of cold fresh water. I poured some onto my handkerchief and laid it on my hot forehead. A single candle, burning lazily in its iron clip, guttered as I lifted the pitcher.

I don't think I heard the door to the Great Hall open.

The first sign I had of any danger was the offensive odour which assaulted my nostrils but by then, it was too late.

The pitcher crashed unheeded to the floor and Squire Tregallas caught me by the shoulders and dragged me back against him, twisting me around; his sweaty fingers clamped hard about my throat so that I had no choice but to face him. I was hardly able to draw breath because of his tightening grip and hardly wished to do so because of his fetid breath and huge malodorous body.

A natural surge of self-preservation made me struggle fiercely against him, but it didn't take me long to realise that he could thwart my pathetic attempts to repulse him with very little effort.

"Be still, my lovely," he hissed, his hot breath against my face, "There be no use in it," and he grinned, baring yellowed and decaying teeth.

"Let me go!", I gasped.

He laughed. "No, I don't believe I shall be doin' that. I be havin' far too much fun. Keep *still* now, will you!" He shook me like a dog shaking a rat until I felt my teeth rattle together.

"What do you want of me?" I demanded angrily.

"Just a kiss or two, for now, my precious. This is not the proper place for what I really desire."

I expressed my deep disgust in language learnt from the stable-lads and found myself slammed up against the wall for my pains.

"Now, listen, Missy! We can do this one of two ways — we can fight all the way or we can be pleasant to each other. The end result will be the same." He loosened his stranglehold, and I felt his fingers stroking my jawline. "There's something else besides," he whispered close to my ear. "What secrets were you sharing with my lady wife?"

I nearly bit through my lip in terror. "Secrets? Oh, you mean the recipe for soused conger eel? We were comparing different methods for its preparation." I could taste blood in my mouth and prayed fervently for deliverance.

"You must think me very stupid, Missy," he snarled and grabbing a handful of my hair pulled my head backwards until I thought my neck was bound to snap in two.

I tried to scream but his hand came down over my mouth and smothered any sound I might have made. I couldn't breathe and started to feel dizzy and sick.

"What did my wife say to you? Tell me now or else I shall be forced to squeeze this pretty neck a little harder." His face pushed closer and I felt his fingers tighten about my already aching throat. I was suddenly filled with a great desire to live long enough to inflict some terrible pain and hopefully death upon my attacker; I renewed my struggles by twisting my head away and kicking at his shins as hard as I could but was much hampered by the panniers of my mother's voluminous gown.

I was failing to make any kind of significant impression on my assailant when a silky voice said, "'Tis my sincere belief, Squire, that your attentions are unwelcome. May I cordially suggest that you release Miss Pentreath while she still breathes and before I am forced to resort to physical violence, which, I must tell you, I abhor. I should hate to risk damaging my new coat but, if pressed, I might just be able to overcome my reluctance to traumatise my tailor; a sensitive fellow, you understand and much given to bouts of depression."

Squire Tregallas, who had spun around to face the intruder thrust me backwards so that I crashed heavily into the sideboard and landed on the floor in an undignified and crumpled heap of grey silk. "What's it to you, Sir Montagu, if I choose to find a little harmless sport with a wench?"

"Why nothin', sir, " replied Sir Montagu lazily. "I came merely to remind you both that dinner is laid out and about to be heartily consumed. I thought p'raps the reason for tonight's gatherin' had slipped your *oh-so-keen* mind and had no wish to see my lady offended." The quizzing glass swung idly between his long pale fingers. "'Twould be prudent in you, sir, to return this instant to your good lady's side. She must be sorely missin' you." The heavily painted eyes showed no emotion as he and the Squire regarded each other. To my surprise, after a tense silence, my attacker capitulated and stormed from the room, slamming the door behind him.

Sir Montagu held out both hands to me. "If you remain much longer down there upon the cold flagstones, you're likely to catch a nasty chill and besides you look dashed uncomfortable."

I wished I could have ignored the outstretched hands but knew I would suffer a serious depletion of what was left of my dignity in my effort to stand up, so I ungraciously put my hands in his and allowed him to help me to my feet. He accomplished the task with remarkable ease.

I smoothed my gown with shaking hands. "I'm obliged to you, sir, for stepping in as you did. Profoundly indebted, in fact." My words sounded stiff and grudging, even to my own ears. He still held onto me and, because I was ashamed of my childish behaviour, I tugged at my captured hands in an effort to free them from his firm grasp.

A smile touched his lips, and he raised my hand and brushed a fleeting kiss into its palm. I snatched it away as though I'd been burned and clutched it to my outraged breast. "I perceive sir, that I have escaped the clutches of one vile lecher just to fall into the hands of another!"

"Methinks you've misconstrued my intentions, Miss Pentreath. Y'see before you a man devoted to only one other above himself and that's his tailor. I have to admit that I take it in devilish bad part that you should accuse me of such boorish behaviour. I am, in the main part, far too idle to force myself upon any unwillin' female. It might crease my coat."

I don't know if I was just exhausted from my traumatic experience, but I actually laughed out loud and saw an appreciative gleam in my rescuer's eye.

"I can see that would indeed be a hazard for such a modish gentleman."

"I'm delighted that your powers of reason have not entirely deserted you," he responded with an answering smile. "And, as you have evidently recovered from your encounter with our charmin' neighbour, I feel 'tis my duty to warn you against becomin', in any way, embroiled with either him or his unfortunate wife; no good will come of encouragin' closer acquaintance with them."

"I thank you for your concern, Sir Montagu but I will do as I please."

"You are a fool, then," remarked that gentleman blandly.

I ground my teeth. "I think we should re-join the party before they draw the wrong conclusions," I snapped.

"Y'r reputation is perfectly safe with me, m'dear. I am renowned for my lack of interest in anythin' remotely tedious. And, just to reassure you, I am quietly confident that I shall be able to deflect any awkward queries and convince them that nothin' is amiss."

"I think I prefer to rely upon my own wits, thank you."

"Yes, I'm sure you do, and we've already seen how successful you have been at that."

"Oh, very droll." I said irritably. "I suppose I *asked* to be jumped on and mauled by — by that revolting person!"

The eyeglass was raised again, "Faith, Miss Pentreath, that gown did all the askin' necessary."

I looked down at the offending item, "There's nothing wrong with it. It belonged to my mother."

The quizzing glass fell, and Sir Montagu turned and walked slowly to the door. I reluctantly followed. He opened the door and stood aside to allow me to pass. I limped by with a swish of the offending skirts but not before I had seen, in his narrowed, painted eyes, such look of torment that I almost stumbled.

Six

The dining-room was a blaze of golden light, every sconce, every candelabra overflowing with expensive beeswax candles that burned away merrily, showing off the beautiful hues of the wall hangings and paintings. The table was elegantly arrayed with decorations of evergreen branches and sweet-smelling herbs which nestled amongst the glittering glass and silverware; there was a fairy-tale atmosphere, the aromas of the refreshments mingled with fragrant woodsmoke from the apple logs crackling in the hearth and the rosemary scented candles used for special occasions such as this.

For a moment I was transported back to my childhood; to other far-away evenings spent at Wild Court, when I'd been allowed downstairs to say goodnight to the guests in all their sumptuous finery, to admire the beautiful ladies and the elegant gentlemen, who smiled down at me and patted my head with amused indulgence.

I returned to the present, but it was like leaving a well-loved friend and made reality all the harder to bear. With muted relief I realised that once again Miles had done his best to alleviate the embarrassment of my situation by arranging that I should sit between Harry and himself. Sir Montagu, having decided it would be prudent to enter the dining-room separately, had rejoined the party first and after a suitable interval I followed. I had no idea what excuse he made for his absence, but I apologised quietly to Aunt Louisa, explaining that I had been called to the kitchen to help with a minor domestic crisis and she seemed to accept my account. Glancing up at Sir Montagu, I fancied I saw him mouth a silent, "Bravo!" but he was placed at some distance from me and the light played peculiar tricks with his face; for a moment I was reminded of someone, but the fleeting thought was quickly banished as he turned away to say something trivial to his neighbour, Lady Anstey.

The meal seemed to go on forever and if hadn't been for Miles, it would have been unbearable, but he made it seem not quite such torture. Baron Rosenberg who was, unfortunately, seated opposite me, spent the evening encouraging Rowena to misbehave but even though he appeared wholly preoccupied by the alluring girl at his side, there were several moments during the interminable evening when I felt his gaze fixed upon my throat and I wondered nervously if the Squire had left his finger marks about my neck. I tried to concentrate on Miles and Harry and the mouth-watering food but even my favourite dessert tasted like ashes. Miles, I noticed, merely toyed with his food with an abstracted air. Hester Jarrett and Lucius were having an animated discussion about the world of theatre in London, while my aunt and Amelia Anstey murmured and laughed together like a pair of naughty children plotting some mischief.

We'd just started on the saffron cakes, which were heavenly clouds of fragrant spice, when it became quite clear to us that there was some sort of disturbance taking place in the Great Hall from whence came much shouting and stamping of booted feet.

The door burst open and a scarlet-coated, rain-soaked, and mud-spattered officer of the Dragoons entered the room in some disarray. He was surprisingly young and appeared to be extremely displeased about something. He made quite an impact standing there framed in the doorway, in sodden scarlet, water dripping from his tricorne, tall and square-shouldered, with a freshness of face that was instantly appealing. He looked as though he'd ridden many a mile already that night and could expect more of the same before he reached bed of any sorts. He looked tried beyond measure. I felt sorry for him as he surveyed the hostile faces, thinking he certainly had his work cut out for him this evening. He cleared his throat, looking flushed and uncomfortable. "I beg your pardon, ladies and gentlemen but we have an unpleasant duty to perform and must crave your indulgence for a short while. We have orders to search your house."

"What the devil do you mean?", demanded Aunt Louisa, outraged.

"We are in possession of certain information which leads us to believe someone in this house may be collaborating with a local gang of smugglers. We have the necessary papers for a random search, milady, if we suspect there may have been dealings with such criminals."

Aunt Louisa fixed the young man with such a look that if it had been directed at me, I would have sounded an immediate retreat.

"Are you insinuating that I am sheltering common thieves?" she asked coldly.

"I am not, Lady Polgrey. Nor am I suggesting that you knowingly accept contraband," he replied rather bitingly, "but, we believe that members of your staff could be in league with the gang, without your knowledge."

"I seriously doubt that."

"You would be astonished to learn how frequently the masters of the house are ignorant of what goes on in the servants' quarters."

"I'll have you know that all my servants have been with me for many years and were chosen for their honesty and loyalty. I will not stand for this unspeakable treatment. It's a disgrace. What is your name and rank? I shall be reporting you to your senior officer!"

"Lieutenant Robin Danserfield, at your service, milady. And I'm afraid it was my senior officer who sent me here."

"My staff would never dare to bring smuggled goods into my house."

"Indeed, Lady Polgrey, I'm sure they're all God-fearing, law-abiding citizens but I'm also sure you're aware that smuggling is not considered to be a criminal offence by many ordinary folk. We all know the locals aid and abet these brigands, otherwise they'd never be able to evade capture as often as they do. There are even Excise Officers who are not above suspicion. Smuggling is considered a noble profession and that attitude only serves to make our task as law enforcers even more difficult and unpleasant." He paused and looked about him at his enraptured audience. "We have to search even the most respectable homes." His searching gaze found Rowena and seemed reluctant to move on. "I must beg leave of you, my lady, to continue. But I must also warn you that we must carry out the search with or without your permission."

"In that case, Lieutenant, you have my permission," said Aunt Louisa in a dangerously quiet voice.

"Thank you, Lady Polgrey, that is most considerate of you. I only wish my first visit to your home could have been under more favourable circumstances," and his keen young eyes strayed irresistibly back to Rowena's lovely face. "I will make sure that everything is left as it is found. We'll not be long — my men are very experienced in these matters and then we'll leave you to enjoy the rest of your evening uninterrupted. Your servant, m'lady." And with a curt bow to Aunt Louisa, as his eyes took in the rest of the room.

There followed a moment of stupefied silence before Aunt Louisa said furiously, "The impertinence of the man!" She scowled down the long dining-table at her husband, "I thank, you sir, as always, for your stalwart support."

"What would you have had him do, Mother? Challenge the Lieutenant to a duel?"

"Don't be nonsensical, Miles. It's entirely reasonable to expect succour from my own husband in a crisis."

As this contretemps continued, it dawned on me that there were guests at the gathering who had apparently more reason to be anxious about the unexpected visit than others. The Squire's forehead was slicked with sweat and his cowering wife could hardly control strong fits of trembling. Lucius, the Baron, and Hester Jarrett all seemed unmoved. Rowena was looking rather pleased with herself, a becoming colour staining her cheeks. Harry and Uncle Joshua were, as usual, keeping their heads down, while Sir Montagu Fitzroy continued to spoon dessert between his painted lips with an air of studied nonchalance, although I had the distinct feeling that he was thoroughly enjoying himself. Miles, however, was not only extremely angry, he was visibly agitated.

As promised, the Dragoons were swift and thorough in their search, although the noise they made rearranging the furniture and shouting audible curses, was quite deafening.

The dinner guests were returning to the Great Hall to play cards and freely imbibe the brandy I was now convinced was contraband, just as the Dragoons were finally quitting the house; some looking rather dusty from rooting around in the attics and cellars. Rowena, I noticed with amusement, dawdled prettily by the exit.

The last soldier had left, and the young Lieutenant was telling my aunt and uncle that apart from the trivial matter of a small bag of tea discovered in a hidey-hole in the kitchen, the house was free from caches of smuggled goods or villains hiding behind the wainscoting. "I'll allow the tea to go unreported and the other minor infringements," he said with a pointed glance at the decanter of brandy, "But next time I may not be in a position to be so accommodating." He spoke very clearly so that Rowena should not miss a word. She was pretending not to listen to or be aware of Lieutenant Danserfield at all, but with very little success.

Uncle Joshua, escorting this unexpected visitor to the door, suddenly looked very much the Lord of the Manor. He slapped the Lieutenant genially upon the back, "Kind of you to drop in! Come back anytime you fancy, young man. Be glad to show you around the place. I have some prime bits'o blood, if you're at all interested." He beamed at the surprised officer and then shuffled away, muttering, "Damned nice fellow. Pleased he could come."

The Lieutenant caught my eye, and I was delighted to find that his earnest blue eyes were alight with repressed laughter.

We smiled and I felt strangely reassured. And it turned out that Uncle Joshua was not completely without understanding, he had seen, even through the fog of his confusion, that the officer was actually a very agreeable young man. With one last sidelong glance at Rowena, Lieutenant Robin Danserfield stepped out into the rain-swept night and was gone.

"By God, someone will pay for this evening's work. I shall have that man's head for this," exclaimed my aunt.

"But Mother, he was only doing his duty," said Rowena uneasily.

"Duty be hanged, my girl. I have had to endure common soldiers tramping all over my house, searching amongst my belongings with their dirty fingers and probably helping themselves to my jewellery. I have influence and I will make absolutely certain that he never holds another command for the rest of his career. Come, our guests await," and she swept majestically back into the heart of the gathering as though there had been no interruption at all.

* * *

The remainder of the evening passed without further incident; Rowena played the spinet with a slightly distracted air, while the other guests formed small groups to play at cards. The talk eventually turned away from the Dragoons' invasion to more general gossip. I was excused from playing cards because of my inability to reckon numbers; I stayed for a short while, listening politely to the conversation and wishing I was in my bed, before making my excuses and escaping to join the staff in the onerous task of clearing up the resulting debris. An extra pair of hands was welcomed, and we set to work with good humour.

Finally, the guests had all left, the family were in their beds, and the servants were seeing to the fires and candles and preparing to retire themselves. It was almost two o'clock when I climbed wearily into my own bed. It was still raining outside, and the wind moaned miserably in the eaves, but even so I fell instantly into a deep and dreamless sleep.

* * *

I awoke at some time during the night with a powerful thirst, brought on, no doubt, by Meggie's rather salty stargazey pie. I slid out of bed and lit my candle to pour myself some water from the pitcher, only to find it empty. With all the extra work for the party I'd forgotten to refill it. I wondered if I could last the rest of the night without a drink but knew I wouldn't be able to sleep. Slipping my wrapper on, I made my way down to the kitchen, my bare feet making no noise on the ancient, polished boards, my sore ankle throbbing painfully. The kitchen still smelled good, of herbs and baking and warmth; so different to my bedchamber with its smell of neglect, of damp and musty bed-hangings. I crossed the room, setting my pitcher on the table, then went to look for the stoneware ewer that contained fresh water. I pulled the pantry door open and was passed by a hissing blur; I span around almost extinguishing the candle and saw Moses, the kitchen cat scurry under a chair, his tail as bushy as a fox's brush. I laughed with relief as he stared angrily at me, his eyes glowing devilishly in the light from the candle. I turned back to the pantry and finding the stone ewer replenished my own pitcher. I took down a pewter tankard, filled it to the brim, and took a long drink.

I was about to make my way back to bed when I heard Moses mewing plaintively at the back door.

"Silly creature. You won't like it out there, you know, it's raining cats and dogs!" I smiled at my own joke. Moses gave me his best pleading look and thinking he must surely know what he wanted, I unbarred the door, picked him up with one arm and stood on the threshold looking out into the wild night. "Look, Moses! You'll get soaked and you know how you hate water." Moses hissed, his tail lashing my side like a willow wand in a gale. "I knew you'd agree once you saw those puddles. It doesn't look so appealing now, does it?"

Moses, rigid with anxiety, glowered out into the yard and growled deep in his throat. He buried his claws in my arm; wincing, I let him drop to the ground and watched as he tiptoed to the very edge of the step, sniffing the air in a way which made the hair on the back of my neck stand on end. "Moses! Come back inside." But the big tabby cat took no notice, so I decided to help him make up his mind by gently closing the door on him. He ignored me. I hardened my heart and gave him his last chance. "Come on, you ridiculous cat! I'm shutting the door."

I was about to carry out my threat when I thought I heard someone cry out. I stopped and listened. Moses was right, there was someone in the yard.

I heard the sound again and this time I was sure I hadn't imagined it. "Who's there?" I whispered, then more loudly, "Is there anyone there?"

I heard a faint movement to my left, followed by a low groan, "Martha! Over — here — by the wall."

I put down my candle, which would have been useless and, ignoring my bare feet and my sore ankle, I felt my way across to the low wall which enclosed the yard, where I nearly fell over someone slumped in the shelter of the peat stack.

I peered through the darkness, trying to make out the face of the prostrate figure. "*Miles?* Is that you?"

"Of course — it is. For — God's sake — help me — inside and stop asking such — damned foolish questions!"

Without another word I did as I was told and with great difficulty and much swearing and groaning on his part, I managed to get him to his feet, thanking heaven he was so slight. His left arm, I noticed hung limply by his side and I could feel the warm stickiness of blood squeezing between my fingers. Biting back the questions, I put his right arm about my shoulders and supported him as best I could as we crossed the yard.

As we reached the kitchen door, another figure materialised from the shadows and silently lifted Miles from me and bore him away efficiently into the kitchen. Somehow, I wasn't in the least surprised and quickly followed, closing the door behind us.

"Light more candles," ordered the smugglers' captain, in hushed tones. "Fetch clean bandages. We must staunch the bleeding, or you'll be one cousin less by morning." With these discouraging words ringing in my ears, I hurried away to search through the linen cupboard, returning as quickly as I could to find him easing Miles out of his greatcoat. Miles was moaning in pain, his eyes squeezed shut and his face contorted from the effort of holding back cries which might give us away to the sleeping house. I tore up sheeting and did my best to assist the Irishman as he carefully washed and dressed the wound. It was clear that the injury had been inflicted by some kind of blade, which had left an ugly gash across his left shoulder and down across his chest. I tried not to think about how he might have come by it. Miles was silent now, his face tinged with grey, his lips bloodless. I cast an anxious glance at the Irishman and saw I was not alone in my fears.

"We must get him to bed. He's going to need expert care."

"How shall I explain — ?" I began uncertainly.

"I'm confident you'll think of something. 'Tis not as though it's a wound from a musket which would have been far more difficult to explain away. A knife wound could have been acquired almost anywhere. A drunken brawl outside a tavern or a cuckolded husband wreaking his revenge upon his rival." I must have shown my doubts for he looked down at me mockingly, "You think your cousin a saint, Miss Pentreath?"

"No, of course, I don't." I said crossly, "I'm not a fool. I'm perfectly aware that young men are apt to behave with imprudence from time to time and I have no illusions about Miles." I looked down at the pale and drawn face which barely resembled my favourite cousin. "But I would trust him with my life, and I'll do all in my power to preserve his." I said simply.

"You'd be wise not to trust your life to anyone no matter how trustworthy you believe them to be," he said, looking at me over Miles's inert body.

He then managed to lift our patient once more into his arms. I grabbed a candle and ran to open the door for him. It was fortunate that Miles had always been on the slender side and not as lanky as Lucius because it was a long way to carry anything let alone such a dead weight. I led the way, holding the candle aloft. I was terrified we'd meet Aunt Louisa around the next corner, and it was with profound relief that I closed the door of Miles's bedchamber behind us. The Irishman laid Miles down upon the four-poster bed and I helped pull off his muddied boots and remove his bloodstained shirt. I then covered him with the quilt and turned to my companion. "I don't know how to thank you, Captain Cavanagh. It was most opportune that you should — " I stopped and frowned, "What exactly *were* you doing out here at this time of night?" I asked suspiciously.

The ghost of a smile played across his lips, "I wondered how long it would be before you started to make accusations. It was a fortunate coincidence that I should happen upon your cousin in this parlous state in the village. I had no choice but to bring him here or leave him to die. Finding the back door bolted I was forced to leave him for a moment while I searched for an open window. Finding none, I returned to discover you had providentially decided to lend a hand."

"Oh, I see. Well, I am most obliged."

"Not at all. Happy to assist. I just happened to be in the right place at the right time," he said, in the politest of voices, just as though we were discussing the weather over a dish of tea.

Miles lay against pillows as white as his face, his breathing shallow. "How did he come by such a serious injury", I wondered aloud.

"I think you should ask him when he wakes," replied the Captain unhelpfully. "I don't believe he'd want me to be the one to tell you. It's a somewhat delicate matter, I understand. You might try talking some sense into that rash young head of his - he may listen to you. He seems hell-bent on getting himself imprisoned or deported to the colonies for some reason."

Miles moaned and I laid a comforting hand on his forehead, stroking his fair hair away from his forehead. "Should we fetch the doctor?"

"To have him bled? I think not. He's lost enough blood already. He'll stand a much better chance of pulling through this if we keep him out of that butcher's clutches. Go and wake the housekeeper. She's experienced in these matters and won't be tempted to cup him or apply leeches."

"I'll fetch her immediately. You'd better not stay here though. I'll have enough trouble explaining things as it is."

"Don't worry. I shall see myself out. It wouldn't do for a notorious smuggler to be discovered haunting the house after dark and with you in that very alluring — er — robe."

I blushed furiously as I remembered that I was wearing nothing but a flimsy wrapper over my nightgown. I snatched at the edges of the inadequate garment and tried to draw them around me as protection against his penetrating gaze. "A *gentleman* wouldn't have mentioned such a thing," I said tartly.

"But I have already warned you that I am no gentleman, Miss Pentreath."

I cast him scornful glance and crossing the room, angrily pulled open the door.

"I'm glad to see your ankle is so much recovered," he added.

I would have slammed the door in his self-satisfied face if it hadn't been essential for the rest of the house to remain undisturbed.

* * *

I knocked timidly on Anne Talbot's door but there was no immediate response. As I felt it was desperately urgent to rouse the housekeeper to enlist her aid, I lifted the latch and entered the room, shielding the candle flame with my hand. I tip-toed to the bed, "Mrs Talbot?" I could see her recumbent form beneath the covers and reached out to gently shake her shoulder. "Mrs Talbot? Wake up!"

She stirred and sighed deeply, "There'd best be a good reason for disturbing me," she muttered, still half asleep.

"There's a very good reason. Miles has been injured in a knife attack and I fear for his life."

In an instant the housekeeper was wide awake and struggling into her woollen wrapper. "Where is he? Does anyone else know?"

"We — I — put him in his bed and you're the only one I've told as yet," I replied, as she pushed her feet into her shoes and rearranged the frilly nightcap over her greying hair.

"Come along then," she ordered and taking my candle from me, she strode past me and into the corridor.

* * *

After examining Miles, Mrs Talbot left to gather together everything she would need in the way of medicines. She returned a short while later with a tisane of chamomile oil and willow bark to soothe and sedate and a poultice of sphagnum moss, honey and comfrey root, which she bound over the wound.

"'Twill hopefully help stop it putrefying," she explained. We then propped him up on more pillows and encouraged him to drink the tisane.

During a night filled with the greatest uncertainty, Mrs Talbot and I never left him alone. The housekeeper asked no questions for which I was profoundly grateful because I would have had difficulty finding suitable answers for her.

As the first shaft of morning light slid slowly over the windowsill Miles opened his eyes. I'd been watching his face with increasing wretchedness but when I saw his eyelids flicker, I looked up at Anne Talbot, hope rekindled, "He's waking. He'll be all right now!" I said confidently.

She seemed unmoved, "It be clear you don't know the first thing about nursing the sick," she said.

Chastened but still optimistic, I took Miles's hand in mine. "Good morning, dearest cousin," I greeted him cheerfully, "You've led us a merry dance indeed! How do you feel?"

He grimaced, "Damnable."

"Poor thing," I said sympathetically. "But if you insist on becoming embroiled in other people's disputes, you must expect to find yourself maimed occasionally and you always were a very inadequate swordsman." This, with a furtive glance under my lashes towards Mrs Talbot and a warning frown for Miles.

The merest hint of a rueful smile touched his lips, "Wooden swords, I seem to recall."

"And you were always easily trounced, by a *girl!*"

A slight chuckle, "It never occurred to you that I may have *allowed* you to win?"

Mrs Talbot fixed me with a speaking look, "Too much idle chatter, Miss Martha. He needs to rest."

Looking down at Miles, I was convinced he was well on the road to recovery. His eyes, although dulled by pain and exhaustion, were brimming with laughter. His words were perfectly lucid, and I couldn't help but feel the housekeeper was being unduly alarmist.

Miles squeezed my hand, "Don't worry your pretty head. I'll be up and about in no time. 'Tis but a flesh wound."

I overheard Mrs Talbot make an exasperated exclamation in the background and murmur something about a dirty blade.

Miles grinned, "She watches over me like a mother hen."

The housekeeper frowned, "That's as maybe, Master Miles, but there's always one chick daft enough to run with the fox."

She then declared that she would go and make some broth for the invalid and left the room, stiff with disapproval.

After the door had closed and her footsteps faded, Miles and I exchanged glances and could no longer stifle our giggles.

* * *

While Miles was forced to finish every last drop of the hearty mutton broth, I was able to dash to my room to tidy myself. I'd changed from the shameful night attire into a sensible dark grey gown earlier but hadn't had time to pin my hair up properly.

I was wondering whether to let anyone else know that Miles was temporarily indisposed and had just decided that it would be wiser to see what Miles had to say on the matter, when I heard Aunt Louisa's stentorian voice raised in anger.

Limping hastily back to my cousin's bedchamber I found there was no need to worry about sharing the news because my aunt was already in the process of reading him the riot act.

Mrs Talbot stood beside the bed, her lips pressed firmly together, and her large hands folded across her stomach. I could feel her pent-up rage from across the room, as her mistress took command.

My aunt, still in her satin and lace morning gown, the prettiest lace cap upon her hair, looked down at her son, the face beneath the becoming ruffles far from cordial. "Exactly what, pray, is going on Miles?" she demanded.

My young cousin, who had never really excelled at the gentle art of prevarication, was looking agitated and I recalled childhood days when it had only been my creative ability with the inconvenient truth that had ensured his most excessive youthful exploits had never been detected. This, however, was a somewhat more serious misdemeanour than being found sampling Uncle Joshua's Madeira in the middle of the afternoon or scrumping apples and plums from Reverend Pender's orchard. As I stepped into the room, I'd not the slightest idea in my head but as in the old days, the words came sliding from my tongue like honey from a hot spoon and with all the ease of a misspent youth.

"Good morning, Aunt Louisa. I see you have found poor Miles. Is it not amusing that he should have been mistaken for a seafarer? Fancy them trying to pressgang him! What a lark! No wonder he should object so strongly and draw his sword." Miles, to his credit, didn't bat an eyelid; he just lay there trying to look like the victim of unreasonable persecution. His boyish face was particularly suited to the pretence of innocence. I never considered myself anything more than an artful dissembler.

"You surely are not expecting me to believe the Navy are using impressment to recruit in time of peace?" uttered Aunt Louisa, thankfully missing the expression which fleetingly crossed her son's face.

"Oh, no, the Navy had nothing to do with it, did they Miles?" I said, improvising wildly. "Have you not heard of the villainous gang roaming our stretch of coast, raiding sea-ports, and capturing locals with the intention of selling them to merchantmen for blood-money? It appears they were idiotic enough to try to press Miles as he returned from escorting Lord and Lady Anstey back to the Manor. 'Tis so fortunate that he is such a *fine* swordsman, or he might, at this very moment, be tied up in the hold of some merchant ship!"

Miles was overcome with a sudden fit of coughing in order to disguise the laughter which had nearly burst out and the housekeeper gazed into the distance with impressive composure. It wasn't such a tall story after all; Miles had indeed escorted the Ansteys and there really was a gang kidnapping unwary locals to sell them into a kind of slavery at sea, but they'd last been heard of much further down the coast towards Polperro. It was, I assured myself, just a little more embellished than the truth. What was important was that my aunt seemed to find it credible and her fit of pique quickly evaporated. Miles and I exchanged a triumphant glance, and I said a grateful prayer.

Seven

I spent the rest of the morning hobbling from kitchen to sickroom, making possets and poultices and reading Tobias Smollett's *"Roderick Random"* to entertain Miles who was quite content, on this first day of his confinement, to wallow in the unaccustomed attention.

I finished the chapter I'd been struggling through and threw the book onto the bed. "Well, if any fool were debating whether or not to join the Navy, this book should simplify the matter! It's no wonder the only way they can man the Fleet is by nefarious means such as press-ganging!"

"Stuff and nonsense. You just don't understand because you're a female. The Navy's a fine and heroic profession. Any true patriot would be proud to serve their country."

"To be cruelly mistreated and then *killed!* Truly, I don't understand how being kidnapped and virtually sold into slavery could possibly be called heroic."

Miles laughed, "If female opinions were acknowledged it would mean that before long, we'd be unable to defend our country at all."

"Perhaps it is so, my dear, but you must own there seems to be more reluctance than enthusiasm to take the King's shilling."

He shook his head in despair, "Martha, have you any idea how terribly earnest you can look sometimes? I'm starting to suspect you may be *bookish*." He reached out and caught my hand in his, "D'you know you quite literally saved my life this morning? I couldn't believe my ears. You are a wonder. It reminded me of the old days." He grinned, reminding me of the carefree boy he had once been.

I squeezed his hand, "'Tis those memories that keep me going. It seems like centuries since my parents were at Wild Court and so very much in love it made your heart ache just to look at them. The sun always shone from cloudless blue skies - or at least that's how it seemed. Perhaps it's just wishful thinking. Perhaps children see things differently."

The boyish grin disappeared. "I don't know what happened... why things changed," he reflected.

"Miles, when we were young, we told each other everything. We were more like confidantes than cousins. You used to be glad of my support then. Could you not trust me enough again?"

Miles regarded me, the doubt plain to see. "I only wish I could, dearest. If only it were that simple."

"But Miles — "

"No, Martha, 'tis best this way, believe me. If anything should happen, you cannot be implicated. I must shoulder the blame for this escapade and become used to the idea that there's no one to shield me with ingenious falsehoods. And that's how it *should* be."

Even though I pressed him further he remained stubbornly reluctant to share his troubles, so I was forced to give in. I read a little more to him and when he became drowsy, I put aside the dreary book and for a long while sat quietly stroking his tousled, pale hair until eventually he fell asleep.

* * *

I was soon to be reminded that one should never doubt Anne Talbot's word.

The next day passed in much the same vein, Miles slept and complained bitterly and slept again. Mrs Talbot tended to his wound regularly, washing it with boiled water and a little of Aunt Louisa's precious gin and then bound it in clean linen. In the evening I wrapped myself in a warm quilt and curled up in the comfortable wing chair beside the fire. After several hours spent watching my cousin sleep, I allowed myself to drift off.

I dreamt about my father. He was standing at the edge of the little harbour at Wild Court, looking out across the estuary, his hand shielding his eyes. I was running towards him but never reaching him. Running and running, yet always staying in the same place. In desperation I called out to him and he turned, his arms outstretched —

I awoke with a start, never having reached him. For a second I wondered what had woken me then realised someone was standing over me. It was Lucius and he was shaking my arm. "Wake up, Martha, you're dreaming."

I sat up and rubbed my eyes. "I'm sorry. I hope I didn't wake you."

Lucius shook his head, "I was just coming in when I heard you cry out. I thought you wouldn't wish to disturb Miles."

I was astonished; if I hadn't known him better, I'd have thought he sounded almost concerned. Up until that moment my least favourite cousin had not been very much in evidence, a fact that had not escaped my notice but for which I was thankful. He had always seemed to exist on the outer reaches of the family, noting weaknesses, listing grievances. He was a stranger to me in this guise and I couldn't bring myself to trust the vagaries of his behaviour when I was used to naught but criticism and hostility.

Miles stirred restlessly and I went quickly to his side. He murmured something in his sleep then suddenly his eyes opened, and he smiled up at me. "I'd very much like some water." I helped him sip from a cup and he sank back with a satisfied sigh.

"Lucius is here," I told him.

Miles looked around a little nervously, "An honour, indeed."

Lucius stood by the un-shuttered window, staring blankly out into the night. A moment passed and then he turned and regarded his brother, who was lying helplessly against a mound of pillows, his fingers restlessly plucking the bedcover.

"Been up to your old tricks again, Miles?"

"Don't know what you mean," replied Miles sullenly.

"Oh, I think you do, brother dear, I think you do. May I enquire how you came by this mysterious wound?"

Miles cast me a desperate glance, "Martha has already explained to Mother — "

"You honestly expect me to believe such a fanciful tale? Come Miles, credit me with a little intelligence. According to my sources that particular gang was twenty miles down the coast pressing the menfolk of Polperro into service. What have you to say to that?"

"Can't think of anything offhand actually," muttered Miles with a rueful smile.

Now we're for it, I thought, as Lucius's expression darkened. I suffered all the usual misgivings when in close proximity to Lucius the Infernal. Lucius the Vile. I used to make up ridiculous nicknames for him to diminish my fear. I occasionally still referred to him by the old names and felt slightly better.

"You'll tell me how you were wounded, little brother, or I'll draw my own conclusions," said Lucius, Prince of Darkness, grimly.

Feeling I should at least make an attempt to protect Miles, I rather rashly stammered that he should be resting rather than being badgered by insensitive siblings. I received a bone-chilling look for my pains and wished I'd kept quiet.

"Perhaps you should leave, Martha."

A return of courage. "A kind thought, Lucius. I think I'll stay, nevertheless. I've been put in charge of your brother's recovery."

A tense silence and then Lucius said, "Enlighten me, please, Miles."

"It sounds very much as though you are already in possession of the facts," said Miles angrily.

"Let us just say I have a desire to hear it from your own lips."

A resigned shrug from Miles as he accepted his fate; Lucius was not to be fobbed off with any more implausible excuses.

"'Twas Ben Fairchild, damn his eyes. Don't like me round his sister."

Lucius clenched his fists and made a move towards the bed. I cried out a warning and stepped between him and his prostrate brother, the one flushed and defiant; the other simmering with a deadly rage and fit to inflict injury.

I didn't understand fully what was beneath these undercurrents but had no wish to see Miles further hurt. They glared at each other like enraged bull terriers. "Would someone kindly explain to me what this absurd display is all about!" I asked while still trying to shield Miles as best I could. Lucius transferred his irate gaze to me as though he were emerging from a dream, his face slowly relaxed and the white-hot anger drained away.

"Ah, sweet coz, what courage! What devotion. You really should have been christened Faith or Makepeace. But wait, was it not Martha who was chided by Christ for allowing her chores to distract her when she should have been listening to His words? Yes, that's right and she was made patron saint of practical females. So, very apt. The perfect little housewife." He made it an insult. I heard Miles's sharply indrawn breath and placed a calming hand on his arm.

"I see no great shame in being good at something or being a housewife and as for my worrying about Miles, *somebody* has to as he seems incapable of steering a straight path at the moment. He's in enough trouble without you saddling him with more." I was angry enough to momentarily forget my fear of him and I reminded myself that it was for Miles. "Anyway, I don't see what it has to do with you," I added for good measure.

Lucifer actually laughed and suddenly my fear resurfaced. "Has not your beloved Miles already told you what ails him?"

"He's told me nothing."

"Then, 'tis up to me to enlighten you as you seem so keen to poke your nose in where it's not wanted." An unkind smile touched his thin mouth. "You see, it has a great deal to do with me." He regarded his brother's flushed countenance with disdain. "Miles and I are unfortunately both captivated by the same village wench."

I looked at them both, seeing that it was the truth, "Village wench?"

"The cause of all the quarrelling and secret outings is the beautiful and yet utterly unattainable Miss Eleanor Fairchild."

Dumbstruck, I sat down on the edge of the bed with a thump. "Eleanor Fairchild? I don't believe it. *Both* of you in love with her? It's not possible. She's hardly your type Lucius!" I exclaimed.

"Who said anything about love?" growled Lucius.

"Well, if you don't love her, why not stand aside? Perhaps give Miles a fighting chance?"

"*I* love her." said Miles softly.

"Then surely the dispute is purely academic? Does not the lady in question have a say in the matter? She must surely favour one of you more than the other?"

Lucius returned to the window, visibly trying to suppress his emotions. "The *lady* will have neither of us. I suspect she's set her sights higher. We're neither titled nor wealthy. There are those, despite their unsavoury reputations, who have more appeal. The charming Baron Rosenberg, for instance."

"Oh, I don't believe that for one minute. She could not possibly consider such man suitable!" I said, aghast.

"I wish I shared your conviction," said Miles gloomily.

This all made very little sense to me. How could Eleanor not love Miles? As far as I could see the only problem was Lucius, whose flinty heart was not in the slightest danger of serious harm. He was only interested because she was unavailable, and he wasn't accustomed to having his desires thwarted.

"So, Miles, as I understand it, you were visiting Miss Fairchild and managed to get into a fight with her brother, is that right?", asked Lucius.

"It could hardly be called a fight — the man's an absolute colossus, with fists like hams! I called at their cottage on the way home and found her brother in residence. Rather a nasty shock, I may tell you. He took exception to my presence and picked a quarrel. Came at me like a madman. Nothing I could do. Never was much of a pugilist. Damned uncivilised behaviour, if you ask me. He went for his knife and it was sheer good fortune that I had buckled on my sword to escort the Ansteys. All the talk of press gangs, y'see?"

"Ben Fairchild has richer pickings in prospect," said Lucius cynically. "Rosenberg is richer than Croesus."

"Appalling manners, you know," said Miles, "Can't think how he came to have a sister as sweet as Eleanor. As I understand it, he was in the Navy. Wounded overseas. Can't have been back in the country more'n a sennight. Fiend seize it! I'm devilish thirsty! All this chatter has dried my throat." He lay back, closing his eyes.

I poured him some water and watched, dismayed, as he gulped it down and asked for more. Lucius and I exchanged glances. I laid a hand on Miles's forehead and had my fears confirmed. His face was flushed, his skin was burning, and his eyes were refusing to focus. I made a quick examination of his wound and found it to be red and inflamed along its ragged edges. "Lucius, fetch Mrs Talbot at once." He needed no second bidding, striding immediately from the room.

I quickly lit more candles and sat down to wait for help to come. I touched his forehead again and his eyes fluttered open, "I'm so cold," he whispered hoarsely. He was shaking and breathing hard as though he'd been running.

I stroked his damp hair, "It's all right, Miles, Lucius has gone for Mrs Talbot, she'll know what to do." But I knew he hadn't heard me.

That night Miles's bedchamber became a battleground as we fought the fever and infection which threatened to take him from us. While the rest of the house slept, we toiled in grim harmony over his rapidly failing body. The housekeeper issued soft-spoken commands which I unthinkingly obeyed, knowing only that my cousin's life depended upon this woman. The sound of his laboured breathing filled the room and as the fever took hold, it was all we could do to keep him safely on the bed; he seemed to have the strength of ten men.

Most of the time his gabbled words made no sense but there was a moment in the early hours of the morning when he seemed almost lucid. I bent closer to hear as I sensed his growing desperation to communicate his confused thoughts with someone.

"The — doors. Got to — open," he thrashed his arm out and clutched at my sleeve, "Mustn't — let them — down," he moaned.

I met Mrs Talbot's even gaze across the bed.

"What can he mean?" I asked.

Her lips drew together in the familiar hard line, "He's delirious, Miss Martha. He's dreaming, that's all."

But I wasn't convinced. I suspected that it wasn't just unrequited love which had been to blame for his uncharacteristic behaviour recently. "Miles! Who do you have to help? Which doors must be opened?"

For a moment his eyes opened, fever-bright and he seemed to look straight at me. "Must — open — much depends upon it. For my sake, do this — for me!"

"Which doors am I to open? Miles? *Miles!*" But he drifted away. Impetuously, I shook him gently. "For God's Sake only tell me what I'm to *do!*"

The eyes, so unlike the rational, kind ones I had always loved, half-opened, "Ask — John." Then he slid back into the confusion and darkness.

The housekeeper became evermore stony-faced when I attempted to extract information from her. "I'm sure I don't know, Miss Martha. Perhaps you'd best ask John, like Miles said," she replied tersely.

The night sky paled and the birds awoke and began their unwelcome and tuneless chorus and still Mrs Talbot and I watched anxiously over Miles, who was stubbornly refusing to show any signs of improvement. Poultices, tisanes, and prayer all had no effect. We bathed his scorching body, regularly changed his dressings and did everything in our power to keep the deadly infection at bay, but I began to to feel that we were losing the fight.

*   *   *

At half past five Lucius appeared, pale and drawn from lack of sleep. "How is he?" he asked.

"Much the same," said Mrs Talbot, "but he's young and has the will to live."

I kept my grave doubts to myself, to me he looked weak and exhausted and as though he had already given up. He couldn't take much more punishment.

Lucius, almost unrecognisable as the demon cousin I'd spent my childhood walking a mile to avoid, suggested that while he remained with Miles, Mrs Talbot and I should go and freshen ourselves, and perhaps try to sleep for a while. He advised us that if we wanted to continue to be of any use to Miles, that rest would be beneficial. Neither of us wanted to leave for even a short time but we knew Lucius was right.

The housekeeper disappeared in the direction of her neglected kitchen and I thankfully retired to my bedchamber. I looked longingly at the bed but knew I couldn't close my eyes until I had spoken with John. I splashed my face with cold water, changed my sweat-soaked gown and tidied my hair, then made my way down to the kitchen in search of the footman.

I found him polishing boots in the scullery. He stood as I entered, anxious for news. "Master Miles? Is'ee — ?" he began uneasily.

"He's no better, I'm afraid," I told him.

John frowned unhappily, "This be terrible," he said, half under his breath.

"Mrs Talbot has great faith in his ability to pull through," I reassured him, and his expression lightened considerably.

"She do? Well, that be good news."

"Indeed," I agreed. "Once the fever breaks, she assures me that his recovery will be guaranteed."

"God willing," I added for good measure.

John looked oddly uncomfortable, "When do'ee think 'ee'll be up and about?"

"If his fever were to break soon, perhaps in a week or two?"

"A *week?*" gasped the footman. "Not for a whole week?"

"Why, of course not. He's still on death's doorstep. It's hardly likely he'll be leaping from his bed anytime soon to resume his normal activities," I said in some surprise. John's pleasant face took on a guarded look.

"No. Of course not. I didn't realise how bad'ee was hurt."

"I'm sure none of us did, John."

He began to buff the boot in his hand once more, but I could tell his mind was elsewhere.

"Miles has been fussing about some doors he's supposed to open. Do you know anything about it?"

He faltered in his boot polishing and caught his breath. "I beg your pardon, Miss Martha?"

"Oh, there's absolutely no point in pretending you don't know what I mean. Miles told me. He doesn't want to let anyone down and said you would know what to do." I tried to look confident and trustworthy. "You know I'd do anything for my cousin, no matter how unusual it may be."

"They won't like it, Miss, but it seems there be no other way. I knows I can trust'ee." He set the riding boot down next to its mate and I crossed the room to sit on the window seat.

"Tell me everything."

"There bain't be an easy way to tell'ee. I don't want'ee to be alarmed but I'll have to speak plain."

"I'd be grateful if you'd do just that. It'd make a welcome change. I'm heartily tired of having to decipher everyone's words."

John nodded, "Some things are best kept quiet."

"Such as?"

"Smuggling, Miss."

I kept outwardly calm. "Smuggling? Of course. Quite commonplace hereabouts. I'm sure most young men of Miles's age and adventurous disposition would find it hard to resist trying their hand."

"Aye, 'tis true but don't'ee think it strange that Master Miles be the one to get mixed up with such things? 'Ee never seemed the sort to me."

I had to admit the same thought crossed my mind. "Nevertheless, he is involved and 'tis obvious his injury will keep him from fulfilling his obligations. So, what are we to do?"

"We got no choice," said John carefully, "They do need someone to open the cellar doors and tend the warnin' lamp at Wild Court. Master Miles has attained the key from Lady Polgrey and keeps it in his room."

* * *

As I returned to the sick-room, I paused briefly on the landing to admire the early sunlight which was gradually dispersing the last silvery ribbons of mist and heard the usual refrain that preceded my young cousin, then saw Harry stride around the corner obviously returning from the stables, whistling Greensleeves loudly, his father's dogs at his heels. I tapped my fingers against the diamond-leaded windowpanes, and he looked up and waved cheerfully to me, the dogs cavorting about him, pink tongues lolling and tails a'wagging. With a jolly grin on his round face, he disappeared from view and I heard the back door open and then close with an enthusiastic thump. One of the dogs barked excitedly and Harry reprimanded the animal at the top of his voice. Then I heard him taking the stairs two at a time. He came racing along the corridor, pink-cheeked, wind-swept, and smelling strongly of fresh air and horses.

"Good day to you, Harry. You're up early."

He beamed at me. "Been out with the dogs. Couldn't sleep. Worried about Miles. Is he better?"

I shook my head, "I'm afraid he isn't."

The smile vanished. "Mama told me he was poorly, but I was sure he'd be well again today. He ain't goin' to die, is he?"

I took his cold hand in mine. "He's a fine strong fellow and you know Mrs Talbot will do her best by him."

"She *did* cure my earache when I was a boy," said Harry more optimistically.

"Of course, we'll both do our best to make him well again. Go and have some breakfast… you must be starving. I'll see you later and tell you how he goes."

Harry squeezed my hand and ambled away downstairs whistling Greensleeves to himself, slightly out of tune.

* * *

There came a moment when I thought we'd lost Miles for sure; the dry, all-consuming heat had raged like an out-of-control forest fire through his willowy young body for too long, devouring his strength and his will to live. When he opened his eyes to stare blindly up at me, it wasn't Miles but a stranger, full of white-hot rage and pain and wild mutterings which none of us could understand. Meggie ran to and fro from the kitchen with pitchers of water for bathing him. On occasion I was hard pressed not to just give in to the hollow despair I felt but the housekeeper would tolerate no such signs of weakness, telling me gruffly that I would be letting Miles down. One minute he'd be gasping through parched lips and tossing off the covers and screaming that he was on fire and the next, shivering convulsively, as though chilled to the very bone.

But, like the darkest moment before the dawn, just when I was ready to give up all hope, the fever finally broke. The relief was so intense that when Anne Talbot looked at me across the crumpled, sweat-soaked bed and smiled for the first time in two days, my knees buckled beneath me and I groped blindly for somewhere to collapse.

"Don't you go and pass out now just when you can make yourself useful," said the housekeeper without irony.

Eight

So it was, at midnight that night, I found myself trudging wearily down the track which wound its way towards my old home, Wild Court. I'd bound my sore ankle tightly so that walking wasn't too difficult, but it was still rather uncomfortable. I'd listened in dismay as John explained as gently as he could, how the smugglers had been using Wild Court as a hideaway for their contraband; it was the perfect place, secluded, and virtually abandoned to the rapid dilapidation usual for dwellings exposed to extreme weather on the coast. Its shuttered windows like blind eyes, its still, empty rooms an ideal haven for the smugglers and their booty. Miles, who knew the house inside out, had been in charge of receiving the goods. Apart from my cousin I was the only one who knew their way around the house and had access to the key.

John had provided me with a dark lantern, but even so it wasn't an enjoyable walk in the dark and, when it started to drizzle lightly, the familiar route became a dismal journey. I'd imagined a very different return home. I remembered how my father had often laughed at my constant perambulations between the two houses, remarking with pride that I'd be able to make the two-mile journey blindfold. As I crossed the Heights, I passed close to Maker Church but couldn't see its statuesque outline through the gloom. I tried not to think of my mother, who lay in her cold and lonely grave and realised that I hadn't visited her resting place since the funeral. It was as though by staying away from the only real evidence of her death, I could convince myself that she hadn't gone forever. There was no time to stop now so I continued resolutely on down the hill towards the estuary.

It seemed, and indeed was, an age since I was last at Wild Court and I approached it with trepidation knowing that I was about to awake memories I'd rather not confront. I pictured the day I'd left for Bristol, so filled with sadness and excited expectations; delighted at the prospect of visiting with our dear friends, Lady Sarah and Sir Aubrey Finch and yet heartsore to be leaving my parents and the home I loved. It had been the first time I'd been away from Wild Court and certainly the first time I'd ever ventured that far out of the county. I remember the mixed feelings I'd suffered as I was handed into the carriage and settled myself beside Ruth, the maid who was to accompany me on the long journey north. Mother and Father stood back as the driver cracked his whip and the vehicle lurched forward, shaking Ruth to the floor; it took me a moment to help her up and make sure she was safely ensconced once more upon the seat but by the time I was able to look out of the window we'd nearly turned the first corner and I was only able to catch a brief, tear-blurred glimpse of my parents standing by the house, waving. My mother was laughing. That was the last time I'd seen either of them. I hadn't had the courage to visit the house since the day I'd returned, I was afraid of coming face to face with the familiar ghosts roaming those echoing rooms.

The house was hidden away on the leeward side of a hook of densely wooded land which stretched out into the neck of the estuary. It stood with its back to the sea, well-protected from the any stormy weather in the Channel, nestled at the base of the gentle hill, in a sheltered but shallow combe, facing its own little harbour, and girded by rustling holm oaks and horse chestnuts. The house was a long colour-washed building of traditional local style, a stepped garden cut back into the hillside at the back. It was homely and beautifully proportioned, yet I knew Aunt Louisa looked down upon my mother for having ended up in a house with no pretensions of grandeur. Sometimes an exceptionally high tide would creep up over the harbour wall to lap gently at the front steps and I remembered how I'd kick off my shoes and splash happily across the flooded lawn, loving the feel of the water-logged grass between my toes. Pink heads of thrift danced above the shallow glassy lake of tidal water. It was like my very own private ocean where I sailed my little wooden boat my father had carved for me; where I could sit for hours watching the sea-breeze send silver and gold ripples shivering across its surface, miniature waves upon which my toy boat, the *Water Gypsy* bobbed, her handkerchief sails billowing, the water politely slapping her blue and white painted sides. I'd sit on the doorstep or on the old wooden mooring bollard at the end of the short quay and dabble my toes in the crystal-clear water and make believe I was a mermaid, combing my long hair with a seashell comb and singing a siren's bewitching song to entice ships onto the rocks. My father had understood the enchantment the fleeting shallow waters held for me; he called it my *Emerald Sea* and smiled indulgently at my intense joy.

I was wet through by now but struggled on, finally coming to the gate in the wall at the side of the grounds. I stopped to shutter my dark lantern, clipping the hinged door shut so no light could escape. The mournful drizzle had ceased, and a slight breeze was clearing the sky. Once through the gate I set off down the grassy track which led down to the harbour, as I neared the last corner before the house, I found I was dragging my feet, reluctant to see the place again. Then, remembering the reason for the journey, I took the corner in a kind of rush and as I did, as though it had been expressly waiting for that precise moment, the moon appeared between the dark scudding clouds and bathed my beloved home in a cold and eerie light. For a moment the house looked sinister and unwelcoming and I could have cried with anger and disappointment. All my dreams were here. Everything I longed for was here. And yet it bore no resemblance to the house I remembered.

Gritting my teeth, I took the key from my pocket, slid it into the lock and tried to turn it. At first it was stiff and uncooperative, I struggled with it rather impatiently, then recalled there was a trick to making it work. I pulled it out a fraction and wiggled it before twisting it sharply anti-clockwise. There was a satisfying familiar clunk, and the door was open.

I stepped quietly into the house, inhaling the sweet musty air with a sense of delight mingled with regret. The hallway was gloomy, but I remembered John's instructions, I was to show no light in the house. The windows, although shuttered, faced across the estuary and I dared not risk any light showing in a house that was supposed to be unoccupied, *unless* I had to warn the smugglers that the Excisemen were around.

It made no difference to me, the house was part of me, like a second skin. I knew every crooked inch of it by heart. I made my way upstairs with all the confidence and relief of a mole that, having found itself stranded above ground in the harsh daylight, manages, against all odds, to find again the comfort and security of its subterranean tunnels. In the darkness, it needs only its acute sense of smell to know it's once again in its element.

Upstairs, in the bedchamber at the furthest end of the house, I sat down to wait. I was wringing wet and could find nothing to dry myself with or even wrap myself in to try to keep warm. I was stiff with cold and fast becoming heavy-eyed when finally, my signal came.

On the opposite side of the estuary, a lantern flashed briefly, and I knew it was one o'clock. With chilled hands I lit a stump of tallow candle from the lantern's flame and set it in the oddly fashioned window; the candle sparked and guttered, and its pale-yellow light filled the long narrow tunnel. I carefully counted five seconds before extinguishing it. It was, John had explained, a smuggler's window; the light from the candle could be seen only from one particular point across the water. Smugglers on incoming vessels, probably inconspicuous fishing luggers like the one I'd recently been on, would be the only people to see the signal and would know if the light was extinguished that the Dragoons had either been led in another direction by decoys or were sound asleep in their beds and if the light stayed steady then there was danger.

I had no idea what to expect but John had instructed me to unbolt a door at the back of the cellar. I'd never seen this door and told John so and he'd explained that while we'd lived at Wild Court my father, believing the tunnel to be structurally unsound, and a danger to his adventurous young daughter, had had it bricked up to prevent accidents. The tunnel, an early exploratory mine, which had ultimately proved not to be a viable prospect, wound for a few hundred yards terminating prematurely in the wooded hillside, giving useful cover to the smugglers.

I was thankful that I could open up my lantern again because the cellar was draped with cobwebs and I had to duck and weave in order to avoid getting them caught in my hair. I'd only very occasionally been allowed to venture into the underworld kingdom of the cellars although I had begged my father often enough for permission, but for once he'd been quite strict with me, forbidding me to ever set foot in them. His words came back to me as I stood with my fingers on the cold metal latch. He wouldn't have approved of what I was about to do but I had to see this venture through if I was going to keep Miles safe. I lifted the latch, pulled open the heavy old door and teetered on the threshold as though about to descend into Hell itself.

I felt for the thick rope handrail, trying to avoid contact with the wall itself, which I had no doubt was crawling with all manner of slimy things. I stayed well away from the other side which had no banister, just a straight drop to the hard stone floor below. I reached the end of the flight and stepped down into a puddle of stagnant water.

John had described exactly where the door was to be found and since the cellars were now empty, I had no trouble finding it. I wasn't surprised to find the bricks had been somewhat hastily hacked out and thrown into an untidy heap against the wall. I drew back the obviously recently oiled bolts, as instructed, and then wondered what I should do next. Was I supposed to wait for the smugglers to arrive with their booty or having discharged my onerous duty, ought I to leave as quickly as possible? I was still trying to make up my mind when the decision was taken out of my hands. A sudden movement in the corner caught my attention and I turned to see a large rat contemplating me. I am not one of those silly females who lose their senses when confronted by a small rodent, but I have to admit it chilled my blood to find myself sharing such a dark and gloomy place with this creature and I decided to quit the cellar with all haste. I picked my way back up the steps, not an easy task with long skirts and a lantern to carry, and reached the top, slightly out of breath and eager for a lungful of fresher air. I lifted the latch and pushed but nothing happened. The door wouldn't open.

For several minutes I fought frantically with it, throwing myself at it and wrenching at the latch until my fingers were sore, eventually falling against its unyielding panels with a cry of frustration, angered beyond measure by my own stupidity. Why had I not thought of wedging the door open? Why had I come at all? How long would I have to stay there in the dank cold with only a glimmer of light to see by? Where was the rat?

Perhaps I had frightened it away. I realised it was only a waste of my energy to beat senselessly upon the door with my fists, there was no-one to hear my cries. There was nothing I could do but await the arrival of the smugglers and pray they wouldn't murder me before hearing my explanation. Were a gang of desperate cut-throats likely to take the time to listen to someone who could easily be a spy? Somehow I doubted it. With a sigh of resignation, I made myself as comfortable as possible on the top step, sitting huddled in the corner with my back against the door.

I must have been blessed with a remarkably robust constitution and a sad lack of ladylike sensibilities because despite the rat and the dankness, my damp clothes and the threat of imminent discovery and possible death, I must have dozed off, with my head couched on my folded arms and rested upon my knees.

I awoke with no idea of how long I had slept, to hear muffled sounds coming from the tunnel. The door swung open on its ancient hinges and the cellar was suddenly filled with flickering light and harsh noises. I quickly looked at my lantern and was actually glad to see it had gone out. I perched on my lonely eyrie, frozen with fear, my heart thumping wildly in my chest, waiting for them to notice me.

I watched as the men filed into the cellar, maybe half a dozen of them, dressed for extreme weather and laden down with kegs and bales. From my hiding-place I could hear what they were saying quite clearly.

A tall wiry man with a shock of unkempt black hair seemed to be dissatisfied with the whole proceedings and was making his feelings known to his companions, in a low grumbling voice.

"S'allus us gets the hard work. Don't see certain folk gettin' their hands dirty, do'ee? No, 'tis left to the likes of us to risk our necks to provide them fine clothes an' stuff." He kicked one of the bales. "What do'ee do, I asks myself, that's so almighty wunnerful? Tells *us* what to do, that's what, as though we couldn't work things out for ourselves." His gaunt face reminded me of the rat I'd encountered earlier.

"Ah, quit y'er bellyachin' Jessel, we've got to get the rest of the cargo in and get the boat back out to sea before dawn. We ain't got long." said one of the others angrily.

"Aye, I know, an' where's hisself, I asks? I'll tell'ee. Sleepin' comfortable an' cosy as a babe in 'is nice warm bed. That's where'ee be. While we be out in all weathers luggin' 'is contraband about, so's'ee can take all the profits and buy hisself another fancy coat. We could pocket the profits if we rid oursell's of him."

"Oh, yes?" said the other man, a solidly built type with white hair caught back in a tidy pigtail. "And how would we know which ships be a'carryin' the most valuable cargoes, without him telling us?"

"We'd find a way," snarled Jessel. "We ain't bloody stupid."

"Of course," sneered a man, I recognised as one of the labourers on my uncle's estate, "I 'spose like him, you be so friendly with the gentry you often be suppin' with them and samplin' their best French brandy!" Their laughter rumbled about the cellar and made me draw further back into the darkest shadows.

Jessel glared about him, sullenly aware that he was outnumbered, "Oh, aye, that's right, laugh if'ee will. Ye're a bunch of old women to be led about by the nose by someone who be no better than the worst of us." He kicked out angrily at the bale again and marched off down the tunnel.

"He'll be back," remarked one of the men. "He needs the money just like the rest of us. Some of us ain't had any wages for months."

Oh, no, I thought, that's Uncle Joshua's doing.

"'Ee always was one to whine about the least thing. We'd be better off without 'im." said the white-haired man.

The muttered conversation grew faint as the handful of men who remained moved away into the tunnel and disappeared from sight.

I waited, holding my breath and listening so intently to the silence that all I could hear was the blood pounding in my ears and my unsteady heartbeat.

How long would they be? Would I have enough time to escape down the tunnel before they returned with the rest of their illicit goods? I made myself sit there while I counted slowly to a hundred. Dare I risk moving? No one appeared, so I allowed myself the luxury of stretching my cramped limbs. Cautiously, I stood up. My left leg was quite numb and would only move sluggishly, the pain of the returning feeling was almost unbearable. Overcome, I stamped my foot to ease the discomfort, caution thrown to the winds.

I was to wonder later, with some exasperation, how I hadn't noticed the man left standing guard. He stood just inside the tunnel waiting for the next consignment.

I found myself being dragged down the steps, like a rag doll, with no apparent consideration for my gender and thrown forcefully into a heap on the dirty floor.

When the other men returned a short while later with more bales and caskets, I was used no less harshly; rudely interrogated and generally made to feel that I was about to be unceremoniously murdered and hurled into the estuary.

Terrified for my life, I could only stammer feeble half-sentences, which, not surprisingly, fell upon deaf ears. I quickly reached the disconcerting conclusion that a violent end was to be my fate unless I could persuade them that I was no threat.

"*Please!* Listen to me!" I pleaded desperately. "'Tis as I've told you. John sent me because Miles is injured. I came to open the tunnel door. No more than that, I swear! The cellar door jammed, and I couldn't get out. Oh, why won't you *listen?*"

There were sullen mutterings from several of the men and the one with white hair scowled at me. "More likely you'm a spy for the revenue officers."

"Oh, merciful heaven, don't be so ridiculous!" I snapped, completely out of patience with their stupid, suspicious faces. "Do you really think I'd willingly sit for hours in the dark, on a cold, wet step with rats crawling over my feet just to listen to your pathetic little squabbles? Do I look as though I've taken leave of my senses? If the Customs men had wanted to spy on you, don't you think they might have sent someone a mite more competent than me? Anyway, do not some of you know me?" I looked directly at my uncle's employee who had the grace to look a little shamefaced. A thought suddenly struck me. "If you don't believe me, why don't you try to open the door?"

This apparently made enough sense to some of them and the man from my uncle's estate took my advice, passing me with a nervous smile and to my profound relief, he found the door to still be jammed tight.

"That still don't prove nothin'," growled the white-haired man

I shook my head in despair. How could I convince them?

There was a sudden commotion from the tunnel and three men emerged from its dark mouth. One was unknown to me, the second was the sailor Colquite and the third was Liam

Cavanagh. I've seldom been so pleased to see anyone in my life. I started forward through the knot of surly smugglers. "Oh, thank heaven, you are come!" I declared. "Would you please tell these imbeciles that I'm not a spy and that I'm free to leave!"

There followed a kind of astonished silence, astonished and amused. I looked up into the Irishman's face. He unclasped my fingers, which had, unbeknownst to me, laced themselves about his arm.

"Let us not be too hasty about this, Miss Pentreath," he said slowly, "I'm not at all sure my men wish you to leave."

I stared at him in disbelief. "But, surely, you understand the reason why? You saw Miles! I was the only one they could trust. I would hardly betray my own cousin now, would I?"

"Ah, gentlemen, she has a point." He sounded unruffled. "Let us pause to consider the facts for a moment. Here we have a young lady who just the other night did everything in her power to save the life of her cousin, who she knew to be a rogue. Is it logical she would then contrive to send this same cousin to the gallows?" He calmly rested his back against the cellar wall and surveyed the scene: the now irresolute smugglers, the untidy heaps of contraband and finally me. Although, I couldn't see his face properly I had the feeling he was inwardly laughing.

"They were going to kill me," I said flatly.

He eyed his men with interest, "May I enquire which one of you fine heroic fellows was going to deprive Miss Pentreath of her life? Could it have been you, Salter?", he asked the white-haired man. "Were you going to squeeze her pretty neck 'til she turned blue? Or would you have tossed her overboard as you rowed back to the ship?"

Salter shifted his weight uneasily, his expression mutinous. "How was we to know she be another of your'n, Cap'n?"

Liam Cavanagh examined his cuffs studiously and something in his manner made Salter take an involuntary step backwards. The Irishman gave the man the benefit of a look that seemed totally devoid of threat or menace yet somehow managed to convey infinitely more than any gesture of aggression. Without taking his eyes from Salter he said, "Colquite, take Miss Pentreath back to the Hall, then return to the ship with the others."

"Cap'n, she could identify us," Salter said anxiously.

"You have my word that she will not inform on us," said Captain Cavanagh equably. I opened my mouth to say something indignant but a speaking glance from him made me swallow the words and without further demur I followed my reluctant escort into the tunnel. Someone had thrust my unlit lantern into my hand, and I thought I could always use it to defend myself.

Colquite marched at a bruising pace along the tunnel, causing some discomfort to my ankle, and only slowed when we reached the entrance, where a string of ponies was patiently waiting. He untied the leader and brusquely levered me onboard. When we reached the Hall, without learning anything more about the other, he took me straight to the kitchen door and turned immediately to leave.

"Thank you, sir," I said, leaning against the door because my legs were refusing to support me.

Colquite stopped in his tracks and turned to me, a look of impatient enquiry in his eyes, "Ain't nothin' personal, Miss but we're all facin' prison an' worse. An' the cap'n more'n most. A careless word an' we be done for. But how could'ee understand how much 'ee's risked for us?" He shook his head, angry that he should have said so much. Then without a backward glance he disappeared into the night, leaving me wondering what it was about Liam Cavanagh that inspired such fierce loyalty.

I was still puzzling over this as I tiptoed to my bedchamber. As I passed Miles's room, I saw his candle still burned, so I tapped gently on the door and entered on his softly spoken command. He was propped up against the pillows, as grey as a washed-out dishrag, his eyes sunken hollows in a face I found hard to recognise. He reached out a thin, shaking hand and I perched on the edge of the bed and took his cold fingers in mine.

"You've been a damnably long time, Martha! I've been worried sick. What the hell happened?"

"Don't worry. I did as I was told. The cellars are now crammed full of silk and tea and tobacco and enough brandy to keep the local gentry inebriated for months!"

"Well done. But what kept you so long? I was convinced you'd come to grief."

"Not a bit of it." I said with a forced laugh, while debating how much to tell him of the night's events. How wise would it be to describe how ill I had been used when in his extremely weakened state he might become agitated and suffer a serious setback. On the other hand, I knew it wouldn't be too long before he heard the truth from someone with less tact, so I told him briefly and without embellishment the less contentious part of my adventure. Even though I had avoided mentioning the death threats and the rough handling I'd received, he still rained curses down on the smugglers' heads and laid a good deal of the blame at his own door. "If only I hadn't let you go! I should have known. When I think of what might have happened had Cavanagh not turned up when he did!"

I soothed him as best I could, but he was determined to work himself up into a frenzy of self-reproach. I found some of Mrs Talbot's sleeping draught and persuaded him to swallow some.

When finally, he slept, I was able to climb numbly into my own chilly bed in the hope of getting a few hours' sleep before work began again.

I was to be disappointed. I couldn't help mulling over my night's adventure and the problems I now faced. I wasn't able to deal with the fact that Miles was so deeply entangled with the smugglers; having been so close to the simmering violence had made me very aware of the danger he was in. I needed help.

But was there anyone I could trust?

After much confused reflection sleep claimed me but just in that fleeting moment between the realms of awake and asleep, I came unexpectedly upon the answer.

Nine

Finding a moment to leave the house unobserved proved to be fraught with seemingly unsurmountable difficulties. Aunt Louisa appeared determined to keep me occupied the entire time with trivial errands. I spent a fruitless morning dancing attendance on Miles who thankfully slept most of the time and Rowena, who was as determined as her mother to keep me constantly busy and ensure that I didn't have a chance to forget my lowly position. I changed linen on all the beds and helped Meggie sew some muslin bags for lavender and darned several pairs of stockings belonging, I surmised, to Harry, if the state of them was anything to go by; he must have worn them through a briar patch, I thought with a fond smile. I polished silver, attempted to clean and tidy Uncle Joshua's best wig, fed the chickens, and swept the kitchen. Then I was summoned to help Rowena.

And so, I found myself on my knees in front of my petulant and fault-finding cousin, fastening the buckles on her shoes and couldn't help wondering what my father would have said to see me treated thus. Pride made me dash away an inexpedient tear from my cheek and I promptly cursed the momentary moment of self-pity when I beheld the look of triumph in Rowena's dark eyes.

"Are you dissatisfied, Cousin?" she asked slyly, "Would you rather be in the poorhouse?"

I bent my head, concentrating on my task, my fingers a trifle unsteady on the jewelled buckle. "No, I'm happy not to have been cast out into the snow. I count myself most fortunate to have found such a thoroughly welcoming home. And I know my father will be grateful too, when he returns. If only he were here now to witness your generosity," I said with false sincerity.

Rowena studied me for a moment, a faintly puzzled expression marring her usually flawless features. "Yes, indeed," she said uncertainly, then laughed and stretching out her leg, arched her pretty ankle, and examined the shoe with satisfaction. "That will do, I suppose. Now, my hair and then you can attend to my petticoats which need some repair. Oh, and you'd better take my rose satin gown because there's a stain on the hem and I plan to wear it tomorrow. I've been invited to The Manor for dinner. 'Tis bound to be a fine affair and the Baron will be there. You'll dress my hair in the latest style, I have no wish to be outshone by that dreadful Jarrett woman. Oh, yes, and I want you to remove the lace at the neck of the gown, I find it altogether too fussy."

Fussy, indeed, I thought; it would be nearer the truth to admit she found it altogether too concealing. And yet, for all my dislike of her, I was still vaguely worried about her fascination with the Baron. She was, after all, just a young and impressionable girl too much under the harmful influence of her domineering and malevolent mother.

Rowena pushed me away with an elegantly shod foot, "Do hurry yourself or I shall never be ready in time."

Taking my queue as intended, I enquired politely about her destination and tried hard not to be irritated by her complacency and entitlement.

"The Baron is taking me for an outing to Millbrook in his new carriage. 'Twill be vastly amusing, he's such an entertaining companion. It must be that dash of foreign blood that makes him so — thrilling," she declared with a delicious little shiver. I managed to refrain from voicing my dismay. I knew that not only would she dislike above all things being lectured by me, but she would probably be spurred on to even greater indiscretions by any strictures I had to offer.

"Who will be your chaperone?" I asked.

She tossed her curls and threw up her hands, "La! As though we need a chaperone! Although, Mama has insisted that Lady Anstey's lady's maid accompany us just for appearances' sake."

I knew there was nothing I could do but keep an eye on her from a distance. I couldn't think why I should care at all. I spent the rest of the morning hoping the Baron would carry her off in his vulgar new carriage and never bring her back.

Eventually Rowena was ready to be dashed through the countryside by Baron Rosenberg and Aunt Louisa and Lady Anstey were settled in the withdrawing room with cups of hot chocolate and a tray of freshly baked marchpain tartlets, dishes of prunellos and chocolate amandes. My aunt was certainly going all out to impress her guest. They would progress from such restrained delicacies and gentle gossip to glasses of Canary and vindictive scandalmongering. I couldn't wait to get away from their maleficence.

I had been granted a few precious hours of freedom by Mrs Talbot, but she warned me to not be late in case Miles needed me. I promised that I would be back before dark and then raced round to the stables where I begged the head groom to allow me to borrow the pony and trap. He was a dear old man who had always had a soft spot for my mother, a naturally gifted horsewoman. He brought out the little grey mare and put her between the shafts, talking to her all the time, his rheumatic fingers gentle. I thanked him and allowed him to hand me into the cart although I was more than capable of climbing in by myself. He squeezed my hand briefly and smiled kindly, "We all misses the dear lady an' your father," he admitted softly.

"Thank you so much, Jedadiah. It's nice to know I'm not the only one who misses them."

"Yes, indeed, Miss Martha," he mumbled and shuffled back to the stable where he was greeted by a fond whinny.

I set out at reckless speed for Picklecombe Point. John had given me the direction and to my surprise I found it was the old tower just south of Maker Church. I had thought it to be in ruins and uninhabited but apparently not so.

It was a beautiful day, crisply cold, the sky bleached white like old bones. My breath made blue clouds in the frozen air. I urged the grey mare onwards and soon I could feel my cheeks glowing pinkly. I gazed upon the wind-tortured trees and bushes and flattened yellowed grass and thought them beautiful. In the distance the sea shone like burnished silver and for a brief moment I imagined myself skimming over its polished surface like a kittiwake with the distant ocean, wide and wild and beckoning, never far from its thoughts.

I shook away the fanciful notion and guided the mare along the narrow track which wound its way to Picklecombe and the tower. Where the track hugged the coast, I could look down on the snowy backs of the gulls as they slid in their endless circles and spirals.

As I approached Holmoak Beacon I wondered for the first time if I was doing the sensible thing; a small voice told me I was being a complete fool, and another egged me on with words of encouragement. My head was like a battleground. But I continued on my way, driving the cart boldly up to the tower and trying not to be intimidated by its looming height. I tied the reins and jumped down.

Holmoak Beacon stood on the west-facing side of the valley which led to Picklecombe Point and the Channel. The square tower was only about a hundred and fifty years old and had been built by a local landowner in a moment of imaginative lunacy. Most people referred to it as Fidgeon's Folly although it was now known as Holmoak Beacon. The building consisted of one large tower of four floors and two smaller adjoining towers, one of three floors and one of two, which huddled together as though for warmth. There was evidence that some larger windows had been recently added to match the fake medieval cusped windows which poor deluded Percival Fidgeon had insisted on incorporating in his original design. Until John had told me about it, I had thought the place to be little more than a ghostly ruin on the point of tumbling down. Last time I'd seen it, the insistent salty sea winds had begun to erode its edges, smoothing them and worrying their way into the cracks to gnaw hungrily at the mortar. Even the sturdiest of buildings could be turned to rubble in a relatively short time.

But now, the signs of decay had been eradicated, the tower stood foursquare and defiant, as though daring the elements to sneak past its renewed defences again. The narrow front door was clearly constructed to repel imaginary Viking hoards and very real tempests. I pulled the bell and waited.

A manservant opened the door and managed to convey deep disapproval in every line of his attenuated body. "And whom shall I say is calling?", he asked in a rigidly polite voice.

"My name is Miss Pentreath, and could you explain it's a matter of some urgency, please?"

He asked me to wait in the library while he informed his master of my arrival. His master, he said pointedly, was still in his bed. This did not surprise me in the least. I was glad the servant was not in my employ but smiled at him nonetheless, in case he thought I might be tempted to make off with the silver.

I found myself, to my utter delight, in a treasure trove, an Aladdin's Cave. Filled with wonder, I tried to take in the unexpected beauty of the room. The panelled walls, the paintings depicting strange lands in rich colours, shelf upon shelf overflowing with ancient books and scrolls, a mahogany writing desk piled high with papers and maps, goose quills and silver inkwells, jewel encrusted boxes and bizarre objects I couldn't even put a name to. In one corner was a virginal, inlayed with mother-of-pearl and elaborately painted with flowers and birds, in another a gilded harp. Much of the furniture was ornately carved, either Oriental or Indian in origin and everywhere there were more untidy towers of beautifully bound books. The shutters were partially closed, presumably to keep the warmth in and the bitter winds from the sea, out. A small fire flickered in the hearth, obviously unattended, so I fed the flames with some logs stacked beside it, supposing that as someone had gone to the trouble of lighting it, they couldn't object.

I removed an open book, written in some indecipherable language, some sheets of music and a lute from the armchair nearest the fire and made myself comfortable with a greedy armful of books. I breathed in their sweet leathery smell and gently, reverently stroked their dry, creamy pages. I had never seen so many, let alone had the opportunity to choose one from such a rare and wonderful collection. I would have been content to remain there the whole day, joyfully absorbing their secret delights, which, as it turned out, was fortunate because my host did not hurry himself to greet me. It was almost an hour later when I heard him approaching in a leisurely fashion. I rose to my feet, still clutching the book I'd been studying and stood rather nervously beside the chair, any bravado I might have been harbouring suddenly having deserted me.

The door creaked open and I was very nearly rendered speechless by the vision of grace and style that drifted so languidly into the room. Purple velvet, silver buttons and a waistcoat embroidered with silver thread. No wonder he'd been so long. The firelight glinted on his shoe buckles and the diamond in his cravat. He held a handkerchief to his lips to partially stifle a yawn.

"'Pon my soul, madam, it ain't considerate in you to call at such an hour. As you can see, I have had to chivvy my valet and now I look a sight," he gestured to his magnificent and perfect ensemble with distaste. "For pity's sake! What time is it?"

I glanced at the lacquered bracket clock on the mantelpiece, "'Tis nearly one o'clock, sir." I informed him. "In the *afternoon*." Pointedly.

Sir Montagu Fitzroy clutched his head, tottered elegantly to the nearest chair and collapsed into its arms, the very picture of lethargy. "Merciful heaven, one o'clock? What can you be thinkin'? I never rise before two. I declare I shall be quite unfit for company tonight," he declared mournfully.

I couldn't help smiling, for I found him delightfully theatrical and vastly more amusing than anyone else of my acquaintance; but at the same time seriously questioned my reasons for turning to this absurd popinjay for help. It seemed a rather desperate and pointless venture when I came to give it sober consideration. Suddenly I wished I'd listened to the other warning voice and hadn't come at all. I started to edge towards the door. "I'm so sorry— I didn't mean disturb you. I looked at your books — I hope you don't mind. I really must go now," I faltered, and to my chagrin turned pink with embarrassment.

There was an almost imperceptible change in the atmosphere, I don't know what altered but it stopped me in my tracks. Sir Montagu tapped a long finger against his jaw and stared thoughtfully at me. "Confound it, m'dear, consider my library entirely at your disposal. Books should be appreciated. Only delighted to find someone who loves them as much as I do."

Surprised and intoxicated by the idea of having free rein in this bibliophile's paradise, I tried to express my thanks. "So kind — I didn't expect — I mean — you don't *seem* — bookish!" I gabbled, wondering how I came to be so lacking in social graces. I was grateful for the dim light because I could feel my face was aflame as I backed towards the door.

Sir Montagu stood up, his back to the fire, "Appearances can be deceptive," he murmured. "Now, how can I be of assistance, Miss Pentreath?"

"I've changed my mind," I said, sounding horridly sullen, because I felt so awkward.

The long fingers undid a silver button on his waistcoat, stroked the raised pattern on its polished face and then did it up again. "D'you not trust me?"

My hand froze halfway to the door handle. "*Trust* you, Sir Montagu? I don't know why I *should* trust you above any of my own relations. I really have no idea why I should," I said softly, almost to myself. "But, for some inexplicable reason, I do. Insanity, I fear. And that's why I came here this afternoon. I trust Miles because I've known him all my life and in all those years, he's never given me reason to doubt him. I've no idea why I should feel the same way about you for you've only ever given me reason to be suspicious. And it isn't because you rescued me from that odious man either, although I am truly grateful. Actually, I really should dislike you intensely after your abhorrent behaviour when I first met you! I am unable to explain such wholly illogical feelings." Fearing rejection or derision, I felt like racing from the room but managed to suppress the urge and face him squarely, chin up.

With the faintest rustle of finest Brussels lace, he rose gracefully and came to stand before me, his expression unreadable in the poor light. "'Tis the very greatest honour y'do me, Miss Pentreath. The very greatest. You can have no idea how affectin' I find your blind faith in me and can only hope 'twill be justified." For just an instant I felt he'd let a mask slip but even as I looked up at him, all was as before.

With a bejewelled hand he led me to a small sofa, and we sat together and for a moment he retained my hand in his.

And there, in that wondrous room, in the warm half-light I confided my fears for Miles. "He's so rash, so hopelessly reckless! He fancies himself in love with Miss Fairchild and it seems to have driven all rational thought from his head. I'm quite certain that as soon as he is well enough, he'll challenge Ben Fairchild to a duel and from what I've heard the fellow is an experienced and callous fighting man. When he was a boy Miles was forever righting wrongs and getting himself a bloody nose for his efforts, but this is different, this is serious, *deadly* serious. He almost died. He won't listen to me — he thinks that I don't understand such matters." I paused to see if my companion was showing any signs of boredom but found him wholly attentive, so I continued, "And now, there's this other business. He seems to have become embroiled with an extremely unsavoury gang of cutthroats and the other night, when I was forced to undertake duties he couldn't fulfil, I was treated in rather a discourteous fashion by these men and now he's threatening to take his revenge and he'll doubtless be killed!' I took a breath.

Sir Montagu idly polished his quizzing glass, looking thoughtful. "These — er — singularly disagreeable gentlemen, would they be smugglers, I wonder?"

"You know about them?"

A look of comic surprise crossed his painted face, "We are cheek by jowl with Cornwall, m'dear! D'you know anyone who has *not* heard of smugglin'? It needed very little deduction to reach this conclusion." He laughed softly. "Not only does everyone know about it but I'll lay odds most of 'em are culpable themselves in one way or another. Turnin' a blind eye. Watchin' the wall. How many would own to havin' a secret supply of rum or brandy? Then, of course, there are those poor souls who are behind on their rent and suddenly and magically are able to pay it and more besides. There will always be those who find it necessary to break the law, as there will always be those who feel 'tis their duty to reinforce it."

"But it is so unlike him. Even though the Polgrey estate seems to be mired in debt now, he said he would approach their benefactor to solve the matter. I can't see how he would think this way of curing their money woes would be acceptable. I mean, I've heard tales of smugglers torturing and murdering those who oppose them. A brutish business!"

"Ah, I'll warrant you're thinkin' of those villains from Kent. A different kettle of fish altogether, m'dear. Cornish smugglers have a well-founded reputation for affability. Now, if I remember rightly, it was The Hawkhurst Gang who besmirched the good name of smugglers everywhere. An uncommonly evil bunch of ruffians. Needless to say, in comparison, the Cornish smuggler is a mild-mannered soul," he said pleasantly.

"I'm not sure that I believe you Sir Montagu. I cannot bear to contemplate my own dear Miles being associated with any kind of criminal activity. He may have a perfectly sound reason but as he's so very miserable I don't believe he's doing it of his own volition."

Sir Montagu took a turn about the room, finally coming to rest beside the fireplace. "An' you think I can somehow persuade him to give up his excitin' new career?" He arched an eyebrow, "Methinks you have more faith in me than I merit. I'm interested to know why you thought, I, of all people, might help. Seems to me a very odd choice."

I had no hesitation in responding. "Everyone else appears to have a vested interest in the smuggling or wishes Miles and myself harm. You may have quite the worst manners of anyone I'm acquainted with but at least you're on the other side of the fence, on the outside, looking in. And, when I came to think sensibly about your performance at the Manor, for I'm quite certain now that it was an act, I felt it had not been entirely for my benefit but perhaps for one or all of the others in that room." I didn't wait to see what effect my theory had upon my host but continued in a rush of words, "Then when you dined at Polgrey Hall, I realised you were, in fact, equally unpleasant to most of the guests and you so gallantly came to my rescue as well." Here Sir Montagu sketched a mocking bow and made a humble face and I laughed, "Most pretty, sir. Truly, you should be on the stage!"

His eyes gleamed and the slightest of smiles touched his lips. I suddenly had the strangest feeling he was about to say something significant but then thought better of the impulse. "How refreshin' it is to be appreciated, Miss Pentreath, although I might be tempted to recommend a little more prudence in your future dealin's with certain shady characters, otherwise you may find yourself in very deep water, quite literally."

"I thank you for your warning, Sir Montagu. I will heed your words. But you have yet to reassure me. Do I need to fear you as well?"

Long, thin fingers adjusted the perfection of lace at his wrist in a curiously familiar manner. "Of one thing you may be quite certain, m'dear — there is absolutely no reason whatsoever to fear Sir Montagu. He's y'r most devoted servant and will do all in his limited power to aid your oh, so hot-headed cousin."

As I was taking my leave I turned back to where he stood shadowed in the doorway. "Have you ever observed, Sir Montagu, how a wild animal in pain or distress, will sometimes willingly surrender itself into the hands of someone it should perhaps have good reason to fear?"

"No, I'm relieved to say, I have not," said that gentleman crushingly.

I smiled at him, "Well, more's the pity because it might explain why I came to you," I remarked sweetly and climbed at once into the cart and drove away at a smart pace before he could think of something withering to say.

Ten

On impulse, I made a long detour on the way back to Polgrey Hall, to call upon Eleanor Fairchild. I was disappointed to find her not at home and wondered where she could possibly have gone. I'd received the impression that she was usually loathe to stray far from the safety of her cottage as the villagers regarded her with suspicion.

In the village I discovered the probable reason for her absence: a winter fair, a rather half-hearted attempt to cheer the drab November days and cheat a few pennies from the tight-fisted locals. Somehow, I knew Eleanor would want to be as far as possible from these roistering strangers, with their sly faces and quick hands.

A few road-weary pedlars and a small, bedraggled troupe of tumblers and jugglers had joined forces and were straining to raise a song and a smile, while providing distraction for the cutpurses and sneakthieves who slid unnoticed amongst the sparse crowd. The miserable locals, who stood shivering in the cold, were showing no huge desire to be entertained. There was a small, but noisy group of boys, intent upon having fun at everyone else's expense; they were taunting a half-starved, stumpy-tailed mongrel, which, unfortunately turned out to belong to one of the more muscular and quick-tempered jugglers. The juggler took exception to their unkind antics and a fight broke out between the travellers and the villagers and before any rational person could calm the stormy waters, the cramped and muddy square was a flailing, bellowing, bloody, cursing tangle of arms and legs and the sound of cracking jaws and bludgeoned noses filled the air.

I watched with a kind of horrified fascination from the edge of the fray. A muddy shoe whistled past, narrowly missing my head; several stray dogs entered into the spirit of the thing and dashed to and fro in a frenzy of excitement, yapping loudly and snapping their yellow teeth at the heels of the combatants.

The original beast, somehow sensing that he had been, albeit inadvertently, the cause of all this commotion, had the good sense to skulk away down the lane out of harm's way.

The villagers, tired of the hardships of country life in the winter, fought with undisguised relish, whilst the travellers, although brimful of bitterness and resentment for the way they were generally treated wherever they went, were in the main, undernourished and therefore it came as no great surprise when the locals gained the upper hand and finally routed the tag-rag troupe of gypsies.

The menfolk of the village, bruised and covered in mud and glory, celebrated their great victory by descending on the only alehouse for several miles and drinking it dry. The reason for the battle was duly forgotten in a haze of alcohol and triumphant exaggeration.

The grey mare picked her way distastefully through the trampled, ploughed mud and the forgotten scattering of battered hats and shoes. It was like a battlefield in miniature but thankfully without any corpses. Knowing it must be going on for three o'clock I urged the mare into a fast trot. I would be late for preparing dinner and Aunt Louisa may already have discovered that I'd been missing for the better part of the afternoon. I need not have worried. The Hall was in a state of complete turmoil, dinner and errant niece quite forgotten.

It seems that while I'd been gallivanting about the countryside the Dragoons had paid another unannounced visit to the house, this time specifically to see Miles. They had expressed grave suspicions about the nature of his injury, and it had been patently obvious to anyone with the slightest intelligence that they suspected him of some extremely nefarious activities. Nobody seemed to know how the Dragoons had come by this information or for that matter how they came to hear about his injury in the first place. They had questioned Miles and interrogated the servants, frightening one of the scullery maids into a fit and maddening my aunt beyond measure. The scullery maid was still weeping copiously into her apron but receiving scant sympathy. According to Mrs Talbot the soldiers had all but dragged Miles from his sickbed in their strenuous efforts to interview him. They had remained entirely unconvinced by his repeated explanations and had only finally quit the house after Aunt Louisa had left them in no doubt that, if her beloved son died due to their ill-treatment, she would personally see them all swing from the nearest gibbet.

Lieutenant Robin Danserfield had not been with them this time; in his stead, there was a new officer, his commission recently purchased, determined to make his presence felt in the district - a young man with ambition, no scruples, and a tactless streak a mile wide. While Lieutenant Danserfield had been called away in search of some known smugglers sighted in an alehouse in Polperro, this young officer, having temporarily been left in charge, had somehow come by information against my cousin and, seeking to advance his career as rapidly as possible, decided to take the matter upon himself. Had he had the sense to discreetly enquire instead of demanding and cleverly insinuate himself into the house with guile and flattery instead of barging in issuing threats, he may have earned respect; as it was, he failed on all counts and was forced to sound the retreat, covered in confusion and blaming everyone else for his incompetence.

The housekeeper was still quivering with righteous indignation. Miles, she told me, seemed to be fretting about something and was far from being the perfect convalescent. His irritability was uncharacteristic and could not but cause concern.

I raced straight to his bedchamber, cursing myself for having left him for so long. I saw that Mrs Talbot had been right to worry; Miles was restless and unreasonably quarrelsome. He demanded to know where I'd been all day and why I constantly neglected him. Without wishing to tell him an outright lie I knew I couldn't mention my visit to Holmoak Beacon, I told him I'd been to visit Eleanor Fairchild, hoping to distract him. But before I could tell him she'd not been at home, he was demanding to know how she looked and whether she'd mentioned him. He was naturally crest-fallen when I explained but I tried to cheer him up with an amusing description of the fight in the village square. To his credit, he at least pretended to find the story diverting but it was plainly evident that his thoughts were elsewhere.

* * *

And so another day passed and then another until it seemed I was sleepwalking through the endless hours. Miles made unsteady and slow progress; too weak to eat well or even talk much, he slept the days away. I watched from my perch on the window seat, worrying about his shadowed eyes and hollowed cheeks; his usually healthy and youthful complexion having disappeared to be replaced by a greyness more suited to an elderly man. My respect for Mrs Talbot grew daily as she bore the brunt of the nursing. Of Aunt Louisa there was little sign bar a fleeting daily visit. Lucius and Harry came regularly to encourage their sibling and to my great astonishment even Rowena deigned to visit the sickroom albeit with a clove-scented handkerchief pressed firmly to her pretty nose. Lucius even troubled himself enough to help Miles while away the hours by playing backgammon and cards, but I noticed there was between them a strained air and hazarded a guess that the tricky question of Eleanor Fairchild had still not been satisfactorily resolved. I was idly pondering the problem, whilst sitting with a peacefully sleeping Miles, when Meggie came running breathlessly from the kitchen with a message for me.

"'Tis Miss Fairchild, come to speak to'ee! She says 'tis im — imp — somethin' tha' she do see'ee."

"Imperative?" I suggested, rising quickly to my feet.

"Tha' be it, Miss Martha. She be all of a-twitter." Leaving Meggie to sit with Miles, I hastened downstairs to find Eleanor just as Meggie had described, in a highly emotional state.

"I must speak with you privately," she said, nervously twisting her fingers together. "Is there somewhere we can talk?"

I showed her into the still room and shut the door. I opened the wooden shutters and sat down on a low bench while Eleanor paced the uneven flagstones, her face pale and drawn.

"Eleanor?" I said after watching her wrestle with her thoughts for a few minutes.

She briefly stopped her pacing. "How is Miles? Is he recovered?", she asked anxiously.

"I believe he is on the mend although for a while we were not sure that he would pull through. The wound became infected," I explained gently. "Is this about Miles? He has told me what happened."

"He will not have told you the half of it, I'm afraid," she said miserably. "I've no business involving you in my problems, but I could not think what to do for the best."

"For pity's sake, Eleanor! Tell me before I go mad from worry!"

"'Tis Ben, my brother. He returned from serving overseas, without a word of warning to discover Miles had been visiting me in his absence." She paused and looked hard at me, trying to assess what my reactions might be. "Before he joined the Navy, he was involved in a small way with the local smugglers, but he got into trouble and had to leave the country with all possible speed. I thought — *hoped* I'd never see him again but now he's back and has taken up where he left off. Only this time 'tis no longer just smuggling." Her voice grew faint.

"Wrecking." I breathed, the very word striking fear into my heart.

She nodded, her eyes wide and frightened, "What are we to do?" she whispered, as though the walls had ears. "If I were sure that 'tis only Ben who has joined them, I think I could bear it." She could not meet my gaze. "Oh, Martha, I'm so afraid Miles has become one of them! That is how he came to be wounded. Ben was attempting to persuade him to help the wreckers and was having no success until he threatened to marry me off to someone else, should Miles not agree to his demands. They fought and Ben drew a knife. I threw myself at him and spoiled his aim, otherwise he would have killed Miles. Ben told him to reconsider his decision or harm would come to me." She grasped my hands. "Ben never makes idle threats and Miles knows this. I just know he'll join them. To save me. He's too good." Tears rolled down her cheeks and dripped prettily off her chin. I patted her hand distractedly. Now it was clear why Miles had been fretting so these last few days; he'd been desperately trying to untangle the web in which he'd been so deftly caught. Either way he found himself trapped; he could not risk Ben Fairchild harming Eleanor and certainly had no desire to see her married off to someone else, nor had he any wish to become entangled with the kind of men who thought nothing of luring ships onto the rocks in order to plunder the cargo. An innocent life meant less than nothing to them, all passengers and crew who survived the wreck and then the sea had to die regardless of age or gender. I'd heard horrific tales of the callous and cold-blooded treatment meted out to those unlucky enough to find themselves washed up alive on the beach.

But, if the only alternative was for Miles to be forced to stand by helplessly while this fragile creature was mistreated by her bullying brother, he'd have little choice but to join the wreckers.

Eleanor stared blindly out of the grimy window, her eyes shimmering with tears. "I couldn't bear him to do such a thing for my sake. He's been so wonderfully kind to me, and I know this would kill him inside, but I can see no way out. What am I to do, Martha?"

"Could you not run away together? Miles could take you somewhere your brother would never find you… to London perhaps?"

This tentative suggestion was met with silence.

"You love each other do you not?", I asked gently.

She gave a tragic, hiccoughing sob and covered her face with her hands. "Oh, my god, 'twould be so easy if it were true! I think he truly believes he loves me but 'tis no more than a boyish infatuation. He'll realise one day we are not at all suited."

"And you, Eleanor, do you love him?"

She raised a tearstained, still beautiful face. "He's the finest, kindest man I've ever known, and I don't deserve his affections," she faltered, "But 'tis Lucius I love."

"*Lucius!*", I gasped, dumbfounded and not sure I'd heard her correctly.

"Are you really so surprised?" she asked, and I found that I was extremely surprised.

I was unable to imagine anyone loving Lucius; he had always been so perfectly unloveable to me and even though he had been a little more approachable recently, he was still not to be trusted. But, no, I could not understand it at all.

"You are astonished that anyone could find anything at all in Lucius to love?" she asked with a damp sniff. "Unfortunately, you cannot love where your head dictates, only where your heart desires. Since the very first day I have loved him, even though I knew it to be hopeless. He has done nothing to encourage my hopes, treating me as he does everyone from duchess to tavern wench — all the same." She turned away from me. "Why can I not love Miles instead, for he is all any sensible woman could desire; loving and gentle and loyal. He would try until his dying day to make me happy; tread hot coals, fight dragons for me. But, no, I have to love someone who cares naught for me, who cares not if I live or die." I sensed rather than saw her wry smile, "I never had much sense as a girl. I seem to have even less now," she said sadly.

I took her hand and tried to think of words to console her but found it difficult, for what had I ever learnt about love or men to pass on? I had loved neither with head nor heart and counted myself fortunate that none of the dashing young blades I'd met in Bristol had stolen my affections. I had no experience in such matters and having observed from afar the havoc romance and unrequited love could bring to the most unsuspecting people, I was grateful to have been spared the pain and humiliation. When and if I married, it would not be for any trumpery reasons but for sound economic ones. A husband with a steady income, a respected position in society was all I desired — a doctor perhaps or a justice of the peace. Intelligent, industrious and undemanding. I had no doubts at all about what I wanted. In the smart drawing-rooms of Bristol, the ladies would gather together like brightly plumed exotic birds, exchanging gossip and scandals, admiring the handsome soldiers in their scarlet uniforms but wishing for some fanciful, fairy-tale knight to carry them off to distant romantic lands. They chased down the latest intriguing novels written by women just like themselves and so fuelled the fires of their passionate and unfilled longings.

Ridiculous that Eleanor could have reliable, affectionate Miles but yearned instead for another not half so worthy of her devotion; an idle, dissolute wastrel, who loved none better than himself. I didn't know whether to feel sympathetic or angry because she seemed bent on ruining her life for the sake of a senseless obsession. But she blinked away tears, her eyes like a wounded fawn and my anger melted away.

"You do not say anything, Martha. Are you so very shocked?"

"Yes, I suppose I am a little. Shocked, and anxious for you. I have no desire to see you hurt and Miles — he seems so very fond of you. I have to own that Lucius is not the man I would have recommended as a suitor — for *anyone*, least of all you."

"I know! I *know*," she cried, her hands fluttering to her face once more.

I comforted her and then advised her to return home, to present a brave and cheerful face to the world, to refuse to see either of my troublesome cousins and to make every pretence of obeying her brother's word as a properly loyal sister should. She was to remain close to the cottage, only venturing forth when accompanied by a respectable married female and she was to do nothing at all that might attract undue attention or suspicion; she was to be as quiet and unremarkable as a mouse in the vestry.

"Do you know what you're about, Martha?" she asked uncertainly, and I laughed, shaking my head.

"No, not really! But for the moment, we just need time to think and plan."

She smiled gratefully and embraced me with real affection. I watched as she walked away and wondered at the coils life threw in one's path. It seemed one could never be wholly prepared for what was in store.

"Well," I remarked to myself as I returned to the sickroom, "At least life is far from dull!"

Eleven

Over a week had passed since the day of the fair. It was the last day of November, Miles was much recovered but still confined to his bed albeit under protest. Aunt Louisa was preoccupied with the planning of a Twelfth Night Masquerade, the magnitude of which, she hoped, would dazzle the entire county. Lucius and Harry continued to take turns entertaining their irascible brother, the visits sometimes ending in laughter, sometimes in raised voices and slamming doors. Rowena, I suspected, spent her time plotting to capture and hold Baron Rosenberg's attention, having unfortunately enjoyed her carriage ride with him so much that she was eager to repeat the experience. Even the vexing presence of a chaperone had not dampened her enthusiasm. The Baron was fascinating to her, a mysterious puzzle to be solved and he, in turn, very cleverly treated her like an amusing little toy, which infuriated her and made her want him to notice her even more desperately.

I was amused to note that Lieutenant Danserfield had called at the house several times on the flimsiest of pretexts and had been unable to conceal the real reason for his frequent visits as he was so charmingly transparent in his intentions. Rowena treated him with arch disdain which had the required effect of fanning the embers of his admiration into a blaze of poorly disguised passion. Her brothers treated their sister and the poor unfortunate officer with fraternal irreverence causing several unseemly tantrums and a smashed Chinese vase. Astonishingly, Uncle Joshua had had the good sense to quit the house saying he had to see a friend about a horse in Tavistock and that he'd be away for a while, thus managing to avoid all the interminable preparations for the Masquerade and the squabbling siblings.

I had seen Eleanor only once since the day she had come to the Hall, when I collected a length of lace for Rowena. On this visit, I had the misfortune to meet her brother and took a not unexpected dislike to him. As far as I could tell he had no redeeming qualities at all. He was a morose individual with huge fists and dark, dead eyes. I found the way he watched me repugnant and objected strongly to his treatment of his sister, whom he spoke to as though she was his property and yet there was in his manner towards her, an uncomfortable over-protectiveness which seemed not quite natural. Eleanor's fear of him was pitiable but completely understandable.

I could easily believe that Ben Fairchild could make her marry someone of his choosing. He seemed to have his fingers and eyes everywhere, he had power over people because of his superior physical strength and now it seemed he had influence. He had been seen, by John, talking with Baron Rosenberg in the village. The Baron, who had been on horseback, had apparently dismounted quite purposefully when he saw Ben Fairchild and they had spoken together at some length before parting company.

The fact that these two men were in collusion did not surprise me but made me even more concerned for Eleanor and Miles.

* * *

I was helping Meggie in the kitchen when there was a knock on the door. It was still early, and we were taken aback that anyone should call at this time of day; not even the most timepressed tradesman would dream of calling at such an hour.

Two women stood on the threshold. Gypsies both, but there the similarities ended. One was almost bent double, as small as her companion was tall. She held out a twisted hand, "Food for a poor ol' woman an' bring 'eeself good fortune."

Meggie glanced back over her shoulder, "Do'ee think I could, Miss Martha? There be no harm in it."

I looked at the old woman's wrinkled face and found her eyes upon me, alert and full of cunning. I was extremely unwilling to allow them into the kitchen, but Meggie had a Cornish woman's healthy respect for all things superstitious and local folk seldom turned a gypsy away from their doors for fear of the curses they might rain down upon them.

So it was that the two gypsies made themselves comfortable at our kitchen table while Meggie, in the hopes of gaining favour, plied them with the leftover crusts of bread, home-cured ham and a little cheese and raw onion. This they washed down with tankards of small beer. The old woman's fingers curled about the tankard like bird claws, dark and sharp-nailed. She downed the last drop with a noisy sigh, wiped her mouth on the back of her hand and set the empty vessel down on the table with slow deliberation. I suddenly felt even less sure that this was such a good idea. Her shrewd eyes looked about her, missing nothing, a puckish expression on her weather-beaten face.

Her companion ate her food as though she hadn't eaten in days but stared at me throughout just as though she were examining me under a magnifying glass. It made me feel very apprehensive. Like the old woman she was dressed in clothes which had once upon a time been brightly coloured but were now patched and grimy and faded like rags left out in the rain and the wind. Her olive skin was smooth, her black hair long and tangled; she reminded me of a wild cat.

Meggie wiped her hands on her greasy apron and held them out to the old woman, who tugged one of the proffered hands across the table, peered into it its calloused palm, shrugged, and pushed it away again. She exchanged a glance with the other gypsy, who held out her hands to Meggie.

I waited, torn between caution and amusement, for the gypsy to closely examine Meggie's palm but she just swayed slightly in her chair, staring into Meggie's flushed face. Meggie was fairly quivering with excitement.

The gypsy closed her eyes. "An ol' woman. Sittin' in a garden. There be children all about her."

"Ma," breathed Meggie.

"The ol' woman bain't be y'r Ma," said the gypsy without opening her eyes. "There be someone else. A man — a very old man. He do have a kindly face and his hair was once the colour of a fox's brush."

"Red hair! Ely Huddy do have red hair! They calls him Foxy in the village," cried Meggie. "The ol' lady — it's *me*. Me an' Ely, who'd have thought!"

"And — "continued the gypsy, "at yer waist 'ee carries a large bunch of keys."

Meggie turned shining eyes upon me, more than content with her fate. "Ely Huddy and I'm a *housekeeper!* Well, if that don't beat everythin'!" She laughed joyously. "Your turn now."

I shook my head, reluctant to surrender my hands. It was rather like dipping your toe into a river, with no idea what lurks below the surface. I told myself it was merely a harmless bit of fun but what had been a pleasant child's game no longer seemed at all appealing. Meggie, however, brimming over with high spirits would not allow me to refuse and having no wish to hurt her feelings by declining, I allowed the gypsy to take my hands. Her skin was warm and alive, the nails dirty and bitten. I felt foolish.

The gypsy's fingers trailed over my palm, but she never took her eyes from mine. She looked at me as though I were transparent, like a window. I had a terrible feeling she could see right through to my soul. She was so long in the looking that eventually Meggie shuddered, unable to contain her impatience any longer, "What do'ee see?" she asked in a sepulchral whisper.

The old woman hushed her, putting a crooked brown finger to her toothless mouth, "Quiet! She be Seein'."

I gazed at the fingers dark against my pale, freckled skin. She smelt of sweat and woodsmoke. I wondered why she bit her nails. Suddenly her pungent scent became stifling and I tried to withdraw my hand from her grasp. It was as though she awoke from a dream. She released me and stood up.

"Well?" barked the old lady. "Tell us!"

"I saw nothin'. We must be away, now."

"What do'ee mean?" cried Meggie, deeply disappointed. "'Ee must have seen *somethin'*."

The young gypsy shook her head and glared at her.

"They've shared bread with us," said the old lady.

The other muttered something in her native Romany tongue. I had always been inclined to treat fortune tellers as little more than thieving tricksters but there was something compelling about this creature, this force of nature, so I put out my hand to her again.

"Will you please tell me what you saw? I swear I will not swoon if the predictions are unfavourable."

She stared at me through the haze of hair, "Be sure. It be dangerous to make fun of Second Sight."

I promised that I would take her reading very seriously and wasn't sure if I was glad or horrified when she approached me again. She looked me straight in the eyes. "Don't say I didn't warn'ee," she said and took my hand once more. She licked her lips, "'You be unhappy. 'Tis y'r family to blame for y'r misery."

This, I considered, was easy to deduce from my face alone and snippets of local gossip. "Is that all?"

To my dismay, she closed her eyes and began to murmur softly to herself. Then she said, "There be troubled times coming. I see betrayal by a loved one an' there will come a time when'ee'll be alone an' fightin' for y'r life in a dark an' terrible place. There be a man, but he be surrounded by darkness. He has no face. There be great strength in him. He can help'ee back to the light. In this man lies y'r salvation. He stands between life an' death."

"Fascinating," I said coolly, "May I enquire who this mysterious fellow might be?"

"I told'ee. I can't see him clear. There be distance of his own makin' 'tween us. There be sufferin'. I see fire. An' blood. I see mortal danger for an innocent."

"Is it Miles?"

"Oh, I can see it plain. 'Tis y'r own sister."

Meggie and I exchanged a significant glance. "I don't have a sister," I said.

The gypsy just smiled, baring her stained teeth. "I never be mistaken. The signs be there. She be in grave danger."

"It's perfectly ludicrous. I am an only child."

"I know this, Miss, but it don't change what be written. There'll be many deaths afore the truth be known."

"Well, I'm sorry to have to disagree but none of this can possibly be true. It just can't," I told her firmly.

"Just as'ee wishes, Miss, but be careful who'ee trusts. Thank'ee for the food." And she strode across the kitchen to the door, where she turned and looked over her shoulder. "Don't'ee despair, mind. 'Tis not all bad. There may also be reward." And she was gone.

The old lady sighed and struggled to her feet, looking up at me from beady bird-eyes. "There do always be good along with the bad, of that'ee can be sure, pretty maid."

"I'm delighted to hear it." I said caustically. 'She seems incurably doom-laden, does she not?"

"She do have good reason," replied the old gypsy as she slowly made her way to the door.

'Oh, I'm sorry to hear that."

The gypsy laughed, a dry creaking sound. "'Ee *will* be sorry when'ee finds the truth m'lovely, yes'ee will," and still laughing, she shuffled out into the early morning mist.

"How very peculiar," I said, falsely cheerful.

Meggie plumped herself down into a chair, "What do she mean, Miss Martha? 'Ee bain't got no sister."

I shrugged and attempted to lighten the atmosphere, "I'm more concerned about her predictions of fire and bloodshed! I *know* I don't have a sister but there may yet be dangers lurking around the next corner."

"Do'ee think she be right, then?"

"I really don't know but she certainly put on an impressive show!"

Meggie grinned happily, "Oh, I do hope she be right about me for I have always had quite the fancy for Ely Huddy!" She frowned. "Although, she never said if all our children will be carrot-tops!"

Twelve

December came with a spiteful chill in the air. The Hall was a cold and draughty house at the best of times but on wintery days it was hard to find a spot where you could keep warm. It seemed like the forceful sea winds, storming in from the Channel, stopped for no man, or wall. It was as though the house, which had once felt so solid and secure, had become riddled with cracks and gaps, where the wind could fiddle its way through to rattle plates on their shelves and lift the worn tapestries away from the walls so that they appeared to be alive, obliging the occupants to move closer to the fire. Unless you were prepared to stand within a few feet of the flames they had very little effect and being so close meant you scorched on one side and froze on the other.

The best thing was to keep busy and therefore keep warm. The kitchen, at least, remained cosy throughout the day, situated at the back of the house, away from the worst of the winds, and with peat fires always alight, it was at times too hot, but in the winter, it was a refuge from the excesses of the bitterly cold weather.

One morning, Miles, who had had a restless night, and I were sitting in his bedroom chatting and playing cards when the door burst open and Meggie almost fell headlong into the room. "Master Miles! Oh, Master Miles!" she sobbed. "'Tis the most terrible thing! You must come at once!"

"What on earth — ? For pity's sake Meggie, calm down and tell me what has happened," said Miles halfway between gravity and hilarity.

Meggie twisted her apron into a knot, "Jenkyns says that the lighthouse be a'fire!"

I thought Miles was going to pass out for a moment but instead he staggered to his feet and uttered a terrible oath which made Meggie clap her hands over her ears.

I went quickly to his side and pressed him back into his chair. "Miles, sit down or you'll make yourself ill again."

Miles sat and buried his head in his hands. "They did it. The crazy fools."

I stroked his hair, but he slapped my hand away.

"Be still, be still. There, don't fret so. It's not good to get so worked up in your state of health. *Meggie*, do stop that wailing and tell us what you have heard."

"Oh, Miss Martha, it be that dreadful! Jenkyns says the old lighthouse on Eddystone Rocks can be seen from Maker. It be in flames an' everyone dead. Jenkyns says that it must've started last night an' they didn't stand a chance. It be so far out an' the seas are awful rough. Jenkyns says — "

"Perhaps we should talk to *Jenkyns,*" I snapped. Meggie's face crumpled and I had to apologise saying that it was all too distressing to be borne.

"He's not here, Miss, he be gone up to Maker to watch the fire. He says 'ee can see it for miles an' even them Frenchies will be warming their toes on it."

"Any signs of the Dragoons yet?", asked Miles urgently.

"Oh, mercy, yes, Master Miles! They was out backalong. All along the coast an' a right fuss they be makin' too."

Miles face was ashen. "The keepers? What of them?", he demanded.

"Jenkyns says they was thinkin' of puttin' out a boat, but they be roasted for sure, he says."

"Dear God in heaven, " said Miles faintly.

"He says no boat could get near an' the sea be so cold — "

"Meggie…" I interrupted her, "Thank you for coming to tell us. I must remember to thank Jenkyns too. You had better get back to the kitchen," and was much relieved to see her scurry away to spread the grisly news.

Miles was staring into space, still painfully changed by his long recovery and now paler still and shaking, his eyes blank from the shock.

"My God, Martha, I could have prevented this. I had an idea they were planning such a thing. I might just as well have murdered those men with my own hands."

"Nothing you could have said or done could have in any way altered the outcome. This is *not* your doing!'

"I never thought it would come to this, truly I didn't. I believed, naively — God what a complete fool — that they were making idle threats. Y'know how they do, bragging in an alehouse, bluffing." He pushed trembling hands through his already tousled hair. "This is premeditated arson, not an act of God nor an accident."

I knelt beside his chair and took his icy hands in mine, "You don't know what you're saying."

"Oh, but I do, God help me. I know who committed this unspeakable act and know I why. I made it clear that I deplored the scheme from the very start and now they'll be afraid that my loyalties, such as they are, may desert me."

"Who are these villains?"

"That's just it, you see, they started out as a band of hard-up locals trying to supplement their paltry incomes with a little harmless smuggling; but half a dozen or so have split away to try more lucrative ventures of their own. Ben Fairchild is one of them and he's promised me a pretty gruesome end should I decide not to play along. And he has threatened to harm Eleanor."

"But it's utterly preposterous," I exclaimed. "Why, you should inform the Revenue Officers."

"And stand by while they arrest and hang my friends! Find myself deported?"

"They're not your friends. They're murderers."

Miles shook off my hands impatiently and turned his face away, "There are men from the village amongst them. Good, honest men who have watched their families go hungry for too long, who have toiled in the mines or frozen on fishing boats, all for a few pennies. Who can blame them for wanting to see their children fed?"

"Oh yes," I retorted, "Who can blame them for wanting more; who can blame them for slaughtering innocent folk to get what they want? Can you not see that by shielding these men you become one of them? Any court in the land would judge you as guilty as those men." I stood up and tried to contain my fury. "What do they hope to gain by burning the lighthouse anyway?"

For a long moment Miles remained silent before replying. "The trouble is they're no longer content to be smugglers. They're hoping without the lighthouse there'll be more wrecks and better pickings for them once the cargo washes ashore."

"So, it's true. You are now involved in wrecking. How could you allow this?"

"I had no choice," he responded angrily. "It was either join them or place Eleanor in an intolerable position. I never meant this to happen. I had planned to remove her from harm's way somehow but when the time came her damned brother saw to it that neither his sister nor his wrecking gang would be in any danger from me. He uses her as a weapon in this deadly game he likes to play. And what good am I to her like this, I ask you? I swear that as soon as I am fit again, he shall be made to pay."

"Who else is in league with him?"

"How the hell should I know? I've had little enough to do with the organisation until now. I merely facilitate the storage and distribution of the contraband goods once they come ashore. I promise you that once they made mention of wrecking, I was plain in my intention to have nothing more to do with them. Bludgeoning men, women and children as they crawl from the sea is a very different matter to secreting a few kegs of brandy from the customs officers."

"We must do something to stop them or we will have blood on our hands!" My head was filled with horrific visions of the battered half-drowned bodies of shipwreck victims.

"There's little we can do, save informing the Excisemen and that will bring the roof down on our heads. I can't do that to those men."

"Can we not reason with their leader? There must be someone higher up the chain who has the final word?"

"I'd like to see you try, cousin, I really would."

An unpleasant thought occurred to me. "Is their leader a stranger to these parts?" A certain dark face coming readily to mind.

"A stranger?" Miles frowned. "No, he's Cornish born and bred. But why on earth would you think him to be a stranger?"

"I don't know — I just thought — "

"Thought he was what? Irish perhaps?" he suggested, suddenly looking more alert.

I looked hard at him. "You know Captain Cavanagh?"

"But of course. He was well acquainted with your parents. I understood that it was your father who brought him here to Devon in the first place. For a while, after you left for Bristol, he stayed with them at Wild Court."

"That's odd. They never mentioned him in their letters to me." I said, baffled. "How would they know such a person? He has unashamedly admitted that he is a smuggler."

"Well, I must say, I did think it a little unusual at the time. He didn't appear to be like their customary run of guests."

He then demanded to know how I came to meet the mysterious Captain myself. I described briefly our first encounter in the churchyard and then the subsequent meetings on the beach and the night Miles had been wounded.

"How came he to bring you home that night, Miles?"

"Now you mention it, it was a most fortunate coincidence that he happened upon me when he did. I'd tried to make my way home but hadn't realised how badly I was hurt. I must have collapsed because I don't recall anything until I came to in the yard, in the pouring rain. Then nothing more until the following day. Apparently, Cavanagh was on his way back to his ship and in order to avoid some drunken soldiers, he took the old track around the back of the village and found me lying face down in the mud. He certainly don't want for much in the brains department for he was quick to act and knew to get me home to Mrs Talbot and above all to keep his own counsel. I owe him my life. It don't bear thinking about. The scandal would have engulfed Eleanor, she would have been helpless."

Feeling he was about to work himself into a state again, I suggested he took a nap and to my surprise he readily agreed, allowing me to tuck him in, plump the pillows and smooth the quilt. Then I dashed with unseemly haste along the landing and up into the tower from where I knew there would be an uninterrupted view of the sea.

* * *

Before the inspired idea of a permanent beacon on Eddystone Rocks, there had been nothing bar skilful seamanship, the power of prayer and good luck to guide vessels past the treacherous reef, around the headland and into the welcoming arms of Plymouth Sound. There had, of course been numerous attempts to assist mariners before but this only amounted to lighting beacons next to St. Michael's Chapel on Rame Head and by the time the sailors were able to see its light through storm clouds or sea mist, it was generally too late.

I gazed out towards the faint glow on the horizon and wondered if John Rudyerd, the London silk merchant who had designed and built this version of the lighthouse, was still alive and, if he were, how he'd feel to know his remarkable feat of engineering had finally been destroyed after nearly fifty years. In the dark and deserted tower, I thought despondently of the poor keepers who had lost their lives.

"Poor beggars," said Lucius, appearing silently at my side.

"Could they have escaped, do you think?"

Lucius shrugged, appeared about to say something, changed his mind and replied casually, "Oh, I daresay they've perished."

"How far away is it?"

"About nine miles, I believe."

"It looks so much nearer. It may have been an accident, do you not think, with the candles?"

His stillness unnerved me. "A wooden structure like that, crammed full of lanterns and candles? It was only a matter of time before something like this happened."

I was suddenly aware that Lucius fully understood the other possible implications. I babbled on, suggesting wildly improbable explanations while Lucius continued to watch the light in the sky, a muscle above his jaw working spasmodically and his fingers drumming the sill. When my words finally faltered and faded away, he said, "If the Revenue Officers should arrive — and I have no doubt that they'll be beating down our door before too long — we must conceal our suspicions or Miles will be spending the rest of his life cooped up in some remote penal colony splitting rocks and digging ditches — unless, of course they discover he has another string to his bow — then he's more likely to swing for it." He grabbed my arm, his fingers biting into my flesh, "Do you have any notion of the danger he's in? If he's arrested and found guilty, we will also be suspects. I don't know about you, sweet cousin, but I have no real desire to have the militia breathing down my neck, hampering my every movement and poking their noses into my business. And you and Miles have always been as thick as thieves; who in their right mind would believe you were innocent?"

I couldn't meet his eyes, wondering how much he knew of my recent exploits.

"Ah, I see I am not wide of the mark. I guessed he would have embroiled you somehow. How typically thoughtless. Reckless young dolt. Now we must try to keep him out of the clutches of the smugglers on one side and the law on the other. 'Tis going to be very taxing. If we're to bring this about you'll have to do as you're told and not argue every little thing."

"I don't — " I stopped, covered in confusion. "All right, Lucius. I will try my damnedest to stay out of trouble."

Lucius rolled his eyes. "Pigs might fly," he said without conviction.

In a moment of both clarity and bewilderment I saw Lucius in a new light. Had I been mistaken in my belief that he was irredeemably wicked? Had the prejudices of others clouded my judgement? My father had spoken with distaste of his exploits and the gossips in the village had been only too happy to share with me some of his worst excesses. After hero-worshipping my older cousin for most of my childhood it had come as a shock to me to find he had feet of clay just like any mere mortal. I had confronted him with a young girl's self-righteous zeal and had been smartly put in my place. I was told, in a clear and measured tone, that I was misguided, infantile and parochial. His disdainful words were seared into my memory. I suppose I had really been looking for reassurance, but he had cruelly made me look foolish and naive. The hurt had persisted, growing and festering and Lucius had fuelled the fire by taking every opportunity to goad or humiliate me.

Looking at him now, his sharp profile silhouetted against the window, I felt as though I had, for some unfathomable reason, been deliberately deceived.

"Why did you do it, Lucius?"

He looked down his beaky nose at me. "God, what am I supposed to have done now?"

"Pretended to be someone you're not."

"What in Hades are you talking about?" he snapped.

"All those years I lived in fear of crossing you. You, treating me as though I had the plague. You made me hate you. Why?"

"You sound fit for Bedlam, Martha."

Goaded once more into anger, I snatched at his sleeve, shaking his arm. "What induced you to do it? All those years, wasted!"

In silence he stared at me, his blue eyes frosty, mouth twisted.

"I don't want us to be like this. I can't bear it."

He grasped my hands in his, his face shadowed, "It's better this way," he said.

"I don't understand — "

"But of course you do, my dear. You've heard the rumours, the scandals, the gossip! Every vile word is true. I am everything they say and worse. Ruthless, cruel, brutal — unnatural. I was a most unpleasant boy, as you no doubt recall, and in order not to disappoint, I have become — the man you see before you."

"Why would you think that?"

"I've seen it in your eyes, cousin, the same golden eyes that look at Miles with slavish devotion. And don't start feeling sorry for me, like one of those damned stray animals you were always bringing home. Ah, yes, you see how well I know you? Remember, I have *chosen* to be as I am. Unlike your beloved Miles, who could never be anything other than honest and true, or Harry, helpless, or Rowena, conniving and selfish. I prefer to observe without attachment. I learned a long time ago that to care is to suffer and I prefer a pain free life."

"You care, Lucius… you've just forgotten how to show it."

"Poor Martha. Do you yearn to save my soul? I'm afraid it's too late for that — far too late. Don't meddle in things you can't possibly understand," and he turned on his heel and left the tower.

* * *

Although the idea of reforming my wicked cousin was tempting, I had other things to think about. The destruction of the lighthouse was all anyone was talking about.

We heard the next day, to our intense relief, that the keepers had been miraculously rescued right at the last minute. The fire was officially blamed on the candles somehow igniting the top of the lantern. After battling the flames for as long as they could, without success, the keepers were forced to take shelter on the rocks. Fortunately, the fire was observed from the shore by Squire Edwards, a man blessed with considerable wealth and a stout heart. He put out a boat and although it was some hours later, and the seas were rough, they were able to throw ropes to the keepers and drag them to safety. On the fifth day it finally burnt itself out.

There was talk of them posting a lighthouse ship out to the rocks to prevent further wrecks. This, of course, would hamper the wreckers and I realised that they would have to act with all possible speed to make the most of the missing beacon. We were running out of time to save Miles.

Thirteen

On the sixth day of December, John stopped me as I was coming out of the linen room, laden with a pile of clean bedding and thinking crossly of all the crumpled beds awaiting me. He handed me a tightly folded and somewhat grimy note and waited with a slightly embarrassed air while I smoothed out the piece of cheap, yellowing paper and tried to read the badly spelt message.

John stood a little apart. His eyes firmly fixed on the floor while I stared furiously at the letter — the words jumping on the page. I wanted to close my eyes and make it go away.

"This is too ridiculous." I said faintly. "They can't expect me to do this. They must be crazy."

"If ee'll permit me, Miss — "

"Yes, anything. I can't cope with this alone."

"It's just that they was relyin' on Master Miles to take the ponies down to the cove — 'ee've proved yourself to 'em t'other night. They can trust'ee." He shifted his feet uneasily. "I be afeared that they won't let'ee be now."

"But I only did it for Miles."

"Makes no odds."

The full import of what he said took a moment to sink in and I realised that by helping Miles I had become an unwilling accomplice too. They now had a hold over me so that I could no longer think of turning them over to the authorities.

"How many ponies will there be?"

"Not many. A dozen or so at most."

"A dozen? I'd be hard pressed to manage two by myself!"

"Young Ned Quick'll give'ee a hand. He be good with ponies."

"Splendid. I feel *so* much better," I said tartly. "You'd think they'd be able to find someone more suited to the job than me."

"They've lost a good few men of late. Five to the Excise Men an' the three to the Pressers up at Polperro. They be short-handed an' it be a difficult run this time."

"Reassuring news. And if we're caught?"

"No chance of that, Miss. They be settin' up two bluff runs to fox the Excise Men. With any luck they'll be off down the coast chasin' ghosts."

"Comforting in theory but there are still a dozen unruly animals to deal with and steep slippery tracks in the dark."

"Them ponies be used to it. They've been doin' it for years. They be old hands."

"*I'm* not though!" I frowned down at the drawn threadwork edges of the linen in my arms, so unremarkable. "They haven't given me much warning. Tomorrow night! Not enough time to run away. When will I be told which cove they're using?"

"Oh, not 'til the last moment. Depends on weather an' tides an' where the Dragoons end up. Always a bit of a gamble."

"So, I have nobody but a young lad to help me, no idea where I'm going and no idea if I'm to be to be arrested. I can't think *why* I should be so worried!"

"They'll let'ee know, don't'ee fret."

"I'll try not to," I said with heavy sarcasm.

* * *

I didn't dare tell Miles about the letter in case it should impede his recovery, he was frustrated at being still confined to his bedroom and champing at the bit, keen to get back to his normal activities. I tried to find Lucius, but he'd left home early that morning without telling anyone when he'd return. Harry, I found slumped in an armchair by a blazing log fire in the Great Hall. His face flushed from the warmth, long pale eyelashes curled against the pink of his cheeks; his mouth had fallen open and he was gently snoring. He looked like a child, a round-cheeked cherubim. His wig had been cast carelessly onto the floor at his feet. His sandy hair was ruffled as though the wig had irritated him and he'd dragged it from his head just moments before he fell asleep. I smiled and wondered if he'd been out rabbit hunting; I rather hoped he hadn't because I hated the messy business of gutting and cleaning their limp little bodies. Just for a second, I contemplated enlisting Harry to help me, but immediately rejected the idea as he was as much use as the rabbits he was so fond of shooting. I picked up his wig, dusted it off and put it on the table at his elbow. He stirred and murmured something but didn't wake. I tiptoed from the hall and went to find Meggie, who was supposed to show me how to make soap.

An hour or so later, I was in the scullery pounding cloves and arras root to powder while Meggie boiled mutton fat in a cauldron over the fire.

"Pooh, this do smell somethin' terrible," she complained as she vigorously stirred the foul mixture, her face shiny with sweat, sleeves rolled up and cap comically askew. "I'd rather clean out the pigsty!"

"Well, I'd rather do this than skin a rabbit," I said, laughing.

"Lucky we don't have no rabbits then!"

"Oh? I thought perhaps Harry may have been out hunting."

"No, Miss, no rabbits."

"Poor Harry, he used to be a pretty fair shot; maybe the rabbits are getting more quick-witted."

"P'raps, but I'm afeared it be 'cause 'ee do spend too much time in the alehouse these days," said Meggie with a grin.

I smiled, "He needs a proper occupation to keep him busy."

"It be the company 'ee keeps."

"Well, of course. A boy his age needs companions. It's not healthy for him to be always with his family. Although, I'm glad to hear he is enjoying life."

As we worked, mixing the aromatics, fragrant resins and wood ash into a paste and rolling them into balls, Meggie chatted brightly, and the combination of toil and local gossip at least stopped me dwelling on the alarming task ahead. She told me about the smugglers captured in Polperro and how she'd obediently turned her face to the wall as a gang of them galloped through the village and how the Excise men had been made to look foolish when they tried to catch hold of packhorses laden with contraband, only to find the animals and been shaved and greased with lard; the ensuing chaos was, according to a witness, a sight to behold. I didn't at all enjoy the stories of the smugglers being captured and severely dealt with by the authorities. I had no wish to end my life as a common criminal. It mattered not that their shameful activities were tolerated by most country folk or that Customs Officers and even magistrates managed to combine their regular occupations with a little smuggling on the side. My father had instilled in me a healthy respect for the law and I could not bear the thought that I might become someone he would have despised.

Miles was reading, cosily bundled up in the wing chair and surrounded by a confusion of papers, books, several empty platters and tankards and Moses, the kitchen cat curled up on his lap. Miles was looking much more like his old self if still a little pale from being confined to the stuffy room for so long.

He threw down his book when he saw me, "Martha! The very person. You must fetch me some meat! I've had enough of gruel and broth! I need red meat and plenty of it!"

"You know full well, that I'd be hung, drawn, and quartered if Mrs Talbot found I had gone behind her back! I'm sorry but I can't bring you any of the delicious, juicy slices of prime beef and roast pork they're having for dinner!"

"Martha! You're heartless! I've eaten nothing but oatmeal gruel and oatmeal pudding for weeks now. If you ever loved me, I beg you, have pity! Bring me anything without oatmeal in it."

"Mrs Talbot knows what's best for you. I wouldn't dare disobey her. Anyway, you're looking so much better that I must conclude that her regime is working, however distasteful it may be."

He contrived to look ill-used, "A spot of brandy then?"

"No, Miles, you'll just have to bide your time. Is there anything else I can do for you?"

"Yes, my clothes. They took them away to stop me escaping. It's just like being in Launceston Gaol." Then suddenly his mood changed, and he fidgeted restlessly so that Moses leapt indignantly onto the floor and started to lick his paw. "I can't bear being cooped up any longer. I shall go mad. I *must* see Eleanor."

"I have told you already, Eleanor is well. I have recently seen her, and she is coping." How could I possibly tell him about Eleanor's feelings for Lucius? I had to hold my tongue and hope everything would sort itself out, without anyone getting hurt.

"I'm glad," lied Miles, gamely. "Gad! I forget always to ask how *you're* coping, dearest cousin. I burden you with all my problems and get you entangled in God knows what and you take it all on the chin."

I smiled because he had, like many young men his age with a fine education and all the privilege money and titles could buy, a rather selfish streak. "I get by, Miles, though I will admit, it hasn't been easy. I miss Papa. I still cannot fathom why he left me here alone."

"I wish I could tell you. Lucius and I had gone to Bodmin Assizes to try to help young William Fewkes; he was being tried for stealing a meat pie from a market stall."

"I remember him. A skinny little lad. What happened to him?"

"He was executed."

"But he wasn't a criminal! He was just a hungry boy, a child! How can they mete out the same punishment for stealing as murder?"

"Lucius and I did our utmost to convince the judge that the boy had only been forced to steal because his family had fallen on hard times, but he would not see reason. Pompous ass! William was nine years old. Lucius begged, he said by all means punish the boy but don't take his life. He said that we'd pay any fines. To no avail. We returned home a week later to find Vida dead and your father vanished. If only we'd not been away — we shouldn't have left when she was so ill, but we had no idea she would succumb; the doctor persuaded us that she would recover well from what appeared to just be some kind of ague, nothing life-threatening."

"You cannot blame yourself. You did what you thought was best. I can better understand your actions than my father's."

"Martha, you must realise — my mother has surely told you — ?"

"Told me what?" I asked fearfully.

"Your father. He is missing, presumed to have been killed on a government mission in France. The circumstances are, to say the least, confusing. I must admit I wasn't convinced by the official report Mother received just recently - it left out some pretty important details. News that the French are gathering troops near the coast reached our government and your father volunteered to go. It was utter madness when relations between England and France are at such a new low. I can't imagine why he would do something so rash. If anyone knows, they are refusing to tell us. Martha?"

I had been listening to him with difficulty, there was a strange rushing noise in my ears and his words seemed to come from far away.

"Sit down! You look a little pale."

"I'm fine, honestly. Thank you for telling me. I didn't want to believe Aunt Louisa when she said he ran away; that he was weak and cowardly. I had always thought that he was above any kind of human frailty, kind-hearted and honourable. Never did I imagine that he could be as selfish as other men. To leave when my mother was so ill — "

Miles was looking exasperated, "Your father *was* honourable!"

"No, he let Mama down. She was beautiful and courageous but died alone. I can never forgive that."

"You don't know the full story. How can you be so quick to judge? Vida *was* beautiful, that is indisputable, but she was also determined to get what she wanted whatever the cost. You couldn't see it. She was more like Mother than anyone would care to admit."

"I know Mama had shortcomings. Everyone does. And, yes, she used her looks to her advantage but who can blame her? Papa was only thinking of himself."

"Your father was brave to volunteer for such a mission, knowing he may never return. We may not know the underlying reason for such an audacious decision, but you have to admire his courage." Miles frowned, "And to be perfectly honest, Martha, I don't believe Vida ever thought of anyone but herself."

"That's a cruel thing to say! You turncoat!"

"You need to open your eyes to the truth. Things are not always how they seem. In loving someone, we can be easily deceived, we are weakened and blinded by that love and blinded to the deceit."

I was silent. His words hurt beyond measure. But deep down, although I would vociferously deny it, I knew there was some truth in what he said.

Fourteen

I found it hard to believe that little more than a month ago I was to be found parading about in Clifton's elegant drawing-rooms, on the arm of a handsome and attentive beau and revelling in the extremely engaging company of dear family friends, Lady Sarah Finch and her husband, Sir Aubrey. It seemed like a lifetime ago. And now here I was about to embark upon a ludicrously dangerous venture which was, in my opinion, doomed to end in disaster, with me languishing in Launceston Gaol and my entire family disgraced. How had my life, once so ordered and ordinary, become this unpredictable shambles?

As I climbed the hill towards Maker Heights, sea fog was rolling in over Cawsand Bay and even though the walking was hard, my face felt clammy and cold and my jaw ached from clenching my chattering teeth. I clutched my trusty dark lantern, but its faint glow was no match for the fog. I kept asking myself why I was struggling through the blurred, grey night in order to assist a band of criminals? But there was no rational answer.

Young Ned Quick was waiting for me at Maker Church and was in good spirits about the night ahead but became noticeably downcast by my evident lack of enthusiasm. He chattered happily as we walked but I contributed little apart from interrupting his optimistic nonsense to enquire about our chances of evading capture.

"There'll be no danger, for'ee anyway, Miss. Ee'll be well away from the action. An' I be just a lookout, although it won't be easy in this ol' roke."

"Where are the ponies hidden, Ned?"

He gestured somewhere into the bewildering greyness.

"The horses be just up here in Ely's Grove an' the ponies are in a spinney near Hooe Valley." He spoke over his shoulder without slackening his pace at all and I was thankful that my ankle had mended sufficiently for me to able to keep up with him. "They change the hidin' places every time to keep the Dragoons guessin'"

The horses stood patiently in the fog; whinnying softly as we approached. When I asked where they had come from, Ned fell silent for the first time, unwilling to share the information with someone he barely knew. After riding for a short while, I came to the conclusion that I preferred the sound of his voice to the sound of my heartbeat thudding loudly in my ears and the voices in my head telling me to turn around and go home.

"Do your parents know you're doing this?" No answer. Just the steady thump of the horses' hooves on the turf, creaking of leather and metallic rattle of their bridles. "If my parents were alive, they'd never understand why I was involved in such a crack-brained scheme. My father would be horrified. You're really enjoying this, aren't you, Ned?"

"There be nothin' in my life to compare to this. It makes'ee glad to be alive," he replied, without turning his head.

"You don't fear capture?"

"Aye. Course. Fool not to. Some folks are forced to help out of fear. Scared their family will be punished if they don't."

"I completely understand," I said, thinking of Miles, caught between his conscience and the frightening consequences of his actions, however innocent the intentions may have been. I gritted my teeth. I was out in the mizzling cold, plodding through the night in this foolhardy fashion because I had no choice in the matter either.

I could smell the sweet musty scent of the ponies before we reached them. A dozen sturdy little animals stood just at the edge of the spinney, their wicker panniers giving them a strangely exotic appearance which would have been comical in a less fraught situation. Ned tied six to his horse and six to mine, ordered me to put out my lantern, remounted and then we rode back down into the fog towards Hooe Lake Point and then the sloping cliffs down to the sea at Warn Sandways, where there was a small beach with easy access from the estuary.

I followed pulling my string of obedient ponies after me and we made our way cautiously along the ridge.

"Do they regularly use Sandways?"

"Oftentimes. But the Customs Officers patrol the whole coast now. When we gets the word, we has to make a late choice dependin' on weather an' tide an' where the law be. Right, we got to be quiet now, Miss. We gettin' near."

The sea mist swirled around us, deadening sounds like a blanket of snow and disorientating me; if it hadn't been for Ned, I would have ended up riding in circles. Ned said it was a good omen as we were less likely to be discovered. The journey took on a dream-like quality; I could smell the sea but felt I was lost in a muffled half-world until I could at last hear the faint whooshing of the waves on the rocks and then I could get my bearings.

Every so often Ned would stop and listen for a moment before urging his horse forward. Finally, he dismounted and signalled for me to do the same. We were in the shelter of some stunted trees, near what looked like the ruins of an old shepherd hut. Ned pulled the ponies up to the wall and tethered them, then we waited in the cloaking, dampening fog. Waiting and listening. Straining to make sense of any sound we heard.

My hair and face were wet, and my feet were frozen. The horses stamped and blew misty clouds into the air. My horse whickered gently so I stood at his head and stroked his velvety nose to keep him quiet. Ned seemed to have a vast reserve of patience because he neither fidgeted nor complained; I don't think he even blew on his fingers to warm them, he merely stared steadily in the direction of the sea. After a while I wanted to sing out loud just to break the tension. I recited poetry to myself and braided the horse's mane and then unbraided it.

We must have waited an hour in that dismal place before they came stealthily out of the banks of fog - dark menacing shapes, moving like wild animals in their element. There must have been eight or so men, swift and efficient, and as silent as the mist. They gathered the ponies, shared brief and mysterious whisperings with Ned and then disappeared back into the impenetrable night. Ned and I were left by the twisted trees.

Wondering what was expected of me, I tugged on Ned's sleeve. "Ned?", I breathed softly, the sound of my own voice making me jump. He put a warning finger to his lips. I pressed my lips together in an effort to keep quiet.

In the darkness I could just see the paler shape of his face. I could hear the waves on the shore, rhythmical and oddly comforting. A small animal scritch-scratched somewhere near my feet, making crisp, nibbling sounds and my horse twitched and whinnied nervously. The back of my neck prickled.

I thought I heard a cry. Probably a fox.

I could make out a faint glow below us. In the far, far distance the mournful sound of a bell. It sounded like a lost soul. Shivering, I looked to Ned for reassurance, only to be greeted by nothing but shrouds of fog. He'd gone.

I suffered a brief moment of panic then calmed myself. He'd be back. He'd just been carried away by his youthful exuberance.

I waited, leaning against my patient horse for comfort and warmth. Five minutes passed and then another five and I began to grow restless. Perhaps he wouldn't come back.

Unable to stand it any longer, I pulled my cloak around me, clambered down the slight escarpment below the shelter and scrambled and slid my way down to where I'd seen the curious light. I could smell smoke. My damp skirts and stockings kept getting snagged on the undergrowth and I impatiently ripped them away and kept going.

After a dozen yards or so I stopped. Which way? The landscape was faceless. The fog billowed like a sheet on a washing line and then parted to reveal the hazy yellow glow again, I stumbled hopefully towards it, unseen obstacles tripping me so that I landed heavily on my knees several times. I drew near and instinctively slowed to assess the danger.

The bonfire was burning fiercely despite the damp; crackling and snapping and sending columns of sparks up into the air. I could feel the warmth of the flames and resisted the urge to rush forwards to warm myself.

A voice, gruff and close by, made my heart skip a beat.

"Keep that damn fire goin'! It'll have to be bright as day for 'em to see it in this."

He spoke again but I couldn't make out what he said.

A beacon lit high on a clifftop could be seen far out to sea. I knew beacons had been lit on Rame Head to guide ships around the peninsular and into the welcoming arms of the Sound but that had been in the days before the lighthouse. Now there was no lighthouse to steer by. The unfortunate sailors were at the mercy of ruthless men.

Another cry, far away. A shout. Muffled and lost in the vastness. I held my breath.

"She be comin' in," another voice called from some distance.

I too heard the bell. Even closer now. Tolling somewhere out in the bay.

I edged carefully down the slope, ending up about twenty feet below the bonfire. The fog seemed less dense there and I could just make out the flat, dark rocks at the bottom of the ridge.

Then, slowly looming out of eerie nothingness, a darker shape, a ghostly apparition.

The bell sounded again, more clearly this time.

The ship's sails hung limply, unable to snatch even the smallest breath of wind.

The fog obstructed my view again and the phantom ship disappeared as though it had been a figment of my imagination, except I could still hear the dismal tolling of the bell.

I could hear that the men had stopped stoking the fire. "We'd better get down to the beach an' help bring her in," said one.

"Aye, Master'll be right glad she's come in as planned."

"Let's hope the crew ain't as troublesome as last time," growled the other. "We lost two good men before we could finish 'em off. "Ee's made sure we be well armed on this run. Come on, or we won't get our share."

For several minutes after they had gone, I stood quite still in case they unexpectedly returned. My thoughts were in turmoil. I had known as soon as I read the note that I wasn't signing up for a straightforward smuggling run. I had entered into this, maybe not in all innocence, but with an idea of what it might entail for my scruples. I knew the smugglers were hoping for a wreck, that they would wait for the cargo to be washed ashore and then beach-comb the contraband away. I also was aware that they may row out to the wrecked vessel and plunder it.

I hadn't quite admitted to myself that the ship might be deliberately lured onto the rocks. As far as I understood it was not normal practice to actively wreck a ship; to harvest the shipwrecked goods from the beach was acceptable according to manorial rights but to intentionally wreck a manned vessel would mean transportation or execution if the perpetrators were caught. I had heard my father talk of a notorious submerged ledge in the bay, just off Sandways where, before the lighthouse, many a ship had foundered in a dangerous south easterly gale. The fog ensured that not only did the smugglers have sufficient cover for their misdeeds but also that a wreck was far more likely.

God forgive me, but I hesitated. I considered the options open to me. I could run, nobody would see me go under cover of darkness and the enveloping mist or I could wait for Ned to return and fulfil my reluctant criminal duties and just blot out the dire consequences of this night.

I was just contemplating a third and far less appealing option when I heard the nightmarish sound of splintering wood and voices crying out in the distance. I stood, frozen to the spot, listening to the agonising sound of the ship breaking up on the rocks.

A moment later I was slithering and sliding down the steep slope, through the scrub and gorse to the beach. I didn't think. I just had to do something, so I pitched headlong into the unknown.

The rocks bruised me, and the furze scratched sharply at my skin, but I felt nothing but a sickening self-loathing.

* * *

The scene which greeted me was like a moment from a terrible dream I'd had, where dark, lumbering shapes had risen from their graves to creep about in the churchyard mist, howling and shrieking as though they came straight from Hell itself.

The fog snaked in ribbons across the beach, revealing brief glimpses of activity, making it hard to understand what was going on, at first. A short way out into the bay, I could just make out the hulk of the ship stalled helplessly on the reef, trapped like a broken toy. I ducked down behind a low outcrop of rock and watched fearfully from my hiding place. Down at the water's edge hunched figures were pushing out the rowing boats in deadly silence. A heavy rope arced out into the hazy distance, towards the stricken vessel; a line of burly men on the beach pulling on it, as though in a tug of war game. Men hauled themselves through the waters, using the rope to guide them out to the ship.

Half a dozen small boats came and went, oars creaking in their rowlocks, their blades softly splashing through the smoothly rolling waves. Then, boats were returning loaded with sacks and casks and crates so heavy it took several men to carry them to shore. It was organised, like a grotesque ballet.

I cringed against the wet rock face unable to look away or escape. I could hear more cries now, drifting inland. Some gruff and belligerent and others fearful. I saw that some of the men were armed with bludgeons and knew that the passengers and crew of the merchant ship would not be allowed to live. There could be no witnesses to this barbaric act. The screams grew more insistent, more desperate, some suddenly cut short.

I closed my eyes and covered my ears to block out the grisly sights and sounds.

Where were the Excise Officers? The Dragoons? Then I recalled Ned telling me about the ghost runs to distract the soldiers. I scanned the cove anxiously but there was no sign of help coming from any direction.

With no clear plan of action, I edged around the rock and made my way gingerly down the beach. I kept my eyes fixed firmly on the men by the shoreline. It proved difficult to focus as the fog rolled and swirled around them.

Suddenly a shout went up. Some of the men pointed in the direction of Hooe Lake. For a moment I couldn't see what they were looking at but then I saw a lonely figure stumbling out of the sea, exhausted by his efforts. He fell and the waves rolled over him, covering him completely. Then, he was on his feet again, wading desperately for the beach. Two smugglers broke away from the rest and ran towards him, cudgels in hand.

Before I knew what I was doing, I was racing across the shingle, my heavy, wet skirts tangling around my legs, my cloak flapping behind me. I could no longer see where the fugitive was, he'd disappeared into the fog.

I shouted and waved my arms and saw the smugglers hesitate. One stopped in his tracks and started towards me. I called out to him, "Soldiers are coming! Soldiers, coming this way!" He looked uncertain, slowed, looked back at his fellow smuggler. "I came with Ned Quick and the ponies! Soldiers must have seen the beacon. They're not far away!"

He made a decision, "Bart! Leave 'im! We got to get out of 'ere." He turned back to me. "How many?"

I made a wild guess, "Thirty or so." The men didn't wait to discuss the matter further, they blundered back along the beach to alert their comrades.

Then shots rang out.

I ducked down and waited. I was in the shallows now, my feet sinking into the wet sand. The tide was coming in. I tried to picture where I'd last seen the man and gathering up my skirts and keeping low, I set off in what I hoped was the right direction. I almost fell over him, lying in the water, face down. I caught him by the shoulders and using all my strength heaved him onto his back. He lay apparently lifeless, his limp hand moving to and fro with the waves. He was a negro, tall and heavily built and dressed in what appeared to have once been some sort of uniform or costume. I didn't have time to look closely, I put my hand on his chest and found he still breathed. I tried to rouse him, shaking him and pulling at his arm. I glanced back but there was no sign of the smugglers so I took a deep breath and slapped the fugitive's face as hard as I could.

He groaned and his eyelids flickered open. I grabbed his hand and tried to pull him to his feet. "Come *on!*" I urged, "Get up! They'll come for us. We must go. Oh, do get *up!* I don't want to die."

"Neither do I," came the answer, in heavily accented but otherwise perfect English.

"Well, now that we've established that, can we please start running?" I begged him. "Do you think you *can* run?"

"Oh, yes, Miss, of one thing I am quite certain, when offered a choice between life and death, I will always choose the former."

He lumbered to his feet and I tried to help him, but it was like a mouse trying to lift a bear. We made our way laboriously to where the rocks jutted out from the base of the cliff. He leaned heavily on me and every few steps I glanced fearfully over my shoulder to see if we were being pursued. The fog had swallowed up any signs of the wreck and the smugglers. I was out of breath, but terror kept me moving, heart pounding, lungs aching. I could hear my companion's ragged breathing and prayed he wouldn't collapse. We were just feeling our way cautiously around the rocks when I tripped over something in my path.

I peered closely at it and reaching down tried to move it. I snatched my hand away. It was a body. I could see the pale face, a dark gaping hole in the middle of its forehead. The breath caught in my throat.

It was Ned Quick.

Fifteen

Shouts from the beach. Another gunshot. We stopped simultaneously and listened, barely daring to breathe. We could hear the sounds from the ship, the sea, the men searching for us. With any luck they'd go right past believing we'd gone further round the headland to where the fish cellars would have provided an obvious hiding place. *Too* obvious. With any luck they'd miss the telltale footprints in the shingle. With any luck.

We'd waited long enough and continued the long climb back to the top. I prayed as we struggled through the gorse; I prayed as we felt our way past scratchy bushes. I could suddenly smell the ashy smoke from the now extinguished fire. We were close to the ruined shepherd's hut.

I lost my footing and would have fallen from the ledge we were crossing had not my companion grabbed a handful of my hair, long since come undone, as I plummeted past him and hauled me back to his side; I didn't complain, and he didn't apologise.

As we slowly progressed up the slope, I was trying to plan. Where could we go? Who would take us in? I scrambled over the final obstacle and turned to see how my friend fared. He was a little way behind me and faring badly, weak from exhaustion and probably hunger. I had no idea what kind of ordeal he had been through but judging by the state of his clothes, it had been long and inhumane.

I stretched out a hand to him to help him up the last incline and he took it gladly. Digging my heels into the turf, I pulled with all my might and we ended up in a heap together, heads couched on prickly furze.

"Are you all right?", I asked his inert form.

"I have never felt better," came the faint reply.

"Then we must find the horses and keep moving. I must be back by dawn or I shall be missed. We must find shelter quickly."

"Then, by all means, let us be off," he murmured. "Might I ask where we're going?"

"I'm not entirely sure yet."

"Why are you doing this?"

"Because I know it's what my father would have done." We helped each other up and headed to the shepherd's hut. "What's your name?"

"Solomon."

"I'm Martha Pentreath," I told him and thought what a very civilised conversation it was to be having in such uncivilised circumstances.

"I'm delighted to meet you, Miss Pentreath, *very* delighted." And we laughed quietly at our own politeness.

"I'm going to see if the horses are still where we left them. You stay here. I'll be back in a few minutes." He dropped gratefully to the ground and I set off along the ridge.

To my profound relief I heard the welcome sound of a horse whinnying a greeting. I quickly untied them and managed to mount the smaller animal by clambering onto a rock and throwing myself across its saddle. Pulling Ned's horse behind me, I returned to Solomon. I couldn't see him but when I called out softly there was an answering whistle and he appeared by my side. I handed him the reins and was surprised when he just stood there.

"We must hurry, Solomon. Is there something wrong?"

"Yes, I'm afraid there is. I have never ridden a horse before. I don't like them very much."

I couldn't help laughing. "Well, the only other choice is being hacked to death by wreckers so — I'm afraid you must overcome your fears, trust in God and pray that your horse will not take advantage of your inexperience. Mount up. All you have to do is stay on."

"I'd rather walk, thank you," said Solomon stubbornly, eyeing the animal with disdain.

"It will take too long. We must get as far away as possible. Catch hold of the saddle, put your left foot in the stirrup and haul yourself up."

Solomon sighed loudly and muttered under his breath; I steadied his horse while he prepared to mount. At the first attempt he failed to swing his leg over because the horse sensing his fear, sidled and threw up his head. Solomon looked accusingly at me but valiantly tried again. This time he landed awkwardly in the saddle and clung on grimly to anything he could reach.

By the time we reached Picklecombe Point Solomon was slumped against the neck of his horse like a sack of turnips. We pressed on, the fog slowing our progress considerably.

Holmoak Beacon came into sight and I stopped arguing with myself about once more taking my troubles to someone I didn't consider to be at all respectable. It just no longer mattered. I was obeying an instinct which took me unquestioningly to Sir Montagu's door.

As we drew near the old tower, I was suddenly overcome by the oddest sensation, a fluttering in my stomach and a constriction in my throat. My heart began to do strange things in my chest. I tried to steady myself which only seemed to make matters worse and I was in a fine state by the time I pulled the bell, wincing at the dreadful din it made. Solomon was leaning against the wall as though his strength had finally deserted him.

"We'll be all right now. Sir Montagu will know what to do." I reassured him.

"That's comforting. Who is this paragon?"

I laughed weakly. "Hardly a paragon. In fact, you had better brace yourself for he can be very rude."

"I look forward to meeting him," said Solomon drily. "He'll not mind us intruding at this hour?"

I didn't have to answer as we heard the sounds of bolts being drawn back and the door swung open to reveal the same manservant as before, his clothes in disarray as though he'd struggled into them without the benefit of light and holding a candle, itself struggling to stay alight. He took in the extraordinary sight on the doorstep with equanimity, just as though it was a regular occurrence to admit two dishevelled characters in the middle of the night.

"Could you please — " I began.

"He's asleep, Miss."

"Well, of course he is. You must rouse him but mind you do it gently! If you don't want to do it, I *will*." I sounded far more confident than I felt.

The manservant took my threat to heart and with a speculative glance in Solomon's direction, he hastily retreated and disappeared upstairs. Solomon and I stood there shivering.

"This is ridiculous," I said crossly and pulling Solomon inside I closed the door. The hall was lit by just two candles in a wall bracket. Seeing a settle against the wall, I stumbled towards it and collapsed onto its hard seat before my legs gave way. Solomon followed and the old wood shifted and creaked under his considerable weight. I leant back and closed my eyes. My head dipped and sank onto my chest. Just for a second. My last coherent thought was that as Sir Montagu habitually took an age to make himself presentable, I would have time for a brief nap.

* * *

Sandalwood. For some reason I could smell sandalwood in my dream, and it reminded me of someone. I suffered an excited flutter of recognition and opened my eyes. There was nobody there.

I was in a large four poster bed, hung with pale grey damask, most beautifully patterned in the Oriental style. The wooden posts were intricately carved, depicting exotic birds and animals I didn't recognise. The feather pillows beneath my head were embroidered, as was the quilt. The walls were hung with flocked wallpaper in shades of silver and sage green. The ornaments and paintings looked rare and expensive. The whole effect was one of elegant tranquillity. I leant over the edge of the bed and noted that the rug was Persian and the ornately painted screen standing in the corner was probably Indian. It was all very modern, and it appealed to me enormously. Used to the heaviness of the Elizabethan decoration at the Hall, I welcomed the lightness of touch in this bedchamber. The wall to my right was lined with books and in front of me long windows in the outside wall looked out over the sea, which was unusual as most people preferred to face inland, away from the fierce buffeting of gales. I knew the owner of this room and was surprised.

And despite the knowledge that I was somewhere I had no business being, I lay back against the pillows and revelled in the luxury of the strange surroundings. I gazed up at the canopy above my head and couldn't help smiling to myself. If Aunt Louisa could see me now, I thought, she would most certainly consign my blackened soul to the devil.

I snuggled down under the covers and gave myself up to an impossible dream. I must have fallen asleep again for the next thing I knew I was being gently shaken.

I awoke reluctantly, stretching my arms above my head, enjoying the last fleeting moments of comfort and security before opening my eyes.

"I'm so sorry." I murmured. "Have I been a nuisance?"

Sir Montagu surveyed me with something akin to vexation. "Confound it, madam! Have you no morals at all? Here you are, after a night spent engaged in, I understand, all kinds of reckless activities and now in a seriously compromised position, behavin' like an unashamed hussy."

I smiled up at him sleepily. "You've been talking to Solomon. Is he all right?"

"He is indeed, m'dear. Thanks to you. Although he's suffered more than we shall ever be able to comprehend. He has a heart of oak. Tell me though, exactly what you were about, roamin' the countryside in the employ of a gang of cutthroats? Devilish bad form, y'know."

I chuckled. "Well, if you must know, I was in desperate need of some Brussels lace for a new gown, so I had some especially smuggled over from France. I was just there to collect it."

Sir Montagu laughed softly, "Very droll. Nonetheless I would like to know the truth. What in God's name were you thinkin'?"

I pulled myself up against the pillows, keeping the quilt tucked tightly under my chin and beamed at him over the beautifully sewn edge. His back was to the bashful dawn light filtering through half-drawn curtains, his face in shadow, his expression unreadable. I became aware, rather tardily, that I was in a strange man's bed, inadequately dressed, without a chaperone of any kind and in the company of a man whose principles were, to say the least, seriously questionable.

"You're perfectly safe with me, Miss Pentreath," said my host, reading my mind with uncanny ease.

"I never doubted it."

Again, he laughed. "Y'r face tells all. I would advise you never to play cards, it'd be like stealin' money from a baby." He turned suddenly and moved to the window. "Come, you are avoidin' my question."

"Perhaps I don't believe it warrants a reply." I watched him warily, noting the squaring of his shoulders as though he were preparing to bear some great weight. He said nothing and the silence was filled with our mute struggle. He turned back to me and leant against the windowsill with a well-practiced elegance and apparently without a care in the world. He idly flicked one of his buttons, undid it and did it up again. I waited.

"You are determined not to confide in me, then?", and I could hear the smile in his voice.

I shook my head. "It's not that, exactly. It's just that I don't know what to do for the best. I mean, there's Solomon. What will become of him? And Miles — I have to consider his safety. I had no choice, you see? It was either help them or they'd have punished Miles in some way."

"I doubt even these villains would have gone that far. After all we're not in Sussex, m'dear. Miles may yet prove himself useful though; your friends have been sadly short-handed of late, grateful for anyone they can lay their hands on, I daresay."

"Well, they must have reached the bottom of the barrel if I'm the best they can coerce. And, in the end, I have proved to them that I am wholly untrustworthy, and they are pitiless and will probably kill me and Miles and Harry and — *you!*" I gulped. "And poor Ned Quick! Shot *dead*. And god knows how many more murdered — and now my virtue has been compromised — I shall be *ruined*. If they don't kill me first." I wiped my eyes with the edge of the sheet, but another tear came and then another and before I could stop myself, I was sobbing silently into the quilt.

Then, without warning, I was enfolded in warmth, my cheek pressed gently against the embroidered silk of Sir Montagu's coat. I felt his fingers at the nape of my neck as he held my head to his shoulder. I drew a shuddering breath and tried to stifle the pathetic noises I was making as I nestled into the sandalwood-scented haven of his arms. I wanted to stay there.

"I suppose I am to show only indifference when I behold the ruination of my once immaculate coat? Sink me, I can hardly bear to look," said Sir Montagu solemnly.

I couldn't prevent a muffled giggle escaping. I sniffed and raised my head from its delightful resting place. "I'm so very sorry. Have I spoiled it? It's such a beautiful coat, too. I didn't mean to cry — it was stupid of me." I wiped my wet face with the handkerchief he produced from one of his pockets. "Thank you, I think I've stopped now. I'm being such a nuisance."

"I desire above all things that you should stop apologisin'. It's not at all necessary. I suppose at least you escaped in one piece and it was exceedin' fortunate for Solomon that you are inclined to be so impetuous. But, if you *ever* — "

Suddenly I felt awkward and pulled away from his enticing warmth and immediately he withdrew his arms and, as the cold seeped through the stuff of my borrowed nightgown, I felt as though for one blissful moment I had been offered something I had longed for, only to have it snatched away before I could fully grasp the joy of it and make it mine.

At that moment I would have given almost anything to have been more like Rowena, to have her flair for getting exactly what she wanted. Sir Montagu returned to the window and I saw it was too late anyway; there was a chill in the room.

"May I enquire how you're going to explain your absence this morning?" He spoke in his usual lazy drawl.

"As long as I'm back before they serve breakfast, I'll not be missed. Meggie will make my excuses for me, should the need arise."

"I admire your confidence. Someone will ride back with you to make sure you don't get into any more trouble." He strolled to the door. "I will see you downstairs when you're ready. Warrick has done his best with your clothes but they were in a parlous state." He gestured to the neat pile on the ottoman.

And he was gone, leaving me sitting in his vast bed, hugging my knees and wondering why I was not more discriminating when it came to falling in love for the very first time.

* * *

I made myself as presentable as I could, dragging my tangled hair into a braid, and gratefully dressed in clothes which must have kept poor Warrick up half the night trying to make respectable.

The tower had no dining room; downstairs there was the hallway, kitchen and the library which is where I discovered my host and Solomon sitting comfortably in mismatched chairs, talking quietly together, the food as yet untouched.

Sir Montagu rose gracefully to his feet, "Ah, Miss Pentreath, we thought you had perhaps fallen asleep again. Pray be seated. Shall I ring for coffee or chocolate, if you prefer it?"

"Coffee would be delightful, thank you." I said politely as though we were meeting for the first time that morning.

"Good morning, Solomon. I trust you're recovering from your ordeal?"

Solomon, who had also risen and proved to be even taller than Sir Montagu and certainly built upon more vigorous lines than his lean and elegant companion, greeted me with outstretched hands. Crossing the room, I lost my hands in his large fists and was able to study his face for the first time without the veils of disguising fog between us. He was strikingly handsome, his large and expressive eyes were smiling, revealing both the pain he had suffered and the relief of his escape. He no longer wore the bizarre uniform of rags but was neatly, if rather too tightly, clad in a fine, white shirt, brocade waistcoat and breeches, all obviously borrowed from someone of slighter stature; his legs below the fastening on his breeches were still bare.

He chuckled, "As you see, attempts to clothe me have been only partially successful. My feet have proved to be beyond even Mr. Warrick's boundless ingenuity." He flexed his massive shoulders carefully within their linen confines and laughed as the material creaked ominously. "'Tis fortunate I am not at full strength or I should surely have split these fine seams asunder."

Sir Montagu steered me to a chair, "I have had a full account of your night's work from Solomon and am suitably awestruck by your escapade, although I feel the need to reiterate that *should* there be a next time, you will apply to me *before* risking your life." He fixed me with one of his blank looks. "And, in case you are at all interested, the Dragoons, Riding Officers, Excise Men, and all manner of officials have been poundin' up and down the peninsula since dawn's first light. They have, accordin' to my sources, captured three of the wreckers, recovered Ned Quick's body, and rescued at least a dozen souls from what was left of the ship and are, at this very moment, searchin' every nook and cranny between Picklecombe and Polperro. Solomon informs me that, without your inspired intervention, he too would have been just flotsam this mornin'."

His praise was almost too much to bear, I felt my cheeks flood with colour, and I disclaimed in a muffled and embarrassed voice and was heartily relieved when Warrick arrived with my coffee.

While I nibbled half-heartedly upon rolls and cold ham, Solomon told us how he came to be upon the doomed merchant ship in the first place.

"My two older brothers and I came from Barbados when I was about nine, to work for our owner in London, as domestic servants; both my brothers perished on the journey. We left our mother behind on the plantation. After I had worked as a houseboy for two years, I was encouraged by the other servants to demand wages for our work. I had a trusting nature and did as they suggested and was thrown out for my pains. Without an official discharge letter no one would employ me. I was destitute and wandered the streets for weeks, living on scraps. I was fortunate enough to be taken in by an eccentric high-born lady who made me her page. I was given a very fine uniform and it amused her to teach me how to read and write and to speak the King's English. She also trained me to eavesdrop and I became a kind of spy for her. I remained with this lady for about ten years, but she was used to keep bad company and the gin and opium took their toll and she died near a year since and once again I found myself cast out but at least I was old enough to take care of myself. I fell in with a gang of pickpockets until I found my feet and then decided to return to Barbados to find my mother. I hoped to work my passage aboard a trading ship, but none would take me, believing me to be a runaway. Another escaped slave was going to try his luck in France, and I joined him. We stowed away on a fishing boat and after an eventful journey, arrived in Roscoff, where unfortunately I was recaptured and put on the merchant ship to Plymouth; where there was some very English fog, a false beacon and — rescue." He shrugged a little sheepishly. "And here I am."

"You were fortunate in more ways than one." said Sir Montagu. "We shall have to look into procuring official papers to secure your freedom and then if you wish, another ship, to take you to Barbados."

Solomon laughed, "At the moment I'll settle for solid ground under my feet! I don't seem to have much luck with boats."

"I don't blame you in the least. Have you ever written to your mother to let her know that you're safe?", I asked.

"It would be pointless and dangerous. My mother cannot read, and such a letter might bring trouble if the Master were to see it. Better she remain in ignorance for now."

Sir Montagu took a turn about the room and I could see it was to calm himself. He was usually impassive, so amused by everything, that to see him so affected was doubly distressing. He stood behind his chair, his long fingers biting into the green and gold brocade and I was aware that he was only just managing to contain his anger. His eyes met mine and I suffered an almost physical pain and had to look away before he could see how much it affected me.

Sir Montagu took a deep steadying breath, "You can stay here as long as you need, Solomon. We will find you clothes that fit and a good pair of boots. Any ideas on that score, Miss Pentreath?"

I thought for a moment, "Uncle Joshua is a large man, and he doesn't take much interest in what he wears; I don't suppose he'd miss a few items."

"That would be ideal. Would you be able to — er — acquire these garments without raising suspicion? I wouldn't wish to see you transported for thieving."

"If I'm caught, I shall not hesitate to implicate you so that you will have to come with me!", I said, smiling and was gratified to see an answering light in his eyes.

"I had no idea you cared so deeply," he drawled.

"Did you not, Sir? I assure you I would enjoy the sea voyage so much more, knowing that you were suffering alongside me."

"Seasickness, bein' high on your list, I suspect!", said Sir Montagu with feeling.

"How perceptive of you," I remarked, enjoying the warmth of his rare smile. Then, as though a goose had walked over my grave, I shivered and tried to capture a fleeting memory which proved elusive. I frowned absent-mindedly at my host.

"Somethin' troubles you?"

I shook my head, "Nothing. I just suffered the oddest sensation, like *déjà vu*. It's ridiculous. Don't mind me. It was when you mentioned — no, disregard me, I'm tired and talking nonsense."

"That might account for it," he said, suddenly bland. I looked up at him but found the tiresome mask was securely back in place.

I stood up, pushing my chair back rather too forcefully, "I really must go. Thank you for once again coming to my rescue and for giving up your bed without a murmur and for breakfast and — "

"Think nothin' of it, madam."

It was absolutely infuriating how he could change so unexpectedly, leaving me mystified. I longed to tell him how inconvenient his mood changes were. Instead, I backed towards the door, stammering farewells, wishing his eyes weren't following my faltering progress; they saw much more than I would have liked. In the hall a small, wiry man was waiting with my cloak, now quite dry; he placed it about my shoulders.

"This is Riordan. He will escort you home."

"I'm much obliged to you, Mr Riordan."

The man's weather-beaten face creased into a grin. He looked like he'd laughed every minute of every day since the moment he drew breath; I liked him instantly.

The horses were saddled and ready and Riordan helped me up.

"I hope you'll forgive the simplicity of our only mode of transport. I do not keep a carriage as I'm not expecting to remain here long," said Sir Montagu, at his most urbane.

"We will be able to approach the Hall with less of a pother. What happened to the horses from last night?"

"I thought it wise to return them to their owner as their rather obvious breeding may have caused tongues to wag. Horse thieves get transported too, y'know. These animals are irrefutably my own — poor stock, y'see?"

"How did you know where they belonged?"

"The less you know, the safer you will be," was all he would volunteer on the matter.

I only once looked back and then wished I hadn't. Solomon stood alone at the door of the tower; he waved a huge hand and then disappeared from my blurred view.

Sixteen

To my surprise, Riordan took several detours on the way back to the Hall, adding at least half a mile to our journey. Suspecting he must have a sound reason, I made no comment. I was happy for the journey to take forever being uncomfortably aware that at the end of the ride would be another scorching lecture from Aunt Louisa. Even though I still ached from the previous night's exertions I was not going to complain if we wasted a little more time before facing the inevitable tirade.

We hadn't got very far when Riordan twisted around in his saddle to watch me guide my horse up a particularly slippery bank; I thought that once I was safely at the top, he would carry on as before but instead he waited for me to draw level with him. His eyes narrowed and he fixed me with a foxy glare. I looked back at him enquiringly, wondering what was on his mind.

"Mr. Riordan? Something bothering you?"

"Indeed there is, Miss," he replied without prevarication.

"Oh, dear, this sounds ominous. Is it to do with me?"

He lifted the brim of his dog-eared tricorne and scratched his wrinkled forehead, "It is, in a way.' He pulled his hat down again and studied me for a moment as though assessing my worthiness. I looked back unflinchingly. He nodded, "Sir Montagu desired that you use a kind of safeguard should you ever again need assistance."

"A safeguard?" I asked, astonished. "Why would I need a such a thing?"

Riordan shrugged, "He says trouble has a way of finding you, Miss. He has a habit of being right. And 'tis not my place to argue. He has suggested that if you were to place a lighted lamp in the smallest tower window at Polgrey Hall, that someone would be bound to see it and know you needed help." He pulled at his earlobe thoughtfully, "Not an unreasonable proposal, I think you'll agree?"

I was about to tell him exactly what I thought about it when I caught the look in his eye and thought better of the impulse. "Well, I'm sure it's very kind of him to be so concerned but there's really no need. I shall be perfectly fine. Thank you all the same."

Riordan shook his head, "At least I've told you and that's all he instructed me to do. Y'know, he's a fine gentleman — you couldn't have a better friend."

"Friend?", I said, suddenly and irrationally cross about something I didn't care to name. "I'd barely call him a friend." Why did I feel so unbearably sad as I realised the truth in this?

My companion sighed and then headed away along the grassy track, leaving me to shrug off a feeling of unaccountable depression as I encouraged my mount to follow the rapidly disappearing figure. When I caught up, he attempted to make idle conversation, but I found I had little to say, my thoughts being wholly occupied with uncharitable sentiments concerning Sir Montagu and his unforgivably governessy ways. What a fusspot! Busybody! Did he really think I couldn't take care of myself? Did he think me such a muttonhead that I needed the constant attentions of a nursemaid? I sidestepped the rather inconvenient truth that it was *I* who sought him out for advice and assistance, time and again.

Riordan left me at the end of the lane, to complete the last short part of my journey on foot. Knowing what was in store, I marched towards the Hall feeling much like a condemned prisoner, bouncing along in a straw-filled tumbrel, *en route* to their execution.

I decided to enter the house via the kitchen therefore delaying the inevitable even further. I was greeted with a surprised and delighted squeal from Meggie, who all but danced around the kitchen to me, clasping my cold fingers in her glowingly warm hands, still sticky with bread dough. "Oh, Miss Martha!", she cried joyfully, "You'm be back!"

Mrs Talbot glared. "That's quite enough Meggie! Get on with that bread before it's ruined." Meggie turned away with something of a flounce and buried her hands in the mound of dough on the table, pounding it with obvious exasperation. Mrs Talbot made a disapproving snort and then turned her attention to me. "I expect you have a mighty fine explanation?" She folded her arms across her chest and compressed her lips into that straight, uncompromising line I was beginning to know well.

I eyed her with misgiving. How much did she know? Was she aware that John had been aiding the smugglers? What could I tell her that wouldn't incriminate both me and Miles? My mind was a blank.

Mrs Talbot suddenly let out a bark of laughter and it was like seeing a rock dance the hornpipe, it was so unexpected.

"There, 'tis just as well you came in by the back way," she said, obviously amused by something.

I frowned in confusion, "Mrs Talbot?" I began hesitantly and was nonplussed when she laughed again.

"If you could only see your face! "You've got no need to worry. We know where you've been. John started to panic when you didn't return, and we'd just organised a search party when the note arrived, and we knew you were in good hands."

"Note? What note?", I asked, bewildered.

"The note Sir Montagu's man brought over early this morning. *Most* thoughtful. We were quite sure you'd had a run in with the Excise Men. I must say it was a great relief because no one fancied telling Lady Polgrey that you'd been arrested. Once we understood how things stood," here a sly look, "We could rest easy. Needless to say, your aunt has no idea — she thinks you've been helping John recover the pig we be saving for Christmas; I told her he broke out of his pen last night and if she wanted bacon and a boar's head for the banquet then 'twould take the two of you a while to catch the wretched creature. A more cross-grained beast I have yet to meet, I told her."

Meggie, still wrestling with the bread-dough nodded energetically behind the housekeeper, "He *bit* me last week. Allus been a brute, that'n. I'll be right glad when Christmas comes!", she added morosely and, picking up the dough, she thumped it into an earthenware bowl, sliced a cross into its domed top and covered it with a cloth. "He's got the devil's eyes!", she added with a shudder.

"Onion and apple pie!", said Mrs Talbot irritably. Meggie wiped her floury hands on her apron and prepared for the next task, one I knew she hated because the onions made her eyes sore.

"I'll slice the onions, if you like, Meggie, they don't bother me as much."

Meggie's fit of the sullens vanished immediately, "Thank'ee! I do dislike onions more'n I can say. But I hate pigs more."

"I'll just go and change my dress," I told her holding out my worse-for-wear skirts. "I'm not fit to be seen at the moment."

"'Ee do look like'ee's really been chasing that evil ol' pig," said Meggie cheerfully.

"Meggie, I do believe, just for once, you've used that brain of yours to some advantage," said Mrs Talbot. "Miss Martha, go straight to your aunt and tell her the pig has been caught and is now properly secured — while you still look the part."

I looked down at my battle-scarred dress and laughed. "I see what you mean!"

"It looks like the pig won," said Mrs Talbot drily.

* * *

Of course, having escaped lightly, the last thing I wanted to do was unnecessarily stir up a hornet's nest. I dawdled for a moment outside the morning room, reluctant to face anyone looking as though I'd been dragged through the mud by the pig. I wiped my hands on my skirts and knocked gently on the door, entering on her command.

Aunt Louisa was seated at her writing desk, she looked up impatiently and observing me standing in her doorway, her expression hardened considerably. She put down the quill she had been wielding and shut the lid on the inkstand with a flick of her finger. "You certainly look a sight," she remarked as she sanded the letter she'd been writing and then carefully folded it.

"I'm sorry for appearing like this but Mrs Talbot said I was to advise you that Christmas dinner is now assured. John and I have captured the fugitive and returned him to his sty. We thought you'd want to know as soon as possible."

"Did you indeed! I believe I could have contained my impatience until you'd changed out of your pig-keeping clothes."

"Yes, Aunt Louisa. I'll go and change immediately."

"Oh, by the bye, Martha, I am in the midst of planning the Twelfth Night Masquerade, as you know. You will be required to attend. I am sure you'll understand that many of the guests I've invited will expect to see you there. Of course, you'll have to be suitably dressed for the occasion. I am sure you'll be able to adapt one of Vida's old gowns and make it fit for purpose. I am sure half- mourning will be acceptable for such an occasion and although many may disapprove of the idea of frivolous amusement so soon after the funeral, I have no doubt in my mind that they will all attend. Curiosity and the fear of being excluded from what is bound to be the event of the season, will guarantee a full house."

"But Aunt Louisa — "

"You will do as you're told, Martha. Now, for pity's sake, take that malodorous garment out of my sight. I can no longer bear to look at you."

"Yes, Aunt Louisa."

* * *

The days that followed melted into each other until I couldn't tell one from the other, but I was more than grateful for a lull in my night-time activities as they were certainly taking their toll on my well-being. I was able to enjoy the menial tasks which became my regular duties and found, to my surprise, that I had a particular talent for making puddings and sweetmeats and was astonished when I quickly became skilled in the delicate procedures required in the still room; the making of medicines and cordials and the preparations of perfumes and washes. I loved working with the different fragrances — rosemary, ginger, lemon, mint, and cinnamon. I was more than grateful to Mrs Talbot who allowed me to concentrate upon this and the making of pastries, seed cakes, and plum puddings for Christmas. I made gilded gingerbread and marchpane both of which she grudgingly admitted were almost as good as her own. I had no doubt that Aunt Louisa would rather I was allotted very different tasks and hadn't imagined that I would spend my time gilding cloves for the gingerbread.

I remembered to make a package up of Uncle Joshua's clothes, which I managed to filch from the clothes chest in his dressing room and John took them to Holmoak Beacon when he was out on an errand for my aunt.

There was a day when I would rather have been elsewhere — the morning the tooth-drawer came. One of the maids had foolishly complained of toothache and the housekeeper sent immediately for the remedy. The poor girl's agonised screams rent the air, driving Meggie to shut herself in the pantry with her hands over her ears and everyone else to creep about with pained expressions upon their faces, all devoutly glad that that their teeth were remaining in their mouths where they belonged. The tooth-drawer, who was also surgeon and barber, handed out various remedies; pills and potions for all kinds of complaints from scurvy of the gums to dog-bites, and although he had the best of intentions, I am sure, we were none of us sorry to see him leave.

Although there were moments when I was able to forget my troubles, I more often felt as though I'd been set adrift on the ocean in a small, rudderless boat. Occasionally, the boredom of my daily chores crept up on me and I found myself wishing for *something* to happen. Then, I'd admonish myself and try to be thankful for the peace and quiet; what with Aunt Louisa so wrapped up in the preparations for her Masquerade and Miles having recovered enough not to need me dancing attendance on him all day, life seemed to have become a bit monotonous.

One afternoon, I was beating a large quantity of eggs and cream together to make Harry's favourite pudding for the third time that week and thinking how I'd happily tip it over his head if he asked for it again, when John arrived at the back door looking very unlike his usual collected self. He seemed distraught and begged a moment of my time. I covered the pudding bowl with a cloth and wiped my hands on my apron. "You look exhausted John. What on earth is wrong?"

The young footman pulled the neatly curled wig from his head and twisted it like a rag in his hands. "My sister just came up from the village, Miss Martha an' she says my mother is very sick." His face crumpled.

"Oh, John I'm so sorry — but of course, you must go to her at once. Shall I tell Mrs Talbot?" I reached out and touched his arm.

"I've already spoken with her, thank'ee, Miss, 'tis all arranged. Mrs Talbot says I can go. She said I can take Amy back with me in the cart. Trouble is, Amy says Ma is askin' to see'*ee!* She says she's been callin' for'ee these last few days. We can't understand it."

"That is rather peculiar, but it doesn't matter any way — of course I'll come. Will there be room in the cart?"

"Aye, Amy's only eleven an' thin with it. 'Ee don't mind then?"

"Not in the least. We'd better make haste. I'll fetch my cloak and meet you outside in a minute."

John went to get the cart while I sped upstairs to collect my things. I met Meggie on the top landing, staggering along under a pile of soiled linen and she promised to finish making the tiresome pudding for me.

Amy was indeed a scrawny little thing, all skin and bone, huge eyes in a tiny, pointed face, a thin hank of dull mouse-brown hair and an air of world-weariness which belied her lack of years. The three of us fitted easily onto the narrow seat. "I told'ee she was just a slip of a thing," said John, with a fond smile.

"Aye," piped up his sister cheerfully, "Herring-gutted, Ma allus says," she grinned up at me, her face haggard and prematurely aged. My heart ached for the poor mite.

"You're not herring-gutted at all, Amy! You're what I'd call willowy. I wish I were willowy instead of being broad in the beam!"

"Ha! I do like willowy. Sounds better'n bein' like a smelly ol' fish!"

* * *

The Pezzacks lived in a narrow, dark lane leading to the village square. The street was so little used it hadn't been cobbled and was awash with evil-smelling debris and I had to resist the temptation to hold my nose, in case I offended John. The street sloped steeply away from the square, the houses tilted at higgledy-piggledy angles. The smells and sounds were an affront: a baby screaming, a woman shouting abuse, frenzied dogs barking, the repetitive banging of metal on metal. The cart finally shuddered to a halt in front of a shabby, crooked little cottage, squashed tightly into the row and I didn't know whether to be revolted by the squalor or ashamed that we should allow people to live like that.

We picked our way across the puddles to the doorway. John opened the door and stood aside to let me go first. I was sad to see that he wouldn't meet my eye. The state of the room struck me like a body blow. The low ceiling and dirt floor, the cold ashes in the hearth, the single yellow candle, the smell of mouldering damp, of sickness. In the furthest corner, in the dark, a bed and in that bed, John's mother, Nell Pezzack. John lifted the candle and held it high, "Did I not remind'ee to keep the fire goin', Amy?" he asked his sister gently.

Amy nodded, "Aye, but there bain't be any wood left," she whispered. "'Ee said not to leave Ma."

"Sorry, love. I should've been here. Why don't'ee go an' take care of the horse an' make sure nobody steals it?" Amy nodded and disappeared.

Holding the candle to light my way, John drew me closer to the bed. He bent over the slight, still form under the thin covers. "Ma, I've brought Miss Pentreath to see'ee. Ma?"

"I'm still here, son," came the feeble reply. "Help me sit up."

John handed me the candle and bent to lift his mother so that she could lean back against the wall. I tried not to stare but she was not the Nell Pezzack I remembered. This was a mere shadow of the wiry, energetic woman I had once known. Her skin was sallow and dark in patches, her eyes sunken and her cheekbones so sharp they looked like they would pierce her fragile skin.

"That's better. I can see'ee now. It be right kind of'ee to come, Miss Martha. I've been meanin' to speak with'ee for a while, but it never seemed like the right time." She suddenly clutched her stomach, convulsed in a spasm of pain. John, kneeling beside the bed cast me a despairing look.

"What can I do, Ma?" he asked hoarsely. "There be no money for medicine yet. I have to wait for the goods to sell a'fore I get my share."

So that's the way the land lay, I thought. John's willing involvement with the smugglers was now a little easier to comprehend.

I perched on the edge of the hard, low bed. Nell Pezzack breathed a sigh of relief as the wave of pain abated. "Nell, do you know why you're sick?"

She smiled weakly, "Oh, aye, I know," she said, "I know."

"If you're able to tell me then perhaps we can find a remedy."

"That's good of'ee but first I have to tell'ee somethin' important. It's been worryin' at the back of my mind. It just bain't be right but they said I wasn't to speak of it." She closed her eyes against the pain again. "I want'ee to know I was allus goin' to tell'ee — right from the start."

I glanced at John, "Fetch the doctor." He shook his head, and I knew what he was thinking. "Don't worry about the cost. I have a few things I can sell if needs be. She needs laudanum. Tell him I sent for him."

He jumped to his feet and casting his mother a frightened look, quickly left the room, the door banged behind him.

"Where's Amy?" asked Nell Pezzack.

"Looking after the horse and cart."

"Good. I want to talk to'ee alone. What I have to say bain't be fit for a child's ears.

I took her trembling hand in mine, "Can it not wait until the doctor comes?"

She shook her head, "No. It be too late already. See, as'ee knows, I was your mother's lady's maid. I loved her, for all her faults. They tried to keep me away from her. But I knew what they were up to. Your father left without sayin' a word to me. Just left. I told them I knew what was happenin' an' then I was a problem too."

"Why? I don't understand."

It increasingly seemed that these were the ramblings of a very sick woman, but she wanted me to hear her, so I remained quietly by her side and listened.

"After'ee left things were not right — I can't really say why. Then your father was called to London an'ee insisted that Mrs Pentreath went with him an' she took me with her. It was a real adventure — I'd never been further than Plymouth before. They rented such a fine place in a beautiful square an' so many quality people came to call. Your mother was the centre of the world. Like a queen. For a while it was perfect. Lords and Ladies an' even an Earl! All dressed so fine." She smiled even though I could tell she was being hit by another violent wave of pain. "Mr Pentreath was away all the time — somethin' to do with his work, I think they said. Then, a new group of people came an' things changed. That Baron an' his doxy. Somethin' not right about them. They went everywhere with them. Always there. Then, your parents had a terrible fight an' we left an' came back here without your father." She paused for a while with her eyes closed. "For some months — it was unbearable. The Baron. That woman. Then your father returned bringin' with him a friend, the Irish captain."

"Liam Cavanagh?" I knew they were connected in some way, but this astonished me. "They were friends?"

"It seemed so. He stayed at Wild Court over the summer an' we didn't see so much of the Baron then. They were happier times. Your mother seemed — so gay an' alive again." She took a deep breath as though the effort of talking was too much for her. "But then, Miss Martha, I noticed — I saw — your mother — " Nell looked directly at me. "She was increasin'."

My heart skipped a beat. "Increasing? You mean — she was with *child?*"

Nell nodded.

My mind was racing. I was having trouble breathing.

"Did my father know? Was he happy about it?" I had so many questions. "It must have been such a shock. Mama was — it would have been a difficult time — she was past the age for a second child."

Nell touched my hand fleetingly, "Your father was at first delighted. But as she quickened — he saw — he *understood*."

I stared at her gaunt face, her sunken eyes no longer meeting mine, "You mean — " I couldn't say it. I couldn't even think it. "The child was not his?"

Nell's face said it all.

In that moment my life changed. It just stopped being the life I was accustomed to and became a frightening world where nothing made any sense; where everything I thought I knew was a lie.

"What happened then?" I asked her as gently as I could.

"I'm so sorry Miss Martha. We had to go back to London to make sure nobody found out. We travelled alone in bad weather — it was terrible. We took the same house again but this time there were no balls or parties. Nobody called. An' then — she engaged a — midwife, but I fear she were no more'n a sham. The mistress was hopin' she would help her — miscarry."

"Oh, dear God!" I cried.

"She gave her drops. Savin and Pennyroyal, she told us. No real harm, she said. Just herbs." Nell's face twisted with pain, or maybe the memory was too much for her. "But it just made her sick. She never fully recovered and remained in bed. That actress woman visited us a few times bringin' medicine for your mother, but it made no difference. She just kept gettin' sicker. It was like she'd given up all hope. She had nothin' to live for. She gave birth in June."

I heaved a sigh, "To a daughter." I stated with absolute certainty.

Nell frowned, "Yes, Miss. A little girl."

"What happened to her? Was she in good health?"

Nell turned her face to the wall and her thin shoulders heaved, "Oh, Miss Martha — ! I can't tell'ee!"

I reached out and put both my hands on her arm as though to imbue her with what strength I had left.

She let out a strangled sob, "Poor little thing. She were healthy — a fair size an' a good loud cry. At first, we were pleased an' your mother held her. She had such dark hair, almost black but when I washed her down, we saw there was a streak of white at the front. It didn't seem so bad to me, but your mother became distraught. Then, the baby opened her eyes an' — " her voice shook, "She had the mark of the devil. Her eyes! One blue an' one brown! I couldn't calm your mother. She flew into hysterics. I thought it might be the effects of the Savin drops but she just kept sayin' over an' over — *'No, no! This can't be! They'll find out!'*"

"But what could have agitated her so?"

Nell just shook her head and shrugged.

"What happened to the child — my sister? Where is she? Did she live?"

It was a moment before Nell answered. "We'd arranged for a wet nurse to come as my mistress was still so sick. An' the child went with her."

"The baby lived?"

"Yes, Miss. As far as I know, she lives still."

"This wet nurse? Who was she?"

"'Twas Fanny Goodall."

"The blacksmith's daughter?"

"Aye. She'd just lost her own baby an' was happy for somethin' to distract her. Her husband, Jem, travelled with her to London to collect the child an' they stayed a while just to make sure it took. An' then they came back here. Fanny kept the baby until she was almost five months old an' then the baby was taken from them."

"Taken? *Who* took her?"

"Fanny say it was a couple she'd never seen before — she had no choice but to let her go. They had official papers." She was again gripped by a cramp in her stomach, she moaned softly and clawed at it in desperation. Each breath she took was an effort. "I'm glad I've told'ee. It was a burden I could bear no longer. I'm sorry for my part in it." Tears trailed down, pooling in her matted hair. "I loved her so. She died with just me by her side. An' I came home with her. Just us."

"Nell, you've been so loyal and brave." I said, trying not to weep, "I swear I will take care of Amy, whatever happens! I promise you!"

Nell stirred herself and squeezed my hand weakly, "God bless'ee for that, Miss. I can go peaceful for knowin' that."

Suddenly the door flew open and Amy burst in, "They be comin'!", she cried and jumped aside to allow her brother and the doctor to enter the room.

Everyone knew the time had come. It was as though Nell had been clinging onto life until she could confess to me and now, with her conscience clear, she was able to let go. We waited while the doctor, a local man with a decent reputation, administered laudanum in increasingly large doses. John sat at the foot of the bed, doggedly refusing to leave his mother and return to the Hall. Amy perched on the worm-eaten stool in front of the empty hearth. She held her hands tightly between her bony knees and rocked back and forth, humming a repetitive tune to herself. She watched us as we, in turn, watched her mother. There was something immensely self-contained about the little figure: no tears, no questions, just the soft, tuneful humming. I could hear John praying and the doctor muttering futile encouragement to his patient, but the loudest sound was Nell struggling for breath, it filled the room. I tried to pray but just felt bitterness for the unfairness of life.

The doctor glanced up, "She's near the end, I'm afraid. There's nothing I can do. Just keep her as comfortable as you can."

John thanked him profusely, "If'ee'll tell me how much — for your time — "

Having no wish to cause embarrassment by offering to pay in front of everyone, I gave the doctor a quick sign and he nodded, understanding immediately and tactfully took his leave.

Nell made a tiny, feeble noise and John leant over her to hear her better, "Aye, Ma, she's still here," and he gestured for me to move closer.

I squeezed past him and took her ice-cold hand in mine, "I'm here, Nell."

Her eyelids flickered, "Find the child." I could barely hear her words. Her voice, nothing but a sigh, bubbled and wheezed. "Find her — *first*." Every sound she made cost her dear, "My mistress named her — Rebecca. She needs'ee."

I pressed her hand, "I will find her. I promise. I'll find Rebecca."

Suddenly I was aware that Amy had come silently to stand by my side. She gazed down at her mother, her bottom lip caught between her teeth. "She be gone, Miss Pentreath," she said in flat little voice. She then went to her brother and put her arms about him, "Don't'ee cry, John. She be with the angels now. Don't worry, I'll take care of'ee."

"I know'ee will," came the muffled reply.

Seventeen

The gipsy's words chanted in my head like a children's rhyme until I wanted to scream with fury. A sister. She'd told me I had a sister and I'd thought her just a trickster trying to hoodwink me into giving her money. I had a sister. Her name was Rebecca. And she needed me. She may be the product of some sordid affair, but she was an innocent child and must be protected. But the recurring questions and the scarcity of satisfactory answers not only gave me an unsettled night but the following day I found I was unable to concentrate on my tasks, so much so, that Mrs Talbot took me on one side and told me that as I was more of a hindrance than help that I was to go for a long walk to clear my mind.

I wasn't going to argue and gratefully threw my cloak about my shoulders and hurried out into a bitterly cold morning; the air was as sharp as broken glass and struck right through my clothes. It was one of those softly misted frosty mornings which transformed all things familiar into objects of ethereal unearthly beauty. The ground was frozen just enough to make walking a little less tiresome, no mud to cling to my shoes and skirts and the grass crunched under foot.

I set out without conscious thought in the direction of Maker Church. I didn't question the strong compulsion which drew me up onto the bleak wintry expanse of the Heights. I just tramped along the tracks with determination, driven on by some inner voice. The air was crisp and clean and soon my lungs were aching from the cold, my cheeks pink and numbed, my eyes smarting. I wished I'd had the sense to find my muff before leaving the house.

Round and round, racing through my mind, like a mischievous puppy bent on eluding capture, Nell's last words would not leave me alone. How was I supposed to find Rebecca and who else was looking for her? It had been quite evident that Nell had reason to believe that no good could come of her being found by the other party. As thought followed relentless thought, I couldn't help shaking my head in disbelief; a sister, I had a sister. I was not entirely alone after all. Surprisingly, it was not altogether a comforting thought. If I did find her, what was I expected to do anyway?

Maker Church loomed above me, the top of its imposing tower shrouded in faint wisps of mist. It always felt like you'd reached the top of the world at this point for there was nothing taller than the church tower as far as the eye could see. I entered the churchyard by way of the stone stile and followed the grass path around to the seaward side and then down the slope to my mother's grave. A crude wooden cross temporarily marked her resting place. I felt nothing but confusion as I looked down at the recently turned earth. Had I known my mother at all? Who was this woman I'd mourned? I wanted to berate her for leaving me, for putting her pleasures above those of her husband and daughter. The sound of footsteps filtered through my angry thoughts and I looked up to see Reverend Pender approaching, his expression one of deepest concern.

"My dear Martha, what on earth are you doing out in the cold? You should be warming your toes by the hearth." He came to stand beside me, reaching out to touch my shoulder but not quite making contact.

"I haven't been able to come since the funeral. I just wanted to — Nell Pezzack died yesterday." I told him flatly.

"Yes, so I heard. I should have been with her at the end, but unfortunately, I was called away to sit with Agnes Legge's newborn. He died early this morning and for a while we thought Agnes was in danger of succumbing, but God saw fit to spare her. I was grieved to hear of Nell's death. So unexpected. She never was one for ailments, always so hale and hearty. I fear your mother's death shook her profoundly. I shall call upon poor John and Amy tomorrow." He shook his head sorrowfully, "How are you settling in at the Hall?"

I really couldn't see the point of answering that question. Neither of us would benefit from the truth. He didn't truly want to know, and I certainly didn't want to tell him. I looked at him closely, perhaps for the first time since I had known him. I had become so accustomed to his face that I didn't see him anymore. He was practically invisible. A man who separated himself from the rest of humanity; living his life parallel to ours, never really touching ours but guiding us with stilted words which had no bearing on our real, unromantic, earthbound lives. Nonetheless, we listened attentively, nodding and making promises we would find hard to keep and never thinking of the man, the ordinary human hiding behind the black robes.

He wore an unfashionably large wig, which had seen better days, probably upon some bountiful nobleman's head some twenty years ago; his skin had a greyness about it which suggested uncertain health, his eyes, a pale watery blue, were kind and concerned yet strangely ill-at-ease. A long nose, mottled blue from the cold, with a tremulous dewdrop hanging from the tip; small, pursed mouth which rarely smiled, yellowing, slightly protruding teeth and limp, sinewy hands only useful for praying. He saw us all at our very best and our very worst, at weddings, christenings, and funerals, in sickness and in health, a witness to our first and last moments.

A thought occurred to me. "Reverend Pender? You know all the happens in your parish, do you not? You must have been aware that my mother and Nell Pezzack left in unusual haste for London and that Fanny Goodall was sent for by my mother?" I watched his face carefully and saw the conflict, the loyalties divided but unkindly I pressed on, determined to extract an answer whatever the cost. "You must have been apprised of the rather irregular situation and maybe even had a hand in helping Fanny Goodall with various issues which may have occurred, for instance — a baptism." He flinched and I knew then that I was on the right track. "Perhaps the baptism of a child not expected to remain in your parish for long? A child with no immediate family and no prospects?"

He was wringing his hands together as though he could squeeze away the deed. "Ah, Martha — I'm not sure — at least — " he faltered.

"You baptised my sister, Rebecca Pentreath, did you not? Perhaps not in the church but at home so nobody would see the child and ask inopportune questions? Yes, I see I am right."

"'Twas my bounden duty to christen the child in case anything untoward should happen," he declared high-handedly.

"Nell described her as healthy, so was it not a little unusual to have the christening without even one parent attending? What were you so afraid of, Reverend?"

He swallowed nervously, his Adam's apple jumping in his scrawny neck. "May God forgive me," he pleaded, eyes raised to the heavens. "I saw your mother before she left for London and understood the reason for her flight but there was nothing I could do to alleviate the situation. And then, when Fanny returned with the — your sister — well, even though she declared the child to be remarkably robust, being possessed of vigorous nature despite —the obvious er — defects. I, of course, agreed to baptise her because her future was uncertain. In order to do this, I had to inform your aunt — "

"You told Aunt Louisa! How — why would you do such a thing?"

The parson looked confused, "Family. Some family had to be there to witness — "

I rolled my eyes, "Naturally. So, how did the woman who *hated* my mother respond to this information?"

Reverend Pender looked smug, "Just as I had thought she would. Lady Polgrey was *magnificent*. She arranged everything. She attended the christening, which took place at Polgrey Hall and she assured me that she knew of a suitable couple who would adopt the baby in spite of her — shortcomings. It couldn't have been more fortunate."

"And did you ever meet this providential couple? Did you interview them and confirm that they were indeed as she said, *suitable*?"

He became a little flustered, "Lady Polgrey was keen to reassure me that their credentials were impeccable. I had no doubts on that score." He took a sidelong glance at the grave, "She said they were friends of your mother's."

"Were they indeed!" I said coldly. "So, Rebecca remained with Fanny until she was weaned and then handed over to this heaven-sent couple? Do you, by any chance, know their names?"

"I'm afraid I never had the good fortune to be introduced to them."

"No? Why does this not surprise me!" I retorted.

* * *

As a child I had often badgered my father into taking me to watch the blacksmith at work; he would playfully protest that he had better things to occupy his time and laughing, I would cajole, knowing all the time that he was as keen as me to visit the forge to witness the fiery spectacle. And when, as always, he capitulated, we would laugh together at our private little joke and he would call for the carriage to be brought round and we would set off with him still pretending to grumble.

I arrived at Thomas Goodall's smithy, breathless and single-minded in my intentions; I was determined to find Rebecca, and nothing would stop me.

Even from some distance there was no doubt that a blacksmith worked nearby; the sound of hammering, metal on metal, the haze of acrid smoke, the puffing and wheezing of the bellows, the snorting of the bored carthorse and the crackle and roar of the furnace. I breathed in the primitive smells pouring out of the open double-doors and for a moment my father could have been beside me, holding my hand, reining me in, warning me not to get under Mr Goodall's feet — and laughing.

The forge was all sooty blacks and blazing reds, clouds of smoke and steam, flashing sparks of silver and gold and the shining, shuddering chestnut mass of the giant horse. The smell of scorched hoof, molten metal, sweat and almost unbearable heat flooded my senses. I shivered with a primeval delight which would have shocked Aunt Louisa and scandalised the parson.

At first, Thomas and his son, Will, were oblivious to my presence as they toiled, both stripped to the waist and smeared with grime and sweat. I enjoyed the ferocity of the scene, almost like watching some Roman spectacle. Then Will spotted me and catching his father's eye, gestured in my direction. Thomas greeted me with an enthusiastic bellow of delight, he beckoned me nearer. I edged forwards, pleased that he remembered me.

He continued to hammer a glowing red horseshoe into shape on his anvil, while Will attended the bellows, keeping the furnace pulsating with heat; every so often he'd glance up and smile amiably through the smoke. For another few minutes he wielded his mighty hammer, pounding the softened iron, reheating it in the furnace, beating it again and then when at last its shape satisfied his critical eye, he fitted it to the horse's hoof and nailed it into place. The smell of burning hoof was terrible but it was all part of the memories I had of the place. Eventually the horse was shod, and Will led it out into the gathering gloom while his father threw down his tools and, shrugged his massive shoulders into a shirt and leather waistcoat and crossed the smithy in three great strides to gather my hands into his blackened ones, beaming down at me like a benevolent giant. "Ah, pretty maid, how we've missed your bright smile all this long while! How's thee been, my girl? Come, tell old Thomas everythin'.

A short while later I found myself settled cosily before the Goodall's welcoming hearth, a small tankard of mead in one hand and a huge slice of cinnamon apple pie in the other. Thomas and his wife, Susan, exuded goodwill and I felt embraced by the delightful aromas of just washed linen and the freshly baked pie. Susan Goodall had been fashioned without a sharp or straight line anywhere on her comfortable person; she was built for dispensing hugs and puddings - a woman unashamedly happy with her lot, content to remain within the gentle bounds of her own small world tending to the things she loved and understood, her family coming at the very top of her short list of priorities. I realised that she was, in essence, the very antithesis of my mother.

I hadn't seen Will since he was stringy youth of about thirteen but was not in the least surprised to find him grown in the intervening years into a young man of lusty proportions, with shoulders almost as broad as his father's. He was a mixture of both his parents, the wicked sparkle in his eye belonged to his father, the steady, unhurried movements were all his mother's, but the saucy grin was all his own. He winked appreciatively in my direction several times while I was nibbling on the pie. Preferring to ignore these bold attempts at flirtation, I smiled in what I hoped was a sisterly fashion and tried not to catch his eye.

Thomas came back into the room, having scrubbed away most of the day's ingrained soot and changed his clothes, and lowered his huge bulk into a wooden rocking chair, which looked too spindly to bear his formidable weight. He stretched out his muscular legs and heaved a noisy sigh; reaching out a plate-sized paw to his wife as she ambled past, he squeezed her dimpled hand in a gesture of such tenderness that my heart lurched with a painful mixture of pleasure in their harmony and envy of their contentment.

"Well, pretty maid." He had always addressed me thus since I was but a dumpling shaped child hanging on my father's hand. "This be just like ol' times. Will and I have missed your visits; fair cheered up our day to see your bonny face when we usually have nought but horses and penny-pinching farmers for company."

Will voiced his enthusiastic agreement in the background, "Bonny indeed, Pa!" he said, giving me another wink.

Susan Goodall liberally refilled my tankard with more mead. "We were so sorry to hear about your mother, Miss Martha. What a terrible blow. We prayed for'ee an' your father an' Thomas has been keeping an eye on the grave for'ee." I started to thank them, but she continued, "We were glad to do it, my dear. We only wished we could do more for'ee knowing a little of how'ee might be faring up there in that draughty old house with no-one for your heart's comfort."

Much moved by her kind words, I quickly gulped down a quantity of mead in the hopes it would stop me weeping in front of them and embarrassing everyone.

Thomas leant forward, causing the rocking chair to creak ominously and took up his clay pipe from its little stone shelf just inside the inglenook and began to prepare it for lighting. While he dealt with the complexities of filling the pipe with tobacco and trying to get it to stay alight, he glanced at me over the spill's yellow flame and the pretty curls of grey smoke, "Now then, dear child, is there anything at all we can do for'ee. 'Ee only has to ask."

Somehow, I knew he understood the real reason for my visit, and it gave me the strength to say the words. "Actually, I was wondering if I could speak with Fanny. I don't know where she and Jem live now."

Thomas exchanged a look with his wife, "Ah, that be no problem." He chewed thoughtfully on the stem of his pipe, "They do live next door but one. Ma wanted them near at hand; and they were more than happy as she's a wonder with babies."

Susan Goodall chuckled, happy that her superior child-minding abilities kept her family close. "They be planning a big family. 'Tis a pity the first one didn't live but Fanny's young - she'll have more," she was clearly thrilled at the prospect of a clutch of noisy grandchildren.

"Now then, Ma, don't go on. Go and fetch your sister, Will," said Thomas, taking charge of the situation. His slow-moving son sauntered out, wondering out loud why anyone would want to waste their time talking to his annoying sibling.

Thomas rolled his eyes in mock despair, "What can you do?", he asked with fatherly amusement.

"He's a good lad, Pa," said Susan, "He just be using all his strength to grow. He'll be taller than'ee, 'ee just wait an' see."

Moments later the sound of hurried footsteps could be heard approaching and Fanny burst into the room.

When I'd last seen her, she had been a thin, rather plain girl with a definite manner, her mother's soft blue eyes, and her father's twinkle. When I'd heard that my sister had started her life in Fanny's care, my heart had lightened considerably; whatever had happened to the poor little creature, she would have had a good start at least. Since I had last seen Fanny, her hips had broadened, her face had begun to lose any defined edges, and she'd filled out in all the right places; she was starting to look more like her mother. She had a wealth of heavy brown hair and an attractive spring in her step. Marriage obviously suited her.

When she smiled widely at me, I remembered exactly why I took to her so readily. "I have something I need to ask you, Fanny, if you don't object." At this point the others - Will, only after a tap on the shoulder from his father - politely made themselves scarce, which I was glad about as I didn't really want to discuss such a delicate matter in front of an audience.

"I wanted to talk to'ee Miss Martha as soon as I heard 'ee'd come home but I remembered that Lady Polgrey said I wasn't to bother'ee. My Jem said 'ee'd find your way to me in your own good time, if'ee wanted to know the truth," she gave me a satisfied smile, "Jem usually knows what's best."

"You know why I'm here then?"

"Oh, aye, 'ee've come about the little one, of course. About Rebecca."

And something about the way she said the name, so easily, so matter-of-factly, left me feeling quite unsteady. I felt blindly for a chair and sat down with a thump. In one swift movement Fanny was kneeling beside me, my hands clasped in hers.

"I swear I cared for her as I would my own, Miss Martha! I loved her, as God is my witness. An' if it'd been up to me, I would have kept her until'ee come lookin' for her. I didn't want them to take her, even though they said she'd have a fine new home of her own with a real family to love for her — just as though Jem and me weren't a *real* family!" she said indignantly, angrily dashing away a tear that had the temerity to slide down her cheek. "I had her for five months before they came for her. I told them that'ee should be told where they were taking her, as'ee were her sister but they wouldn't listen. I even tried to make them take me with her, but they said another wet nurse had already been hired to take my place. It fair broke my heart." Another tear followed hard on the heels of the first and received the same brusque treatment.

"Who took her Fanny? Did you know them?"

Fanny shook her head, "They weren't from round here, that's for sure. Lady Polgrey didn't tell me their names; she didn't say much at all. Just sort of stood there. They didn't take much interest in Rebecca. The woman leant over the baby basket and asked if she'd had any illnesses, but that's all."

I reflected upon this for a moment, "It doesn't seem as though she was the motherly type, does it? You'd think she'd have been more pleased to see her. What were they like? Can you describe them?"

Fanny shrugged, "Hard to say really. The man didn't say anythin', just stood with his arms folded, like this, an' stared at me. I didn't like him much and I didn't like *her* at all. She was as tall as me, with very fine clothes an' spoke different to us, not like Lady Polgrey, or any round here, not foreign, just different. It was as though she were pretendin' to be someone she wasn't. I'm sorry, I didn't look at them as hard as I should've. I was so upset an' the baby seemed to know she was bein' taken away an' cried somethin' terrible." She jumped up, her skirts bunched in her fists, her whole body rigid with fury and suddenly I felt quite sorry for Aunt Louisa being forced to negotiate with Fanny in full flight. How very vexing it must have been to be faced with such vigorous and unexpected dissent from someone who was supposed to be a biddable hireling.

"Did they mention where they were taking the child?", I enquired gently.

"No. But your aunt did say somethin' odd — as they got back into their fancy carriage, the woman said somethin' to her, under her breath an' Lady Polgrey fairly snapped back at her, sayin', *"I would have thought you already had reward enough, Madam."* At first I thought she must have meant the joys of findin' a child to adopt but now I'm not too sure."

"I have to agree with you, Fanny. It sounds to me as though this woman, whoever she is, was in Aunt Louisa's employ and not as we have been led to believe, a lady of good family, with honest intentions."

"What can we do?" asked Fanny despairingly.

"That my dear, loyal Fanny is a good question. I can see that Aunt Louisa holds the key to this mystery, which is even more perplexing. You know, I'm so grateful to you for caring for Rebecca and for standing up for her in the face of such intimidation."

She dismissed my thanks with a wave of her hand, "I only hope that if'ee ever finds Rebecca that'ee'll consider me should'ee have need of a nursemaid."

"The job is yours!" I said gladly. "If I ever find her. Tell me, Fanny, what did my sister look like?"

"She were proper healthy, she always fed well. There was somethin' a bit strange though," she faltered, "Her hair was as black as a raven's wing an' there was a white streak above her forehead. An' her eyes — one was blue an' the other brown. I thought they were beautiful, but some think it's the mark of a witch." She eyed me with some anxiety.

"Yes, I was already told this by Nell Pezzack. 'Tis something she will no doubt grow out of in time and does not mean she's a witch! That's just foolish nonsense."

"That's what I told that Silas Leake when he said I'd be needin' some eye of newt a'fore long."

Eighteen

That night I dreamt of my father again — the same dream but this time the sky was black and the air cold and I was filled with dread. I had a struggle to wake myself up and shake off the clinging darkness of the nightmare.

The frost still lingered, so that you couldn't escape its sharp nipping fingers; Meggie wrapped her head and shoulders in a woollen shawl and was reluctant to take on any outside chores, begging John to step in for her. John had been allowed a little time off to deal with his bereavement but was now back and although subdued, he worked just as hard as ever. We all wore mittens in the house and ice had to be broken on the pails of water left out in the yard. Regimented rows of buckets stood before the fire to warm. Aunt Louisa announced that she would be taking to her bed until the weather improved, which made several members of the household bless the weather. Harry and a stable lad took the new colt, Nonpareil, out for an airing, much to Miles's disgust; he roundly told them that any fool would know the ground was too hard and would only do damage to the young animal. Miles felt strong enough to dress for the first time and I was pleased to see the colour returned to his cheeks. When I popped in to see him, he was reading Robinson Crusoe, only pausing to rain brotherly insults upon the absent Harry's head. I returned to the kitchen to start peeling the potatoes.

We heard from a passing tinker that Henry Hall, the ninety-four-year-old lighthouse keeper who had been injured in the fire, had finally departed this earth. I was much saddened by the news, but Miles seemed to think that at the ripe old age of ninety-four the keeper had very little to complain about.

Having already ascertained that Aunt Louisa was the leading player in the drama of the missing sister, I realised that with her safely tucked away in her bed, there might never be more favourable conditions for instigating a search for information. The coast would be clear for me to search the house for clues. Delighted for this unexpected opportunity and feeling that at last God was on my side, I arranged that I should be given the weekly chore of waxing furniture in the morning room where Aunt Louisa kept her papers locked away in her bureau. The lock would not be a problem as I had known since childhood that the key was kept hidden inside one of the secret panels in the wainscoting, which had been added by a Royalist ancestor during the Civil War.

On the allotted morning I took up my rags and pot of beeswax and began to dust and polish the furniture in the Great Hall, the dining-room, the library, and eventually the morning room. While vaguely wafting a rag over the furniture I listened intently for any sound of footsteps on the other side of the door, my ears practically out on stalks. Imagining that at any moment I'd be discovered, my heart was racing, and I was jumping at my own shadow.

I worked my way around the room until I came to the panel beside the fireplace. I listened for a moment before running a shaking finger down the side of the panel until it came to the join in the wood, then sliding it along the moulding on the edge came upon the hidden trigger, pressed it, and sighed in relief when the secret door opened silently to reveal the little gilt box I remembered. I took out the key and quickly opened the bureau.

Bills for wine and confectionary jostled for space with invoices from milliners and drapers for brocade and damask, striped lustring and sarsenet, yards of ribbon, superfine chip hats, lace and Cyprus aprons. Bills for powder, pomade, and Hungary water; I gasped at the cost of a green velvet riding habit made for Rowena and only worn once. I wondered at the amounts paid for mere fripperies such as macaroons, limes, and flowered jelly glasses. I had no idea that everyday items were so costly and was astonished by the quantities of unpaid bills that were accumulating in the desk.

Then I found a separate parchment folder containing letters. I thumbed through them, noting with mounting elation that they were all in the same hand and contained unambiguous demands for immediate remuneration; with an inward shudder I read the signature in thick, ill-formed lettering. For some reason Squire Tregallas was blackmailing my aunt.

The threats were thinly veiled; demands for increasingly large sums of money were couched in oddly flowery terms and made reference to a scandal and his invaluable services. In the last letter I found a cryptic reference to Nell Pezzack; mentioning how tragedy could strike without warning. There was then a surprisingly polite enquiry about Fanny Goodall and her state of health which made my blood run cold.

In a panic I put the papers back in order and returned them to the bureau; I locked it and put the key back in its hidey-hole.

The parson's words about Nell's usually good health came back to me and I realised that having been so close to the centre of the events, she had unwittingly put herself in grave danger. And now dear Fanny was also in the firing line. I knew enough about Squire Tregallas's lack of moral fibre to be certain that he would stop at nothing to achieve his own ends.

Letitia Tregallas's peculiar behaviour at the dinner party was becoming more understandable. I was beginning to see that she was the weakest link in the chain. Somehow, despite the disordered state of her mind, she seemed aware of her husband's murderous inclinations but was unable to warn anyone in a lucid enough manner to be believed. It wouldn't take long for Squire Tregallas to discover I'd been talking with Fanny and realise that their secret was out.

What had Letitia Tregallas said? *"They'll all die."* At the time it had seemed just the ravings of a sadly disturbed woman but seen in this new light, it didn't seem very far from the truth.

I found out that Squire Tregallas spent a good deal of his days in taverns or at cockfights and dogfights or watching pugilists boxing for a paltry prize. I decided I had to contrive a visit to Letitia Tregallas without rousing suspicion, while her husband was away from home. I didn't dare ask Mrs Talbot for more free time as I'd already exploited her generosity as far as I could, so I had to come up with a good enough reason to leave the house. Two days later I was handed the perfect excuse.

Rowena had been invited out for another drive with the Baron and had decided right at the last minute that although it might be very daring and stylish to be seen out in a racy new curricle with a man whose character was decidedly questionable, such antics might well damage her reputation. So it was that she insisted I should accompany her on the outing but warned me, that once out of sight of the scandalmongers in the village, I would be surplus to requirements and would have to make myself scarce as the whole point of the exercise was for her to be alone with Baron Rosenberg. I wanted desperately to prevent this ill-judged escapade but had no choice but to pretend that I was happy to aid and abet her. I suggested they might drop me just outside the village in the lane leading to the vicarage, leaving Rowena to suppose that I was calling on Reverend Pender. From there it was but a short walk to Millbrook Farm and I would hopefully be back at the rendezvous point in time for them to collect me.

Rowena made me swear that I wouldn't tell anyone of her brilliant plan and bearing in mind my ulterior motive I wasn't inclined to go against her wishes.

It was another briskly frosty day and we made sure we were warmly wrapped up. The shiny black and yellow curricle drew up at the front door; the Baron as always dressed in his rather restrained fashion. Rowena clapped her hands and pirouetted like a child opening presents on her birthday. I observed her, dismayed; torn between my need to interview Letitia Tregallas and the unbidden thought that there was no one who cared enough about my headstrong cousin to keep a watchful eye on her. She was so determined to do as she pleased, I doubt anyone could have influenced her anyway.

The Baron's unctuous charm and unnecessary concern made my skin crawl and I wondered how Rowena could bear to be near him. As he handed me into the curricle, I realised too late that the vehicle was designed for just the driver and one passenger and however we arranged ourselves we would be crushed against each other. I could barely prevent a shudder of revulsion as I shrank away from his touch and cursed my stupidity as I endured the bumpy but thankfully not overlong journey.

I couldn't bring myself to speak to him or even meet his icy gaze because he filled me with a dread I couldn't explain. In other circumstances I might have found him attractive as he had an air of self-assurance and was handsome in a flat-cheeked, strong-jawed kind of way; the sabre scar across his blind side lent him an even more compelling mien. He was certainly putting himself out to win Rowena's affections, although it was cleverly done with a hint of condescension, which was doubly effective in engaging such an inexperienced girl's obsessive interest. There was nothing to confirm my instinctive mistrust of him and yet with every particle of my being I knew he should be treated with the utmost caution. Rowena was, however, at pains to prove how enlightened and sophisticated she was but only managed to show just what an ingenuous child she was. I had to bite my tongue to prevent myself from telling her to stop uttering such idiotic nonsense. She took no notice of me until we were nearing the Parsonage and then she said, with a sly, sidelong glance, "Did you not say, Martha dear, that you wished to call upon Reverend Pender?" and without waiting for an answer, she continued, "We shall almost be passing by his gate in a moment. Would it not be convenient if we dropped you there and picked you up on our way home?"

I really didn't want to leave her alone with this man but had to agree with her scheme.

I waited until they were out of sight and then picking up my skirts, I raced in a most unladylike manner in the direction of the Squire's ramshackle farmhouse at the foot of Clarrick Woods, overlooking Millbrook Lake. A long, low house with crumbling whitewashed walls, various barns and outhouses; a few bedraggled chickens scratched forlornly in the yard, a robust horse stood saddled and tethered to a post and half a dozen miserable-looking cows huddled together under a sagging shelter and from the smell I deduced that there was at least one pig in the vicinity.

I knocked loudly on the splintered, weather-beaten door and stepped back to look up at the windows. They were all shuttered. I waited but no sound came from within the house, so knocked again. I was just about to go in search of another entrance when I heard the rattle of metal on metal and the door opened a crack and an eye peered at me through the gap.

"What do you want?" demanded Letitia Tregallas in a fierce whisper.

"I'd like to talk with you, if you could spare the time, Mrs Tregallas." I replied.

"I'm very busy. Go away."

"I really need to ask you something."

"He mustn't find you here. Please leave me alone!"

I inserted my foot into the opening and placed a hand on the door. "If you don't let me in, I shall still be here when your husband returns. It won't take long, I promise."

The eye stared at me, unblinking; I gazed back with a nonchalance I was far from feeling. I folded my arms across my chest and tried to look indefatigable. The eye disappeared and the door swung open to reveal Letitia Tregallas, in her nightattire, a crumpled and grubby calico wrapper and ancient mob cap which had slipped down over one eye.

"Better come in, then," she said grudgingly and stood aside to let me pass into the dark and narrow hallway. She carefully closed the door as though it were the most important task she had ever undertaken and then led me into the parlour. She seemed not to notice that the shutters were still closed and stood in the centre of the room, swaying slightly and staring at the empty fireplace.

"Did I not light the fire? I was sure I had," she said faintly, "I know I brought in the wood." There was not a stick of wood to be seen.

"Shall I light some candles, so that we can see properly?", I asked, wondering if she was just forgetful or truly crackbrained. She didn't answer, so I found the tinderbox on the mantlepiece and lit two tallow candles in a wall sconce and one in a pewter candlestick. She gazed into the light like a child, as though seeing candles for the first time.

"I've come to ask you about your husband's business with my aunt, Lady Polgrey. I feel sure you must have some idea of what kind of dealings they have together." I said gently. "I expect he confides in you."

At the mention of her husband, it was as though she woke from her dreamworld, looking fearfully about her. "I know nothing of his affairs. He doesn't trust me." Her hand fluttered to her cheek where I imagined there were often bruises to show for her husband's uneven temper.

"There must be times when you can't help overhearing things, Mrs Tregallas. You see, I've found some letters and it appears that your husband has been receiving payments from my aunt. He's been blackmailing her. She's buying his silence." I watched her face keenly for signs of comprehension, "I wouldn't want to put you in danger, but I believe he knows something about my missing baby sister."

She stared blankly at me for a long while and then back at the fireplace, "I was so sure about the wood," she said. "But then nothing is as it was. He says I'm of no use, living or dead. He says I don't understand — But I *know*. I heard her say she would pay to have the child removed from the county. No word ever to be heard again."

I tried to contain my mounting impatience, "Did they say where they were taking her?"

She frowned in an effort to remember, "He said it would be a waste of time and that he should get rid of the problem once and for all. For a price."

Was my search in vain? Had my sister's life already been extinguished? The gipsy's words came drifting back again; *"fire and bloodshed"* — the lighthouse and the wrecked ship — all true. She had said Rebecca was *in grave danger* — did that mean she had died? "Did you hear anything else?"

She inched closer to me until our skirts brushed together, "He's taken the wood away," she whispered, "He wants me to lose my mind. He tells me I do strange things, but I never remember doing them."

I half-heartedly patted her arm, "I'm so sorry," and felt guilty for wishing she'd stick to the point. "Forsooth, Mrs Tregallas, if there's anything I can do to help you, you must let me know. But, before I go, I must know about my sister — "

"Poor child. Poor little thing. I never had a child. They let me hold her for a while." She began to rock, cradling an imaginary baby in her arms, crooning to it and stroking its face, "They said people would talk. Lady Polgrey said she didn't want the child's blood on her hands. Poor little thing."

"Where did they take her?"

"God forgive them — they've taken her away where she'll never be found. He says I will join her soon."

My heart sank as I began to suspect the truth of the matter. "Mrs Tregallas, do you have any family who could give you shelter? A sibling, perhaps?"

"I have a sister, Matilda. She has seven children. All girls."

"Oh dear. Where does she live?"

"York," she replied despondently.

"That won't do then. Far too many mouths to feed and too far away. There must be somewhere you'd feel safe — "

"Safe from what, my pretty?"

I froze. There was no mistaking that voice. I'd delayed too long. He was back already. How much had he heard? I steeled myself and turned slowly to face him.

"Good afternoon, Squire Tregallas. How very — " I began, without much hope.

"How very *unexpected?* How *inconvenient?* Pray, don't let me interrupt you," he insisted with chilling politeness. Out of the corner of my eye I saw his wife shrinking back into the shadows. "Do finish what you were sayin', Miss Pentreath, I'm dyin' to hear what you think. You were sayin' my wife isn't safe here?"

"Not exactly. We had been discussing the recent outbreak of — of violence in the district — the dreadful wreck the other night seems to have very much perturbed Mrs Tregallas." I said impulsively.

"Perturbed!" he bellowed, his face contorting with rage. I took a few steps backwards, joining his wife in the corner of the room. I realised that as Sir Montagu had so unkindly pointed out, trouble had, once again, found me. And this time I would have to rely upon my own scant resources to save not only my own skin but the pitiful woman at my side. Before I could put any brilliant plan into action, the Squire lunged forward and grabbed his wife by the arm, hauling her across the room and holding her up for my inspection. "Look at her! No more sense than a chicken! Bird-witted. She be of no use to anyone." He shook her like a dog might shake a rat and she hung limply in his grasp. Whilst alarmed for her safety, I also wished she had a bit more fight in her so that we might have stood a chance. Two against one. I wondered if I could talk my way out of it, but realised I could never appease him now, his fury was out of control.

"Perhaps she'd be better off in someone else's care?" I suggested placidly.

"I'll tell you somethin', Missy!" he shouted, jabbing his finger at me as though I were a side of beef in the market. He still held his unresisting spouse in one huge fist, with all the ease of someone who was used to disposing of livestock with his bare hands. "I'll tell you what you can do with your advice! I don't want no witless girl tellin' me how to handle my own wife, d'you hear me?"

Letitia Tregallas made a small whimpering sound and without warning was hurled against the wall, she slid to the floor, silent and alarmingly still. Her husband then turned back to me and I thought he was sure to lash out, but something stayed his hand and for a moment he stood glaring at me as though trying to decide what to do with me. In that brief respite, I acted. In one swift movement I reached towards the sideboard and snatched up the pewter candlestick and before he even realised I had moved, I span around, swinging the weapon as hard as I could at the side of his head. It made contact with a transfixing thud. He looked momentarily nonplussed, his wig slipped sideways and then he slowly crumpled onto the floor, where, apparently rendered insensible, he lay breathing heavily, just as though asleep. I waited for a split second, to be sure, then threw down the candlestick and dashed over to Letitia Tregallas. She was still breathing so, as speed was of the essence, I decided delicacy was not the answer. I gave her a good shake. She stirred and opened her eyes. I wasted no time waiting for her to regain her senses, I dragged her to her feet. Fortunately, she was feather-light, and fear gave me added strength. She seemed not to understand what was happening, so I took advantage of her acquiescence and holding her against my side, half-carried her out of the house. All this I accomplished in a kind of trance, knowing only that I had to put distance between us and Squire Tregallas. I had no idea what kind of damage I had done to his solid skull, but I was taking no chances. Desperately looking around I saw the horse tied to the post.

It took me a moment to steer my companion towards the barn, where I found a wooden pail which I used as a step to heave her up onto the horse, I then managed to climb up behind her and we set off with great difficulty in the direction of the estuary and Wild Court. Something told me that it represented sanctuary.

It took a rock and a broken window to get into my old home and some praying and brute force to get her upstairs and into my parents' old bedchamber. I found bedlinen in a cedar chest, a little musty but thankfully not damp. I made her as comfortable as I could and then hoping the jackdaws hadn't blocked the chimney since it was last in use, I filled a basket with logs from the outhouse, found sticks and tinderbox, and ran back upstairs to light the fire. She hadn't moved. She was breathing steadily and seemed to have been shocked into a deep sleep. I felt uneasy about leaving her alone but knew in the long run it was better to seek help as soon as possible. I tucked her in, banked up the fire, and placed the guard in front of it.

As I rode Squire Tregallas' horse to Polgrey Hall I felt bone-weary and had to concentrate hard so as not to fall asleep in the saddle. It suddenly hit me that I had been unforgivably stupid. Squire Tregallas, of course, would have been riding his horse if he'd been away from home; he had no cart or carriage and always rode about the district. I could have howled with frustration.

I may have killed a man, I thought. What if he really were dead! What if they accuse me of his murder? I'd be imprisoned or executed even though it was self-defence. It would make no difference that he had nearly killed his wife - by law a man was allowed to treat his spouse like a chattel. People would believe that it was his unassailable right to pamper or abuse her as he saw fit.

I hoped I *had* killed him. At least then Letitia Tregallas would be safe. At least then he would be unable to molest any other defenceless females.

I reached the Hall, tethered the horse, and peered in through the windows to see where everyone was. The Great Hall was empty, so I crept in through the front door, ran quietly up the main staircase and along to my own room, where I shut the door behind me with a sigh of relief. I got my breath back, grabbed my candlestick and tinderbox, and slid back out into the corridor and silently made my way up to the tower.

The candle flickered faintly in the little triangular window that looked westwards over the sea. It looked so feeble. Perhaps I should have risked awkward questions and asked someone for a lantern. What if they didn't see it? I closed my eyes and tried to will someone to see the signal. I could think of no better course of action. Twenty minutes passed so slowly; I grew colder and more despondent as I waited. Then I heard the faintest whistle below the tower.

I opened the window a crack and peered out; I could see nothing but the dark tops of the trees against the slightly lighter sky. Then another whistle, a softly tuneful warble, unlike any nightbird I'd ever heard — someone had come. I shut the window, blew out the candle, and fairly flew downstairs again. On hearing voices in the Great Hall, I swiftly changed tack and slipped out by the side door and edged cautiously around to the front of the house. I was just wondering if I should whistle to attract their attention when I was suddenly aware that someone was approaching. I held my breath. The figure stopped about twenty paces from me, looked all around, then advanced steadily, his boots snapping and crunching the frozen grass.

"Another moonlit tryst, Miss Pentreath?" came the amused whisper.

My heart lurched in a rather deplorable fashion and began to race like a mad thing. I stepped out of the shadows, "Why, Sir Montagu, how very unexpected," and congratulated myself on the steadiness of my voice.

"Unexpected? Did you not send for me?" I imagined one of his painted eyebrows arching quizzically.

"Well, *yes*, but I expected you to send Riordan," I explained, glad that he couldn't see my face.

"I may well have sent him upon a less important mission but the moment I learned you had lit the signal, I knew it must be a matter of some urgency, understandin' as I do, that you would never stoop to ask me for help unless it was absolutely necessary. Am I not right?"

"I suspect you are always right," I snapped, ungratefully. "It must be very irksome for those who have to live with you!"

He laughed softly and then suddenly his mood changed and he took my hand in his, "Come, we can't stay here flirting all night, someone may see us. Then I'll be forced to make an honest woman of you, and we'll fight every single day of our married lives because you keep falling into scrapes," and he pulled me across the lawn into the little copse of trees where Miles and I had built tree-forts in more carefree times. I could feel my face flaming under cover of the darkness; his mocking words bruised me, and I pushed them away. Once sheltered from the house, he released my hand; I felt my fingers grow cold again and tried to ignore the irrational sense of abandonment I felt.

"What made you light the signal?" he enquired.

"Um — I don't really know how to explain — it's a bit awkward — " I began uncertainly.

"May I suggest you leave out all unnecessary detail and stick to the bare facts?"

I scowled at him, "Well, if you insist! I've killed Squire Tregallas — with a candlestick — and his wife is, at this very moment, asleep or unconscious at Wild Court."

He actually laughed out loud. "Killed him, have you? I know many full-grown men who would have formed an orderly queue to do just that! I congratulate you, Miss Pentreath but have to admit that I doubt, even with the weightiest candlestick that you would have been able to make much of an impression on that dense skull. Still, I shall immediately bestir myself and investigate the murder scene and hope for the worst! But first we must find a doctor for the fortunate Mrs Tregallas."

"Fortunate? I would hardly call her that!"

Sir Montagu started away through the trees, "I would say she's exceedin' fortunate, m'dear, for she could not have been in better hands," he said over his shoulder. "Come along, my horse is by the gate."

I rushed after him, my aching legs and hunger pangs quite forgotten. With one easy movement he was in the saddle and reaching down for me. With blind faith I put my hand in his and was swung up behind him without the least sign of exertion. He invited me to put my arms about his waist and as soon as I had happily obeyed, he urged his horse forward and we set off at a brisk pace for the village.

Nineteen

The doctor was easily found, sitting with his cronies in his favourite tavern and Sir Montagu seemed to have no difficulty in persuading him to give up comfort and a tankard of good ale for a hard ride, frosted fingers, and a patient injured in extremely suspicious circumstances.

Sir Montagu, having seen us safely to Wild Court, rode forthwith to Millbrook Farm to discover if I had indeed committed murder. While the doctor examined Letitia Tregallas, I tended the fire and waited anxiously for his verdict. He finally pronounced his diagnosis; the lady was suffering from a blow to the back of the head and the shock had rendered her senseless, a state which was difficult to assess. He nevertheless prescribed treatment; various concoctions of herbs and an efficacious course of fomentations, which he hoped would prevent the onslaught of pneumonia. He also recommended a diet of caudles, junkets, and broths until she was out of the woods. He warned me of the dangers of allowing her to become chilled or agitated and confided that he did not at all approve of the practice of bleeding where a head injury was involved.

Before he left, I reaffirmed my intention to pay for his care of Nell Pezzack and now Mrs Tregallas, but he waved his hand airily, saying that my friend had already paid all debts incurred. I protested and he reluctantly explained that whilst in the tavern he had happened to mention the outstanding amount, upon which, the gentleman had paid him five guineas in advance and instructed him to keep a tally of his accounts. I bit back an unkind retort about Sir Montagu's propensity for high-handed interference, thanked the good doctor and returned to the bedchamber to impatiently await Sir Montagu's return.

When I eventually heard the sound of a horse approaching the house, I was hard pressed not to hurtle downstairs to greet him. I sat before the fire with my hands clasped tightly in my lap; I didn't even jump up at the sound of his light footfall on the stairs. With considerable restraint I merely looked up as he entered the room and did not batter him with a barrage of questions. His face was such that I found it difficult to tell what he was thinking. Under one arm he carried a bag, which, he informed me, contained provisions he had *acquired* from the Squire's own kitchen. I took the bag and peered into its depths, discovering nearly all the things I would need. I still didn't ask what he had found at Millbrook Farm, not trusting my voice. He came to stand before the fire and looked across the room to the bed, where Letitia lay as still as a statue.

"Your patient will be safe for a while, at least," he remarked, "Her husband is a little confused. He seems to be suffering some kind of misapprehension, I'm afraid," and he paused, seeming to enjoy some memory which obviously remained fresh in his mind.

As I was expecting him to be angered by the terrible deed I had committed I was disconcerted to observe what could only be described as levity.

"Is he — ?" I whispered and his eyes glinted in the firelight.

"Squire Tregallas is nursin' an extremely sore head and a lump the size of a hen's egg. I do believe that his rather eccentric taste in wigs saved him from a cracked skull — however, it has not prevented some slight memory loss which is most fortuitous."

"He doesn't remember how he got a sore head?"

"He's not entirely sure of his own name, m'dear!", replied Sir Montagu, having clearly been hugely entertained by his visit to the Squire.

"Will he recover, do you think? Will he eventually remember what happened?", I asked, trying not to be too euphoric that I'd only severely injured my victim.

He smiled, "Let us hope that if he does recover his senses it will be gradually or not at all. Perhaps he will never discover why he has the imprint of a candlestick in his head. Perhaps he won't even remember he ever had a wife and will wonder at the female clothes in his house. Perhaps he will be a changed man." He paused and said in a more serious vein, "What are we goin' to do with Mrs Tregallas? She will need constant attention for a while yet, will she not?"

We, I thought with ridiculous delight - not just me. "I was thinking about that while you were gone. She could go to her sister but annoyingly she lives in York and Letitia is too poorly to travel all that way even if her sister didn't have so many children. She has seven girls, you know!"

"No, I'll freely admit I had no idea," said Sir Montagu happily.

I glanced up at him to see if he was mocking me, but his face was as inscrutable as ever.

"Well, anyway, there's really only one solution. She must stay here at Wild Court and I shall take care of her — and be damned!", I added for good measure.

He chuckled, "Will your aunt allow such folly?", he enquired with interest.

"Oh, I'm quite certain that Aunt Louisa will do everything in her power to make our lives as uncomfortable as she can. I shall ask Fanny Goodall to come from the village — I like her *very* much."

"And how will you pay for her services?"

I hadn't quite resolved this problem; I had no money of my own and no method of acquiring any in the near future unless I sold something. Fanny had said she would like the position of nursemaid but nursing the Squire's fugitive wife was a very different matter. My dilemma must have been apparent.

"May I offer a suggestion?" he asked.

"I would be glad of your counsel, sir." I admitted.

"I think your plan is, on the whole, quite sound but it might be wise to allow me to deal with the financial side for a while at least. I see no reason why you should shoulder the entire burden when all you did was defend yourself. I think you would be better off livin' here but these are dangerous times, and you will most certainly need more help."

Yes, I thought to myself, what with wreckers abroad in the district and smugglers making free with my cellars! "That's most kind in you, Sir Montagu, and I will accept but only if you allow me to repay you in full." A wry smile from my companion made my cheeks colour. I rushed on, "I do thank you though for settling with the doctor and it's possible that Fanny's husband, Jem Liddicoat, might be able to help out although they wouldn't be able to live in as Mrs Goodall is looking forward to grandchildren and likes Fanny living nearby. She loves children, you see?"

"'Pon my word," said Sir Montagu vaguely.

I bit my lip, realising that I was being garrulous in order to cover my discomfit. "Oh, I do beg your pardon, I didn't mean to run on so — "

"No, indeed, no need to apologise, it don't signify," he said handsomely.

It suddenly seemed to me that he had withdrawn somewhat, and I couldn't understand what I'd said to make him change. I tried, without complete success, to conceal my disappointment and continued talking as though I hadn't noticed the difference. "There's someone else I could ask to come; I'm sure she'd be delighted to leave the village and she could do her work anywhere."

"Ah, I take it you refer to Ben Fairchild's sister, the lacemaker? I agree, she would make a very suitable companion," he allowed.

Letitia moaned gently in her sleep. I crossed to the bed and put my hand on her forehead. She twisted away, whimpering in terror; she was still asleep. "Poor thing," I said sadly, "What chance did she ever have? I can't fathom why she married him in the first place, they're so ill-matched." She moved restlessly so I spoke soothing nonsense to calm her, "There, don't fret — you're safe now. No one can hurt you. Hush, Letitia, just sleep." She gradually relaxed and her breathing deepened again. I knew I would have to try to get her to drink and eat before long in order to build up her strength but for the moment warmth and safety were of the first importance. I looked back at Sir Montagu and, as I did, he turned swiftly and kicked a log back into the fire with the toe of his boot. I watched his straight back and once again suffered a fleeting recollection, a memory just out of reach and then it was gone, and I was left staring at those square shoulders and wondering if I was in need of an early night and a slightly less harrowing life.

"I think I shall prepare a herbal tisane for her and find bedding so that I can sleep in here tonight to keep an eye on her. I'll need to keep the fire in all night. I don't know how to thank you for all your help. You have been invaluable."

"Delighted to be of service. Don't hesitate to ask if you need anythin'. I am entirely at your disposal. Attempted murders are my strong suit."

"That's very thoughtful of you. I don't know what I would have done had you not been here — with Miles still out of action — I hope — " What did I hope? That he didn't mind watching over me as though I were his responsibility? That he quite *liked* watching over me? "I *will* repay you, somehow," I declared.

"I'm sure you will," he said rather too bluntly for my liking. He strolled to the door. "Will you send word to your cousins?", he asked, as an afterthought.

"Indeed, I must tell them my plans. Miles will be concerned, and Meggie — I dread to think how my aunt will react though." I could imagine, all too clearly, the resulting fit of pique. "Would it be too much trouble to send someone to tell them in the morning?"

"Faith! 'Twould be a pleasure, ma'am. "Tis not too late, I shall send Riordan this very evenin' with a note."

I murmured my thanks again. He made an elegant leg and left.

* * *

I brewed the tisane, from the herbs Sir Montagu had purloined, by heating the water on the fire in Letitia's room. I left the jug beside the fire to keep warm and went in search of bedclothes. Even though it was suffering from neglect, the house seemed to wrap itself around me like an old familiar shawl and it soothed my tangled emotions. I breathed in the smell of it and rejoiced in the well-worn, the frayed, and the shabby, all so wonderfully dear to me; every cobwebbed corner held memories and stirred up mixed feelings. I was back where I belonged, roaming the corridors where I had once been Queen of England, duelled with a wicked pirate, and made Miles walk the plank. I came across some things belonging to my mother, a pair of cherry-red gloves, a lacy handkerchief embroidered with her initials, a book she hadn't finished, and found myself reduced to tears by the faintest drift of her scent.

I made a makeshift bed on the floor in front of the fire and when Letitia woke just before midnight, I managed to persuade her to sip some of the warm tisane and then she slept again. I slid into my cosy bed wearing an old nightgown I'd found tucked away with the bed linen. It was too small and smelt of cedar wood.

I dreamt I was pirate queen, standing on the fo'c'sle of my ship, the wind in my hair, a sword at my hip, the cries of the gulls in my ears, and dolphins cavorting in the sparkling bow-wash.

I awoke twice more in the night when Letitia cried out in her sleep; she took some more tisane and just for a brief moment held my hand before she slipped away again. After stoking the fire, I got back between the covers and listened for a while to the mice scratching in the wainscoting. Eventually I slept without dreaming.

The first sound I heard on waking was faint sobbing. I scrambled up and stumbled to Letitia's side. She was awake, lying curled into a ball like a terrified child, her thin arms over her head as though to defend herself from heavy blows, her knees drawn up to her chest.

I reassured her, as gently I touched her hand, hoping not to startle her. She flinched away, whimpering.

"I'm a friend. My name's Martha Pentreath. You're safe here with me," I told her. She didn't seem to be able to hear or understand me, making herself even smaller under the bedcovers. I sat on the bed and took her in my arms even though she tried to shrink away. "Don't be scared my dear Letitia. Sir Montagu has seen your husband and assures me that he has no recollection of what happened. I promise I will protect you."

She gradually relaxed, the shivering lessened, her breathing steadied, and at last there was a glimmer of recognition in her eyes. After talking to her for several minutes to ensure that she remained calm, I went down to the kitchen to make a start on creating some order. The first thing I did was light a fire, then I set about cleaning away dust and woodlice from every surface, and a desiccated mouse from the empty larder, and began preparing some wholesome food for my patient using the stolen ingredients.

As I made a caudle with newfound expertise, I finally had reason to be grateful for the domestic training I had received at Polgrey Hall. I found a bottle of port wine in a cupboard and added a dash to the mixture for good measure. Mrs Talbot always said a tot of alcohol made everything taste better.

Letitia was awake when I took the drink up to her. I propped her up on a mound of pillows and watched as she sipped the piping hot drink, I was pleased to see a little colour return to her pallid cheeks.

"Thank you, it's delicious," she said timidly. "Where are we?"

"We're at my old home, Wild Court. Down on the estuary. It's been closed up since my mother died. It's far enough away from the village and prying eyes to be safe. Sir Montagu is going to hire some help for us, and we shall take care of you until you're fully recovered and then you shall decide whether you want to return to your husband, go to York to be with your sister, or stay here with me. It will be entirely your decision." I tidied the bed as I spoke and then brushed and braided her wispy tangle of hair. I brought warm water for her to wash her face and, pleased with my efforts, I suggested she rested until I'd made some breakfast.

I had almost reached the kitchen when I thought I heard a noise outside. My stomach turned. I tiptoed to the morning-room and peeped through a crack in the shutters. I couldn't see much, just a narrow and tantalising view of the little harbour. There was someone there. A gentle knock on the door made me nearly jump out of my skin. Knowing that the Squire would have knocked the door down with his fists rather than tap so politely, I flew to open the door.

Sir Montagu bade me a good morning and I was so relieved that he wasn't Squire Tregallas that I welcomed him rather too warmly, forgetting how frosty he'd been with me the night before. He stepped into the hallway and I smiled up at him and found him peering at me through his quizzing glass, eyebrow arched.

"Sink me, m'dear! D'you greet all your visitors in this er — informal manner?"

I looked down and beheld the wretchedly crumpled nightgown which barely reached my calves and strained uncomfortably across my chest. I let out an anguished shriek and hurled myself up the stairs but not before I heard the hateful man laugh quietly.

Merciful Heaven, I grumbled to myself, what was *wrong* with me? I dragged on my clothes and quickly braided my hair with shaking fingers. How could I have done such a vexing thing? What must he have thought? I covered my glowing cheeks with cold hands and cursed the impetuous streak I'd inherited from my mother. It took several minutes to work up the courage to go downstairs again, I stood on the landing hoping he might just go away and then I realised I was being childish, took a deep breath and marched down as though I hadn't a care in the world.

Sir Montagu had removed himself to the morning room and having opened all the shutters was sitting on a window seat, staring pensively at the view. He stood up when I entered the room and not for the first time, I wondered why he did himself up like some ludicrous peacock when he didn't seem at all the kind of man to give a fig for the way he looked. Why would he wish to ape those risible beaux who preened and swaggered for everyone to admire or ridicule? He no longer seemed the conceited coxcomb I had thought him when we first met.

"Ah, Miss Pentreath, I was just admirin' your harbour. What a perfect spot, I found myself thinkin', for a smuggler's hideaway," he remarked idly, as though making trifling small talk at a tea-party. "It feels a little less chilly today, d'you not agree?", he asked, swinging his quizzing glass on its blue ribbon. "We could have snow before Christmas. How is your patient this mornin'?"

Taking his lead, I acted as though I hadn't already appeared before him in a state of embarrassing deshabille. "She's quite well, thank you, although she had a restless night — which is hardly surprising in the circumstances. She knew who I was and has taken herbal tea. She's resting now. I think she'll be all right as long as we can keep her husband away from her."

"Yes, indeed. You may safely leave that aspect to me. I'm of the opinion that the Squire's attentions will not be too hard to deflect for a while — at least until he regains his senses." He paused and flicked an invisible something from his sleeve, "Oh, by the bye, I hope you won't object, but on my way here this mornin' I called upon the Goodalls and advised them of your plans. Fanny was most enthusiastic and said such an arrangement would suit her admirably. And, last night Riordan delivered a note explainin' your whereabouts to Miles."

We stood facing each other, Sir Montagu with his usual sang-froid and me with the feeling that we were talking about something other than everyday banalities. There seemed to be an undercurrent which I couldn't quite put my finger on, as though I were being tested in some way.

"Of course, if we do have snow, it will be somethin' of a hinderance to certain people. Very awkward indeed," he reflected.

I could see no point in prevaricating any longer; he had asked me to trust him before and each time I had cause to, he had proven himself to be entirely dependable despite my misgivings. However, what I desired to tell him now was a far cry from asking for his help with Solomon or Letitia. How could I allow anyone to know how badly my mother had behaved? While I was still considering my limited options, Sir Montagu delicately cleared his throat.

"Would it not be a most welcome relief to share this burden you carry? I am perfectly prepared to listen without passin' judgment," and he raised that damned eyebrow at me. "After all, did I not take in your stowaway without battin' an eyelid, and although it grieves me to mention it, was I not ready and willin' to aid and abet you when it looked as though you were a cold-blooded murderer? I cannot think how you would find my conduct anythin' other than sympathetic and wholly cooperative." He eyed me with lazy amusement, "You see how tactfully I make no mention of the night you spent in my bedchamber or for that matter this mornin' — "

I raised both hands in surrender, "Please, I beg you do not speak of this morning. I am utterly cast down. But, as for the night of the wreck, you can hardly lay the blame at my door, I was under great stress," I chided him. "I will allow that you have been the very soul of discretion and have behaved with extreme fortitude at every unexpected turn although I do find your continued support quite baffling."

"I am fortunate to be blessed with an unquenchable thirst for adventure."

I couldn't help laughing at the thought of this dedicated exquisite being addicted to anything that might muddy his beautiful coats.

"You mock me, madam!" he said, looking pained and I had to hide an unladylike grin behind my hand.

"So, Miss Pentreath, apart from smugglin', wreckin', a spot of attempted murder and, oh, wait, kidnappin' — what else have you become embroiled in?", he asked without preamble.

I struggled to speak.

"*Trust* me, my dear," he said softly and taking my hand, he led me to the sofa. I sank gladly onto its worn seat as he retreated once more to the window. He waited patiently for me to begin.

"I hardly know how to explain. I'm finding it hard to make any sense out of it myself." I was reluctant to admit my mother's shame.

"As I believe I have said before one is always advised to begin at the beginnin'. I will do my level best to help unravel any knots we may come across," said Sir Montagu helpfully.

"You are quite right, of course. I'm being ridiculous. Please forgive me if I am not wholly intelligible — "

"Naturally, I will make allowances," said my companion in such an avuncular tone that I couldn't help my heart sinking just a little.

So, I told him the whole labyrinthine tale, as succinctly as I could and tried to keep my emotions under control. I got muddled several times and had to retrace my steps, worried that my meandering and sometimes incoherent account was causing him to lose patience I checked to see how he was contending with the flood of revelations. Each time I found him to be alert and attentive. I rushed through the difficult parts and knew I was gabbling but I just wanted to get past the painful episodes.

When I had reached some sort of conclusion, I closed my eyes for a moment. Sir Montagu was silent. I took a deep breath and looked at him. He was contemplating me from faraway eyes; as though he were in another place altogether, as though I were someone else.

I waited. The silence grew. I looked back at him.

"Sir Montagu?"

He seemed to come back to the present, as though slowly waking from a dream.

"Yes. I was listenin'. I was just — attemptin' to take in all that you have told me and to make some sense of it. I have a number of questions, if you don't mind. I shall, for the moment, set aside some of the minor characters and their questionable conduct and get straight to the salient point of your story. The child. Rebecca. Have you managed to establish where she may have been taken?"

"Only that Letitia told me Rebecca had been *shut away where she would never be found* and that Squire Tregallas said she, Letitia, would soon join her there. Oh, and I'm a little embarrassed to tell you —a gipsy said Rebecca was in grave danger. Of course, I don't really believe in fortune-telling - it's absurd."

Sir Montagu looked thoughtful, "A gipsy? How divertin'! And you say that Lady Polgrey is herself deeply mired in this perplexin' business?"

"Yes, she is paying blackmail money to the Squire to keep quiet and, according to Fanny, Aunt Louisa was present when Rebecca was taken by this *suitable* couple."

"And do we have any description of this mysterious couple?"

"I feel for certain that they were in my aunt's employ rather than the well-heeled people they were made out to be. Fanny said she spoke to them as though they were merely hired to convince her that Rebecca would be well cared for. She said there was talk of the woman being rewarded for her work. She also said the way the woman spoke was odd. I think she meant her accent. The man made little impression upon her apart from the fact that he didn't say anything. Oh, and she said the woman appeared to be *pretending*."

"Is that so?" said Sir Montagu keenly. "Pretendin'? Well, that most certainly provides food for thought." He tapped his quizzing glass against his thigh while he considered something. "I am beginnin' to understand how and why this has all come about."

"You don't think they would have — hurt Rebecca in any way, do you? I mean, Letitia said my aunt didn't want *blood on her hands!* Do you think that might mean — ?"

I had a brief glimpse of a man in a towering rage before he said in a strained voice, "At the moment we have no way of knowin', I'm afraid, but my feelin' is, that if Lady Polgrey is still payin' Squire Tregallas, then the problem, your sister, must still be an issue and provin' vexatious. In other words, my instincts tell me that Rebecca is still alive, somewhere."

I took a deep breath to steady myself and leant forward over my knees, covering my face with my hands. It was all just too much. I felt completely torn at the edges.

I heard him move across the room and felt the slight movement of the settee as he sat down next to me. "We *will* find her, Martha, I promise. I have resources and they are all at your disposal. I think, from what you have already gleaned, that they have placed the poor infant in an institution of some kind. I think I might know of someone who can supply us with the addresses of likely establishments."

I expressed my muffled thanks but unusually I had no desire to argue with him about his inclination to interfere.

He continued, "On a slightly different tack, it strikes me that the three females livin' here are under threat from those who fear being unmasked. Letitia is in possession of pertinent information even if we are unable to coax it from her; Fanny was the last person to see Rebecca and saw the abductors; Rebecca is the centre of the storm and you, m'dear *are* the storm. All of you are in grave danger. Wild Court is remote so I shall send you a guardian as soon as I am able. And, before you feel the need to disagree, I must remind you that you have no say in this. Consider it a personal favour. I would be able to rest easy in my bed if I knew someone was watchin' over you."

"Well, as long as it makes *you* feel more at ease."

He smiled wryly, "Thank you for being so understandin'. There is a great deal to do, so I must regretfully take my leave. If you should need anything you have only to mention it to my man and he will get word to me. If you can persuade your patient to surrender more information about her oh so, delightful husband, that could be advantageous. And take care of yourself; *try* not to get into any more scrapes."

I thanked him again and he shrugged his elegant shoulders and fixed me with an inscrutable look. "'Tis entirely possible that one day soon you may wish you had never had dealin's with me, m'dear."

"Nonsense!" I declared roundly, "I shall always be indebted to you."

He shook his head and taking my hand in his, turned it palm upwards and examined it thoughtfully, running his finger lightly along the mound of my thumb and into the centre. "Confound it, Linnet, you are impossible. *Please* be careful whom you trust."

"But you *said* I could trust you!", I laughed and tugged at my hand in a half-hearted sort of way. "I am very careful as a rule, but it becomes somewhat more difficult when strangers *will* keep thrusting themselves into my path — "

"I'm serious, Martha!", he said gravely, "You must be vigilant at all times."

"I implore you to stop, sir! I promise that I will suspect everyone I meet of fiendish intentions! Young and old alike."

He glared down at me, his eyes narrowed and then he roughly pulled me towards him, and I found myself pressed hard against his chest; I could feel his quizzing glass digging into me and was just hoping the undue pressure wouldn't shatter the glass or bend the ornate frames when Sir Montagu tipped my chin up and planted the softest kiss upon my unguarded lips.

"Oh." I said feebly and not knowing where one was supposed to look in such circumstances, I stared hard at one of the buttons on his beautiful grey satin coat. "Oh." I said again.

Then just as suddenly, he was putting me away from him as though I were something he didn't quite understand or like. I closed my eyes and was almost relieved when I heard the door close behind him.

"Oh, God, oh God." I whispered to the empty room. "How could you be so unkind? What am I to do now?" But there came no reply.

Twenty

The first thing I did after the door closed behind Sir Montagu was dash to the window to watch him ride away. He had kissed me against his better judgement, that much was obvious. But he *had* kissed me. The only other time in my life I'd been kissed was in Bristol when the Honourable Andrew Temple had stolen a fleeting kiss from me as we returned from the theatre in the company of Lady Sarah and Sir Aubrey. It was raining and we were racing pell-mell to hire sedan chairs to carry us home across the slippy cobbles, when Andrew had snatched at me, pressing his cold lips to mine in a hasty embrace which had both startled and embarrassed me. I was never quite able to be the same with him again; the ease with which we had previously conversed vanished and I couldn't recapture the lightness of our friendship and was saddened that all I could feel when he appeared was alarm that he might try to kiss me again. My feelings about my second kiss were slightly different.

Later that afternoon Fanny arrived, bearing a basket containing eggs, suet, flour, and some chicken sent by Susan Goodall and I was, for a short while, able to put Sir Montagu firmly out of my thoughts. As soon as I had explained our peculiar situation to her, she was keen to start and once introduced to Letitia, she immediately took over the care of our patient and began setting the house in order. She was like a very chatty whirlwind. Within hours of her being in the house there was a marked difference not only in the cleanliness of the place but more importantly, the atmosphere. It became more like the home it had once been: aromas of cooking, dishes clattering, buckets clanging, doors banging, and half-heard snatches of song. It gladdened my heart. Fanny and I worked well together, laughing as we scrubbed floors, sharing experiences and talking about everything except what really tied us together, Rebecca.

I took Letitia up a little chicken broth for her dinner, hoping it might tempt her to eat and whilst she drank the broth and nibbled on a piece of bread, I sat down at the little writing table and penned an overdue letter to Eleanor Fairchild. To try to seal the deal I told her that we would have a guardian and that I really couldn't manage without her delightful company. I begged her to, at least, consider my proposition and, folding it and sealing it, I gave it to Jem when he came to collect Fanny at the end of the day.

Jem said he would be more than happy to help out where he could at Wild Court and promised to deliver the letter to Eleanor the next day.

I was forced to explain to Fanny and Jem that I would be short of funds until I had sorted out my parents' affairs, but they brushed my words aside and said that they were being employed by Sir Montagu, who was, by their fulsome accounts, a real *gentleman*, despite his eccentric taste in clothes. I refrained from criticising him in any way because they seemed genuinely taken with him and I wondered if perhaps his meddling was in fact well-intentioned.

I then made a list of things we would need but could not possibly afford. Wishing I could buy lamp oil which was ten shillings and fourpence a gallon and therefore out of the question, I wrote instead: Three Pounds of Tallow Candles. Then feeling this was unnecessarily extravagant, I scratched it out and wrote: Make Do With Rushlights. I added: Salt, Oatmeal, Mutton, Turnips, Cheese, Herrings, Cabbage, Tea, Coffee, Sugar, Oranges, and Apples. Then, I stopped and threw down the pen because it all seemed so impossible.

I knew that to support a household containing three or four people we were going to need so much more than I could provide even if I sold everything I owned. Even tea bought from the smugglers would cost nearly nine shillings a pound. How on earth could I afford to feed everyone when we didn't have a cow or chickens or a pig of our own? I had no clue about animal husbandry but there was no other way; I would just have to find a way to make ends meet.

The following morning Jem brought Fanny across in the cart and handed me a note from Eleanor Fairchild, clearly penned in some haste but nevertheless quite forthright in its contents. She wrote of her delight at my offer and said with luck and a following wind she would have her meagre belongings packed and ready to transport by late afternoon. An under-footman from Polgrey Hall arrived bearing a hopelessly scrawled and rather petulant letter from Miles and my portmanteau containing all my belongings, for which I was very grateful as my dress was now only fit for dressing a scarecrow.

When Jem could spare the time from his proper job at the fish cellars, he cheerfully set to mending anything that was broken or dilapidated, oiling hinges, washing windows, chopping wood, and clearing the chimneys of jackdaw debris and soot.

As soon as he had finished the last task I rather unkindly packed him straight off to collect Eleanor Fairchild. Fanny and I had put freshly washed and aired linen on her bed, swept away all the cobwebs and dust in her room and then with a great deal of difficulty we struggled to carry in a small chest of drawers which had been banished to an outhouse by my mother for its lack of style; I thought it might be perfect to house lace-making paraphernalia. We laughed a good deal as we bashed it against walls and got it wedged in the doorway. I picked a spray of winter jasmine I'd found in the sheltered garden behind the house and arranged the straggly branches in a vase and put it beside the bed. I looked at it for a moment, moved it to the writing desk, then after considering it, moved it back beside the bed. Fanny laughed at me from the doorway, "Anyone would think we were expectin' bloomin' Royalty!" It was such a relief to be light-hearted; it was as though the pressure which had built up over the past few weeks had, like pent-up steam, finally been released. And then, mid-laughter, I suddenly thought of Sir Montagu and the unexpected kiss and I very nearly told Fanny but decided I wanted to keep it secret for a while.

Finally, Jem returned in the cart, which was laden with bulging sacks and there was Eleanor Fairchild, a small wooden box on her lap and her hat askew. She looked frail, thinner than when I'd last seen her, violet shadows under her eyes. We embraced and I could see she was struggling not to cry. I welcomed her and she looked about her, taking in the little harbour and the pretty house and murmured, "Not a moment too soon. I was at the end of my tether and so afraid — "

"Pray, do not say another word!" I begged her. "This arrangement is as much for my benefit as it is for yours. Come, we will get you settled in and then have something to eat. You must be exhausted."

We ate a hearty bowl of soup and then we sat around the table and discussed our plans. Jem and Fanny were happy to come and go but admitted they were hoping to begin a family before long, so Jem would have to keep his job at the fish cellars where they gutted and salted the day's catch but was not averse to some extra work to help out. We then had to fathom a way that Eleanor could continue to make her lace and sell it without her brother discovering her whereabouts. It was Fanny who came up with a solution when she suggested that any lace Eleanor made could be taken across the estuary to Plymouth to sell. I pointed out that it was all very well in theory, but one would have to have some sort of legitimate outlet. It would not be appropriate to sell it from a market stall. Fanny smiled triumphantly, "Well, course, I have thought of that! My cousin, Prue, do work as a seamstress for one of the smartest mantua-makers in town. Her employer, Mistress Kent, is alway keen to acquire the best for her clients. Everyone knows the superior quality of Miss Fairchild's work. I am sure it will work!"

"What do you think, Eleanor?" I asked.

"It sounds a splendid idea, and I will then be able to repay you for — "

"Your being here is mutually beneficial," I interrupted her, "We stand together in adversity! We will have no more talk of repayment, I beg you."

After Fanny and Jem had left and I had settled Letitia Tregallas for the night, Eleanor and I retired early to our beds, weary from our day's exertions and I expected to fall into a deep sleep almost immediately.

I was, however, to be disappointed because almost before my eyelashes touched my cheeks a certain face managed to insert itself between me and Sleep's outstretched arms. It reminded me of Moses, the kitchen cat, when he was in pursuit of a dish of milk and I smiled to myself, wondering what Sir Montagu's reaction would be to being compared, none too favourably, to a disreputable old tomcat. I turned over and furiously pummelled my pillows. Sleep eluded me. After battling for a while against his persistent and unwarranted intrusions, I decided it would be better just to allow him access to my thoughts and then maybe I might be able to rest. Sleep continued to evade me as I helplessly endured Sir Montagu turning away from me and silently leaving the room —time and time again, until I could have wept with frustration. It was mortifying to think that although some whim had made him kiss me in the first place, he had almost instantly regretted the impulse, putting me away from him as though he'd kissed me much against his better judgement. How could I face him without shrivelling with embarrassment? And, once again, he turned away from me and left.

The morning found me heavy-eyed and miserable and my misery was to be compounded by an unexpected early-morning visit. Fanny was energetically taking down the curtains in the morning-room and Eleanor and I were engaged in removing all the mildewed and moth-eaten rugs to the garden, where we threw them over bushes so that Jem could beat them with an elderly besom; clouds of dust billowed and drifted out to sea and the sound of rhythmic pounding was punctuated by Jem's loud sneezes.

Eleanor and I had bound our hair in clean rags and Fanny was wearing a battered leghorn hat, which having lost its shape over the years, made admirable protection for her beautiful hair. We all wore old gowns, with the skirts pinned back for ease of movement and I noticed that Eleanor had dust smudged across her cheeks and brow and presumed I was probably looking no better.

We had just rolled up a particularly badly mouse-gnawed carpet when our visitor arrived. Fanny ran to the door, still laughing at a frivolous jest I'd made about having to find new homes for all the displaced rodents; she opened the door and the smile faded from her dirt-streaked face as she stepped back to allow the caller to cross the threshold. Eleanor and I stood as though struck by lightning.

Aunt Louisa, silhouetted against the cold morning sky, surveyed the scene before her as though she had suddenly come upon Sodom and Gomorrah in her drawing room.

"So, here you are and in such company that even your mother would have had the grace to blush!" She looked me up and down with contempt, "I have never admired this new fashion for aping country modes. Homespun can never be acceptable," and before I could answer her or divert her, she marched imperiously into the carnage that was the morning room.

The three of us exchanged speaking glances, Eleanor's eyes round with dismay, Fanny's positively warlike.

"Are'ee going' to let her come a'stalkin' in, just like that?", she hissed at me. I could do nothing but make a face and shrug helplessly, before following my aunt.

I heard a brief burst of whispering from the hallway and realised that my companions were valiantly determined to stand by me. My chin went up and my shoulders went back; I was not to be browbeaten in my own home.

"What have you got to say for yourself, Martha?", my aunt asked coldly.

"I don't have anything to say, Aunt Louisa. This is my home and I have every right to be here."

For a second she fought her temper, breathing in through pinched nostrils. "It appears you have found your true level at last," she said with a sweeping glance which took in my doughty companions, "An incompetent serving wench and a local oddity. What was I to think, pray, when Rowena returned without you? We were all desperately concerned for your welfare," she said piously. "Miles has been nearly out of his mind with worry. I need hardly remind you that you owe our family a considerable debt of gratitude. We took you in when you had nowhere else to go and this is how you repay us! Of course, it's your mother's bad blood coming to the fore. I have come to take you back to the Hall."

I somehow managed a hollow laugh at this absurd idea, "I think not, Aunt. For a start, Eleanor and Fanny are friends not servants. As for being concerned about me, I find that impossible to believe. I would have thought you'd be delighted to be rid of me. I'm truly sorry to have worried Miles, although I think he's sensible enough to realise I am capable of looking after myself and would understand that I will be better off here. As for your unkind reference to my mother, I shall not waste my breath trying to change your mind because I have more productive things to do with my time. And, finally, I wouldn't return with you to Polgrey Hall even if I were completely destitute."

I had the small satisfaction of seeing her fleetingly discomfited.

"My word, you've become very sure of yourself in the last few days," she said, quickly recovering her balance. "I wonder if you will still be so confident when you hear all the facts? Somehow I doubt it." She shrugged, "We shall see. Truth has a way of working its way to the surface."

"You wouldn't know the truth if it were staring you in the face."

"Is that so? I must remind you then to whom you owe your allegiance."

"There's no need. I know very well where my loyalties lie. They are not just tied to blood but to friendship, based on mutual respect and affection. This is something, unfortunately, you will never know, because you have no notion of how to love even your own children and for this, I pity you, Aunt, truly I do."

Aunt Louisa's face was like the surface of a frozen lake, cold and hard and potentially dangerous. A smile twisted her lips, "Such fine words and particularly brave when you have no idea what cards your opponent may be holding."

"Well, I'll admit I had no idea we were playing some kind of card game," I murmured.

I saw she made her mind up then and I braced myself.

"'Tis obvious that you are now somehow aware of Vida's bastard child," and she sent Fanny a spiteful glance. "But it seems you still have no idea who the father was. Vida's lover! The man who brought shame upon our family and cared nought for the consequences of his actions. No breeding, no gentility — one would have expected no more from such a man. The Irish of course are a wild and uncivilised race."

My breath caught in my throat and I made a small choking sound, "Did you say Irish?"

"The very worst kind," she said with evident satisfaction.

I felt a pulse fluttering in the base of my throat and felt everything grow distant but then a supporting hand at my elbow steadied me.

"What is this man's name?", I asked, with deep foreboding.

She gave me a calculating look, "Why, Martha, what an odd question. You are already acquainted with Captain Cavanagh. I understand you were seen with him after your mother's funeral."

I saw that haunted face again, heard the cryptic conversation we'd shared in the churchyard, the lilt of his brogue, and finally began to understand his words; his sense of duty towards me. His demeanour had certainly suggested a burden of guilt and he had clearly been affected by the sight of my mother's grave. It all rang true; he was Rebecca's father and was, indirectly, the cause of my mother's death.

"Captain Cavanagh? You're right, I have indeed had the misfortune to meet him although I don't suppose I would have been so polite had I known his history. He offered no explanation for his presence and I only found out a few days ago about my sister. I understand I have you to thank for finding the child a good home. It was the best thing for her." The awful lie nearly made me choke again.

She started to say something and then thought better of it. A smile of sorts touched her lips, and she inclined her head graciously, "It was best done swiftly before the child became too attached. I felt it was my responsibility to make sure no more scandal tainted the family name."

I stood back and gestured to the door. "It was kind of you to call but we really must be getting on, we have so much to do," I said affably and after a moment's hesitation, she swept from the room. A deafening silence followed as we held our breath and then heaved a collective sigh of relief when we heard the carriage bearing her away.

"Has she *gone*?", whispered Fanny and her eyes were filled with barely suppressed mirth; she bit her lip in an effort to control herself.

"Fanny! It's not in the least amusing," I told her disapprovingly and then caught Eleanor's eye, who was also having a job keeping a straight face.

"It's just that it all started to seem a bit, well, funny. I was imagining how our faces must have looked because she's so terrifying and we were all so terrified and I just wanted to laugh," she admitted.

I smiled reluctantly, "Do you think we looked as nervous as we felt?"

"Scared little rabbits!", giggled Fanny and suddenly we were laughing, the kind of laughter that bordered lunacy.

It wasn't until much later, alone in my bedchamber, that I allowed myself to think of my aunt's words. Captain Liam Cavanagh. What kind of man could so carelessly cause such wanton destruction to a family — to an infant? To abandon his mistress and child so callously? How was he able to live with himself? I swore that, come what may, I would find a way to pay back the mischief he had done.

There were, of course, no answers, just another sleepless night and heavier shadows under my eyes in the morning.

Twenty-One

The next interruption we suffered was equally if not more unwelcome than the first. A thundering of horses' hooves alerted us to yet another visitor approaching; this time, it seemed, it was not to even slightly resemble a polite social call. Eleanor, peering out of the window, gave a terrified cry, and recoiled across the room as though fired from a canon. The look on her face was enough to set alarm bells ringing from Plymouth to Land's End. The visitor hastily dismounted and marched up to the house. Eleanor's terror became infectious and Fanny and I also retreated away from the windows in a very poor-spirited manner. The sound of a large fist beating on the door made us jump.

"Is Jem here?", I whispered urgently but Fanny shook her head.

"'Ee's down the fish cellars an' won't be back 'til later."

A loud voice bellowed an all too audible string of profanities and then demanded that Eleanor should come to the door before he was forced to break it down and forcibly remove her.

"Dear God, 'tis Ben Fairchild. What'll we do Martha? 'Ee can knock down that door with one hand."

"Does *everyone* know we've moved into Wild Court? Can *no one* keep a secret?", I asked nobody in particular. "I shall go and talk to him in a civilised manner and you will stay here with Eleanor and should anything untoward occur you must make sure no harm comes to her." Eleanor had turned her face to the wall as though by shutting out the source of her terror she could make it go away. I realised that fear of her brother had driven her very nearly to the edge of madness.

Standing by the solidly built door, I wondered if it would make more sense to leave by the back door and go and find help, but I would have to leave Letitia and Eleanor with no one to defend them but Fanny. My thoughts of flight were interrupted as Ben Fairchild thundered his fists against the door once more. I gritted my teeth and pulled it open, to find Ben Fairchild's muscular arm poised above my head ready to batter the wooden panels again, he was unable to stop the course of the blow and I had to dodge sideways to avoid his flying fist.

"Where in damnation is my sister?", he raged at me.

I attempted to stay calm, managing a smile of sorts. "Mister Fairchild, what an unexpected pleasure. I'm afraid Eleanor is very busy at the moment and is unable to come to the door. However, she'd be only too happy to see you another time. Perhaps you could come to tea later in the week?"

His face darkened and I forced myself not to take a step back, "Don't you try being clever with me, Missy. I know all about you and your cursed family and I'm not having my sister mixing with people like you. Now, go and get her or I'll drag her out here myself."

"No." I said clearly. "I will not. You have made her life a godforsaken misery and she will not be returning to it." This time I had no choice but to jump back as he lunged towards me and grabbed at my hair, twisting it painfully.

"What do you have to say now, eh?", he snarled into my face.

"I say that as long as there is breath in my body Eleanor will not go with you. 'Tis just like a bully to pull a girl's hair." I remarked calmly, all the while wondering how I was going to stop him.

"So, you like a fight, do you? I like a wench with a bit of spirit. I suspected when we first met, we might have something in common."

I glared at him, "We have absolutely *nothing* in common and I do wish you'd stop panting in my face because your breath is as foul as your language."

And then I wasn't alone. Fanny and Eleanor emerged into the hall.

"Ben, release Miss Pentreath at once!", said Eleanor shakily. "There's no point in threatening her because nothing will change my mind. I'd no more live with you than a rabid dog. And I'll not marry anyone I don't want to either so you can forget your ridiculous scheming. Now, let her go!"

Her brother just laughed, "What will you do if I refuse, sister dear? Will you strike me with your tiny hands?"

"She won't need to do anythin', Mr Fairchild," said Fanny, drawing a deadly looking knife from somewhere under her apron, "Because I will stab'ee through your evil heart before'ee can blink an eye. And just in case'ee thinks I wouldn't do it, let me remind'ee that I can gut a fish with my eyes closed and to my mind'ee has less worth than a herring that's been dead a fortnight."

Observing the relaxed way she handled the knife I didn't doubt her and seeing the dangerous glint in her eye I was only mildly surprised when Ben Fairchild wrenched my head back and growled into my face, "I'll get you for this, mark my words. Keep looking over your shoulder because one day I'll be there and there'll be no one to help you." He then released me with such violence that I caught my side on the edge of the door and was briefly winded. Out of the corner of my eye I saw the redoubtable Fanny start forward to my defence, knife at the ready; Eleanor gave a startled shriek and I turned to see Ben Fairchild being hauled backwards, a sinewy arm clamped around his throat, a dumbfounded expression on his half-strangled face.

"*Jem!*" cried Fanny, jumping up and down, "Knock 'im down, Jem! Knock 'im flat! Oh, Jem! Jem!" In her excitement she was waving the knife around with scant regard for anyone's safety, so ecstatic was she at the timely return of her heroic swain she seemed to have forgotten she was still armed with a deadly weapon.

Jem dragged Benjamin Fairchild out onto the quay where he kept him pinioned, helpless, and raging against his captor.

"What do'ee wish me to do with him, Miss Martha? Throw him in the harbour?"

Although the idea greatly appealed to me, I saw it would hardly improve relations with him. "I think not — *this* time, Jem. Mr Fairchild, it seems I must explain to you in simpler terms that your sister has permanently left your house, not just because of the unpleasant flaws in your nature but first and foremost because you have failed in your duties as her brother; you have failed to protect her as you should, so you had better become accustomed to making your own dinner from now on. I do hope you'll understand." Jem slackened his grip on his victim's neck just enough so he could look me in the eye and what I saw there didn't fill me with confidence. "Oh, let him go, Jem. 'Tis no use."

Jem was disappointed but let him go. "Seems a waste of a God-given opportunity, if you ask me," he said sulkily.

Ben Fairchild tugged his coat back into place and tried to salvage the last tattered shreds of his dignity; he stuck out his bristly chin, "You'll pay for this, you filthy scum!", he shouted at Jem. "It was a dark day when you and your harlot joined forces with the Pentreaths. I'll see you dead. I've got friends in high places — you've made a serious mistake." He untied his horse, threw himself clumsily into the saddle and galloped away up the track.

"There's just no reasoning with some people," said Jem dolefully.

* * *

Two days passed without serious incident apart from the arrival of Riordan, Sir Montagu's man who quietly made himself at home saying he'd been sent to keep an eye on things, he seemed happy to sit at the kitchen table with a piece of pie and a cup of coffee and regularly went on patrols around the grounds, he told us that Sir Montagu was organising something a little more permanent for the future. It was a comfort.

Jem mended the roof, replaced three broken windows and started organising the outhouses, which were crammed to the eaves with rubbish of every conceivable kind. Fanny and I continued our war on the accumulated dust and decay while Eleanor took charge of washing and darning all the curtains, covers, and bed linen. Letitia remained in her bed, mostly lying supine, gazing at the canopy. On the third day, I decided that something had to be done about her so I discussed the problem with my companions, and it was decided that the best person to consult would be Mrs Talbot. This meant a visit to Polgrey Hall which was not something I really wanted to do, but at least there was a chance I might be able to see Miles. I managed to put it off for another day until Fanny pointed out that Letitia was not going to improve without some proper medical intervention. I had to agree.

* * *

It had been a mild, blustery day, the frost having finally abated, and I set off on foot to the Hall rather later than I should have, just as dusk was approaching. After ten minutes walking, I had to stop to take off my cloak as I was becoming a trifle overheated. I stopped at the top of the ridge above Wild Court and looked back at my home; cobalt blue smoke curled from two of the chimneys which made it seem alive again.

Mrs Talbot's sound good sense was about the only thing I had really missed since I left the Hall along with Meggie's bright little face and of course, Miles. I was looking forward to seeing them again.

Of course, Miles and I had not been so close in recent weeks; I couldn't help feeling he was not the boy I had once known. In some fundamental way he had become a stranger to me; we talked and laughed together but there was a part of him I no longer understood. This didn't make me love him any less, but it did mean that I could not rely upon him as I once had; my trust in him had to be qualified.

I marched on across the hill, the wind buffeting me in a friendly fashion and after a while even the closely cropped wintry brown grass and the wind-tortured trees looked beautiful to me in the fast-fading winter light. My father had always said, 'A breath of fresh air could work wonders for a fit of the sullens.' I started to sing *Greensleeves*, at first to myself, and then so loudly I wouldn't have heard a pack of wild dogs bearing down on me, so it wasn't surprising that after clambering over the wall onto the Polgrey estate, I had no idea there was someone fast approaching from behind me.

"Your family seem singularly fond of that song," commented Captain Cavanagh cheerfully as he fell into step with me. I was so taken aback, I nearly tripped over.

My aunt's words immediately came flooding back and I found I couldn't speak. I just stared at him, wanting to break him as he had broken my mother; to make him suffer. I wanted to wreak revenge upon him.

"Miss Pentreath, this is very unlike you. Have you nothing to say for yourself?" He looked so amused at my expense I could have hit him. Instead, I turned and marched away as fast as I could, but he didn't take the hint, merely adjusting his pace to mine.

I stopped and scowled at him, my voice returning rather too loudly, "Do you *mind*!"

"Not in the least," he replied affably. "Are you late for an appointment?"

Seething, I clenched my fists; at that moment a gentle breath of wind swirled around us and I caught the faintest scent of sandalwood; momentarily distracted, I tried in vain to place the memory it brought with it.

Recollecting my anger, I urged him to leave me alone. "I have no desire to talk to you."

"My word, you're in a terrible temper this afternoon. Is there anything I can do to help alleviate this dark mood of yours?"

"Yes! You can leave me *alone!*", I shouted at him, wishing I didn't sound like a fishwife.

"Merciful Heaven!", he remarked, looking as though he were going to burst out laughing "You sound uncommonly like a fishwife."

That was all I needed. I flew at him, like something demented. I wanted to hurt him in any way I could. He fended me off with ease, holding me at arm's length as he would a spitting, hissing, but ineffectual wild thing.

"Miss Pentreath! *Martha!* Stop this. What has got into you?"

"I'll tell you! You — you wicked, cruel — how could you *do* such a thing?"

His grip on me tightened and through the red haze of my rage I was aware that he had stopped looking amused. "Ah, I begin to see the light. What gossip have you been listening to?", he demanded.

I was struggling with my pent-up emotions and couldn't answer so he shook me, "Martha Pentreath, stop this nonsense and tell me what this is about."

All the fight just drained out of me and he had to hold me up. "I can't. It's too dreadful."

This time he let me go, his expression unreadable, "So, the rumours have finally reached you. I wondered how long it would take before some helpful soul whispered a word in your ear. What version of the story have you heard, I wonder?"

I couldn't bear to look at him for fear of seeing the guilt in his face.

There was a moment of complete stillness, as though the earth stopped turning.

"I *know*," I said.

"What do you know, Martha?"

"The child. Rebecca. She's yours."

The air seemed to shiver around us. I looked up at him.

His countenance had somehow softened. I got the distinct feeling that some of the strain had suddenly dissipated.

"May I enquire how you have reached this interesting conclusion?", he asked.

"My aunt kindly informed me a few days ago."

"I think Lady Polgrey should get her facts straight before making such wild accusations. And you shouldn't be so damned gullible." He moved several paces away from me and looked out over the darkening estuary. "The child is not mine, of that I can assure you — unless it was an immaculate conception."

My thoughts began to race, all the allegations and suspicions and deceptions tussled in my mind, tying themselves into knots. Who could I believe? Was Aunt Louisa telling the truth or this unprincipled smuggler? I just didn't know what to think; I felt as though I was trapped in quicksand.

He had turned his back on me. The breeze caught at the black ribbon in his dark hair and toyed with the edges of his moss green frock coat, fluttering them like butterfly wings.

I felt like I'd been spinning round and round for too long until I got dizzy; my head was whirling. I felt so exhausted that I dropped down onto the grassy bank, my skirts settling about me in dull brown folds and furrows, like a ploughed field. I wrapped my arms around my knees and buried my head in them. I really just wanted to stop the heartache, for me, for *everyone*.

Or to wake up and find this had all been a grim dream. I wanted my old life back; this one did not agree with me.

"If you're not her father — then who is?", I asked, my voice small and muffled.

A pause, a slight sound as he turned, "I have my suspicions of course but they're hard to substantiate but, you have my word, I intend to unmask him, whoever he may be." He looked down at me, "This child? Do you know what has become if it?"

"As far as I am aware, the baby was removed from the wet-nurse, Fanny Goodall, and instead of being adopted was, in fact, left in some kind of institution. I don't as yet know where."

"If you wish I will ask some discreet questions around the district; I know a few handy souls who might know a thing or two, for a few guineas."

"I'm sure you do. In the local alehouses? And — "

"Don't you dare say brothels," he interjected.

"I was going to say houses of ill repute, actually."

A slight smile, "*So* much more acceptable." He came to stand in front of me and held out his hand, "Come, let me help you up before you get rheumatism. You seem to have a penchant for sitting around in dark, damp places; you'll catch a chill. Why don't you let me take you home?"

"I'm on my way to the Hall to consult with Mrs Talbot about Letitia Tregallas, who is still not improved after an accident befell her."

"Well, then, I will happily escort you the rest of the way." He took my hands and pulled me to my feet with ease. "I find myself at a bit of loose end today."

"Well, in that case, thank you - that would be kind. I don't feel quite myself."

We stood surveying each other for a moment and he reached out to flick an escaped curl out of my eyes.

"No arguments, Martha? That's unusual."

"I *told* you, I'm not feeling quite myself!"

He laughed and headed off towards the nearby copse. His long stride was too much for me, I was damned if I was going to break into an undignified trot, especially hampered by my skirts, I stopped in my tracks, hands on hips, "If this is your idea of escorting — !"

He immediately pulled up, turning back to me with a wry smile, "My apologies. My mind was elsewhere. I am used to moving at speed — to evade capture, you know."

"That doesn't surprise me in the least. However, as my legs are a deal shorter than yours, it would be helpful if you could take smaller steps."

He waited until I caught up and then handed me his coat-tail. I laughed and grasped it firmly. My fingers curled about the green material and I thought of my father, walking ahead of me along the shore, telling me stories of derring-do at sea, while I clung onto his coat, so that he couldn't get away from me. I found myself smiling like a fool.

"Your father often talked of you, y'know. He told me about you paddling barefoot on the flooded quay, your petticoats hitched up above your dimpled little knees, how you demanded that he should always bring you back a book from his journeys and that you always clung onto his coattails when walking. I know a good deal about you, Martha Pentreath."

Again, he'd been able to read my thoughts and I wondered what else he'd seen in my unguarded moments.

"Do you know what happened to my father?"

"Ralph persuaded me to work with him on a venture he was planning and although I was reluctant at first for either of us to become involved in such a reckless scheme, he somehow convinced me. His arguments were always compelling. Then his life became untenable and by all accounts he sailed for France, on this fool's errand. I have heard nothing since, despite digging as deep as I dare into his work. I'm sorry to be the one to tell you but I have several sources over there who all attested to having witnessed him being executed — as a spy."

"Executed! That can't be! It's preposterous. Why would they —? He would never risk his life! He was such a cautious man — so terribly opposed to impulsive behaviour of any kind. He was forever scolding me for my impulsiveness. He would never have considered anything so audacious. You are mistaken."

"I wish I were, Martha, but I fear there may be some truth in it. He undertook an exceedingly dangerous task, and it made no sense until I realised his once perfect life had just crumbled to dust." He glanced up at the sky behind me, "The weather appears to be on the turn."

Looking at the bank of dark cloud rolling in I knew he was right. "I'd best get to the Hall quickly — I don't want to have to spend the night there. If I hurry, I might just be home by nightfall."

"It might be a good idea to postpone your visit," he said.

'Oh, no, I've come this far, I may as well carry on. I'll be fine. I'm used to this kind of unpredictable weather; I've lived here all my life."

"Of course you have. However, I think I shall wait for you to make sure you get back safely."

"What an absurd idea! I assure you there is no need," I protested.

"I will wait by the gate for you," he said resolutely, so I argued no more and set off through the small unkempt wood which lay behind the Hall. Just once, I allowed myself to look back and was reassured to see him still standing where I'd left him, watching me. I waved and turned away quickly in case he didn't respond.

Twenty-Two

The commotion from the kitchen assaulted my ears from the other side of the yard; the clatter of pots and pans, the din of voices, all heralding the imminent creation of dinner. I knew what sounded to the untrained ear like chaos would in fact be a disciplined military campaign. Some things could be relied upon to never change. I was hoping that my relations would be so distracted by the arrival of dinner they wouldn't notice me running around at large in their house. There was no point in knocking; nobody would hear. So I pushed the door open and stepped back into Polgrey Hall.

It was like walking into a madhouse. I paused on the threshold, seeking a familiar face amongst the kitchen staff toiling in the smoke and steam; there was John Pezzack bearing a tray, as ever, and dear Meggie, round face shining and over on the other side of the kitchen, Anne Talbot was loudly berating one of the scullery maids who had apparently dropped a dish of cream in the buttery; the poor girl stood biting her lip, tears trickling down her crimson cheeks, while her faults were enumerated for all to hear.

"I'll give you *mouse*! If you drops anything else I'll tan your hide!", she thundered and the unfortunate girl nodded miserably and scurried off to clean up the mess she'd made. Anne Talbot rolled her eyes heavenward, then turning to bellow an order at a passing footman, she caught my eye. Before I could say a word, she was cutting a swathe through the hordes of servants.

"And where have you been, Martha Pentreath? Have you been blown in by the storm?", she said surveying my windswept hair critically. "It looks as black as sin out there now."

"The weather looked fine when I left home."

"Did you come alone?"

"In a way." I said cautiously.

"Ah, I see. Do you want a bite to eat? You're looking as thin as a rake."

I laughed because this couldn't have been further from the truth. "Thank you, but no, I've really come to ask your advice — about a rather sensitive matter."

"Right," she said, "Come with me. Meggie!" she roared, "Meggie, bring food to the stillroom."

Once closeted in her inner sanctum, Mrs Talbot lit some tallow candles and a few minutes later Meggie came with a plate of roasted pigeon, bread and some cider. I thought guiltily of the smuggler captain waiting outside in the worsening weather but remembered I hadn't eaten anything since breakfast and tucked in regardless.

"Firstly, Mrs Talbot, I'd like to apologise for leaving without due warning — it all happened rather suddenly. You could say I was overtaken by events. Anyway, I'm at Wild Court, with Fanny and Eleanor Fairchild and — "

"That muddle-headed Tregallas woman," said the reliably informed housekeeper. "You be careful dealing with her — that husband of hers is unstable to say the least."

I explained that Letitia had been injured by a blow to the head and wasn't recovering as quickly as I'd like; I described her symptoms as best I could.

"Sounds to me like she don't *want* to get better. Nothin' to live for. Maybe a touch of brain fever. I'll have to see her for myself. Leave it to me. I'll get John to take me over in the cart tomorrow if this storm blows over." She gave me a very straight look, "Now, tell me your other troubles."

I chuckled, "Which ones do you have in mind? I have so many!"

"Why, the important ones, of course. I've heard 'bout a certain new man in your life — "

"Ah, you mean Jem Liddicoat? Fanny's husband."

She fixed me with a penetrating stare and left me to flounder like a fish out of water.

"I can't think who you mean, Mrs Talbot." I muttered, turning pink.

"I be talking about that fine and fancy fellow from Holmoak Beacon, the one that's been so friendly with them up at the Manor."

"You can't mean Sir Montagu Fitzroy?" I exclaimed in horrified accents, "He's certainly not — I don't — no, not him —*especially* not him."

She smiled benignly, "Finish that food up," she said.

The cider loosened my tongue and made me a bit too chatty and I was soon telling her about life at Wild Court, about Fanny facing up to Ben Fairchild, and Aunt Louisa's terrifying visit, and then I was running on about Sir Montagu this and Sir Montagu that until I heard the words spilling from my mouth and ground to an embarrassed halt.

"Sir Montagu has been kind enough to come to my rescue when I've found myself in the occasional scrape. He's very — odd." I added.

"So I've heard," said Mrs Talbot. "There's no accountin' for taste."

Before she could say anything else, I jumped to my feet, thanked her profusely for the food and her offer of help and leaving her smiling smugly, I went to find Miles.

The door to the library was closed but as I tiptoed towards it, I could hear uproarious laughter from within and it stopped me in my tracks. I hadn't imagined Miles would have company and was disappointed. I wanted to see him alone. I started to retreat the way I had come when the door was wrenched open and Lucius was there, his handsome, dissolute face still wreathed in uncharacteristic good humour.

"Well, bless my soul!", he remarked. "If it isn't little cousin Martha! Come and join us. We could do with a female point of view."

I shook my head and backed away.

Lucius raised his eyebrows and tut-tutted, "I'm disappointed in you. D'you really think I'd let you stumble headlong into a trap? Look, 'tis just Miles and Harry swapping tall stories by the fireside encouraged by some rather good brandy. Are you going to just stand there? Mother will find you still rooted to the spot when she returns."

I stalked past him into the library, still hating how he always made fun of me for his own amusement.

"What a prickly hedgehog," he said. "Perhaps I'll stay after all; this promises to be far more entertaining than the stables."

Harry leapt to his feet and rushed to greet me with kisses for my cheek and a stammered welcome, while Miles remained seated beside the fire. He didn't even look up and I knew by the stiff line of his shoulders that he was out of humour with me. He was in one of his full-blooded but thankfully rare sulks. With years of experience, I was hopeful I could defuse it, I went straight and knelt beside him.

"Miles. *Beloved* Miles. I do most humbly beg your forgiveness for all my transgressions. For regularly defeating you in sword fights, for telling Reverend Pender you were the phantom scrumper when it was really me, for locking you in the cellar and not allowing you out until you promised me your new tin soldier, for putting a toad in your bed, for — "

"That *was* unforgivable. You knew I had a morbid fear of those vile beasts. And the cellar incident still gives me nightmares," he said accusingly. "You were shameless and, to be perfectly honest, I'm glad you left. You really have always been a damned nuisance."

"Thank you," I said, laughing, "I truly *am* sorry I didn't tell you I was leaving but I didn't know myself until it was done." His shoulders had already relaxed, and I thought to myself how easily manipulated he was. "I've missed you so much, Miles," I declared with absolute honesty.

"Yes, well, all right. I suppose I must be thankful you didn't pretend to cry like you were used to, just to get your own way. As a child you were utterly ruthless."

"I will admit, weeping did cross my mind, for a very brief moment."

"I still wouldn't have forgiven you for leaving me at the mercies of my mother. Indefensible."

"I hate to own but it's been pretty dismal here without you, Martha," said Lucius. "Harry and I were on the brink of tipping Miles into Hooe Lake."

"He'd be better off in the lake. Nobody likes it here, y'know!" announced Harry. "We should all leave really."

Lucius blew out his cheeks and tried to contain his irritation, "Oh, do stop prating on in that absurd fashion. You didn't used to be such a dolt."

"Lucius!" exclaimed Miles and I in unison.

Lucius threw up his hands in defence and swore roundly, "Don't pretend to be on the side of the angels! You know as well as I do that he wasn't always this feather-brained."

"Behave yourself, Lucius. He can't help it, the accident wasn't his fault," Miles snapped.

"Of course it was his fault. What other fool would ride a half-baked animal like Pax at that ditch? Good God! Was ever an animal so unsuitably named! It was a damnable waste of a good horse too."

"Let us not forget that we could have lost Harry as well. He was dead to the world for nearly two days."

Lucius glowered at Miles and kicked a log in the hearth with such violence it sent a shower of sparks across the room, he stamped on them angrily before they burned holes in the rug.

"I can see no earthly reason for talking about this now," I told them crossly. "What's done cannot be undone."

Harry was occupied picking one of his teeth with a silver toothpick and appeared to be oblivious to the conversation.

"Anyway, I'm not here to listen to you two bicker. I'm here to tell you that we had a rather alarming visit from your friend Benjamin Fairchild. He came to forcibly remove Eleanor from Wild Court."

"Did he indeed! What an out-and-out blackguard. Y'know, it's time we did something about that fellow, he really is starting to irk me," said Lucius.

"And, while we're on the subject, it's also time we did something about extricating Miles from the tight spot he finds himself in thanks to his smuggler friends — before he's in too deep," I added. "You may have thought it perfectly acceptable to help them out when you thought them to be honest men fighting to keep their families fed but you must surely find their recent activities harder to stomach? I find it difficult to believe you have lost all sense of what is just. You cannot have changed that much."

"There may an easy way to solve this whole debacle," said Lucius thoughtfully, "Miles can give up his pursuit of Eleanor and then her brother will no longer have a hold over him."

Miles glared at his brother; his face was now suffused with colour. "What the hell do you mean by that, Lucius?" he demanded, jumping to his feet.

"I *mean* if you hadn't made your feelings for Eleanor so blatantly obvious you wouldn't be in this bloody mess. You gave Ben Fairchild a stranglehold over you and a man like that would never pass up a chance to use you for his own ends and gain control over his sister into the bargain. He wins all round." Lucius sneered, "And, of course, you lose."

"Let *go* of me Martha! I'm going to wipe that smug smile off his blasted face once and for all."

Lucius, quite prepared to provoke his convalescent brother, laughed in his face, "All this fuss over a village wench — it hardly seems worth falling out over."

I held on tightly to Miles's arm. "Lucius stop tormenting everyone just because you want them to be as unhappy as you are, and Miles *sit down* and stop being so childish!"

Lucius shrugged carelessly and pulling out a filigree snuffbox, took a pinch and snapped the lid shut. "I simply cannot support my brother making such a complete ass of himself."

"I'm going to marry her."

"Are you out of your mind?", barked Lucius and he sent the pretty gilt snuffbox flying into the fireplace where it smashed against the wall and fell into the ashes, with a little puff of dust, forever misshapen.

Miles slumped back into his chair again, "It's no damn'd use anyway. She won't have me."

Lucius grinned, "Well, at least *someone's* showing some common sense."

"This is getting us nowhere," I told them impatiently, "We need some kind of plan."

Miles's chin sank into his cravat, "I'll admit I'm in over my head."

"Of course you are, you feckless half-wit," sniped Lucius.

"So, what can we do?" I asked.

Lucius contemplated me in a way I didn't much care for, "We're going to bait a trap and have Mr Fairchild walk right into it."

"And what are we going to bait the trap with?" enquired Miles with a frown.

"Martha," replied Lucius blandly.

"I don't wish to put a damper on your plan but I'm not offering myself up as bait," I said.

"All you'd have to do is entice him away from home and keep him busy for an hour or so while Miles and I plant some contraband in his cottage. We then inform the Excise Men, and he gets transported to the colonies, with any luck."

"It's a dreadful plan. Utterly hare-brained."

"It won't work," agreed Miles.

"D'you have a better idea?"

I looked at Miles and he shrugged eloquently. "All right," I said reluctantly, "I'll do it. But it must be properly planned, and we must execute it without a hiccough, or I might just be tied up in a sack and tossed in the estuary."

Lucius sat down and stretched out his booted legs before the fire. "Don't worry, someone will be near you at all times in case something goes awry. I still think that if you were sensible, Miles, you'd give up your quest for Eleanor's heart and then Ben Fairchild would loosen his grip on that stringy neck of yours." He thrust his fists deep into his breeches pockets and scowled, "Besides, Eleanor isn't a suitable match for you. Even if she were a fitting bride, it would still be ill-advised because you're too alike. It'd be an unmitigated disaster. You'd end up killing each other."

"You cannot dictate where your brother, or for that matter, Eleanor, should love; it's beyond even your wide-ranging capabilities. I believe I may have an answer to part of our problem though. It has come to my attention that our new and most diligent Dragoon has a very marked preference for volatile raven-haired beauties, and I feel we may be able to turn it to our advantage."

"Devil take it! Are you telling me that Danserfield has taken a fancy to Rowena? Is he mad? She'd grind his bones to make her bread. Poor fellow." said Lucius gleefully. "I can't say I've noticed."

"You may not have been aware of much because the Dragoons were making you exceedingly agitated — for someone with nothing to hide."

Lucius gave me a level look, "One day you will have to apologise for your unjustified accusations."

I returned his gaze with equanimity, "If you say so, but I should warn you that I am unlikely to change my opinion without a deal of evidence to the contrary."

Lucius smiled, "You always were mule-headed. An unbecoming trait in a female."

Miles was listening to all this with interest, Harry was dozing, sprawled untidily on the settee, his pale hair coming loose from its ribbon and his cravat trailing in loops across a rather grubby waistcoat.

"I must go before Aunt Louisa discovers me and the weather gets any worse. I shall leave you two to decide how the trap will be set. Just send me word when you have worked out my role in this farce but please remember that although I am reluctant to risk either life or limb, I am *profoundly* opposed to endangering my virtue."

"Noted, cousin," said Lucius solemnly.

"Now I must away to Wild Court and my little troupe of misfits. I will probably have to continue my receiving duties for the smugglers. Now that I've been truly compromised, I don't suppose they'll allow me to cease my night-time activities." Opening the door a crack, I peeked out to see if the coast was clear, "I'll see you all anon. Be good to each other and tell Harry, if he ever wakes, that I said goodbye."

As I tiptoed through the house to make my escape by a side-door, I remembered with a sudden clenching of my stomach, that Liam Cavanagh had said he would wait for me. I doubted he'd kept his word as I'd been gone far longer than I'd imagined.

The sky had darkened considerably, and the wind was bullying its way around the house, looking for something to knock over. It barged into me, grabbing at my skirts and shoving me forcefully against the wall. I steadied myself against the solid stones and waited for my eyes to accustom themselves to the gloom. It was a battle to pull the hood of my cloak over my head and keep it there, while feeling my way gingerly along the inner boundary wall. Why hadn't I thought to bring a lantern?

Finally, I reached the gate which led into the woods and reached for the latch, expecting my fingers to find cold rusty metal but instead discovering the unexpected warmth of material.

"You certainly took your time. I've been kicking my heels out here for the best part of an hour and a half," complained Liam Cavanagh. "I do congratulate you however for not screaming and alerting every soldier for miles. It would have ruined your already sullied reputation to be found alone in the dark with a notorious smuggler."

"I have no idea why you find it so amusing that, should I ever need to, I will never be able to find gainful employment anywhere in this county."

He laughed softly, "Employment? Were you thinking of becoming a governess or perhaps a companion to some cantankerous old dowager? I can't see that ever happening; you'd be thrown out on your ear within the first week."

"I have to find a way of making enough money to keep everyone at Wild Court."

"May I suggest a temporary measure? I will pay you to continue aiding my — ah, enterprises. You would only have to turn a blind eye — maybe open a door, light a lantern — nothing too taxing. Then, at least, you'll not be forced to suffer the indignity of looking for employment and being summarily ejected by the mistress of some fancy house because she thinks the temptation too great for her lecherous husband."

"Are you insinuating — ?"

"No, I'm not suggesting that you would *deliberately* seek their attention, but I do suspect there might be a bit of a stumbling block when the mistress of the house sees your shiny copper curls and alabaster complexion. Although, I understand freckles are not at all in vogue this season, so she might relent."

All I could manage was a muffled sound of exasperation before stamping away from him towards Maker Heights, and home. I'd only taken a few steps when he caught up and to my chagrin, handed me the hem of his coat to hold. "I wouldn't want you to get blown away by this wind - it's rather ferocious," and I knew he was smiling.

It was by now too dark to see very far ahead and the sky was sullen with black rolling clouds and I wasn't keen on the idea of being abandoned to the encroaching night without a lantern, so I took the corner of his coat in my frozen hand and wondered if all the recent alarums had not slightly unhinged me. Unaccustomed as I was to being in such perilous and bizarre situations, was I now in danger of becoming immune to the risk? Lucius had persuaded me to take part in his madcap scheme with alarming ease. It appeared that the more peculiar the circumstances, the more out of character I was beginning to behave. The man walking just ahead of me, for instance, should be my sworn enemy and yet here I was trailing after him like a mindless sheep. I should have reported him to the authorities as soon as I found out the truth about his nefarious activities but for some reason I hadn't.

"A penny for your thoughts, Martha," said the object of those thoughts and again the fleeting idea that he could read my mind made me nervously bite my lip.

"They're worth at least a guinea," I said. He chuckled to himself and walked a little faster.

Rain started to fall, pitter-pattering onto my hood and sliding into my eyes, it was gentle at first and then the heavens opened, and it came down as though its only desire was to hammer me into the ground like a tent-peg.

The smuggler's coat was like a lifeline, and I hung on as we crossed the Heights and made our way down to Wild Court; somehow he seemed able to see in the dark which, of course, would be a prerequisite for a smuggler.

It wasn't until we reached the wood behind Wild Court that I felt able to let go of his coattails, finally trusting my feet to recognise the familiar ground. We came to the high folly wall and I thanked him for escorting me home.

"It was my pleasure. I will be seeing you before long anyway, so 'tis *au revoir* not goodbye." And with that he vanished into the storm.

Twenty-Three

The following morning, I was rudely awoken by someone pounding on the front door. Sleepily, I struggled out from beneath my tangled bedclothes, a sure sign of a disturbed night, dragged on my wrapper and staggered downstairs. Fanny, already in the hallway, looked thoroughly put out.

"Who can it be, at this hour?"

Stifling a yawn, I drew back the bolt on the door, "The only person who believes dawn to be halfway through the working day." I pulled the door open and Anne Talbot marched into the house at full speed. John followed close behind, carrying the cedar chest I knew contained herbs and potions and the mysteries of Mrs Talbot's almost magical healing abilities.

"We've been knocking for an age. Why are you not dressed?"

"I was asleep, Mrs Talbot. 'Tis not even six o'clock."

She looked at me with disapproval, "You mustn't let your standards slip just because you're head of the household now. It's up to you to set a good example."

"You are quite right. I will try harder in the future. Fanny, please take John through to the kitchen and make coffee for our guests and I'll take Mrs Talbot up to see Letitia."

Letitia was lying half-asleep, her mousy hair unpinned and fanned out across the pillows; she looked like a child. Her blue-veined eyelids fluttered open and she frowned as she tried to focus on my face and work out where she was.

"Letitia, it's Martha and I've brought Mrs Talbot from Polgrey Hall to see you. She's going to see if she can help with your recovery." I patted her hand as she observed Mrs Talbot anxiously.

"I'm pleased to see you, indeed I am," she said politely, in her reedy voice. "I feel I should offer you some refreshment, but I don't think this is my house."

Mrs Talbot gave me a speaking glance and moving closer to the bed, took Letitia's other hand in hers. I could tell by her concentration she was feeling for the pulse in Letitia's wrist. She then laid her large hand against her patient's forehead and looked pensive. "Martha, ask John to bring up my box. And I'll need a pitcher of boiled water. Oh, and do you have more candles? The light in here is not at all satisfactory."

To be truthful I was glad to hand over the care of my patient to someone else. I had been finding Letitia's limp grip on reality quite difficult to cope with.

An hour later Mrs Talbot rejoined us in the kitchen and swallowed her cup of coffee down in one powerful gulp whilst still standing. She put the delicate porcelain down into its saucer with such force I was sure it would be cracked. "In my opinion, Mrs Tregallas is suffering from weak nerves and the sure and certain knowledge that her husband will more than likely kill her one day. I've given her a sedative and a restorative and something to ease her mind. She'll be well enough to travel in a day or two as long as she's heavily dosed with the sedative. I have written out instructions for her sister."

She waved away my thanks, "I have much to do. The Twelfth Night Masquerade isn't going to organise itself. Come, John, we must away before Meggie burns my kitchen down." She gave me one of her forthright looks, "I wasn't sure, but I see you'll be all right now, Martha. You're stronger than you think."

The front door thudded closed after them and then the sound of the rattling cart faded away.

* * *

"I'm not sure you're well enough to take part in this Miles. Please go home," but my stubborn cousin would have none of my pleading, although he had the look about him of a man who was about to faint at any moment. "'Twill do us no favours if we have to stop our endeavours and carry you home," I said unkindly.

Miles curled his lip, "I am perfectly capable of playing my part. There is no need to coddle me. We need Lucius to plant the goods and I must stand lookout, not exactly a strenuous task, you must agree. Once Ben Fairchild receives the letter from Eleanor, he will be as keen as mustard to see her. He'll think she's given in. That's where you come in; you must detain him for as long as possible so that we can find his secret hiding places and load 'em up with damning evidence. We've come up with an even better idea for making absolutely sure he's arrested. I'll be lookout for Lucius and Harry will keep an eye on you. We can't be too careful."

"Oh, have no fear, I have no illusions about the risk we're taking but you should see your face - you look like a pale imitation of Banquo's ghost. Mrs Talbot will have my guts for garters if she ever finds out."

"She'd do even worse if she heard you using such coarse language!", laughed Lucius, who appeared to be thoroughly enjoying the idea of the forthcoming adventure. "Where did you learn such unladylike terms?"

"From you, I have no doubt," I remarked, with a wry smile. "I used to listen to you talking with the stable lads. It was extremely enlightening."

Miles drew our attention to the rapidly fading light, "We must set off or we'll miss him and the whole plan will fall apart. 'Tis nearly time for you to keep your appointment, Martha. 'Twould be a pity to spoil all our careful plotting especially after lurking in this copse in the freezing cold for so long. I can barely feel my fingers."

"You should have stayed at home," I told him testily.

* * *

As I neared the disused windmill above Wild Court, I wondered if I should just turn around and run home, leaving Lucius and Miles to their own devices. Skirting the building with caution, I approached the door, which hung crookedly from its rusting hinges. Lucius had chosen the rendezvous because it wasn't too far from safety and there was ample cover nearby for Harry to lurk in. I had little faith in my ability to outrun a fit young smuggler whilst hampered by heavy skirts and the gathering gloom; so I had dressed accordingly, borrowing some breeches, waistcoat and a coat from Miles, who was slightly built, and a pair of boots which had belonged to Jem Liddicoat when he was a boy.

The rotting wood was soft beneath my hand and the door groaned loudly as it swung open. Stepping into the lower room, I decided not to venture too far into its sour-smelling dankness; a prickling up the back of my neck warned me that all was not well.

"Hello? Is anyone here?"

There was no reply. Not even the sound of mice or beetles scrabbling under the floorboards. Nothing but the sound of my shallow, panicky breathing. I kept the dark lantern closed so no light could escape and alert the Preventative Officers who might be patrolling the coast.

I was just wondering where I should place myself to keep the upper hand, when the sound of ancient wood giving under a heavy weight made me shrink back against the cobwebbed wall. Someone was already in the building and creeping down what was left of the stairs that curved around the inside of the circular room. I held my breath and peered into the shadows, trying to make out who was approaching. The movement stopped. I drew a shuddering breath, filling my lungs with the foul dusty air. My ears strained to hear any sound; my legs braced to run. I had started to edge nervously towards the door when a familiar voice broke the silence.

"Well, well, Miss Pentreath, as I live and breathe! Now, what would you be doing gadding about in the dark without any protection — and disguised as a boy? And where is my sister?" There was a distinctly chilling edge to his words, and I cursed Lucius and his persuasive skills.

"Eleanor is safely at Wild Court, Mr Fairchild. May I ask what you are doing hiding in a windmill? Are you using it to store some illicit kegs of brandy?"

In a few aggressive steps, Ben Fairchild crossed the room to stand over me menacingly, "And what would you know about such things, a pampered little brat like you?" He gripped my shoulder, his fingers biting through the fabric of Miles's coat like pincers. I tried to shake him off, but he wouldn't release me.

"I am not such a fool, Mr Fairchild, that I don't know you are involved in some exceedingly suspicious activities. 'Tis well known in these parts that you are a deeply unsavoury character and to be avoided at all costs."

"If this is so widely known, why have you sought me out?" His fingers tightened and I bit back a pained yelp as I wondered how long I could keep him distracted. At least Harry was hiding in some gorse bushes not fifty yards from the windmill and would hear me scream.

"I came to bear upon you that Eleanor will not be returning to the cottage. She can longer suffer your uncontrollable temper and the dangers you bring to her door. She has decided that it will be a better arrangement if she stays at Wild Court. Also, she has repeated that you will *never* persuade her to marry against her will."

His smouldering rage intensified, "Is that so, Missy?" His breath reeked of strong alcohol. "You obviously don't credit me with much intelligence. It occurs to me that you seem willing to risk your own safety by arranging to meet in an isolated location to divulge information I am already familiar with. What could you possibly gain — ?" He stopped suddenly and laughed. "I think I'm beginning to understand. Either you were keen for a romantic tryst with me or there is some other, more likely, explanation that you are so eager for my company." He let out a sudden low growl and an explosion of obscene curses. Suddenly I was being dragged through the door and out into the night. I tried to take a swing at him with my lantern but only succeeded in flinging it away.

My first thought was that he was going to kill me there and then and when I realised, I was still being half-pulled, half-carried around the windmill; my second thought was Harry.

The scream that came right after that thought was much louder than I'd expected although it ended abruptly as Ben Fairchild clamped his hand over my mouth. I felt certain that it had been loud and long enough for Harry to hear and come running. I fought my captor, hoping to slow him down enough for Harry to catch up and threaten him with the pistol I knew he was carrying.

A horse whinnied and I was flung across its saddle as though I was a bale of hay. To do this, he had to remove his hand from my mouth, so I sucked in a lungful of air and shouted for Harry again.

Harry didn't come.

* * *

I clung onto the horse for dear life while thinking perhaps I should fling myself to the ground and try to run but Ben Fairchild would easily outrun me, and the fall would probably kill me. We were riding with breakneck speed in the direction of his cottage and my unsuspecting cousins.

The horse, by now blowing hard from the long mad dash across the Heights, was pulled to a violent halt a discreet distance from the village, far enough away for my cries to be useless. I found myself deposited on the ground and my mouth tightly bound with his neckerchief then holding my arms behind my back, he forced me to walk in front of him down the narrow lane towards the cottage. I stumbled on the uneven surface and got a brutal shove for my pains. Eventually I could see the building ahead but there was no light in the windows but then I didn't expect Lucius to be stupid enough to broadcast his presence to the world. Miles would be hiding nearby but I couldn't expect him to run to my rescue in his still weakened state; I was on my own.

In the moment when Ben Fairchild had swung himself into the saddle behind me, I had noticed something without being aware of its significance at the time.

Without stopping to think, I deliberately threw myself to my left with such force that Ben Fairchild had no choice but to release my arms. As I hit the ground, he immediately bent to drag me up again and as he did so I lunged forward and grabbed the flintlock I'd noticed tucked into his belt; at the same time, I kicked out with my leg, wonderfully free of the complication of skirts, and smashed my boot heel as hard as I could into his knee. Scrambling to my feet, I pointed the primed and loaded pistol into the air and pulled the trigger as my cousins had often shown me. There was a loud explosion, sparks shot forward like comets and I was thrust backwards onto the ground by the force of the report.

The horse squealed in fright and galloped off into the spinney and Ben Fairchild lay on the ground holding his leg in agony.

I took the pistol by the barrel end and before he could even think to defend himself, I clouted my captor on his head. As he collapsed, I thought grimly that this sort of thing was fast becoming a habit with me.

Scrambling up the slippery bank beside the cottage, I breathlessly yelled for my cousins.

"Martha, for pity's sake, stop that blasted caterwauling! You'll have the Dragoons down on us."

"Lucius? Is that you?"

"Of course it is, you silly goose. Come on, take my hand. Miles is over yonder with the horses. We must make haste before Fairchild regains his senses."

And once again I was being dragged along in the darkness but at least this time I was in relatively safe hands.

Miles was concealed in the copse above the cottage, he held two horses by their reins. "Where the hell have you been? Oh, you've got Martha! Where's Harry? What was that gunshot?" he babbled anxiously. "I thought you'd been discovered and were being shot at by Ben Fairchild or Excise Men."

"Had it not been for Martha's quick thinking I would have been run to ground, but she fired his pistol to warn us and then whacked him on the head with it. Cousin Boudica! All the evidence is in place. All we have to do now is inform Lieutenant Danserfield and stand back and watch the show," said Lucius with relish. "Of course, the Lieutenant will, this minute, be at Polgrey Hall wondering why Rowena isn't showing the promised enthusiasm for his latest appearance."

Miles laughed, "Not realising, poor beggar, that we sent him the enticing missive. I wonder how long it will take for him to twig. We'd better get there before he leaves in a fit of pique or he discovers how awful Rowena truly is! He's going to be very interested in our information I think."

I eyed the two horses with misgiving, "If I am to endure another ride in the dark, I insist that I have an entire horse to myself this time. You two can share."

* * *

John looked at me with sympathy as he handed me the much-folded, rather grubby piece of paper, "This came for'ee to the Hall, Miss Martha," he sniffed expressively. "'Twas brought to the back door." He sounded deeply disapproving.

'Thank you, John. Did you see who delivered it?"

Another sniff. "Yes, indeed, I did. An' I must say, Miss, that I had no idea that'ee was acquainted with such persons - a hussy by the looks of her 'Twas fortunate Mrs Talbot was upstairs at the time or she'd have chased her away with a broom. It takes some nerve to stroll up to God-fearing folks as though'ee be one of the gentry yourse'n."

"I'm sorry you've been so put out, but I am delighted to hear all the news from the Hall." I sensed he had something else to add and gave him an encouraging look, "Is that all?"

"I think so. Although, 'ee might want to prepare 'eeself for a call from the Hall 'afore long. I overheard Lady Polgrey tellin' Mrs Talbot that what with Christmas an' the Masquerade they'd need all hands on deck."

I sighed, "I had a feeling that might be the case but I'm happy to assist if it eases Mrs Talbot's workload."

"An' Miss Rowena is bein' a bit of a handful too. That Lieutenant came by last night all unexpected an' there was quite an undignified scene, with a bit of shouting an' Miss Rowena flouncin' about the place an' the Lieutenant lookin' confused but then Master Miles an' Master Lucius took him to one side an' talked quietly to him an' he seemed to calm down an' then dashed off lookin' very pleased. Miss Rowena was even angrier then an' blamed her brothers for ruinin' her *whole life*!" He grinned, "It was quite funny."

"That's very interesting. I wish I'd been there!"

"Miss Rowena an' Lady Polgrey have been at loggerheads for days now. Arguin' 'bout the guest list an' gowns an' such. They were shoutin' so loud we didn't have to eavesdrop, 'ee could hear 'em all over the house."

"Kindly tell Mrs Talbot that I'd be happy to lend a hand when the time comes."

"She said 'ee'd say that. I'd better get back to the Hall." He glanced at the letter in my hand, "Be careful, Miss Martha, there be folks who'd be happy if some harm were to befall 'ee."

"Thank you, John. I shall be vigilant. I'm well aware that not everyone has my best interests at heart. I must say that since my return I have had my eyes opened to the dangers lurking in the most unexpected places!"

As soon as John left, I unfolded the grimy letter and smoothed it out. It was in such a poor hand that it was difficult to decipher. Eventually, to my dismay, I was able to understand the message.

"Miss, I must warn thee that if thee shud think my man Liam is for the taykin, I will make thee sorry. I am watchin thee an so are my frends. Be thee warned. No mersy. Mary Yates."

I read it again, just to be sure and then crumpled it into a small ball in my hand. I had never heard the name Mary Yates and I had no idea why a complete stranger should send me such an explicit warning. I supposed that she was one of Captain Cavanagh's doxies; he was bound to have at least one in each port like most sailors. She clearly felt I was some kind of threat to her. If she had been here, I would have taken great pleasure in setting her straight. She was welcome to him. The brazen effrontery of the woman!

I wandered distractedly into the kitchen and stood in the middle of the room staring into space.

"Has something happened, Martha?", asked Eleanor, who was preparing turnips for the pot.

I sat down with an exasperated sigh, "If only you knew!"

"Perhaps if you tell me what is making you so flustered, I might be able to help."

I thrust the crumpled letter at her as though it were likely to poison me if I held it any longer. She was silent for a moment and then she carefully put it down on the table. Her expression filled me with immediate foreboding.

"Martha, I *know* of this woman. I have heard of her through my brother and have heard much about her exploits. She is the very worst kind; an unprincipled trollop with a reputation to match any ruffian you might find carousing in an alehouse. If she believes you to be her enemy — she will find a way to do you harm. There was a rumour in the village that she poisoned Thomas Carter's herd of dairy cows with hemlock because he refused to let her stow contraband in his barn. She is thoroughly treacherous. She is more lethal than any man."

Sudden exhaustion flooded me, and I rubbed at my eyes with my knuckles, "This is just intolerable. What am I supposed to do? I seem to be making enemies at every turn."

"You could talk to Miles and Lucius?"

"Ha! They are like two silly schoolboys bickering with each other. That would be a waste of time."

"Well, there is only one other solution."

"No."

"Why not?"

"I cannot. Not again. He will think I've run mad if I go to him again."

"And why should you mind so much what such a peculiar fellow might think of you? I had thought you unimpressed. Surely, you have not formed an attachment, my dear?"

"Dear God in Heaven! No, I have not! Such a notion could not be further from my mind. He is the most maddening of men. He has a caustic tongue and thinks nothing of using it to entertain himself at my expense. Yes, he has been — very helpful — at times but I feel he didn't do it out of any sense of chivalry but merely to occupy his lively mind whilst isolated here in the back of beyond. He's more used to the hustle and bustle of London life and must find us so very parochial. How he must laugh at our dowdy country ways and when he leaves, he will, no doubt, regale his sophisticated friends with tales of our peculiar customs such as taking our meals so unfashionably early and not wearing hoops in our skirts unless it's a special occasion! No, I will not turn to him for help again. I will not."

Eleanor looked up from her task and smiled at me, "Is that so?" was all she said.

"What do you mean by that exactly?"

She lay down the knife and rested her chin on her hands, the same playful smile hovering upon her lips, "Dearest Martha! Why so defensive?"

"Indeed, I am not in the least defensive! I was just explaining why I cannot trouble Sir Montagu with my plaguey problems because he must be weary of them and me." I spoke sharply and was sorry that I should speak so to my friend, but she was, I felt, being uncharacteristically insensitive.

She suddenly let out a delighted laugh, "If you could only see your face! The very picture of innocence and outrage. You remind me of a child caught with her hand in the sugar jar and despite the evidence still being upon her lips, she denies the truth with all her might because she is scared of the consequences. Why you should be scared of what I might think of your attachment to Sir Montagu, I have no idea, but you have assured me that he has always behaved in the most gentlemanly manner towards you and I believe despite his rather theatrical style, he must be an honourable man."

I tried to laugh with her to show that it all meant nothing, "He is certainly a kingfisher amongst sparrows. But I cannot comprehend why a man of his obvious calibre, a man of wit and intelligence, should dress so outlandishly, and behave so abominably."

"I have thought the very same but then I know very little about modes in London. He would probably not be in the least out of the ordinary in a city where they don't retire to bed before dawn and the ladies have blackamoors to cool them with ostrich feather fans and even the poor eat swan and peacock every day. My feeling is that in some way we are all wearing masks — his is just more detectable than most."

I had to smile, for although I knew very little about life in London, I understood that the poor in a city were as unfortunate as the poor in the countryside. Although I had always had a yearning to see the sights of London, I knew that not all that glitters there was gold. I had heard my father talking many a time about the injustices he had witnessed and how frustrated he'd felt that he and those in power could do nothing to alleviate the suffering of those whose lives were a constant and fruitless struggle against the ignominies of poverty. Even knowing this, I could not disappoint Eleanor by telling her it would probably mean a stiff fine if anyone was found eating one of the King's swans, however poor and needy they were.

Eleanor picked up her knife again, "You know he is the answer, my dear," she said doggedly, "If you won't ask him for help, I will."

Twenty-Four

So, it was, once again, against my better judgement, I arrived at Holmoak Beacon and was greeted by the manservant, Warrick. He fixed me with a studiously blank expression and told me that his master wasn't at home. He explained that he'd left after breakfast and hadn't yet returned. Then he invited me in to wait a while.

I found it momentarily difficult to gather my thoughts, which had been scattered like leaves in a gale. I only seemed able to focus on my disappointment and the scale of that emotion was an unwelcome revelation to me.

Warrick showed me into the library, as before, and gestured to the comfortable armchair, saying he would fetch some refreshment for me. "Master'd wish'ee to stay, Miss. I'll not be long."

I did as I was told and tried in vain to collect my wits but succeeded only in becoming more mired in confusion. I stood up and took a turn about the wondrous room, which despite my inner turmoil I noticed was in a state of remarkable disorder, every surface being hidden beneath teetering stacks of books and papers. I wandered between the beautiful furniture, trailing my fingers across the worn leather-bound volumes with their gilded edges. There were books I had never seen before, familiar books, books on every subject I could possibly imagine; novels and poetry, history and religion, great atlases, and to my delight, open on his writing desk was a copy of a book on herbs and their usage with detailed illustrations. I drew up Sir Montagu's chair, sank into it and began to carefully turn the pages of the treasured tome.

Warrick came back a short while later with a tray of tea, bread and butter and a slab of gingerbread large enough to have fed several grown men.

I continued to browse through the herbal book for a few minutes and then gently closed it, pushing it out of harm's way and turned my attention to the tea and gingerbread. I was quite hungry and despite the fashion for females to affect delicate appetites, I tucked into the unexpected collation with relish and almost no shame.

After finishing the tea, I eagerly worked my way through several other books, wishing enviously that I had ready access to such a wealth of information and amusement. I was idly tidying a pile of papers on the desk when I came across a small, dog-eared notebook, with a marbled cover. Curiosity got the better of me and I flicked through the pages. Inside were some indecipherable notes written in an elegant hand, some small ink drawings of what looked like fortifications, some of which were slightly smudged as though hastily created in the open air and rows of numbers and columns of words in some foreign language. I could make neither head nor tail of any of it.

Then I came to a page where a tiny pen and ink drawing stopped me in my tracks. It looked like my mother. It was tenderly wrought. I stared at it, unable to comprehend what I was seeing. Who had drawn this exquisite miniature? She had obviously meant a great deal to them.

And what were all the strange notes and lists about? They looked deeply questionable to me. There was only one reason I could think of that would require information to be in code and that would involve an act of treason and the punishment for treason was execution.

I leapt up and put the book back exactly as I had found it, with shaking hands. For a second I looked at it and then dashed to the door.

I stepped blindly into the hallway and ran headlong into Sir Montagu's embroidered waistcoat.

"Confound it, Linnet! 'Tis no way to treat a veritable work of art. I take it in devilish bad part that you should use my new waistcoat as a buffer and my tailor would most likely fall into a swoon. Now, why are you in such a hurry, as though all the hounds of hell are chasin' you?" He set me away from him and looked down at me with wry amusement, "Warrick says you have been waiting for my return for two hours. It must be very important. Tried to murder any more upstandin' members of the community? No? Then what can it be?" he drawled.

I could barely look at him as I prepared to dissemble, "I — I have been looking at your books. You are so fortunate to be in possession of such a comprehensive library." I licked my dry lips and continued to talk just to fill the empty air between us. "Warrick brought me tea which was very kind of him, and I was quite content to wait with so many wonderful books to occupy my time."

"Faith, m'dear, as I said before, it gives me great joy to share the library with you. What is the good of having so many books if no one reads them? Are you goin' to tell me why you came now?"

I felt my face flame, "I called to thank you for sending Riordan to Wild Court and for your invaluable assistance the other night. I don't think I expressed my gratitude sufficiently at the time."

Sir Montagu was silent and looking at me with avuncular tolerance. "Indeed, it does not signify. Any gentleman worth his salt would have done the same. I would wish you to think no more of it. Now, before I lose all patience with you, tell me the truth. Why are you really here?"

I knew by the inflexible note in his voice that I could prevaricate no longer. I sank down on the nearby settle, clasping my hands together in a bloodless knot, "Eleanor insisted I should come. I didn't want to vex you again. I would have asked Miles and Lucius, but they are a little too hot-headed to be relied upon."

Sir Montagu swung his quizzing glass on its ribbon as though we were discussing the state of the weather.

I delved into my pocket and pulled out Mary Yates's letter and held it out to him. He took the soiled piece of paper with obvious distaste, his lip curling slightly.

As he read it his face became an impassive mask.

"Eleanor is acquainted with this woman and believes she truly means me harm. If I could, I would reassure this Yates woman that I have absolutely no interest in such a callous villain as Captain Cavanagh and then perhaps she would leave us in peace. Does the name mean anything to you?"

Now that the mask was back in place I could not even guess at his thoughts; he slowly folded the letter up and strolled to the fireplace and threw it into the flames. He watched until it caught and then turned back to me. "There is no need for you to concern yourself anymore with this matter. I will deal with it. Do I make myself perfectly clear? It is imperative that you obey me in this one thing, Martha."

I nodded mutely, not at all liking his dispassionate tone.

"I shall set Solomon to watch over you at night. You will not try to give him the slip or coerce him into helpin' you meet this woman," he flicked an imaginary speck from his sleeve and observed me from narrowed eyes, "If you decide to go against my wishes you will be putting yourself in danger. Now, let us find Solomon and he will take you home." He crossed the hallway, and I schooled my face into an expression of abject obedience and followed him without enthusiasm.

* * *

We found Solomon in the kitchen plucking a large goose with gusto and singing a beautiful but unfamiliar song which made the hairs on the back of my neck stand on end.

"Miss Martha!", he exclaimed and jumped to his feet scattering a blizzard of white feathers about him. He was across the room in two giant strides, shedding feathers as he moved and grasped my hands in his, "I am pleased to see you. I wanted to properly thank you for your kindness and bravery that night. I will always be indebted to you."

"Please, I wish you would forget it."

"I believe I have the answer to that, dear fellow," said Sir Montagu. "Miss Martha has managed to get herself into yet another scrape and is in need of an extra bodyguard. I can think of no one better to ensure her safety."

"This is good news! Better than kitchen duties. Bah! Women's work," declared Solomon with a speaking glance for Sir Montagu, who merely laughed and reminded him he had volunteered for the task. Solomon glared at the half-naked goose, "I had hoped to warm myself by the fire. Accursed country where the sun never shines and folk stare as though I have two heads and horns. I will never get used to it. But I look forward to being of service to you, Miss Martha." He pointed to his dark blue coat with amusement, "And thank you for sending your uncle's clothes. As you see, I have not yet split the seams!"

"You are most welcome, Solomon, I hope they keep you warm."

"Excellent," said Sir Montagu, "At last an outin' for the new chaise we have invested in for just such an occasion. If you would drive her home Solomon? Miss Martha will provide you with temporary accommodation until this latest scare is behind us. You will make sure that her reckless heart does not overrule her pretty head. She is inclined to be wilful, my friend. You will need your wits about you at all times and eyes in the back of your head."

I took immediate exception to this unflattering description and huffed crossly but on meeting his penetrating gaze I made an effort to disguise my displeasure.

"You are not foolin' me, Martha. Mind my words or you will find yourself in my bad books."

My thoughts flew to the scruffy notebook in the library and I averted my face as it flamed a traitorous red again. Let him believe that I disliked his peremptory tone rather than betray the fact that I had been prying and seen things I shouldn't have.

I had no doubt that if I wished I would be able to give my two guardians the slip. I had not spent a wild childhood with my wayward cousins without learning a trick or two in the art of throwing the hunter off the scent.

Sir Montagu handed me into the shiny new chaise and managed to restrain himself from lecturing me any more on the flaws in my character and the hazards of being impulsive. I muttered my farewell into the hood of my cloak, pretending to be much occupied with arranging myself upon the seat. The chaise bounced off down the track and I grabbed the leather strap to keep from being hurled onto the floor, Solomon obviously having no sympathy for his passenger's internal organs. Several times my teeth actually clashed together from the sudden impact of wheel against stone boulder; I had to clamp my jaw shut in order to prevent tooth damage.

We miraculously reached Wild Court and Solomon handed me down onto the wonderfully solid ground, "Thank you, that was a most invigorating journey. I believe I might be able to persuade Jem to give you some lessons in driving such an equipage so that should we go out again, I am not terrified for my life."

Solomon gave a deep chuckle, "I have been told I am not a natural horseman and Sir Montagu did mention to me the need for caution. Just before we left, he said, 'Precious cargo, Solomon, no cutting corners, please.' But that horse was rather too fresh for my limited skills."

Precious cargo? What had Sir Montagu meant by that? Solomon smiled down at me from his great height, his expressive face full of understanding. I tossed my head and marched into the house leaving Solomon to follow, carrying a small, banded portmanteau which I assumed must contain his belongings. On further consideration I realised that as he had lost any personal possessions in the wreck so that Sir Montagu must have provided him with all that he would require for daily life in this unfamiliar land along with the clothes I had pilfered from Uncle Joshua.

At the rear of the house, where the garden rose steeply up the hill in shallow terraces and a high wall contained and protected the plants that had been coaxed to grow there, there was a single-story cottage, which had once housed the elderly gardener and his wife. It was a modest home although easily big enough for two, with unusually high ceilings which was fortunate for Solomon. I felt he would be more comfortable in a place of his own and it would cause less scandal than being found staying with three females.

"Help yourself to anything you need from the house. We all eat together, and you are most welcome to join us. Oh, there is a tin bath somewhere. I will set Jem to discovering its whereabouts. I am vastly reassured to know you are here to keep an eye on things."

Solomon was peering into the cupboards and making contented noises. "That's not what Sir Montagu said. He thought you would be, as he put it, *mad as hellfire* for being treated as though you needed a nanny to watch over you."

"Did he indeed? Well, he was wrong, as usual." I snapped.

* * *

Later that evening, when everyone was settled, Letitia was tucked up in her bed, Fanny had gone home with Jem, and Riordan had handed over his daytime vigil to Solomon, I sat down with Eleanor to discuss the new arrival. She and Fanny had received Solomon with admirable equanimity, accepting the arrival of this exotic giant into their home as though it were an everyday occurrence. I had already told her a little of his origins after the wreck and now filled her in with a more detailed account of his history. I also decided to tell her about my discovery in the library at Holmoak Beacon, which clearly took her aback, having previously been an advocate of Sir Montagu's, but she was determined that there must be some perfectly reasonable explanation and that I was not to leap to any ill-conceived conclusions as I was inclined to do.

Solomon proved to be worth his considerable weight in gold; he could turn his hand to almost anything as long as it had nothing to do with horses. His particular expertise turned out to be skinning and gutting rabbits and fishing, which pleased me immensely. We soon established some kind of routine and muddled along quite nicely, with only the occasional hiccough.

It was perhaps because I had been lulled into a false sense of security that I allowed my guard to drop and tripped headlong into what Sir Montagu would have called another one of my scrapes.

Preparing Letitia for her forthcoming journey kept me busy and prevented my thoughts from dwelling too much upon subjects best avoided; I found a small trunk in the attic and packed it with all the personal items and clothing retrieved from her home by Sir Montagu and other items I was able spare of my own: a shawl and a fur-lined cloak belonging to my mother to keep her warm on the tedious journey north. Mrs Talbot paid us another visit just to make certain that the patient's health was improved enough to cope with the fatiguing time ahead. The day before the planned departure I had received a note from Sir Montagu, a disappointingly brief missive, which informed me that he would be hiring a suitable post chaise for the trip and had hired a local woman to keep Letitia company and act as her maid, for the sake of propriety, if nothing else. Instead of being grateful for this, I found I was decidedly put out, annoyed that I had not thought to hire someone to care for Letitia during the gruelling journey and infuriated that he should foist a carriage upon us as though I had not the ability or the foresight to organise one myself.

Letitia's sister, a Mrs Matilda Jessup of York, had answered my letter expressing her delight and anxiety in equal measure; delight that her sister should wish to stay with them and anxiety that Letitia should feel the need to leave her husband in such inauspicious circumstances. She had hinted between the lines that she was not really surprised that Letitia should wish to escape the Squire's intolerable traits but at the same time found it hard to comprehend how a wife could desert her spouse without a deal of heart-searching. I had carefully explained that there were irreconcilable differences and that her sister's well-being had suffered considerably in the last few months, leaving me to conclude that it would be most advantageous for her to remove to York to be nursed back to health by those who loved her. Mrs Jessup had heartily concurred but there was an underlying air of disapproval that went some way to explaining why Letitia had not applied to her for sanctuary before.

A few days before Christmas, Sir Montagu's hired carriage arrived, with two seasoned footmen and a postillion and bearing a plump, efficient lady from Millbrook, who took control of the patient and everything else within minutes of being introduced. I had my suspicions that they were all being paid above and beyond for their efforts and I therefore had no qualms about handing my charge over to them, with a list of instructions which would have made even the stoutest heart quail. I slipped Mrs Talbot's sedative into a sweet cordial, which Letitia happily took, and then instructed the nursemaid to give another dose mid-afternoon and another when they reached the first staging post, to help her sleep. The maid fussed about, making her charge comfortable in the luxurious carriage, tucking a large fur rug around her knees, wrapping the shawl about her thin shoulders and placing a hot brick under her feet. She then poked her head out of the window and assured me that Mrs Tregallas was safe in her hands and told me not to fret because her new employer had seen to absolutely everything - nothing had been left to chance. With no doubt she had been well chosen; I was able to smile and wish her all the luck in the world.

With a crack of the whip, a loud rattling of metal on metal, some thumping of hooves and impatient snorting from the very well-bred horses, they were off. As they drove away up the lane one small burden lifted from my shoulders and I silently thanked Sir Montagu for his uncanny ability to see what was required.

In the kitchen Fanny was sniffling; poor Solomon was doing his best to comfort her, and Eleanor was smiling at the theatrics. "What a splendid thing Sir Montagu has done.

Every comfort for Letitia and bedchambers already booked by an outrider! I've never heard the like."

"No, indeed, he is extremely — high-handed," I said crossly, forgetting my gratitude.

Solomon looked at me with amusement, "Admittedly he has extravagant ways, Miss Martha, but I don't believe he means to offend with his generosity. He was only thinking of Mrs Tregallas's well-being and hoping to please you, I am thinking."

"Oh, I am sure you are right, but he has a habit of riding roughshod over people — *me* — and to be frank, I am a little tired of such cavalier behaviour." I didn't like to add that I also suspected Sir Montagu of something, I wasn't quite sure what, but I certainly had some serious concerns about the baffling contents of his notebook.

Twenty-Five

That delicate, lovingly executed drawing of my mother haunted my thoughts. It had captured her looking straight at the viewer, her tangled hair windswept and snaking across her face, passionately expressive eyes alive with promise and behind her a glimpse of the storm-tossed sea. She looked tantalising and irresistible. A knot of emotion I dared not put a name to was tightening uncomfortably in my chest.

If the artist was Sir Montagu, I supposed it was possible that he had met her at some local event, a dance or an evening of cards at the Manor or at any number of local entertainments. Few men would have been able to resist my mother's alluring personality and beauty. Her legions of fawning admirers had been legendary, and it was more than possible that Sir Montagu, despite his world-weary languor, was just another of her conquests. I almost felt sorry for him.

* * *

A very welcome letter arrived from my dear friend Lady Sarah Finch, expressing surprise at not hearing from me for an age and hoping that I was in good health; she also desired that I should return to Bristol should I not be happy with my lot. They had always promised me a home should I find my situation desperate. I promised myself that as soon as I found the time I would sit down and pen a quick response to set Sarah's mind at rest.

* * *

Two days before Christmas, in the early morning, Miles, on his way to Plymouth, paid us a visit, to bring news of his father, who had returned from Tavistock with two fine fillies from a renowned breeder and was very puffed up about his purchase. There was quite obviously another more pressing reason for my cousin's visit and I encouraged him to share it with me. He finally admitted that Uncle Joshua had in fact been trying to agree some financial support from his benefactor in order to prevent the family's imminent ruin. Miles buried his face in his hands and tried not to let the despair engulf him, "Instead, he returns with a pair of beautifully matched horses which will only drive us further into penury. He has become such a liability, Martha, I scarce know what to do. There are stacks of demands on his desk, all unpaid, all bound for the fire. I have even had the family mantua-maker and the carriage maker apply to me for settlement. I cannot pay them. Mama has such extravagant plans for her wretched Masquerade. I cannot fathom how we are to come about; indeed, I fear we are bound for Newgate Prison. If our creditors turn against us and we become insolvent, we could be imprisoned indefinitely. The family have no idea how deeply sunk we are and now these damned horses! I am at my wit's end."

I put my arms round him, "I had no idea it had become so serious, Miles. I am sure we shall contrive a way forward. Have you spoken with the creditors?"

He nodded, misery etched in every line of his boyish face, "Of course! I have pleaded with them to no avail. They have been put off so many times with empty promises that they have lost faith in us. One cannot blame them. We, as a family, are all guilty of increasing the debt without due consideration; Lucius and his gambling and drinking and women making demands and even Harry who has had to be bailed out of several sticky situations and then there is Rowena with her expensive tastes in gowns and shoes, which my mother wilfully encourages. I am not blameless either, I could have done more to arrest the squandering of our funds, but I chose to ignore what could not be easily remedied."

I stroked his back absentmindedly, "We will find a way to right ourselves, I swear."

Miles was on his way to speak to another creditor in Plymouth, hoping to persuade her to wait for settlement. He would take a ferryboat from Cremill to Admiralty Steps and from there a sedan chair to Madame Pascal's Mantua-Makers and hopefully gain a reprieve from the fearsome French seamstress. Having met her on several occasions I had my doubts about him succeeding in his mission for she seemed a particularly humourless creature with a firm grasp on business matters and an aversion to anything which might reduce her income. I had heartily disliked her but realised that as her work was vastly superior to most local dressmakers, she would need to be cajoled, and more importantly, paid on time. I pitied poor Miles, who now had no choice but to become saviour of the Polgrey honour.

* * *

Even at Wild Court we could feel the tense emanations from the party preparations going on at Polgrey Hall. Eventually my aunt could bear it no longer and sent John for me. Knowing the day would come, I was prepared; how could she possibly manage without a scapegoat? I was aware that my presence would, at least, deflect censure from the staff who would be under ever-increasing scrutiny as the day drew nearer. She was to have a Christmas Day dinner party - nothing too elaborate as the real spectacle would be the Masquerade. No expense was to be spared for either party. The provisions had been ordered from the best establishments in Plymouth and the most fashionable dishes were to be served; Aunt Louisa had no wish to be thought provincial by people she clearly regarded as her inferiors. New gowns had been designed and fashioned with great attention to detail and Rowena and her mother had already suffered several tedious dress fittings with Madame Pascal or her terrified minions. The materials, heavy brocades and watered silk, shot taffetas and embroidered gauze were mainly from her homeland as Madame said one could not compare such fine fabrics to the poor quality found in England. The gowns for the party were extremely stylish and flattering but when I saw the costumes for the Masquerade I was dumbfounded - never had I seen such wondrous creations.

No mention was made of what I was to wear although I was undoubtedly expected to attend both parties, much to my dismay. I had had a quick search through my mother's gowns but the only one that was even remotely suitable had been nibbled by mice. The one useful item I found was a black domino, beneath which I could hopefully hide any lapse in dress sense.

* * *

Mrs Talbot put me in charge of making sure the Hall was decorated in a manner befitting the Polgrey's social standing. John and I set to finding boughs of holly, ivy, and mistletoe on the estate, to be brought into the house on Christmas Eve, and Meggie and I enjoyed an afternoon making decorations from apples, coloured paper, sweetmeats, and gold foil. We gilded nuts and gingerbread and barley sugar twists in the kitchen, which ended up covered in fluttering spangles of gold leaf and petals of scarlet paper all glued into the sticky mess. Mrs Talbot grumbled away in the background about the terrible shambles we had created. "Why can't you tidy up as you go? Sugar everywhere and so precious too! What a waste."

John stood the greenery in buckets of water ready to be arranged the following day as was customary and then was sent out again, even though it was growing dark, to help bring in the Yule log for the main fireplace in the Great Hall. It took two men to carry the huge apple bough and there was a little round of applause from the staff who had gathered to witness it being set in place.

John stood up and rubbed his sore back, "Right, that be all done an' now I must see to the guns for the Wassailin'. I'll sleep well tonight after all this."

* * *

An hour or so after returning home, I finally found a moment to hastily scratch a note to the Finches, full of reassurance and a short explanation for my silence and telling them all about the preparations for the prospective Masquerade. I added a postscript wondering if they might be able to help me with a charitable scheme I had in mind, for which I would need some generous investment. I sanded the letter, folded it, and sealed it and, leaving it on the hall table for Jem to collect, I wandered into the kitchen to stoke the fire.

On the table there was a note from Eleanor, in which she apologised for retiring early with a bit of a headache and saying she would take a strong sleeping draught. She also said that earlier that evening The Wicked Mary Yates had called to speak with me and explained that she had sent her away with a flea in her ear thinking that I would have no wish to speak with such person. She wrote that Solomon would stay awake all night if need be, so not to worry and that Fanny had decided to stay the night as Jem was visiting his mother in Plymouth and had been away all day.

After reading the note I flew around the house and made sure that all the doors and windows were shut and bolted but it made me feel no more secure. For a while I sat at the table and wondered if I should get Solomon to stand guard and then ran back into my father's study and rummaged in the old sea chest he kept there; amongst the maps and sheaves of curling yellowed papers I found his old flintlock pistol. It was an unwieldy, old-fashioned weapon of walnut and silver and had not been fired in many years. Thankfully my incorrigible cousins had made sure I could handle such a firearm, as I had already proved during the Ben Fairchild incident, so I was able to find the shot and with admirably steady hands, load it, using the silver ramrod. Somewhat reassured, I blew out the candles and went to bed, the pistol primed and ready for action.

* * *

The high tide was lapping gently about my bare feet, the grass under the rippling water was emerald green, out across the estuary the sun shone brightly, and I shielded my eyes against the glare. I felt a surge of joy and then someone screamed.

Pulse racing, I listened but there was no other noise. However, the silence was somehow too silent, so I reached for my wrapper and having retrieved the pistol, I tiptoed to the door. On reaching the top of the stairs, I wondered what I was doing creeping about with a loaded pistol in my hand. I was about to turn back to my bedchamber when I heard something.

The sound was so slight, so innocuous that I wonder that I heard it at all. Every sensible instinct urged me to run to my room and bolt the door but instead I silently descended the stairs, being careful to avoid the creaky step. In the hall, I listened again, tilting my head this way and that, like a wild animal. Some sixth sense told me to tread stealthily towards the kitchen. I could hear Sir Montagu's voice in my head, and it wasn't being complimentary. But something was wrong. I knew it. Every nerve ending was tingling because I was certain there was danger beyond the kitchen door.

I gently lifted the latch and peered through the narrow opening; the darkness was broken by the faint cold blue of moonlight coming through the windows. I could see nothing out of the ordinary and slowly let out my breath.

Then I heard the sound again.

My blood ran cold and I froze to the spot. My breathing was so shallow I was becoming a little light-headed. The little window by the back door was smashed and ajar. Someone had managed to get into the house. My fingers tightened around the handle of the pistol. Saying a silent prayer, I opened the door and stepped into the kitchen. As I did so my foot nudged against something on the floor. Something solid and human.

As soon as my fingers felt the cold metal studs on his belt, I knew. Solomon. Apparently dead to the world. I felt all around him until I touched a pool of sticky blood, still seeping from the back of his head, quickly grabbing a cloth, I pressed it against the wound. He still breathed.

I realised the noise had not come from Solomon; he was in no state to make a sound. From the position of the wound I guessed he'd been attacked from behind, with what must have been quite a blow to fell a man of his stature.

The moonlight made the dark corners of the kitchen seem darker; I couldn't see where the threat might be hiding. Then I thought I heard muffled movement. Rashly coming to the conclusion that it was as dangerous staying where I was as it was actually doing something, I began to crawl across the cold stone slabs towards the pantry door. My nightgown kept getting tangled around my knees which slowed my progress. I positioned myself so that I could open the door a crack without it making its usual loud creak. The little room was lit by thin moonlight filtering through the dusty window. Objects took shape, dangling hams, a net of onions and bunches of herbs, then an unfamiliar silhouette on the floor in the middle of the room.

The strange form suddenly moved and emitted a soft groan. Suddenly I knew what I was looking at.

"Fanny!" I whispered and wriggled through the gap.

The poor girl had been securely bound and gagged and thrown to the floor, where she lay helpless but thankfully unhurt. I put the pistol down but the ropes about her wrists were expertly tied and hard to loosen. Fanny made another muffled sound which sounded impatient and made a dramatic gesture with her head. It took a moment before I realised she was still gagged.

"Oh, I'm so sorry — I wasn't thinking — " and I pulled the scarf from her mouth. She let out a stream of unladylike language which at any other time would have made me laugh.

"Knife!" she said hoarsely, "Cut them. S'quicker."

A flash of cold light on the blade guided me as I groped along the shelf beside me. I hadn't quite managed to cut all the way through the first loop when the pantry door creaked loudly behind me.

The light from a lantern blinded me, the knife slipped from my grasp and clattered to the floor. I heard it skitter out of my reach. Fanny let out a little squeak of fear. Surreptitiously, I felt behind me for the pistol, but I couldn't find it. I kept my eyes on the lantern, trying to see who was concealed behind its ochre glow.

"I've been lookin' forward to this meetin' Martha Pentreath, f'r quite some time." A woman's voice, broad Cornish and containing a level of threat and satisfaction that caused me to quickly stand up in order to face my foe on as equal terms as I could.

"Mary Yates," I said, and some feminine instinct told me not to let my guard down just because she was a woman. Part of my mind was on the pistol. Under cover of the hem of my nightgown, I felt about with my bare foot.

The lantern lowered and I could finally see my adversary. Even in the unkind light of the flickering candlelight, I could see that underneath the dirt and tumbled mess of hair was the makings of a great beauty — no, perhaps not a beauty but she possessed a kind of smouldering wildness which was beautiful in its own way. She was too tall, too dark, too strong for the fashion, but she seemed to exude the very essence of life. I discovered in that moment that I envied her freedom, envied the raw, stormy life she must lead. She made me feel weak and insignificant, a colourless shadow in comparison. Her dark eyes flashed brightly, catching sparks from the lantern, showing both a kind of native intelligence and burning hatred. She was smiling, showing her sharp, little teeth, which did nothing to alleviate my fears because of the degree of menace behind that cat's smile.

"You were kind enough to write to me recently," I remarked, "and if I remember correctly, you were a little concerned about being unable to hold the attention of a local criminal — now, wait, his name will come to me! Ah, yes, the crude and boorish Captain Cavanagh." Fanny made a small warning sound, but I recklessly chose not to hear her. "I am rather surprised that you think he might be interested in *me*! Or I in him, for that matter. Have you not seen your reflection lately? How could such a man be interested in a pale and inconsequential creature like me when you are *clearly* so much more to his taste?"

She took a step towards me and I steeled myself for a blow of some kind but refused to flinch. I would not give her the satisfaction of seeing me cower. "I don't think'ee knows who'ee be dealin' with. I can make'ee disappear, just like that," she snapped her fingers, "an' no one will be any the wiser," she arched her lovely neck and tossed her mane of windblown hair, "I've got men who'll do anythin' for me."

"I have no doubt," I muttered. "So, what do you want with me?"

Mary Yates lifted the lantern again, blinding me, "I want'ee out of my way." The lamplight lit up her smile, lending her face a feline cruelty.

"So, you've gone to all this trouble just to ask me to leave?"

She laughed then, "Leave? It's goin' to be more lastin' than that!"

Keeping my inner turmoil hidden, I forced a smile, "Ah, you're *that* afraid you can't hold on to him! It's amusing to think you would consider that I could ever be a rival for his affections. I would never be interested in him. I may not be up to snuff myself but the very idea that I might wish to associate with such a person is laughable! The lowest of the low and destined for the Tyburn Tree. And if I have anything to do with it, you will swing alongside him," I added for good measure.

Her beautiful top lip curled with disdain, "Oh, 'ee'll be dead long 'afore that an' I'll have sailed to the New World with Liam, so don't'ee count y'r chickens too soon."

I saw the harsh flash of silver in the lamplight and allowed myself the luxury of taking a step back and as I did so, my bare toes touched the heavy barrel of my pistol. Heart racing, I prepared myself. Fanny was still partly tied up and unable to help. She caught and I hope, understood, my quick glance. She had no idea what to expect but knew to be on her guard.

Beneath the folds of my nightgown, I eased my foot towards the pistol and feeling cold metal, I curled my toes around it and pulled the gun nearer, while trying not to show any intention in my upper body.

Mary Yates seemed to be listening for something beyond the walls of the pantry, her attention, for a fleeting second, was not on me. I bent and swiftly grabbed the gun by its handle, straightened up, cocked it and fired in one movement. I had no idea of my aim and was taken aback to hear a shrill scream until I realised it was Fanny. There was dull thud and the sound of a body crumpling to the floor and the lantern crashing down was extinguished by the fall.

"'Ee's bloody well hit 'er, Martha! She's down!" shrieked the ever-over-excitable Fanny in croaky triumph.

I could see nothing; the flash of the pistol had blinded me. I edged over to Fanny and began fumbling with the ropes again, "Oh, damn these knots, Fanny, they're so tight! Where is that knife? No, wait, they're loosening, I think, There! I have it. Oh, do stop wriggling, you're not making this any easier." Then Fanny was shaking herself free of her restraints and staggering to her feet. She quickly located a tinderbox and lit a candle and the lantern. We then stood and stared down at the inert body of Mary Yates.

"'Spose we ought to see if she's dead," said my companion reluctantly and nudged the body with her foot. Nothing happened so we took a closer look.

"She's alive," I whispered, afraid she might hear me and wake up.

"Pity," said Fanny callously. "What are we to do now?"

"I shall see where she is wounded and then — we must tend to her, I suppose."

"Tend to 'er? Is'ee mad? She was goin' to kill us without turnin' a hair. I'll *tend* to 'er all right!"

After examining Mary Yates, I found a dark graze along the side of her forehead that ran into her hair. It was bleeding only a little as it wasn't very deep. It was a lucky shot in many ways. I had been fortunate to hit anything at all, aiming so wildly and fortunate not have killed her outright. However dastardly she might be, I had no desire to become a fugitive from justice.

"It seems the shot has struck her a glancing blow and knocked her out. If you get a wet cloth, I will clean the wound as best I can."

Fanny tossed her head and muttered under her breath about wasting our time.

After I had quickly seen to her wound and we had found more clean cloth to bandage her head, I tried to rouse her. There was no response. "I hope she's not going to be damaged in the head after all this, that would be unfortunate and would not please Captain Cavanagh. I am already in his bad books. Keep an eye on her while I go and check on Solomon."

Solomon hadn't moved. I put the lantern and the pistol beside his huge body and once again knelt beside him, unable to avoid the pool of blood. I was just tenderly feeling the back of his head when the kitchen door opened, hitting the wall with some force. I grabbed the pistol and jumped to my feet, levelling the empty flintlock at the intruder.

It was Liam Cavanagh flanked by two unsavoury looking ruffians. I gasped but continued to point my weapon in his general direction.

"You're too bloody late," I said crossly.

His dark gaze took in my dishevelled appearance, my hair hanging down my back and my ripped and bloodstained nightgown. He took an impulsive step towards me, "Martha, you're hurt."

"No, indeed, I am not, sir, but our brave guardian, Solomon, I fear, is badly wounded."

He seemed to drag his eyes way from me to the body on the floor and gestured to the men beside him to attend to the wounded man. He then crossed the kitchen and gently removed the pistol from my shaking hand. He examined it and allowed himself a small chuckle, "'Tis not loaded, you little fool."

I stepped away, out of his reach.

He sniffed the barrel of the gun and frowned, "This has been fired. What have you done?"

I took another step back, "I had no choice — she left me no choice — " I glanced towards the pantry.

"I say again, what have you done?"

"I shot her."

"Her? Who the hell are you talking about?"

"I shot Mary Yates."

He grabbed me and dragged me across the kitchen, kicking open the door to the pantry and assessing the scene before him. Fanny stood over the motionless form of his lover, still brandishing the knife.

Liam Cavanagh swore roundly, using words that brought colour to my frozen face. He let go of me and pushing Fanny aside, bent over Mary Yates. He straightened and sighed, "She's alive. Just stunned by the blow to her head. Who taught you to use a gun, Martha?"

"My cousins," I replied.

"I might have guessed. Halfwits. You could have killed her."

"I'm beginning to wish I had," I muttered, thinking he was far too concerned about someone who had intended to murder us. A noise escaped him which I could have sworn was a snort of laughter. His eyes were darkly shadowed, and the flickering candlelight cast sharp triangles from his cheekbones and made his face looks like it was carved from unyielding granite. I must have been mistaken.

"What in God's name were you thinking? Shooting at people in the middle of the night in your nightgown!"

I bristled, "It's not as though I had much choice in the matter. I heard a noise and investigated it. Solomon was out cold, and Fanny bound and gagged. I couldn't just abandon them to their fate. 'Tis not my fault your esteemed mistress, for some reason best known to herself, finds me entirely *de trop*." I glared at him, "I don't fit in with her plans."

"Oh, and what plans are those?"

"Suffice it to say that I think you'll do very well for yourself in the New World. It will suit your adventurous spirit. From all accounts 'tis a wild and lawless place filled with naked savages bent on murdering innocent people in their beds. It sounds ideal."

"Innocent? I suppose that depends which side you're on. Rather like with this incident — "

Fanny cleared her throat, "Perhaps not the time for such a discussion," and she gestured to Mary Yates who was stirring at last.

Liam Cavanagh gently lifted the injured woman up in his arms as though she weighed nothing at all; she rested her head against his chest and put her arms about his neck. He carried her out of the kitchen and into the night. The two ruffians had somehow removed Solomon and we could hear them grunting as they manoeuvred his considerable weight across the yard.

Fanny and I stood motionless.

"Well," said Fanny, "What a to-do."

I couldn't help it, I laughed. But then I couldn't stop laughing until Fanny started to look quite concerned. "Sorry, Fanny! But he was so — *worried* about that woman. Captain Cavanagh. He must be very fond of her. I was starting to — well, I had thought — but it appears my first impressions were nearer the mark. Poor Solomon, I hope he'll be all right. I wonder where they've taken him?"

"I'm sure the Captain will let'ee know. Come, Martha, let us tidy up an' get to our beds. Oh my, to think, Eleanor has slept through the whole thing! She'll be so relieved, she really don't like pother of any kind. 'Twill be dawn before long an'ee has a hard day at the Hall tomorrow — today." Her eyebrows went up in surprise, "Oh, my! 'Tis Christmas Eve!"

Twenty-Six

Christmas Eve morning arrived with a half-hearted flurry of gritty snow, which dusted the fields and gathered in the corners of the yard against the walls as though it was afraid of the light. Frosted cobwebs hung like Eleanor's lace from the gates and puffs of frozen breath misted my face as I hurried to feed the handful of scraggy chickens Jem had rescued from a local smallholder, who was being forced to sell up; he had also been given a small pig, the runt of the litter, by one of his co-workers at the fish cellars. The chickens fluffed up their feathers and huddled together for warmth and the pig refused to come out of her sty preferring her steamy bed of straw and filth to tiptoeing through the frozen puddles. I scattered corn for the chickens and filled the trough with slops for the, as yet, unnamed pig, then raced to clean myself up, gather my cloak and freshly laundered apron and with a despairing glance at the grandfather clock, dashed up the iron-hard track to Polgrey Hall.

Mrs Talbot was quick to point out that they'd all been hard at work since dawn, but I knew she was glad to see me and that her mood was more about the enormity of the task ahead of us.

Another day of amusing, triumphant, catastrophic, and mundane moments flew past; the camaraderie in the house at least made the work seem less insurmountable. We even managed to share a joke or two at my aunt's expense, which lightened the mood. Slowly, the house came together and began to look fit to host the grandest party and when the table was laid with linen and sparkling glass and silver and the walls hung with holly, ivy, and mistletoe, fires in the grate, and sweet smells of puddings baking, we couldn't help feeling rather pleased with the result. However, it didn't stop Aunt Louisa from casting her critical eye over everything and insisting on several last-minute alterations that were wholly unnecessary but reminded us that she was in charge.

It was late afternoon when Mrs Talbot finally allowed us to stop for tea and a slice of plum cake and while the staff were enjoying their well-earned rest, I went to find Miles.

He was in the library and the second I entered the room he was enthusiastically regaling me with the story of how Ben Fairchild finally got his comeuppance.

"Our plan worked, Martha! Better than we could have hoped. Lieutenant Danserfield came up trumps at last. What a rattling good show you've missed! I've a good mind to add my brotherly backing to his doomed campaign for Rowena — poor beggar. All it took was a word in his ear and Danserfield was on Ben Fairchild's trail like a hungry fox after a fat chicken." His eyes were sparkling for the first time in weeks.

"Someone witnessed these events?"

He chuckled wickedly, "By Jupiter, yes, as luck would have it our groom was in the village and saw the raid on the cottage. Danserfield isn't one to give up easily, he persevered and after tearing the place apart, found the contraband Lucius planted. Oh, *and* the extra special parcel of maps of England's coastline, letters *en français* talking in easily decipherable code about tide times and crossing times and phases of the moon. We threw in a few sketches of important buildings and locations of defences on the coast, major army posts for good measure. Danserfield found them and now Ben Fairchild is where he belongs, under lock and key in Mill Prison. And for all that Eleanor has had to endure, may he rot in there for all eternity." His eyes fleetingly darkened but he shook himself out of it, "What an adventure! Just like the old days."

*   *   *

John kindly drove me back to Wild Court in the cart and I was grateful as darkness had brought a biting wind which sliced right through even the thickest cloak.

Fanny greeted me in the hallway, fidgety with excitement.

"Martha! At last! 'Ee've been an *age*. Eleanor an' me have been waitin' for'ee all afternoon. We've been beside ourselves!"

"What on earth — ?"

Fanny pointed with high drama to the table, which was stacked high with pretty boxes, tied with ribbons.

Eleanor arrived in haste, practically tumbling through the door in her eagerness, "Ah, there you are! Finally!" Her cheeks were pink and her eyes wide. "Come, for pity's sake, put us out of our misery. Open them at once."

I laughed at them both and drew nearer the heap of parcels.

"Who sent them? When did they arrive?"

"Never mind that! They're for you."

My hand was drawn of its own volition to one of the parcels, tied with a green satin ribbon - it hovered, unsure.

"If'ee don't damn well open them, I will!", declared Fanny impatiently.

Taking the box, I sat down with it on my knees and slowly pulled the ribbon. It slid gracefully to the floor, curling like ivy across the rug. I lifted the lid.

There, nestling in layers of tissue paper, was a gown. The most beautiful gown I'd ever seen.

It was as black as the night sky and shimmered with a lustre of inky blue like the wing of a starling. Tiny beads of faceted jet glistened. A delicate mist of black lace edged the neckline. The stomacher had a vertical row of black velvet bows like butterflies. The fabric of the robe and petticoat was silken and floated like a cloud as I lifted it from the box.

Eleanor and Fanny inhaled a collective gasp, and my hands shook, making the gown tremble as though alive. I laid it gently over a chair and stood back to look at it. I could think of nothing to say.

In another, smaller box I found a black lace fan, a black ribbon choker, black kid gloves with jet buttons, a black lace half mask which would cover everything but my mouth and in a separate velvet pouch, an *en tremblant* hair-clasp with a crescent moon of pearls and tiny diamond stars which quivered as I moved it.

Fanny pushed the final box towards me. It contained a pair of exquisite mules in black silk with little curved heels in a shocking shade of scarlet.

Feeling rather shaky, I closed my eyes for a moment and took a deep breath to try to steady myself.

Nobody said anything. We looked from the boxes and their ruffled petals of tissue paper and extraordinary contents to each other.

"I don't understand — " I said, "Why — who sent these?"

Eleanor was stroking the gown as though it might be afraid of her and shy away. "'Tis beyond anything I have ever seen — 'tis the work of a true artist. I think it must have come from Madame Pascal, but the work is not by one of her usual seamstresses, this is made by a special hand." Her eyes were misty, "Whoever ordered this — must be — "

"Must be — ?"

"Either mad — or in love with you."

My heart thumped loudly, and I couldn't seem to catch my breath.

"Don't be — ridiculous! This must have been sent by Lady Sarah and Sir Aubrey. That is the only logical explanation."

Eleanor looked at me as though I were not very quick-witted, "This is not from a *friend*, Martha. Can you not see? This is from someone who wishes to win your heart — to be your lover. This is from someone who *sees* you."

My hand was over my mouth, holding back the sounds I wanted to make, the little laugh of delight, the terrified moan of fear in case she was wrong, the hope — the painful surge of *hope*.

I stood up, tissue paper falling around me, "Well, I cannot accept it! 'Tis too much! 'Tis most improper and it must all be returned. At once."

"Are you not even tempted to try it on?" said Fanny irritably. She picked up the velvet pouch and peering into it pulled out a small square of deckle-edged paper, which she handed to me.

In a flowing hand, it just read, "Wear your hair powdered."

"Oh!" I said, infuriated, "How — how typical! Imperious, obnoxious, meddling — outrageous. How *dare* he? Pack it all up! I shall ask John to take it to the ferry and send it back to Plymouth."

"Sometimes Martha, you can be so provoking!" exclaimed Eleanor. "You have a stubborn streak as wide as the Tamar which makes it very difficult to reason with you. You really must own that you can be quite irrational particularly about matters of the heart."

"I have no 'matters of the heart' as you call them," I muttered, "Although, I will allow that I can be a little obstinate. I attribute it to a childhood growing up alongside my cousins and having to fight for my rights, otherwise I always ended up with the broken sword or the smallest cake. It was a matter of survival."

"Yes, I understand but this gift — it is not just a matter of the immense cost of it, which, must have been prodigious, but the thought that has gone into it. He has taken into account that you are in mourning. He has attended to every detail — the heels of those shoes are just the sort of gesture of defiance *you* would make! It is as though he has seen into your heart, Martha. I know that may sound far-fetched, it is, after all, just a gown, but there is a message here, if you care to see it."

* * *

Later, as I made myself ready for bed, I had plenty to think about. My mind was racing, and I was fairly certain I had a sleepless night ahead of me. I kept thinking of the astonishing array of carefully chosen things which were still lying half-hidden in their wrappings in the morning room. I wanted to go down and look at them again, to imagine him choosing them, insisting, in that dictatorial way he had, that everything should be just so. What had made him do such a thing?

I climbed into bed and pulled the covers around me tightly, trying to stay in the warm patch that the warming pan had left. It was past midnight and Christmas Day now, and I knew my life had just taken an unexpected turn and that it was up to me what happened next. I felt a thrill of excitement in my chest and curling up into a tight ball, I fell asleep immediately.

* * *

Christmas morning and there was a hectic air at Wild Court. Amidst a whirl of gift giving and receiving, my thoughts would not stray very far from the gown still draped across the chair in the morning room. We had agreed to make do and mend with the presents as we were all short of funds. My present for Eleanor was my mother's favourite bergère straw hat with sapphire blue ribbons and, even though not new, she was clearly delighted; and for Fanny a forest green silk shawl my mother had given me. Fanny, who had been collected late last night by Jem on his way back from Plymouth and, I suspect, by way of the alehouse in Cremill, had returned that morning to bring some little gifts for us, quince paste sweetmeats, which she laughingly admitted her mother, Susan, had made. Eleanor had made us all lacy handkerchiefs with our initials embroidered in one corner.

The Christmas dinner party was to begin at half past four and to continue into the evening as usual but first we were all to attend Maker Church for the Christmas service. I had rummaged around in my mother's press and found a pelisse in fur-trimmed black velvet which almost made my black day dress look respectable enough for church and a lace cap, over which I tied a black velvet scarf. I'd be warm but not at all fashionable; happily, the church would be crowded so there was little chance of critical scrutiny.

We had no choice but to walk to church as the four of us couldn't all fit in the cart but fortunately it wasn't far and the weather, although frosty, was kind, the sun filtering through the mist, giving the day a suitably festive silvery luminosity.

The church was full to bursting and looked a picture with all the candles lit and the pillars hung with greenery. We were greeted by a few of the parishioners; with cool nods from those who had obviously listened to the rumours, a few friendly smiles from others and a vigorous hand shaking and warm embraces from the Goodalls, Anne Talbot, Meggie, and John Pezzack. John held little Amy by the hand, and I recalled my promise to take care of her and resolved to honour that pledge as soon as possible. Reverend Pender gave a good account of himself with his sermon, raising his normally modest voice to the wagon-shaped rafters to berate his parishioners for their vices and remind them to be more caring to the poor and needy amongst them.

After the service Aunt Louisa, dragging Uncle Joshua in her wake, came to exchange curt greetings, quickly moving on to find more exalted company. Miles, looking so much more himself, Lucius, as sour as ever, and Harry gathered around and chatted noisily about horses and dogs and the coming Masquerade. Rowena, I noticed, was making straight for the small group of Dragoon officers who had made a special effort to attend. Standing in the centre of them was Lieutenant Danserfield, who was watching her approach with obvious delight, his face lighting up and his eyes gleaming; he took her hand, kissed it in a crisply military fashion and introduced her to his fellow soldiers. She blushed prettily but only had eyes for one of them. The Ansteys were there but thankfully there was no sign of Baron Rosenberg or Hester Jarrett. I found, to my dismay, that I was scouring the faces of the gathered worshippers, looking for a particular pair of laughing eyes. Of course he wasn't there, and I tried not to notice that my heart sank a little.

Lucius blatantly ignored Eleanor and flirted ostentatiously with Kitty Anstey and I resolved to tell him later just how shabby his behaviour was. Miles was attentive but slightly distant with Eleanor and Harry paid more attention to the horses waiting outside the church than any of the humans who might be about to ride them.

Eventually the congregation dispersed, and we were able to return to Wild Court to discuss who we had seen at the service. Eleanor was a little subdued, but Fanny made up for it by regaling us with the all the titbits of gossip she'd picked up while Jem brought in the logs and lit the fires and then took Fanny home to have Christmas dinner with her family.

Eleanor had already offered to help me dress for the Polgrey Christmas dinner and I was happy to accept. I wore the same grey gown as before but this time, bearing in mind, Sir Montagu's criticism, I tucked a gauzy black fichu into the neckline. Eleanor pinned my hair up and added a pale grey ostrich feather and some black ribbons. With the addition of a shawl and the pelisse, we decided I looked perfectly acceptable and when John arrived in the carriage, sent by a thoughtful Miles, I was almost excited to be going, although I was not going to readily admit the reason why.

It was a token gathering of local dignitaries, those with titles or great riches, large estates or influence, and those Uncle Joshua hunted with and Aunt Louisa considered to be almost her equal and wanted to cultivate in case they could be useful to her. The Ansteys, Baron Rosenberg, and Hester Jarrett were there alongside a rather nervous looking and very out-of-place Reverend Pender, who barely said a word the entire night. But once again, the only face I sought was not in evidence and all I had to look forward to was an interminable evening of watching Rowena make a fool of herself with Baron Rosenberg again, Kitty Anstey make hopeless sheep's eyes at Miles, and Hester Jarrett get steadily more intoxicated as the evening wore on and begin to lose the refined accent she'd obviously been affecting. Edmund Anstey made a half-hearted attempt to engage me in conversation, but he kept having to stifle yawns which I tried not to take amiss as it was exactly how I was feeling myself. Lucius didn't put in an appearance at all although Miles said he had faithfully promised his mother that he'd be there to support her.

The evening ended with a few hands of cards and a late supper, a collation of cold meats, cheese, pastries, and plenty of champagne by which time Harry was asleep in a chair as usual.

A very tired John drove me home at two in the morning and I was more than glad to see my bed after such a disappointing day. I snatched up the box of quince sweetmeats as I passed the kitchen and sat in bed and ate the whole box until I felt quite sick.

Twenty-Seven

He was *here*? At Wild Court?"

"He was."

"But I don't understand. *Why* was he here?"

"He came to talk with me."

"You're not exactly being very forthcoming, Eleanor. It must have been quite serious for him to miss the party at the Hall."

"He wanted to ask me about Miles."

"This be like tryin' to get blood from a stone," said Fanny gloomily.

Eleanor sighed, "He — wanted to ascertain if I had feelings for Miles."

"And you told him — ?"

"That I felt friendship for Miles. Nothing more."

"And his reaction to that was — ?"

"He seemed — pleased."

"And then — ?"

"He left."

Fanny and I exchanged a speaking glance.

"He just *left*? Without saying anything else? Without *doing* anything else?"

Eleanor blushed.

Fanny crowed with triumph, "He kissed'ee! I knew it! 'Ee looked like'ee'd been kissed."

"Goodness. How — extraordinary. Who'd have thought! While I was having an absolutely ghastly time at Polgrey Hall — you were being kissed by Lucius!"

"Is'ee a good kisser?"

"*Fanny!*", cried Eleanor and I in unison.

Fanny shrugged, "It be an important consideration. 'Ee don't want to end up spendin' the rest of y'r life with a man who kisses like a lamprey!"

"Fanny! What a monstrous image. I will never be able to rid myself of it."

Eleanor smiled secretly to herself, "He is, indeed — good," she said.

Fanny let out a squeal of joy, "The quiet ones always be!"

"So, did he say anything of interest?"

"He did."

"Which was — ?"

"He loves me."

"Oh, Eleanor! That's — that's wonderful. You must be so happy. Are you? *Are* you happy?"

Eleanor seemed to consider this for a moment, as was her way, "Yes. I am. Although I realise that there are still many obstacles in the way of lasting happiness, not least of which is Lady Polgrey. But now at least I know that my feelings are returned, and it makes everything bearable. He says he has always loved me but that he thought I would be better off with Miles. I had to reassure him that although I am very fond of Miles, it had always been him — even when he treated me so carelessly." Her eyes glistened, "He became very agitated when I said that and took me in his arms and with every kiss, he apologised. He said that I was too good for him and that he would spend the rest of his life trying to be a better man for me. I told him I didn't care because I loved him regardless. He said that it was seeing me at church on Christmas morning that tore his heart into pieces — when he was flirting so deliberately with Kitty, he saw the sadness in my eyes and knew he couldn't bear to see me so hurt."

"Well, I never," I said. "I honestly thought he was a lost cause."

* * *

Later that morning Riordan arrived to inform us that Solomon had been returned to Holmoak Beacon and had pulled through the worst of his injury and with good care was thought to have every chance of a full recovery.

"Sir Montagu thought ee'd want to know," he explained, "He said ee'd be concerned."

"I am so relieved to hear that. That is most kind of you to bring such good news. Please give my regards to Solomon and tell him that I shall visit as soon as I am able."

Riordan smiled, that foxy, knowing smile, which made me feel a little awkward.

"I don't suppose you have heard any word of what happened to that woman, Mary Yates, the one who injured Solomon?"

"Aye, Miss, I heard from someone down at Cremill that she already be on a ship goin' to the New World or some such place. No more'n she deserves."

"Did they say if she went by herself?"

Another foxy glance, "Aye, Miss, by herself. Good luck to the Americas, I say," said the little man with an impish chuckle.

"Do you know Captain Cavanagh, Mr Riordan?"

"Aye, I do, in a manner of speakin'."

"Did the Captain not want to go with her?"

"As I understand it, Miss, he be lookin' forward to havin' an ocean between them."

"Oh, I thought — "

"Things change. Not sayin' it never were that way but — things change."

"Oh," I said, wondering why I felt an inexplicable wave of relief and a certain amount of unsatisfied curiosity.

"I don't know the Captain that well, nobody does, but I do know that there be another side to him. Don't'ee believe all the talk."

* * *

Eleanor and I spent a leisurely Boxing Day in and around the house, talking of what could be expected from Aunt Louisa's

Masquerade and every so often I would catch Eleanor staring into space with a half-smile on her beautiful face. I was happy for her but could not help but wonder if Lucius would come up to scratch when the time came. He was so used to getting his own way and had never been in the habit of taking anyone else into consideration in anything he said or did. If he could somehow learn to curb his naturally wicked impulses it might be the making of him but having had years of experience dealing with the darker side of his character, I had my doubts about his ability to change, or perhaps his *willingness* to change.

Fanny was still with her family and now that we no longer had Letitia as a patient, there was not so much for her to do at Wild Court, but she said that if I needed her to send for her. I missed her raucous laughter and unguarded tongue.

Eleanor and I were just eating some bread and cheese in the kitchen when we heard a horse approaching and Miles arrived at our door in a state of high excitement.

"Martha! Eleanor! Good day to you both. A fine Boxing Day indeed. Oh, to hell with the niceties! You will never be able to guess what has happened!"

"Well, that goes without saying, dear Miles. Do not prolong the suspense for a moment more by making us speculate." I said, laughing.

Miles rolled his eyes at me, "Never could tolerate too much drama! I'm sorry to talk about our wretched money matters in front of you, Eleanor, but this morning, a messenger came from our benefactor in Plymouth with a substantial packet of correspondence saying that all our debts have been settled and that a new sponsor has come forward and taken over all liability for any future loans or debts we may incur. Is this not the most staggering news?"

"A new sponsor? Miles, who in their right mind would take on the Polgrey debts just like that? And pay off all your outstanding obligations. It makes no sense. I could understand it if they just took over your accounts because they'd expect to make a profit by raising the interest but there is no reason to pay off those debts. Unless — "

"Unless, what oh, disbeliever?"

"Unless someone has something personal to gain — something they want and are willing to pay over the odds for. I think you should be very careful because nobody does something like this out of the goodness of their heart. Perhaps you should ask around and see if you can discover who it might be."

"For pity's sake, Martha! Must you always think the worst of everyone? Can you not just be happy for us? Don't you see what this means? I am free of the smugglers! I no longer need to sell my soul to the devil to pay for Father's horses and the damned Masquerade."

"Yes, I see that and I'm glad, but I just wonder why — "

But Miles was having none of my naysaying and he was so exuberant that in the end, I didn't have the heart to continue with my argument even though I was unable to quell a growing sense of foreboding.

"Oh, by the way, did Harry ever explain why he didn't come to my rescue on the night of our raid on Ben Fairchild's cottage?" I asked, deftly changing the subject.

"Yes, he said he fell asleep, which of course, we all know he's likely to do as quick as a wink. Since his accident he falls asleep several times a day without warning; he'll nod off standing up sometimes, or when he's out riding; he has the luck of the devil though, should have been killed a dozen times but, like a drunkard, he's seldom gets hurt when he falls."

"Well, fancy choosing Harry to be lookout! What a lamentable decision. Have you heard any more of the fate of the wreckers?"

"Yes, our tame Dragoon officer has informed us that four more have been captured, two for trying to sell a hogshead of wine to a judge and another one who had been bragging rather too loudly in an alehouse in Plymouth. The last one has been arrested on suspicion of murder; for the killing of Ned Quick."

"I'm glad to hear it. That poor boy, so full of life. I feel guilty for not trying to stop him."

"He would have still been on that beach, Martha, even if you hadn't been there. And, anyway, you had no choice in the matter."

"That's as maybe but perhaps if I'd said no — "

"He would have gone alone. He was well-known for his sense of adventure."

As he was leaving, he turned to Eleanor and wished her happy and said to notify him at once if Lucius didn't turn up trumps.

* * *

As I stitched a repair in my petticoat, I was wondering about Amy Pezzack, who had been on my mind ever since I had witnessed her mother's suspicious death and seen the tiny child bravely take on the mantle of carer. It had broken my heart to see the Pezzack's hopeless situation and particularly to realise that Amy would have no future to look forward to apart from hard toil, illness and an early death. It dawned on me that I had enjoyed a privileged and sheltered life and had never in my twenty-one years really understood what it was like to be poor; I had, of course, seen poverty at close quarters but the idea of living in a sweet little cottage like the Goodalls had seemed romantic and idyllic. When I was a child my father had explained to me that something should be done about the inequality the working classes were forced to suffer and often berated the government for being more interested in lining their own pockets than helping their constituents. He frequently reminded me that if the "haves" did nothing to help the "have-nots" society would disintegrate and there would be civil war again. My father was not a man who wore his religion on his sleeve, he had a quiet but deep faith which provided him with the foundations upon which he built his life. I suppose I could blame the callowness of youth for my lack of understanding of worldly things, but it was also fear of the unknown, fear of knowing that if you noticed something unjust then it was up to you to rectify it or live with the guilt and the consequences.

I had decided that Amy wouldn't just be a problem I would lose sleep over intermittently; she would be the beginning of a new way of life for both of us. I had made her a promise. Amy and Rebecca would have a future to look forward to. I now impatiently awaited a response from the Finches about my proposal and news from Liam Cavanagh about Rebecca's whereabouts.

Eleanor eyed me over the top of the book she was reading, "Martha, you are all of a fidget. What is making you so restless?"

I heaved a theatrical sigh, "Everything."

Eleanor smiled, "That's a little too all-encompassing for me to be able to advise, I'm afraid. Could you be more specific?"

I laid down my sewing, "It's just so hard to have to sit and sew when I'd rather be *doing* something. Something to resolve all the questions that remain unanswered however hard I try to unravel them."

"About your parents?"

"Yes, I know the barest facts about what happened. I can hazard a guess that my father somehow found out that Rebecca wasn't his child and it tipped him into a reckless act and according to Captain Cavanagh it ended with his death in France. Who *is* Rebecca's father? I thought perhaps it was the Captain himself, but he swears 'tis not possible. I believe him, although I don't know why - he is a smuggler and therefore should not be trusted. Where has Rebecca been hidden? Who took her? Was Nell poisoned? Who is behind all of this? I only have questions! Nothing but questions and I have to sit here mending a rip in my petticoat. 'Tis so futile. I want to be out there finding the answers!"

Eleanor carefully closed her book. "It seems to me that you are in need of some fresh air. A walk around the harbour or up over Maker. You've been cooped up all day and you need to clear your head and to be perfectly frank, my dear, your stitches are suffering, they look as though they were done by a bear wearing mittens."

"Oh, very amusing. I have never liked sewing; 'tis a tedious occupation without suitable reward and I must say that I do admire you for your fortitude in that area. You are right, I shall take myself out for a quick walk to blow away the cobwebs before it gets any darker." I gave her a wry look, "And you can finish your book in peace."

* * *

The first deep breath of wintry air hurt my lungs but with every step I took I became ever more light of foot, until as I reached the top of the hill above Wild Court, I just couldn't help myself, I gathered up my skirts and broke into a run, I wanted to drive away all the questions circling like buzzards in my mind. I was so unused to any kind vigorous exercise that after about twenty yards or so, I was completely out of puff, my heart racing and my face glowing. I bent double and tried to get my breath back, laughing at my own silliness.

"Have you lost an earring?"

Oh, for heaven's sake, I thought, must he be everywhere? I straightened up and tried to not sound too breathless, "I was just — taking a walk — before nightfall." I could see Liam Cavanagh leading his horse and behind him some other figures, shadowy in the dusk "Oh, good evening, Jeckie! Is that indeed you? And Mr Colquite? Well, fancy seeing you all up here and not a boat in sight!"

"Cap'n? What'ee goin' to do now? If she ain't there an' she be here, ain't that goin' to be a problem?"

"No, Jeckie, it won't. Miss Pentreath is about to allow us to escort her safely home for 'tis not a night to be out and about."

"Pshaw! You're all — *out and about*," I said pithily.

"I was, in fact, on my way to see you, Miss Pentreath. I have brought you some news which I believe you will be interested to hear. Shall we make our way back to Wild Court? Jeckie and Colquite have business in the harbour which will keep them busy for a while. There is not much of a moon tonight - you should have brought a lantern."

"I had not intended to be out for very long. I thought I would be home easily before dark."

"Perhaps you ran further than you meant," said the Captain with an infuriating smile in his voice. "Come, let us go back this way. Would you care to ride?"

"No, I would *not*, thank you, sir."

"Tetchy."

"Cap'n, what if — ?"

"Jeckie, we have nothing to worry about. Miss Pentreath is already up to her pretty neck in the smuggling business and will therefore keep her counsel should she happen to see anything untoward, is that not so, Miss Pentreath?"

I said nothing in case my words should incriminate me. I was intrigued to find out what they were plotting. I had noticed that there were three of them but four horses. They were probably going to collect some smuggled goods.

As we walked the short way back to Wild Court, Jeckie chattered and Colquite answered him tersely as though swatting away a particularly persistent insect.

The harbour was hard to see with so little light to illuminate the water, the copse was as black as pitch and as we drew nearer, Jeckie stopped talking. He took the horses and held them while Liam Cavanagh and Colquite walked down to the harbour's edge. I stood and watched.

"Damn," the Captain muttered as my ears suddenly picked up the sound of quiet sploshing and the creak of oars.

Around the headland, from the direction of the open sea, a jolly boat appeared. I could just make out four men in it. I moved closer.

Liam Cavanagh and Colquite pulled the boat in, tying it to the mooring bollard and helped one of the men ashore. There was a muffled exchange of words, some handshaking and then I thought I caught a few words. They were speaking French. They were smuggling a Frenchman into the country! I let out a tiny gasp and saw Liam Cavanagh turn to look at me. He said something to the stranger, and they made their way towards me.

"Miss Martha Pentreath, may I introduce to you, Monsieur Gilles de Thou."

I held out my hand and had it handsomely kissed by this, as far as I could see, rather elegant Frenchman.

"Bonsoir, Monsieur, bienvenu sur nos côtes. J'espère que vous avez fait un bon voyage?"

"Merci, Mademoiselle, ce fut une traversée difficile, mais vous avez rendu toute cela intéressante!"

I laughed and had the satisfaction of seeing Captain Cavanagh look mildly displeased.

"Colquite!" he barked, "Please make sure our friend gets to his lodgings safely. I will join you in a while."

* * *

Eleanor's eyes widened as I ushered the smuggler captain into our home and made the necessary introductions.

"I was sorry to hear about your brother, Miss Fairchild," said Liam Cavanagh.

"Well, I can assure you that I was not in the *least* sorry," replied Eleanor crisply, "I was only too glad to see the back of him. He doesn't have a good bone in his body. He was always going to end up on the wrong end of the law and I can only suppose that the world is a better place with him gone. I think I shall go up to bed, Martha, my eyes are tired after reading for so long."

I tried to dissuade her, but she would have none of it, leaving me alone with Liam Cavanagh with one of her speaking looks.

"May I get you some refreshment, Captain?"

"Thank you, but no." He removed a small drawstring pouch from his pocket, "This is for the last shipment you were kind enough to store for us. No arguments, please." He tossed it carelessly onto the table.

We sat and for a moment there was silence.

"You came to give me some news?"

"Indeed. I have heard that Solomon continues to improve daily."

"That is good news. I feel responsible because he was injured whilst guarding us."

"I'm sure it was a necessary measure. I think you have already heard that Mary Yates — "

"Your *mistress,* Mary Yates, you mean?"

"Martha! Sometimes your expressions are not in the least ladylike. Mary Yates, whatever she may have insinuated, was never my mistress," he shook his head in despair, "I cannot believe I am having this conversation with you. I have been away for the last few days to make absolutely certain that she left our shores for good. After the other night I could not risk her trying to hurt anyone again."

"That's most kind in you, sir, if a little tardy."

He swore under his breath. "Truly, you could try the patience of a saint!"

"You're certainly no saint."

"I will own, regretfully, that my past has not been entirely blameless, but I have never claimed I was a saint."

"Just as well, really."

"About Monsieur de Thou. I would be eternally grateful if you would not mention his arrival to anyone, not even your cousins."

I looked at him curiously, "Is he a spy?"

"You believe I would bring an enemy agent into the country?"

I shrugged, "I know you to be ruthless. You are a smuggler after all. Hardly a reassuring career choice but — I will admit though, I do not believe you would betray this country."

"Thank you for your trust. I probably don't deserve it. I don't want your expectations to be too high, but I have made some progress with the search for Rebecca. I have discovered that she was taken from Fanny Goodall to Plymouth where the kidnappers hired a wet-nurse and then from there they travelled to The White Hart in Exeter and eventually to The Swan with Two Necks in Cheapside. I think I can determine where they were heading."

"I cannot believe you have found so much. It is beyond anything. I never thought — hoped — I — " I cast around for the right words, feeling overcome with a sudden wave of emotion but I would not cry in front of him. "How can I thank — ?"

He held up his hand, "One day, I'll think of a way but until then we have not yet found the child." His Irish brogue was intense, "My source is hopeful and sent news that he is on their trail. 'Tis our belief that their destination is the Foundling Hospital in Bloomsbury where one can, in all good faith, abandon an unwanted child and have it disappear to some country wetnurse for several years. Very convenient. The worry being that if she has already been moved on — "

"We will never find her."

Liam Cavanagh frowned, "We *will* find her. I swear to you, Martha, on my life."

His eyes were dark and fathomless and for a moment he held my gaze, and I froze, suspended in time, unable to look away.

He took a step towards me and my heart leapt anxiously in my chest, I had to break the spell, to escape this confusion I was feeling. I took a deep breath and turned away to open the door.

"It has been a most enlightening evening, Captain Cavanagh and I thank you most sincerely for bringing such hopeful news, on all accounts. I hope that whatever purpose Monsieur de Thou is meant to serve is worth the risk. I will, of course, say nothing about his arrival. Your secret is safe with me."

He followed me into the hall in silence but as we approached the front door, his coat brushed my hand and I instinctively recoiled, as though I'd been burnt. He glanced down at me and something in his expression made me want to reach out to him, but I seemed unable to speak or move.

He looked at me for a long moment as though committing my face to memory and I returned his gaze as fearlessly as I could.

"Someday soon, Martha, you will see but until then — " he made an abrupt bow, "Your servant, as ever."

And I was alone.

I stood rooted to the spot for far too long staring at the closed door and listening to his horse's hooves thudding away into the distance.

Twenty-Eight

December continued frosty, keeping us mostly at home near a fire and even though Jem diligently kept the woodpile stocked and brought in peats and gorse faggots when wood was in short supply, we were bundled in so many layers of woollens we looked like a small flock of fat sheep.

Very little of interest occurred and I found I was actually bored with my life, pacing the floors and pestering the usually patient Eleanor with unanswerable questions and posing ridiculous notions until she told me quite succinctly that I was driving her to distraction.

"Martha, I understand that you are at a loss, being caught in a kind of limbo where everything seems to have come to a standstill; but you have said yourself that the search for Rebecca goes on even now and no amount of agonising will hasten the outcome. 'Tis a pointless waste of your energy; besides, I am inclined to think that this is not wholly about Rebecca and 'tis perhaps more to do with your inability to disentangle your own feelings."

"I'm sure I don't know what you mean, Eleanor," I said moodily.

She laughed, "You're acting like a lovelorn adolescent and 'tis most unbecoming in a girl your age. I suggest that instead of moping about the house you might address the problem face to face."

"I cannot — "

"Well, then, take up your sewing and sew like a bear!"

I rolled my eyes, "All right, I'm going. Had I realised that you were such a despot I might have thought twice about sharing my home with you."

* * *

I might as well not have bothered. A brisk walk and cold feet were all the reward I got for my pains. Holmoak Beacon was silent and shuttered; nobody answered the door and a sullen stillness hung over the place as though it had never been inhabited. I sat on the low parapet beside the steps and pondered for a while, finally coming to the conclusion that I had been abandoned and without a word of explanation. Quietly seething, I turned back and headed towards Maker Church, its tall tower beckoning to me against the bright sky. I wandered the churchyard, reading the names on the headstones and wondering who all these dead people were. I stopped for a moment beside my mother's grave and told her about our search for Rebecca and may have mentioned my forlorn hopes and fruitlessly asked her what she would do in the same predicament but on receiving no response I rounded the church to the leeward side facing the estuary and sat on a low tomb, out of the wind, to contemplate the view.

Voices penetrated my muddled thoughts and for a while I listened without hearing.

"It cannot be helped, if we are to avoid being discovered something must be done."

"But must it be this?"

"'Tis the only way."

"Perhaps, we will not be found out. Perhaps it will blow over and nothing come of it. My part was small. I did my duty and would do it again."

"You think you have God on your side, Reverend? I think you have the most to lose. Are you not worried that you could forfeit your precious soul? Mine is already lost. Nobody would believe I had anything to do with it, anyway. I can guarantee that I am not thought in the least dishonourable these days. My alibi is sound. They think me nothing but a fool. You had better keep looking over your shoulder, my friend."

"But you were the instigator of the whole affair, I was just there in a minor role. I was performing God's ordinance in accordance with my beliefs."

"You aided and abetted, Reverend Pender, aided and abetted."

"I will not take the blame — nor will I hurt anyone."

"Say what you will but it must be done and *soon* before that meddling creature exposes us all and our esteemed colleague decides we too are surplus to requirements. I would not trust him not to have us thrown down a mineshaft and left to rot."

There was the sound of footfall and then fading into the distance, a whistled tune, a snatch of lyrics, "*Greensleeves was my delight, Greensleeves was my heart of gold —* " and then silence.

I slid quietly off the tomb and on hearing the church door close, I tip-toed away from the church and into the nearest copse, where I stopped for second to look back and seeing I was not being pursued, I raced down the hill to Wild Court.

* * *

Once in the safety of my bedchamber, I was unable to sit still; my head was pounding, I couldn't think straight at all. A jumble of words flew around me like bats, and I couldn't make head nor tail of them.

Reverend Pender and Harry! My young cousin, sounding like the Harry of old, before his riding accident. I just couldn't even begin to understand what was happening. It seemed that we had all been hoodwinked; Harry had been a bit of a rakehell before his fall and his rackety ways had been widely known but it wasn't apparent to me why he should have acted out this entire crazy scheme and what he hoped to gain from the deception. Now, I could see why he hadn't come to my rescue that night at the windmill: he hadn't wanted me to survive and he had hoped Ben Fairchild would be my undoing. Suddenly I was looking at everything differently, it was as though someone had given me enchanted eyeglasses and I now saw more clearly. I realised that I had been distracted from the truth, by a conjuring trick; Harry had used sleight of hand to make us all look the other way. We were easily gulled like children believing only what we thought we saw. I ground my teeth together.

Then the words of the gypsy came back to haunt me.

What had she said? Betrayal by a loved one. Was this it? Was Harry the betrayer? And, she'd said that an innocent was in danger — well, it didn't take a genius to work that one out. Rebecca was the only innocent in all of this.

I considered all my options carefully.

I discovered, to my dismay that they were limited. One of them seemed to have left the county without so much as a by-your-leave. My two remaining cousins would be no help: Miles didn't need another adventure so soon after the last and Lucius was now much taken up with Eleanor. I could ask Liam Cavanagh but had no idea how to find him; he was an elusive shadow, turning up when least expected but with no place of abode apart from, as far as I could tell, a ship, which could be anywhere. I could hardly write him a note for Jem to deliver. And now Reverend Pender was out of bounds for advice, not that he had ever been of much assistance in that department, being more concerned with saving souls than helping his parishioners in an everyday, practical fashion. My safe little world was rapidly shrinking and to add to the uncertainty there was now the threat of Harry's *"esteemed colleague"* to worry about.

I had only myself to rely upon and it made me feel desperately alone. I made a decision.

* * *

By the next day I was as prepared as I would ever be. The note I left for Eleanor, who had left very early to deliver some lace in the village, was brief and reassuring but, because I had no wish to alarm her, lacking in any specific detail, apart from the salient fact that I would be away for a few days and she shouldn't worry. I added that I had asked Jem if Fanny could come and stay to keep her company. Feeling that I had covered every possible angle, I packed a few things, including my now trusty pistol, into a small bag and threw on my warmest cloak. I dashed into the morning room and reluctantly picked up the drawstring purse Liam Cavanagh had left on the table which, until now, I had refused to touch, but I could no longer afford the luxury of feeling insulted. To my delight it contained ten guineas and a handful of very useful smaller coins — a fortune in anyone's eyes and certainly much more than was deserved for just hiding some contraband in the cellar. Ten guineas would buy me a great deal and had come at a most heaven-sent moment, but this didn't mean that I was grateful: I was furious and would let him know in no uncertain terms that I could not be bought — if I ever saw him again.

Jem was waiting outside for me with the cart and looking a little disgruntled because I'd sworn him to secrecy. He was, by nature, a fairly taciturn fellow so I had faith that he could maintain a few days of silence as long as Fanny didn't suspect anything and turn her eagle-eyes upon him; nobody could withstand the onslaught of one of Fanny's inquisitions.

It had been an age since I had used the ferry boat from Cremill to Plymouth, but I quite enjoyed the journey once we were out on the estuary.

All the time I was plotting my journey and hoping that the weather held fair while I was out in the open; I really didn't want to travel in sodden clothes.

I hired a sedan chair and was taken, for what I considered a reasonable fee, to the coaching inn where I was to catch the stagecoach to London. I'll freely admit my heart was arguing with my head and there were forceful and compelling imaginary interruptions from a certain meddlesome busybody. I ignored them all and continued on my journey.

As I waited outside the inn for the stagecoach to arrive, I watched the people passing by, busy with their ordinary lives, buying eggs and cabbages and wondering their ordinary thoughts and here was I setting out on a madcap adventure with danger at every turn. A cold shiver slid down my spine and my eyes were drawn towards the other side of the street where a group of rather ostentatiously noisy people were leaving a grand town house; a raucous laugh caught my attention and made me shrink back into the shelter of the doorway behind me. As I peered out from my hiding place, I saw Hester

Jarrett being handed up into a familiar carriage, with shiny black and yellow paintwork. I pressed myself flat against the pillar and held my breath. Her companion, dressed in his customary sombre black, was Baron Rosenberg. She shouted something loudly to someone leaning out of one of the upstairs windows and waved. The Baron flicked a glance around the street and I quickly ducked out of sight into the entrance hall of the inn. After a few minutes the carriage pulled away and was driven off at speed, scattering passers-by like autumn leaves. I let out a sigh of relief and eased my way back into the short queue forming outside.

The stagecoach filled up quickly and the passengers weren't perhaps as polite as they should have been as they stowed their bags and found their places - I had my toes trodden on several times and a sharp elbow jabbed into my eye. A jovial looking man in a bright red waistcoat winked at me and rolled his eyes at the commotion going on around us. I clutched my bag to my chest and wished for the end of the journey to come fast as it was going to be unbearably long and not very comfortable. One very thin, elderly lady had a tiny dog tucked under her arm that yapped at anything that moved and was obviously incensed at not being able to run around and bite ankles at will.

It was, as I had anticipated, a disagreeable experience because of the close proximity of strangers, which meant a good deal of jostling, and the violence with which the coach lurched along the rutted tracks with no consideration for those unfortunate enough to be confined within. The journey to Exeter was just over forty miles and hilly with several stops to change the horses, the first being in Ivybridge. I had optimistically brought a small volume of Shakespeare's sonnets to read but found that I could not look down at the words without feeling quite ill. The jovial man tried to strike up a conversation with the dog lady but had his cheerfulness rudely curtailed when she haughtily asked him not to address her in such a familiar manner. After the first stop two passengers disembarked and I was able to take a window seat and from then until Exeter was somewhat entertained by the countryside bouncing by. At one point near Ashburton, we were overtaken by a speeding carriage which forced our driver to take to the verge and send a volley of curses after the flashy racing vehicle. He had to stop the coach and inspect the horses to make sure they hadn't been injured during the incident. He apologised for the delay and promised they would make up the time quite easily.

My companions were all agog and spent the next few miles discussing the rules of the road and our near-death experience which at least distracted us from the tedium of our journey for a while.

We arrived in Exeter at just after nine in the evening, crossing the old bridge over the River Exe and finding ourselves deposited at the White Hart near the cathedral, feeling rather dazed and bewildered. I followed the other passengers into the inn and was relieved to see that it was a well-tended establishment. The bustling landlady hurried up to us and began allotting bedchambers and advised us to make ourselves at home before coming back downstairs to have a little repast before retiring to bed.

My bedchamber was perfectly satisfactory, the bedlinen clean, and the mattress soft. I tidied myself and made my way down to join the others in the parlour but was waylaid by the landlady in the hallway.

"Oh, Miss? There's a gentleman wishes to speak with you. He has a private sitting room at the back. If you come with me, I'll show you the way."

My heart quickened and I beamed at her, "A gentleman?"

"Yes, indeed! A very refined sort of fellow."

I happily followed her through the warren of corridors to a room at the rear of the inn. She opened the door and ushered me in. The room was lit by a few candles and a fire glowing in the grate.

The only occupant was standing before the fire, his booted foot resting on the iron fender. I took an eager step into the room and heard the door lock behind me.

I span around to find Hester Jarrett smiling at me.

"Miss Pentreath, how very fortuitous that we should cross paths," said Baron Rosenberg, "It seems we are all going to London, no?"

I stood stock still, a rabbit amongst foxes. For once my enchanted eyeglasses worked perfectly and I knew immediately what I had done. In my impatience to find answers, I had walked right into a trap of my own making. It was in this moment that I knew I was going to have to be as wily as the foxes that had me cornered if I was to remain unscathed. And I knew, without doubt who Harry's *"esteemed colleague"* was and the indifferent lady who had *adopted* Rebecca was standing behind me blocking my escape route. And predictably I was the *"meddlesome creature"* who needed to be silenced.

I saw it all so clearly now as though veils had been lifted from my eyes — but I also knew it was too late.

* * *

Baron Rosenberg was all false geniality as though we were enjoying afternoon tea; I adopted an expression of mild disdain in order to cover the shock and the fear which I did not want to share. On no account was I going to allow him to see that I was terrified.

"Miss Pentreath, you have led us a merry dance. Your sudden flight caused us some consternation to begin with, but I must own that in the end it has very much turned to our advantage. 'Tis fortunate that I keep the very latest racing curricle for just such an occasion and that my driving skills are second to none. Of course, once I saw your direction, I knew what you were about. I realised it was only a matter of time before you happened upon the truth, or at least, some version of the truth. As luck would have it your precious Sir Montagu is not at hand either — really, it is as though the angels smile down upon our endeavours. I heard how he wrested you from the arms of Squire Tregallas; for a rather ineffectual sort of fellow, he has inadvertently managed to thwart several of my carefully laid plans. This time, I think, I have the upper hand."

Listening to this I was remaining outwardly calm whilst trying to think of some way to escape. Screaming for help did not seem to be an option; we were too far away from the public rooms and I was fairly sure a man famed for his duelling prowess would be able to overcome me in a matter of seconds.

"I have absolutely no clue to what you are referring, sir. You appear to be under the illusion that I am part of some sort of plan. I can assure that you are very much mistaken. I am merely in Exeter to find a suitable gown for the Masquerade, as frivolous as that might seem. We females will do anything to ensure we are the most fashionably dressed even if it requires enduring a few days of discomfort in a stagecoach and getting bitten by fleas in a coaching inn. You will have no doubt noticed that we are very vain."

He eyed me coldly, "Sit down, Miss Pentreath and have a glass of ratafia and something to eat, you must be famished." He gestured to the table where there were some dishes of food, some bottles and glasses. He poured a glass of the liqueur and handed it to me and pushed a plate of small pies towards me. I suddenly felt extremely hungry and took a pie, without thinking. The ratafia was sweet and delicious, fragrant and tasted of bitter almonds. I was grateful for it. Realising just how exhausted I was, I seated myself in a chair by the fire from which I could keep a wary eye on my captors.

Twenty-Nine

It was the smell that awoke me. And then a growing feeling of nausea which made my stomach churn. My head throbbed and my mouth was so dry I had difficulty swallowing. I tried to sit up but found I was unable move my limbs. For a while I lay still, trying to get my bearings. Above me, a ceiling, rafters, not much light; the stench, all pervading and unnameable but including human filth and possibly a nearby pig; noises, crying, groaning and sounds I couldn't identify. It all added up to despair, the sound and the smell of it. Whatever this place was, it was a place of suffering and desperation. I tried not to panic, keeping my breathing steady, and focusing on the fact that I was still alive.

I was lying on a thin mattress filled with straw and covered with a threadbare blanket. There were others in the room with me, but I couldn't see them, only hear the terrible sounds they made; the uneven breathing coming from my neighbour made me think they were not long for this world and somewhere on the other side of the room, someone was making repetitive sobbing noises like a small child would and lost in the general din there was a babble of words, nonsensical words without punctuation or end.

After a while - I have no idea how long exactly - I found I was able to move my arms a little, and with some effort managed to heave myself up into some sort of sitting position against the wall behind me. Even that slight amount of movement made my head reel and caused me to feel extremely nauseous. I felt far less vulnerable though and was able to gather my thoughts in order to rationalise what was happening to me.

The room was lit with two feeble rushlights in wall brackets, but no light came from the small window, which I could just make out was barred and shuttered. I couldn't tell what time of day it was. I had no idea how long I'd been there.

In the next bed there was nothing but a slight form under the coverings; I could only assume it was human. And beyond, only darkness and the interminable noises.

I tried to speak but was only able to make a sort of whisper. I cleared my throat and tried again.

"Is there — anybody there? Hello?" There was no answer, but the childlike sobbing ceased for a moment before starting again.

"Hello? Can — you speak?"

The sobbing paused, "I'm here," said a high female voice, "I'm here."

"My name is Martha," I told her, "Do — do you know where we are?"

"I'm here," she said again.

"Yes, I know, and I'm here too. Do you know where here is?"

"Madhouse."

"We're in a — madhouse? A lunatic asylum?"

No answer.

"But why? Why are we here?"

"I'm here," said the disembodied voice.

I realised I wasn't going to get very far with this conversation. I tried a different tack. "What's your name?", I asked.

"I think it used to be Patience. Before."

"Then — you are still Patience. 'Tis a pretty name. Why are you in this place?"

A slight pause, "My baby — she died. I cut all my hair off."

I heard a metallic rattling sound. "Patience? Are you chained to your bed?"

"I am. In case I try to escape again."

"Is escape possible?" I whispered.

"Only if you die," came the answer.

Time meant nothing. I have no idea how many hours passed and in the foul-smelling darkness knew only that I must somehow survive whatever this was. The effects of the drug the Baron had obviously given me had gradually worn off and I was able to think more clearly and move myself around on the bed. It was bone-chillingly cold, and the blanket provided little comfort. My companion had stopped communicating with me but the noises from the other inmates continued unabated.

At some point during that time a man and a woman came into the room and inspected everyone; the man was apparently a doctor of some sort and I heard him recommending bleeding and purges for someone. He came to look at me; he asked my name and then questioned the woman with him about why I had been committed.

I quickly replied, "I have been wrongfully confined, sir. I was kidnapped and have been shut away because they want to silence me. Please, if you apply to Sir Montagu Fitzroy of Kingsand in the county of Devon, he will vouch for me. Or my cousin, Miles Polgrey of Polgrey Hall — "

He stared at me, "Delusions. Cold baths."

Later still an elderly woman came with bowls of food, if you could call it that - torn bread in water. After she left, Patience roused herself enough to advise me to eat whatever they brought as I would need my strength. I had a hard time doing as she said even though my stomach was now grumbling with hunger. I took a few mouthfuls and then could eat no more.

More drugs were administered, a bitter tasting fluid which was forced down my throat. I didn't have the strength to fight them. I slept.

Then, I presume it was the next day, but I couldn't be sure; they took me to have a cold bath, wearing nothing but my shift. They threw buckets of cold water over me, until I shook convulsively and begged for them to stop. Nobody talked to me or listened to what I said.

As I lost track of time, I found myself drifting in and out of an endless nightmare and as my mind wandered, I tried desperately to hang onto something solid, to anchor myself in reality; I clung onto the idea of Sir Montagu's beautiful fingers stroking my palm and the feeling of his quizzing glass pressing against my chest and the ensuing kiss. I relived it over and over in my mind, using it as a shield to keep the growing fear at bay.

Whenever I could, I spoke to Patience and tried to encourage her to tell me about her life. She told me she had been married to a farmer in Okehampton and they had been happy until she found herself with child. She became increasingly disturbed at the thought of the impending labour, having lost her beloved sister to childbirth and when the time came had obviously had a difficult time, ending in the loss of her first-born child. The doctor had at first declared her to be melancholic and had suggested treatments of bleeding, brisk walks, and prayer but when Patience had chopped off her long hair the doctor had diagnosed her with acute mania, and they had locked her away. Her husband had fought the decision but under extreme pressure from the authorities had finally given in. I told her a little of my circumstances but found that her interest waned quickly, and she could not fully understand what I was saying.

Talking helped me remain calm. It was in those moments when I could hear that the others were asleep that my thoughts crowded in and I became confused.

The next visit from the doctor and his assistant brought a flurry of activity when they discovered the patient in the bed next to me had gone to meet her Maker. I hadn't even noticed that she had stopped making any noise. I found I was a glad for her. Her suffering was at an end. I was almost envious.

The smells grew ever more unbearable. They brought food but I couldn't eat it. They forced me to take more of the drug which made it impossible to move and made my mind sluggish.

I tried to sleep as much as possible, but it was difficult because day had become eternal night.

I woke up crying. I knew nobody would come for me. I would die in this room, in the dark, alone.

Patience was calling to me. "Martha? Are you here?"

I tried to answer but hardly had the strength to move my lips, "I'm — here," I whispered.

The darkness seeped into my head and I no longer felt hunger or sadness or hope.

I could feel myself fading away.

Time meant nothing.

* * *

"Martha! Wake up!" Patience's soft voice floated like mist around me. "Martha! *Listen!*"

I tried to do as she said and listen. There was no sound.

Then, somewhere, far off, I heard shouting.

Suddenly, there was a commotion, inexplicable noises and lights. Banging doors and a ferocious altercation nearby. The lights came nearer, and I felt a hand touch my face.

"Thank God," breathed a familiar lilting voice. Then, "Take the lantern! Here, give me a hand."

I was being lifted. I couldn't bear the thought. "No! Don't *touch* — me. *Please* — I'm filthy — " and I started to weep and feebly tried to evade his hold.

"I don't give a damn," he ground out, "Stop *fighting* me. You're safe now. I have you."

I was being carried at some speed through dark corridors; someone was being threatened with a certain and grisly death if they interfered with our progress. Sounds of a scuffle. There were other voices I vaguely recognised but I couldn't seem to open my eyes. I was so tired.

The chill of the night air hit me, and I must have fainted because the next thing I was aware of was being held tightly as the vehicle we were in moved fast across cobbled streets. There was hushed talking around me and I tried to place the voices, but nothing made sense. Then the sudden movement of the carriage began to make me feel ill.

"Uh oh," said a voice that I knew well, "She be goin' to cast up — "

"Be quiet, Jeckie, or I'll throw you out and you can find your own way back."

* * *

I remember only small snippets of the next few hours. Being held so close I could scarcely breathe. Carried like a child from the carriage into somewhere warm. Then, softness under me, warmth above. Some fiery liquid being dribbled between my cold, chapped lips. Someone stroking my matted hair.

I awoke with a cry.
Instantly, warm fingers touched my face, soothing.
A soft voice reassured. Told me what I needed to hear. I believed them.

I slept once more.

When I awoke again, it was still dark, the room dimly lit by candles and a fire in the hearth. It took me a moment to realise that I was not still imprisoned in that godforsaken place. It dawned on me that I was somewhere safe, and I started to cry again but when I was gathered into his arms, I attempted to push them away, "No! Don't! I can't bear — need to wash."

"Stop fighting me, Martha," the brogue was pronounced, his voice, hoarse and low.

The arms released me, and I felt bereft. The door opened, curt orders were given, the room was suddenly filled with movement and sound. Something heavy being moved, water being poured, people coming and going.

Some delightful fragrance filled the room, I think it was roses. And the air was heavy with steam. I was still half-asleep and acquiesced to being gently lifted and carried and lowered, still in my shift, into heavenly scented warm water.

Then the shift was being lifted and I obediently raised my arms and let it be pulled up and over my head and then allowed myself to slide down under the water, letting it cover me from top to toe. I wanted to stay under until I couldn't breathe anymore, until the water had washed me completely clean. I came up with a gasp and pushed the wet hair out of my face. I kept my eyes shut, too afraid to open them in case I found I was still back in that hell. Too afraid that if I could see him, the shame would catch up with me and overwhelm me. Just beneath the shield I was hiding behind was a flood of terrifying emotion and humiliation waiting to engulf me. I could feel it pushing at my frayed edges, hoping to demolish me piece by piece. I wouldn't let them win. I concentrated on this moment, on the warmth and the relief of knowing I was safe and protected.

The water splashed and a warm sponge slowly trailed down my back, reaching every part, my shoulders and neck and down my spine, my arms and my hips. A little pressure pushed me back against the end of the tub and with a shuddering sigh, I let myself relax. The sponge continued on its meandering way, over my breasts and stomach, under the water and slipped gently into areas which made me gasp again, this time with such a surge of pleasure, I felt hot tears mingling with the sweetly perfumed water. Then on it went, down my legs and finally to my feet, which curled away from the tickling sensation. There was a husky chuckle from my companion and his other hand firmly held me still while each foot was thoroughly washed.

Then, almond oil was rubbed into my hair, my head and scalp very efficiently massaged, and my hair combed through, easing out the knots. I exclaimed a few times as the comb got caught and my hair pulled a little but was told harshly to hush.

When all was done, I slid under the water again and came up clean. Still with my eyes tightly shut, I was helped to stand and step out of the tub and rather roughly dried. A clean shift was pulled over my head, I was guided to the bed where I collapsed, my knees shaking with weariness; my hair was loosely braided by inexpert hands and I rather weakly leant back against him while he struggled with my now unruly curls, he swore under his breath and then I was briskly tucked back between clean sheets.

He started to move away, paused, then came back to stand over me. I felt his nearness like the heat from the fire. He sat down on the bed, slid his hands under my back, I could feel the heat of them through the thin material of my shift and then his mouth covered mine in a kiss which lingered, revealing anger and relief, tenderness and superhuman control.

I didn't open my eyes until the door had closed behind him.

Thirty

The journey home was a blur, I barely noticed what went on around me. I was still feeling utterly exhausted and shaky but was now able to drift in and out of sleep without being scared of either state. I felt his continued presence beside me and found it comforting and yet a little unnerving at the same time. I found my emotions were a bit tangled and because I was so tired, I felt it was probably best not to try and sort them out until later. So, I closed my eyes and gave myself up to peaceful slumber. I came to when they were changing the horses at one of the coaching inns *en route* and found that I was lying curled up on the carriage seat under a warm rug, my head in his lap, his hand gently resting on my waist. For a moment, I thought I should sit up and behave with some kind of suitable decorum and then thought that it was a little too late for bowing to convention. I must have let out a small laugh because his hand moved to my shoulder and gently squeezed, reassuringly. I reached for his hand and put it firmly back on my waist, holding it, until the movement of the carriage lulled me into sleep once more.

* * *

Then it was night-time again and I found myself in my own bed and Eleanor and Fanny were there. And I could hear my two older cousins quarrelling loudly, Lucius swearing and Miles reasoning. Miles came and hugged me until I thought my ribs would break and Lucius berated me for being a thoughtless halfwit, which made Eleanor admonish him for his lack of sensitivity, while Fanny explained how she was going to kill my kidnappers with her bare hands when she caught up with them.

And, just as suddenly, they were all being removed from the room and there was just me and him.

I opened my eyes and looked up at him and couldn't help a rush of embarrassment staining my cheeks.

"I — I don't know how to thank you. You saved my life."

"You led me quite a dance, Martha Pentreath. There was a time there when — " he paused, looked away, "I thought — " The brogue was strong.

"How did you find me?"

He smiled, "You are most fortunate to have very loyal and persistent friends. Eleanor found your note and deduced that you had gone upon one of your harum-scarum adventures. She didn't like the sound of it and told Miles and Lucius. John overheard as they were planning to chase after you and suggested I should be informed. As luck would have it, I was just returned from — my own little adventure and I was easily found as John discovered Colquite having a quick ale in the Cremill Arms. Because you left a trail, hiring a sedan chair and buying a ticket for the stagecoach, we were able to follow in your footsteps; once in Exeter a red-waistcoated fellow staying at the White Hart remembered you *very* well and the landlady recalled the couple who had been seen with you there. I blame myself for giving you the pertinent information — I should have damn well known better. It was to our benefit that your kidnappers are rather memorable and his curricle, unmistakable. We were able to ascertain their direction after a few miscalculations and using nothing more complicated than brute force and outnumbering them, we — found you."

"Patience!" I suddenly exclaimed.

"I'm afraid I don't have much," said he, frowning.

"No! Poor Patience, she is an inmate in the madhouse. I cannot leave her there. She must be set free. Can you — ?"

He sighed and shook his head, "Really Martha, another lame duck? Must you collect them wherever you go?" He smiled, "Patience? Does she have a surname?"

"Oh, I am so stupid, I didn't ask! But she was married to a farmer in Oakhampton and lost her baby, poor thing."

"I will do my best then to find her. You have my word. I am blessed to have a leading judge in my pocket; he might be able to obtain her release without too much fuss."

"That would set my mind at rest, thank you."

"Now, against my better judgement and against the wishes of your friends and vociferous relations, I am going to have to ask you if you are well enough to attend Lady Polgrey's damned Masquerade tomorrow?"

"Tomorrow? Is it already Twelfth Night? How can that be?"

"Because you have been Sleeping Beauty this last week and have not noticed the days passing. If you can bear the idea of putting in an appearance at the wretched ball, I can assure you that not only will you be watched over at all times, but you will hopefully be a witness to the conclusion of this terrible series of events."

"Well, I have no idea what you're alluding to, but I will do as you wish. 'Tis the least I can do. I believe I will be perfectly well."

"You do not have to stay for the whole affair as I am sure it will be long and tedious, and you are not yet sufficiently recovered. But, with guardians to keep you safe, I feel certain that your appearance would be unexpected enough in some quarters as to give us a welcome advantage."

"Well, in that case, it would be churlish to refuse."

"How are you feeling now? Strong?"

"Indeed, stronger by the minute."

"Good. I will be back in a moment. Don't go to sleep again in the meantime." He met my eyes as though assessing me. I regarded him with what I hoped was a steady gaze. He nodded and left the room.

A few minutes later, slow and considered footsteps approached up the stairs. The door opened and there was Captain Cavanagh, accompanied by Eleanor and Fanny and somewhere out of sight, Miles and Lucius.

The Captain advanced into the room, carrying some sort of parcel, or bundle of clothes. I sat up in bed and prepared to receive another gift probably to wear at the Masquerade.

As he transferred it into my arms, it moved a little and for the first time I felt the solid weight of her against me; I buried my face into her soft, sweet-smelling neck and sobbed silently.

"I *told* you she wasn't ready," said Miles furiously.

"She's ready. This will help," said Eleanor calmly.

"Yes, shut up Miles. What would you know about such things anyway? You've never shown any interest in babies at all — ever!" sniped Lucius.

"Oh, and I suppose you *have*! What an utter dolt! Youngest female you've ever taken an interest in was that opera singer — I say, take your damned hands off me!"

Eleanor serenely stepped between the warring brothers and separated them, "This is neither the time nor the place! Miles, pull yourself together and Lucius? — we shall discuss the opera singer at a later date."

"Dash it, Miles, now look what you've done!" exclaimed Lucius. "Fallen at the first hurdle."

"I have no doubt there will be many more insurmountable problems yet to come," said Eleanor wisely.

Liam Cavanagh sat on the edge of the bed and gently raised my head up and I made an attempt to stop crying as I looked at the face of my sister for the first time.

Her eyes were open, and she was looking back at me.

"Rebecca," I whispered.

She was small for her age and unnaturally quiet, not a sound did she make, not a gurgle or cry. I knew it to be unusual and glanced up at Fanny, "Is she — ?"

"She be fine, Martha. She been through a lot an' hasn't had a chance to be an ordinary baby. She be bit underfed an' she don't yet try to sit up but given time — "

I gazed into the eyes of my mother's child and wondered at those eyes, one so dark and peaty brown, the other a bright icy blue. I pushed back the blanket wrapped around her face and revealed her hair; jet black and streaked with white from her forehead. I was a little startled because against her delicate pink skin, it seemed such a jarring contrast. I stroked her tiny nose and when she wrinkled it, I began to cry again.

"Do'ee want me to take her?" asked Fanny.

"No, thank you, I shall never let her go now," I sniffed, "What about a wet-nurse? Is she weaned?"

"No, not completely. Captain Cavanagh has brought a young wet-nurse from Exeter an' she will stay with Rebecca 'til she be properly weaned."

I met Liam Cavanagh's eyes, "How on earth did you find her?"

"Discovering her whereabouts was the easy part frankly. Once we had established who had taken her, we were able to extract the information from one of the culprits, who put up very little resistance once he knew he was, as that rapscallion Jeckie would so succinctly put it, *in the basket.*"

"Who was it?"

"I'm sorry to tell you that it was your damnable cousin, Harry."

"I could murder him!" raged Lucius. Eleanor's delicate hand on his arm silenced him.

"Harry? *He* was the man with Aunt Louisa who pretended to adopt Rebecca?"

"Yes, I'm afraid so. He has willingly betrayed his cohorts and tomorrow we will have our revenge in more ways than one. It promises to be quite a night. I hope you are up to it, Martha," said the Captain.

"I am ready for anything now. Now, I have Rebecca I could face the very devil himself."

Liam Cavanagh smiled, "Hopefully it won't come to that. I was only just returned from retrieving her from where she had been placed by the Foundling Hospital, when I heard that you had disappeared. I am only sorry that I could not have known this as I came back through Exeter. I could have found you sooner — "

"You could not possibly have guessed. 'Tis a miracle that you found me at all. I thought — " I stopped, the horror of what might have happened had he not been able to find me fleetingly overwhelmed me but suddenly there was a movement from the bundle and a small pink fist popped out of the swaddling blanket and opened like a starfish. I put my finger into it and her fingers curled around it tightly. I looked up at the man beside me and beamed at him. "Look! She's holding my hand."

"One can hardly blame her," murmured the Captain.

I blushed and returned my gaze to the extraordinary wonder that was my infant sister.

* * *

That night Eleanor and Fanny set up a makeshift cot by my bed, made from a large laundry basket on a box, and Rebecca slept beside me. Fanny made a bed for herself by the fire so that she could call the hired wet-nurse if necessary. Rebecca had still not made a sound, but Fanny reassured me that any small child would take a while to find her voice again especially after the ordeal she had suffered.

I found it hard to get to sleep because I was listening to Rebecca breathe. If there was a slight falter in the rhythm I sat up and peered at her to make sure she was all right. Fanny eventually told me I was making mountains out of molehills and to stop bothering the poor little mite.

* * *

Twelfth Night was finally upon us and after a rather slow start to the morning, where we all stood around and watched Rebecca a good deal too much and got to know the new wet-nurse, Jenny, we began to realise that we didn't have long as the Masquerade started at five o'clock. Lucius had surprised Eleanor by asking her to accompany him and she had flown into a panic over what to wear. Happily, we found the perfect gown of rose silk for her in my mother's linen press and she was able to quickly replace the cream lace at the neck and sleeves with silver instead to make it look as good as new. Lucius thoughtfully acquired a silver-grey domino from Rowena without her noticing and left it at Wild Court that morning and Eleanor made herself a domino mask from the silver lace to complete her costume.

My bedchamber became a whirl of silk and feathers and drifts of hair powder as Fanny helped lace us into our gowns and dressed our hair.

The gown Sir Montagu had sent fitted me beautifully and when I saw myself in the looking glass, I have to admit I was taken aback by my reflection. I hardly recognised myself.

Eleanor eyes opened wide, "Oh, Martha! 'Tis perfect. It looks as though you are swathed in the night sky. I have never seen anything so exquisite. Nobody will recognise you with your hair powdered and that mask. Look how the little stars quiver in your hair, 'tis so clever! You look like a nocturnal goddess." She tweaked the skirts of my gown, "He was quite right to instruct you to powder because it would have revealed your identity as sure as if you had your name on your forehead! Let us fix your mask in place now and that will disguise your freckles."

Once I was safely corseted and laced, masked, bejewelled, and powdered, and they had cleverly hidden the dark shadows under my eyes, Fanny finished Eleanor's toilette for her and we both agreed she looked like a damask rose, the deep pink brought colour to her pale cheeks and set off her golden hair to perfection.

Finally, I perched on the edge of the bed and lifting my voluminous skirts, I pushed my feet into the extraordinary mules with their shocking scarlet heels. I pointed my toes and admired them with mischievous delight; if my aunt caught sight of those wicked heels, I would be turned out of the Polgrey Hall immediately! It was bad enough that my gown shimmered when according to mourning convention it should have been made of material with no lustre at all. Sir Montagu clearly had no sense of propriety and was willing to flout the rules of acceptable behaviour whenever it suited him even if it meant that I was shunned by the whole county for my immoderate conduct. I twisted the indecent little heels this way and that, so they caught the light and decided I didn't care.

* * *

Fanny was to stay behind with Jenny and Rebecca while Jem would stand guard over them, armed with my pistol.

Miles was sending Jenkyns in the Polgrey carriage to collect us and I found I was as nervous as a kitten. Eleanor had to remind me that I was not recovered from my ordeal and said it was hardly surprising that my legs were like jelly. Eleanor seemed to be quite sanguine about the whole affair and when questioned about her enviable serenity she explained that she knew Lucius would be there to guide and protect her. That set me to wondering and I was thrown into an even worse state of confusion by my disordered thoughts.

I kissed my sister goodbye, and Eleanor and I were handed into the carriage by a most unusually punctilious Jem. We tucked the fur blankets around us and chatted uncertainly about the night ahead and about how curious it was to have a child living with us at Wild Court.

Our carriage joined a slow-moving procession of vehicles wending their way towards Polgrey Hall. The driveway was lit with lanterns hanging on poles and every window in the house glowed yellow. My aunt had obviously spared no expense in hiring extra staff as there were liveried footman at every turn, all eager to help in any way they could, or just stand staring into space like statues.

The carriages disgorged an endless stream of illustrious persons who could claim to be part of the local *haut monde,* and they were slowly making their way up the steps and into the house.

Eleanor and I exchanged wide-eyed glances as we joined the throng of guests swarming towards the wide front doors. We reached the top and suddenly there was Lucius, easily recognisable even though masked, splendid in dark grey and silver, the small portion of his face we could see wreathed in unaccustomed smiles, mainly for Eleanor. They stood gazing at each other for so long that I coughed discreetly to remind them to be on their guard whilst under such close scrutiny. Lucius was expounding on Eleanor's radiant beauty when Miles arrived and taking my hand, he escorted our little group into the Great Hall.

Thirty-One

The Great Hall was a wonder to behold. A cacophony of sounds assaulted the senses first; the chattering voices made a sort of deep rumbling murmur punctuated by sharp exclamations, effusive greetings and laughter with a background of lively music coming from the orchestra in the minstrel's gallery. The sound of swishing silk as they all curtsied and bowed at each other reminded me of waves on the shore.

Then one's eyes had to cope with the hundreds of candles in the chandeliers and sconces, the huge room was ablaze with golden light which sparkled and gleamed on the myriad jewels decorating the guests. And then came a sensual wave of warm scents, floral and spicy and the everyday smell of humanity *en masse,* mingling with food, rich wines, and candle smoke. It was like nothing I had ever experienced before.

Amongst the crush of people, there were those I could recognise even though they were masked; Aunt Louisa, haughty in heliotrope brocade, holding court, greeting a line of eager locals with cool self-satisfaction and there was Uncle Joshua looking lost and confused and Rowena, in cherry red with a black mask, her dark hair unpowdered, resembling a Spanish señorita; she was surrounded by a group of young gallants in dark dominos and masks who all looked unmistakably military in their bearing.

As we made our way further into the crowd, we saw goddesses and shepherdesses, nuns and Ottoman Turks, dairymaids and Harlequins, and Miles mockingly pointed out Queen Elizabeth I with a ruff so large she was barely able to get her glass safely to her mouth. Above the sea of people, ostrich feathers nodded soundlessly, like smoke.

Eyes followed me, people conferred trying to guess my identity, whispering behind their hands; they bowed and nodded but I could see that my disguise was foolproof. I felt strangely invincible, my beautiful gown swirling around me like stormy clouds. Lucius was making wicked comments *sotto voce* about some of the costumes and snorted with laughter at some poor lady dressed, we assumed, as Aphrodite, a fake dove perched in her wig and the gown rather too diaphanous for someone of her advanced years. Eleanor tapped his arm sharply with her fan and after that he tried, wholly unsuccessfully, to keep his unchivalrous opinions to himself.

It was difficult for me to see very far ahead past the wall of revellers and I was concentrating on making sure nobody stepped on the trailing hem of my costume.

Just as I was wondering which direction to take, the barrier of people parted in front of me and there immediately ahead of me was a solitary figure standing at the edge of the room, observing my progress. He wore a long, black domino cloak, the hood draped about his face, a black tricorne and full-face gold Bauta mask, a sword dangling from his hip. Beneath the cloak I caught a glimpse of black satin with elaborate golden embroidery and the hard sparkle of diamonds. He leant against the linen-fold panelling, white stockinged legs crossed at the ankle, the very picture of nonchalance.

I stopped and stared, uncertain. Then, my heart skipped a beat as his long fingers idly strayed to a gilt button on his waistcoat, undid it, then did it up again.

I didn't hesitate. I pushed my way through the crowd towards him, ruthlessly elbowing a portly Tartaglia out of my path when he wouldn't give way and sliding inelegantly between various other characters who stood between me and my objective.

I reached him slightly out of breath and suddenly not quite as sure as I had been. He cocked his head at me and straightening up, made the most elegant leg. I curtsied low, my inky black skirts billowing.

"Well met, fair *Nyx*," drawled the oh, so familiar voice, softly. "Goddess of the Night. You are lookin' radiant — as ever."

"Only thanks to you, Sir Montagu! I cannot believe — will never be able to — "

He raised a beautiful hand, "There truly is no need, m'dear. Happy to oblige. Knew it'd be fetchin' once you were wearing it. Causin' quite a stir too, I see." His impassive golden mask nodded vaguely over my shoulder and I peered behind me discreetly, to see a man in a smiling, black full-face mask and black cloak apparently looking in my direction. "Seems you are turnin' heads, Linnet, as I knew you would. Although, I'm not at all sure I approve."

I cast him an impudent look under my eyelashes knowing that the black lace mask protected me somewhat from his languid but all-seeing gaze. "But Sir Montagu, you only have yourself to blame. I am but the ivory statue to your Pygmalion. You can do with me what you will."

His sharp intake of breath made me smile up at him innocently.

"Martha," he said silkily, "Don't you *dare* — just because you are in disguise — you cannot behave like one of the doxies at Vauxhall Gardens — "

I pouted saucily, "La! I am sure I have no idea what you mean, sir."

He leant closer, the candlelight glittering on his mask, "Miss Pentreath, you are playin' with fire, I would be *very* careful if I were you."

I laughed, enjoying myself immensely. I fluttered my fan coquettishly, "I am not at all well acquainted with the ways of the world but find that I am suddenly more than willing to learn."

He made a low sound in his throat, and reaching out, drew me in, holding me tightly against him, I gasped from a heady mix of fear and excitement, biting my lip, wondering just how far I could play this thrilling game without finding myself in serious trouble.

I found myself enfolded in his cloak, his warmth permeating my gown, his hand hard in the small of my back, pinning me; I could hear his rough breathing and realised I had no intention of pulling away or fighting. I pressed myself against the length of his body, looking up at him all the while. Daring him. Taunting him. Realising that I had some kind of primeval power over him was exhilarating. I felt giddy, triumphant, my heart was racing in my chest and I could barely breathe.

I wasn't aware of anything else, the revellers faded away, the noise no more than a distant murmur; we were in a world of our own.

"Devil take it, you shameless minx! I'll make you pay for this night's work, mark my words." His voice was ragged and no more than a whisper.

I laughed and reached up to touch his mask, "You could take this off — "

He pulled away, "Not now, m'dear. The night is yet young and I suspect you are merely bewitched by the excitement of the evenin'."

Slowly the world drifted back in around us and we were returned to the Masquerade with all its boisterous tumult, once again surrounded and buffeted by the loud and rather obnoxious merrymakers. As he released me and I reluctantly moved away from him, he stroked a fingertip gently over my lips — it was like a kiss. I shivered and quickly turned my back on him in case I betrayed the true depths of my feelings.

* * *

He didn't abandon me but escorted me to where my cousins were gathered together with Eleanor. Rowena had joined them, Lieutenant Danserfield at her elbow and beside Miles, a pretty little shepherdess dithered, awkwardly brandishing a shepherd's crook. I didn't recognise her until she spoke then realised that it was Kitty Anstey. An Elizabethan gentleman, possibly Henry VIII, whom I took to be Edmund Anstey, was chatting animatedly with Lucius about horse racing and the perils of riding to hounds. I thought it to be an extremely dull conversation so chatted with Eleanor instead; she gave me quite a look, her eyes wide and amused. I blushed furiously, understanding that despite the volume of people shielding us, my wanton behaviour had been noted.

"Where is Harry?", I asked, in order to change the subject.

"Miles says he's gone to ground. He knows there will be a reckoning for what he did. Lucius asked him why he did it and he replied that he was bored." She shook her head, "Silly boy. Spoilt and lazy. And without scruples."

"I think his accident was the turning point. He was never the same after that."

"You are too generous, Martha."

* * *

A little later I saw Sir Montagu in conversation with a tall gentleman, in the simplest costume of cloak and mask, they looked to be discussing something of importance and I watched them for a moment wondering what could be so urgent.

When Kitty Anstey was barged into by an intoxicated monk, I was pleased to see that Miles jumped immediately to her defence, seeing off the swaying friar with some pithy words; Kitty beamed up at him as though he were a knight in armour.

There was dancing, exuberant country dances and sedate minuets; the participants stimulated by some excellent wine and vast quantities of champagne, entered into the spirit of it all with unbridled enthusiasm, the ladies flinging up their skirts and kicking out their dainty feet as they circled their partners. There were several accidents as trains got caught under heels and the drunken monk staggered into the midst of the dancers, throwing them off their complicated steps, he apologised profusely but incoherently, bowing so low he nearly toppled over and then continued on his way through the centre of the dance, causing havoc as he went.

The gentleman in the smiling mask sauntered up to our little group and asked Rowena if he could have the next dance but she was far too enamoured with the Lieutenant to be persuaded to leave. I thought she was rather dismissively rude to him so when he then asked me, I felt obliged to accept. As he led me out, I caught Sir Montagu looking in our direction and sensed some tension in him and then just as we began our first steps, I noticed him talking with a couple of the military types who had earlier been Rowena's satellites.

My partner didn't converse as we danced, the movements of the dance making it difficult and for that I was grateful because under cover of my mask I was able to observe some interesting manoeuvres in the crowd.

At the end of the dance, he bowed, I curtsied, and as I was about to thank him, there was a slight commotion amongst the guests. I made to step away from him, but he snatched at my hand, holding me fast by his side.

"Sir! I beg you will let me go at once." I said as calmly as I could, trying to pull my hand free. He paid no mind to me, his attention firmly fixed upon Sir Montagu and the growing circle of gentlemen gathering at the edge of the assembled onlookers. The guests were slowly becoming aware that something unusual was happening and they were beginning to take an interest. Conversation was dying down and although the music still meandered along in the background, an eerie hush was falling in the Great Hall.

The smiling man tightened his grip on my wrist, his fingers digging into my flesh. I felt the desperation in him, and my heart quailed as finally I recognised him and because I knew that desperation would make him even more unpredictable. I tried harder to escape by pulling at the strong fingers around my wrist but to no avail.

I frantically searched the sea of masks for a golden one and found it. He was slowly advancing, his cloak thrown back to reveal his sword. He was within a few steps when my captor said clearly, "Come any nearer and I will kill her."

"That would be extremely foolhardy. It cannot have escaped your notice that you are surrounded, Baron? There is nowhere for you to go. 'Tis over. You have shown your hand, very nicely, although, perhaps, a little earlier than expected. Gilles?"

At this, the tall gentleman Sir Montagu had been talking with earlier stepped forward and removed his mask. I felt the Baron stiffen beside me. It was Monsieur de Thou, the man I had suspected was a spy.

"*Bonsoir, Monsieur le Baron. On se revoit.* I have been waiting a long time for this day. *Enfin*, we find you and now we will be avenged. Murderer. *Traître*. *Et maintenant,* you have been betrayed by your own; Harry Polgrey and Monsieur Fairchild have given information against you. *Alors*, for the murder of Madame Pezzack and Madame Vida Pentreath — "

A shout went up, there were several cries from the crowd and a few surged forward but were held back by the ring of gentlemen at the front. I caught a glimpse of my aunt's face amongst the spectators, she was ashen and staring fixedly at the Baron.

I felt faint. I couldn't seem to take in what was happening. I swayed a little and Sir Montagu took a step towards me.

Baron Rosenberg drew his sword in one easy movement and stopped Sir Montagu in his tracks.

Someone shouted, "Have a care, he's a duellist!"

My startled gaze flew to Sir Montagu who, of course, knew exactly what he was up against. I remembered hearing that Baron Rosenberg was a master swordsman, famously unvanquished in duels.

Sir Montagu slowly drew his own sword, "We will fight, dear Baron, *if* we must, not because you betrayed this country, or because you have been so very willin' to murder innocent people who get in your way but because you kidnapped and imprisoned Miss Pentreath — in the hopes that she would no longer be such an impediment to you — and also, an innocent newborn child, her sister, Rebecca Pentreath."

There was a shattering scream from somewhere and a scuffle in the crowd, then silence. Everyone was waiting, expectantly.

"You cannot hide behind her. Release her. I think we will now discover why you were so keen to dispose of the very inconvenient evidence, yes?"

Without warning, Sir Montagu lunged, and I found myself suddenly liberated and pushed carelessly to one side by the Baron. Miles and Lucius were there dragging me back out of harm's way.

Baron Rosenberg's sword arced through the air, Sir Montagu evaded it and backed away. With a gesture of impatience, the Baron ripped his cloak off and tore at his mask, throwing them aside, followed swiftly by his wig.

As the Baron span to face Sir Montagu, Lucius let out a volley of astounded curses. We saw for the first time that the Baron was no longer wearing his customary eyepatch. The scar from the sabre slashed over his brow and down onto his cheek. His eyes, startlingly different — one light blue, the other dark brown.

"Devil a bit! Look at his hair!" exclaimed Miles.

"We see now why he was so keen to be rid of the child," said Lucius grimly.

Those who had seen my sister understood at once — Baron Rosenberg was, beyond doubt, Rebecca's father. They suffered from the same strange affliction, the eyes, the hair, it was unmistakeable.

My whole body shook as though fevered and I looked to Sir Montagu who was advancing again. He paused and with an ironic little bow to me, he too removed his disguise.

"I'll be damned," said Lucius, under his breath.

Captain Liam Cavanagh saluted us by raising his sword and then turned to face his opponent.

"Martha!", someone shouted, and I felt arms supporting me, preventing me from sliding senseless to the ground.

The sharp clash of steel on steel, the stinging hiss as the blades slid against each other, the thumping sound of heels on ancient tiles, the grunts and exclamations; it seemed to go on forever.

Everything I knew was in ruins.

I watched them as though sleepwalking. I watched the man I loved fighting for his life. But I didn't know him. It seems I had never known him. I couldn't stop reliving moments with him and seeing them with new eyes — now all I had were lies.

The crowd gasped as Baron Rosenberg steadily advanced, cut and thrust, cut and thrust, forcing Liam Cavanagh back against the panelling, the guests scattering in a mad flurry of skirts and fluttering cloaks to find safety but retain a good vantage point. The Captain parried, narrowly avoiding the downward slice of the sword against his shoulder. Rosenberg was clearly the finer swordsman, but the Captain had an advantage in height and stamina. Then, they were battling hand-to-hand, locked together, Baron Rosenberg struggling to get his sword free and Liam Cavanagh trying desperately to gain the upper hand.

Suddenly, a few feet away from us, a female in bright canary yellow and a towering wig, forced her way through what was now resembling a human barricade, but they held her back, she screamed abuse at them and fought like a hellcat. I recognised her. She tried to shake off those restraining her, pulling this way and that, her wig toppled to the ground, revealing a shock of dyed red hair.

And in that moment when her captors were momentarily distracted, she threw herself forward, breaking free of their grasping hands.

I don't really know what happened next, I couldn't see clearly but the bystanders nervously drew back to reveal Hester Jarrett brandishing a pistol.

She was aiming it in the direction of the two fighting men. I knew who she was hoping to injure.

I knew.

She wasn't far away. I didn't even have time to think, I flew at her, full-tilt and knocked her arm just as she fired.

There was a loud report which echoed around the Great Hall and I saw the shocked faces around me.

Filled with the greatest fear imaginable I turned to see what everyone was looking at.

People were cautiously edging forward, blocking my view. Lucius grabbed me and pushed me through the excited rabble, threatening those who didn't move out of the way fast enough with all kinds of terrible violence.

There was someone lying on the floor, crumpled, bleeding.

"*Liam!*" someone screamed. It was my voice. I fought my way through, sobbing and flung myself down beside the body.

Lucius was next to me, "Martha, it's not Liam, it's Rosenberg. Martha, for God's sake, listen to me! It's *not* Liam."

I could see the plain dark frock coat, stained even darker with blood and the black hair with the white streak at the forehead. I could see but couldn't believe it.

Strong arms were lifting me. I was being held against a black and gold waistcoat. I breathed in heavenly sandalwood. I put my arms about his waist and cried into his chest.

I could feel his warm breath on my neck. I could feel his rapid heartbeat under my cheek.

"You saved my life," he whispered, the brogue intense and lilting. "That shot was meant for me." His arms were wrapped tightly around me, and I felt so safe and yet — and yet —

I pulled away from that haven, pushing my hands against his chest. He reluctantly let me go.

Looking up at him, the tears still storming down my face, I shook my head, trying to find the words, "Who — are you?"

He reached for my hand, but I snatched it away.

"I can explain. I didn't want to deceive you."

"Who *are* you?"

"Sir William Montagu Dracot Cavanagh Fitzroy, 6th Baronet," he said, looking hard at me, "County Galway. Anglo-Norman. Naval officer." He sighed, "It's complicated."

Around us the soldiers who had formed the barricade were removing their masks and cloaks, they were guiding and organising, making sure that everyone left the Hall in an orderly fashion.

Lieutenant Danserfield had taken charge with commendable efficiency. The body of Baron Rosenberg had been covered with a cloak; Hester Jarrett was being questioned and nearby Aunt Louisa was weeping into her handkerchief whilst being led away by two Dragoons.

Eleanor was next to me, looking concerned and Lucius had his arm protectively about her waist. Miles and Kitty were talking quietly together, and Rowena was hovering nearby, pale and frightened. Gilles de Thou was pacing nearby, clearly impatient to talk to Captain Cavanagh.

"You'd better go. They need you," I told him flatly.

"Martha — "

Eleanor took my arm and led me away from him. As I passed Rowena I reached out and took her hand, she squeezed my fingers convulsively. "Miles! Look after your sister!"

Eleanor found a way through the dwindling crowd to a window seat. We sat together, holding hands, trembling, not speaking.

Around us, chaos.

Gilles de Thou and Liam Cavanagh supervised the removal of Baron Rosenberg's body by the soldiers. Lucius had discovered poor Uncle Joshua somewhere and was comforting him as best he could and slowly the Polgrey staff appeared and started clearing up.

The orchestra had given up and were packing up their instruments and making their way out into the night, a good deal earlier than planned.

Everything was strangely muffled, voices kept low and movements carefully considered.

My mind didn't seem to be working at all. I felt dead inside. I looked down at my beautiful gown, the jet beads still gleaming forlornly in the candlelight, the clouds of black silk shot with indigo — I had had such hopes and now they were in tatters and the gown was just another disguise that had only worked for a while. And perhaps, in the end, it had only fooled me.

Tears started to slide down my face again and Eleanor put her arm around me.

"Martha, my love, what do you want to do? Shall I get Lucius to send for the carriage?"

I wiped my face on my petticoat and tried to pull myself together. "I truly don't know. I suppose we should return to Wild Court. To Rebecca."

Eleanor nodded, "Well, I can't see that we are needed here. They seem to have everything in hand. I'll go and tell Lucius."

Lucius's face lit up when he saw her approach and I was glad that there was still some happiness to be found amongst all the despair.

A shadow fell over me and I looked up into Liam Cavanagh's exhausted face.

"Martha, will you hear me now? I must explain."

I said nothing.

He sat beside me on the window seat.

"You must understand that I had no intention of lying to you in the beginning, but I was involved in a plot already in progress, sanctioned by the government to stop Rosenberg from selling state secrets. He was suspected to be spying for the French, but it was hard to prove. The French are, as we speak, amassing their troops and making the politicians extremely uneasy. Relations between our countries are strained at the moment and Newcastle's ministry has been working to stall what looks like plans for an invasion. Lord Anson, First Lord of the Admiralty, particularly desired that we protect our shores and Gilles, under our auspices, was certain there was an undercover operative working here. Unfortunately, we had no idea at the time that Rosenberg had become embroiled with — Vida — and was so ruthlessly disposing of everyone who might stand in his path to glory. It seems that your impetuous exploits distracted him enough to make him let down his guard and make some unaccustomed errors. He momentarily took his eye off the prize."

He rubbed his hand across his eyes, and I felt a brief wave of sympathy.

"Gilles had had dealings with him in France and therefore had to be smuggled into England so that he could confirm his findings and force the Baron's hand. My initial part was to intercept dispatches which is why I was posing as a smuggler, it made it easier. And, in my other guise, to work my way into his circle and find out what I could from the inside. I happily played the fool and aroused no suspicion. All went according to plan until, regretfully, your mother became a victim of his machinations and you were forced to return ahead of time. It complicated matters. You certainly did your best to divert my attention."

I glanced up at him and saw his lips curve in a slightly bitter smile.

"For a while I began to wonder if you were colluding with the Baron but was soon made aware that you were just inclined to fall regularly into scrapes because of your impulsive nature. It made my job all the more difficult. I have to say my powers of concentration have been severely tested. Your father took me in, in the beginning, knowing what my objective was; he made it possible for me to infiltrate Rosenberg's inner circle, both here and in London. Unfortunately, Vida became yet another victim of Rosenberg's inexplicable but deadly fascination — we could not have foreseen that. And Hester Jarrett seems to have been her final undoing, plying her with minute amounts of poison, probably Pennyroyal, which eventually killed her, the same way that Nell Pezzack died. They hoped to abort the child, but your sister was determined to live. Hester would have done anything for Rosenberg. In her own way, she too was a victim of his thrall. The poisoning looked, at first, like childbed fever so suspicions were not immediately aroused. Luckily, Nell thought to tell you what she knew before she finally succumbed, however, this brought you to the fore and made you a very obvious target. It also precipitated you into a search for your sister, which as we know might have ended very differently. I did my utmost to keep watch over you, but I have to admit that your behaviour was, at times, wholly unpredictable and strained both my patience and resources."

The Hall was almost empty now, just a few soldiers and footmen lingered. The candles burned low and a few guttered before going out. I wondered what Mrs Talbot and Meggie were doing. Miles had escorted Kitty Anstey out to her carriage and Lucius, having ordered our carriage was waiting with Eleanor beside the main door.

"We kept your release from the asylum a secret because we knew, if it was known abroad, that Rosenberg would realise the game was finally up and try to flee. We were waiting for him to recognise you and realise his plans had come unstuck and try to make his escape — when you somewhat hastened our plans by accepting his invitation to dance. It put you in a dangerously vulnerable position and I had no choice but to challenge him. We had no idea that Hester Jarrett would do as she did or that you would — be foolish enough to risk your life — to stop her." His voice was husky with emotion, the telltale brogue pronounced.

I stood up without looking at him. He caught my hand in his and I allowed my cold fingers to rest in his briefly before gently pulling away.

As I walked away from him, my heart broke.

Thirty-Two

The next few days passed without me noticing. I had been put to bed by Eleanor the night of the fated Masquerade and there I stayed.

It was as though my mind couldn't cope with the recent events and my body, weakened by the days in the asylum, decided that it could take no more. Even as I found myself unable to move or to think clearly, I was aware that I was slowly turning into Letitia Tregallas. I lay all day and most of the night staring at the canopy of my bed.

A very subdued Fanny brought me delicious dishes of food which I could barely eat, and Eleanor brought Rebecca for me to hold hoping to anchor me. I stared down into her peculiar little face and wondered what was to become of us all.

Miles and Lucius visited and spent the time bickering about trivial things, horses and dogs and what they'd had for dinner.

Solomon brought me a little bouquet of primroses, tied with the same green satin ribbon that had been tied about the box containing the gown.

"I don't know what they are called, these little flowers but they reminded me of you. They are pretty and extremely brave and persistent even in such inclement weather. I found them in the woods."

I held the flowers and wept.

Solomon was distraught that his gift should make me so upset and I couldn't tell him that it was the sight of the green ribbon that had pierced my carefully constructed armour.

After a few days had passed thus, there was a timid knock on my bedchamber door. Eleanor, who had been reading to me, jumped up and opened the door.

Rowena stepped hesitantly into the room. Eleanor showed her to the chair beside my bed and my cousin perched nervously on the edge of it, as though poised for flight.

She cleared her throat delicately, "I expect you wonder why I am come? Indeed, I too wonder but felt compelled to see you." She coughed again, "I know we have not always seen eye-to-eye, but you *are* my cousin and after the night of the Masquerade I have begun to consider that I have perhaps been, at times, a little — unkind — "

"Heartless," suggested Eleanor helpfully.

"Indeed — heartless, thank you, Miss Fairchild. *Heartless*, in my dealings with you, for which I am — "

"*Heartily* sorry?" Eleanor again.

"Well, yes, that is so. I am. Sorry. I never meant — I am afraid I have realised — Lucius has been at pains to *point out*, that I am shallow and weak-minded, and that Mama had too much of an influence upon the way I behaved, and I wasn't brave like you Martha — I should have stood up to her, but I failed."

I watched in astonishment as two jewel-like tears slid prettily down her perfect cheeks. She dabbed at them with a lace handkerchief and sniffed daintily.

"But I am determined to become a better person. Lucius said that pigs might fly but I can be quite stubborn and promise you that I will make an heroic effort to be more like you. More — ordinary."

I covered her shaking hand with mine and held it for a moment and then obviously overcome, she snatched up the book Eleanor was reading to me, "I know! I will come every day and read to you! It will be my *punishment!*"

My eyes met Eleanor's and hers were brimming with suppressed laughter.

* * *

I noticed particularly, as the nameless days drifted by, that nobody mentioned anything of importance. Nobody told me what had happened to Hester Jarrett or Aunt Louisa. I had no clue if Harry had been found or if I was to be arrested for being partly responsible for Baron Rosenberg's death.

Nobody mentioned Liam Cavanagh.

Eleanor sat beside me making lace on a little pillow; the rhythmical clack of the bobbins was a soothing lullaby, and I would sometimes fall asleep while she worked.

At some point the doctor came and pronounced me perfectly well, merely suffering from a bout of hysteria which would heal itself with time.

Anne Talbot and Meggie came and bustled about making tisanes and all manner of caudles.

But still nobody said anything.

Miles brought a chess set and carefully set it up to entertain me and then had to play both our parts until it was checkmate and I had won without lifting a finger.

Fanny washed and brushed my hair and braided it whilst gossiping about what was happening in the village, telling me amusing stories about an escaped cow and some stolen laundry.

One day I was holding Rebecca against my knees and she suddenly pulled herself up into a sitting position and reaching out, grabbed my hair and tugged it as hard as she could. I cried.

* * *

Then one day I heard a carriage arrive and a commotion downstairs. There were shouts and laughter and then thumping steps on the stairs and my door burst open to reveal Lady Sarah and Sir Aubrey Finch, still in their travelling clothes, looking a little dusty and dishevelled.

"What's this now, m'gal!" bellowed Sir Aubrey. "Lyin' abed in the afternoon! What? We're come to winkle you out into the daylight. No more slugabeds! No, t'won't do at all, will it my love?"

Lady Sarah, with a hatful of nodding ostrich plumes and a coat of pale blue velvet, was already kissing me and patting my hand. "No, indeed, Aubrey, we shall have her up and about in no time and get some colour blooming in those pale cheeks. What a to-do! We should have come sooner. I suspected something was amiss, I felt it in my bones. My bones never lie. But, still, here we are and now things will change."

I gazed happily from one to the other and cried. Sarah mopped my face with the end of her gauzy fichu and laughed. "There, there, dearest girl, we're here now and you'll soon be back to your old self. No more languishing in bed like a hopeless invalid! We've brought the clothes you left behind in Bristol, although you look too thin to fit them now!"

Sir Aubrey thundered downstairs to find himself some reviving brandy and I recalled fondly that he thundered everywhere, being an enthusiastic sort of fellow with rather large feet.

Sarah consulted with Eleanor and quickly went off to change and wash the travel dust away. Fanny brought a basin of water and washed my face and hands and then she and Eleanor unpacked the portmanteau of clothes and shook out the creases in a pretty pale grey gown with black braid and by the time Sarah came back, in stylish violet silk this time and a little white lace cap, I was sitting on the edge of my bed wearing proper clothes for the first time in many days.

"Ah, that's an improvement," said Sarah cheerfully, "We will soon have you up to snuff."

Snuff, I thought miserably and tried not to cry again without much success. Sarah gathered me to her bosom and rocked me like a baby. "Come, let us go downstairs and have some dinner together. I am famished! The food in the coaching inns is much improved but still not like homemade. I am longing for some good, boiled ham."

* * *

After this welcome invasion, I started to feel a bit more like myself, I talked a little and even laughed at Sir Aubrey and his boundless exuberance. Fanny and Eleanor had somehow rustled up a very worthy dinner and Sir Aubrey remarked particularly on the quality of the pastries which made Fanny blush with pleasure as they had been made by her own hands.

Still, somewhere in the darkest recesses of my mind, lived the memories I was determined to kill with neglect. But they were obdurate and refused to be banished. They came to me in the middle of the night and haunted me. They mocked me and my pathetic attempts to oust them. They were like sticky burrs and clung to me however vigorously I tried to shake them off. Wherever I went I felt their sharp little hooks digging into my flesh.

* * *

Lady Sarah and Sir Aubrey took me out in their carriage first for a short run along the coast road and then to Millbrook and Plymouth where they bought me a beautiful hat which Sarah spotted in the milliner's window. They talked to me about my plans for Amy and Rebecca and promised me financial support for my fledgling idea for a small village school for orphans.

Miles and Lucius were regular visitors and Rowena came even though I swore that I no longer needed reading to; she sat and listened to the conversations with her hands clasped tensely in her lap. She fetched and carried for me until I could bear it no longer and beckoned her to sit beside me.

I took her hand, "Rowena dear, I *forgive* you. Now please will you stop acting as though you have to be good for the rest of your life! It really doesn't suit you and I have no wish for you to be my personal dogsbody. I would much prefer it if you sat here and complained about how ill Lucius treats you."

To my relief she laughed and squeezed my hand. "Thank you, cousin, I must say I was finding it a great strain and hard to keep up."

"Good, well that's settled then. Now, tell me about your charming Lieutenant. Has he declared himself yet?"

*   *   *

The next time Miles and Lucius came I demanded to know what had happened to their mother and Hester Jarrett. They exchanged a glance and clumsily tried to evade the question.

"If you don't tell me at once I shall scream and throw things at your stupid heads," I threatened.

"Oh, all right, but it was agreed that we wouldn't trouble you with such things," said Miles, "Mother was arrested for kidnapping but has since been acquitted because, remarkably, kidnapping a child is, according to our ridiculous laws, not a felony. She apparently had nothing to do with the poisoning. She will, however, never live down the ignominy and I suspect may never leave the house again. Father, rather to our astonishment, has turned up trumps and seems to have gathered his wits enough to take charge of the situation, in his own muddled way. At least now there are no insurmountable debts for him to contend with. Hester Jarrett has been indicted for three murders, Aunt Vida and Nell Pezzack and the inadvertent shooting of Baron Rosenberg. She will be executed eventually I expect. I don't think they will even take into account that she was coerced into the first two murders by the Baron."

"And Harry?"

"Ah, yes, *dear* Harry. He has disappeared entirely. Absconded. Probably fled abroad. Cowardly to the last. He played a leading role in Rebecca's kidnap and I'm sorry to say also had a hand in the murder of Nell Pezzack and he was planning to be rid of you next. There are also suspicions that he may have been working with Rosenberg on behalf of France, which means he may have committed criminal acts of a traitorous nature. He would be a fool to come back to England any time soon. I shall miss his stupid face despite everything." Miles gave me a considering look, "Is there anything else you wish to know, Martha?"

I shook my head, "No, nothing else. Thank you for finally enlightening me. I feel better for knowing."

Lucius shrugged at his brother and they left it at that.

* * *

One afternoon at the end of January, the sun came out and gilded the water in the estuary, turning it into rippling cloth of gold. It stirred in me a memory which made me put down the book I had been reading and go to stand in the window, gazing out across the tiny harbour. The sky was kingfisher blue and strangely cloudless.

"What is it, dearest?", asked Eleanor, stopping her lace-making.

"I don't know really. I just feel — "

Lady Sarah stretched her arms above her head, "'Tis a beautiful day. Would you care to go for a drive in the carriage? You seem a little restless. I could fetch Aubrey and we could rattle along the coast while the weather still holds fair."

I sighed, "No, I think I shall just walk down to the water's edge. It seems to be calling me."

Sarah asked if she should accompany me, but I said I was happy to go alone and would not be long.

I threw on my cloak and stepped out into the cold sunshine.

* * *

There was a cormorant sitting on the mooring bollard at the end of the quay; it hooked its shining black wings and lazily took off. I watched it fly out over the estuary.

The sun was so bright on the water I had to squint my eyes a little so that I could see.

I was aware of a splashing noise and watched as a rowing boat made its way around the headland, the oars scattering brilliant gems as they lifted and dipped.

The boat pulled round into the harbour and nudged in against the wall. Someone jumped out and secured it and then turned back to help another passenger onto dry land. I shielded my eyes with my hand.

The sun glinted ferociously making my eyes water. The two figures stood at the end of the quay, dark against the dazzling light.

One tall and elegant, the other shorter and slightly bowed, leaning heavily on a cane.

I started to run.
"*Papa!*"

He held out his arms to me and I flew into them, nearly knocking him over. Sobbing and laughing. Stroking his wonderful face. He was crying too, his frail frame shaking. I looked into his kind eyes and saw the pain and suffering; I saw the effort it was taking for him just to stand upright.

"Come, let us go into the house, my own beloved Papa."

I glanced up at his companion and tried to smile but failed miserably. He stepped forward and helped my father, with great patience, slowly make his way across the emerald lawn to Wild Court.

* * *

Liam Cavanagh carefully guided my father into the morning room and made him comfortable in a chair beside the fire. After brief introductions, Eleanor sped to the kitchen to make refreshments and Lady Sarah tucked a woollen rug around my father's knees before tactfully making her excuses.

"You have quite a houseful, my dear," said my father and his voice was thin and wavering, not at all the firm but gentle voice I remembered. Seeing how much he'd aged in so short a time I couldn't imagine what he had been through, but I could see it etched in every line of his face.

"The Finches are here and of course, Eleanor, who has become my dearest companion. Fanny Goodall helps with — with Rebecca. We muddle along." I knelt beside him, his hands clasped in mine, "Where have you been all this time? We feared the worst."

"We have so much to talk about but I'm afraid I will have to leave it to Captain Cavanagh to explain for now, I am feeling a little weary. But I would not be alive today, if it had not been for him. I would have died in a French prison. Don't let him play down his part in my rescue either, there is no man I would rather have by my side in a fight."

A few moments later Eleanor came in with a laden tray for my father and his rescuer. The Captain moved the card table in front of the fire and Eleanor laid the hastily prepared food out for them with glasses of wine. I watched them settle and begin their meal and then Eleanor and I went to make beds.

We put my father in one of the spare rooms as I didn't feel he would want to sleep in the bedchamber he used to share with my mother. Eleanor said nothing when I suggested we make up a bed for Liam Cavanagh. "He's probably very tired after making the crossing. It's the least we can do," I said.

She nodded and together we quickly accomplished the task and then I returned to the morning room. They had finished their meal, neither eating very much. I could see my father's strength was fading.

"Papa, would you like to retire now? Your bed is ready. We can talk again tomorrow when you are rested."

He readily agreed and Liam Cavanagh helped lift him and together we half carried him up the stairs to his room. It took both of us to undress him and get him into a nightshirt, by which time he was already half-asleep.

The Captain went downstairs leaving me to tuck my father in. I kissed him on the forehead, "Goodnight Papa. I love you so much." He held on to my hand and I stayed for the few minutes it took for him to drift into an exhausted sleep, then tiptoed out and quietly closed the door.

I found Liam Cavanagh in the morning room, looking out of the window and it reminded me of another time when he had been in a different guise and I hardened my heart.

"We have prepared a bed for you, should you care to stay. I'm sure you must be worn out after all the travelling and worry."

"Thank you, that is kind of you. I will gladly accept your offer as I told Colquite to anchor the ship further around the headland, just in case the wind gets up and it's a little too far to Holmoak Beacon — "

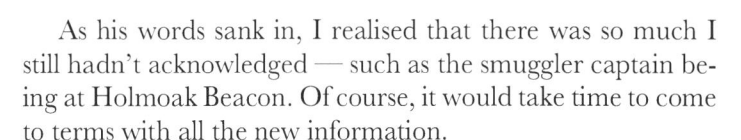

As his words sank in, I realised that there was so much I still hadn't acknowledged — such as the smuggler captain being at Holmoak Beacon. Of course, it would take time to come to terms with all the new information.

I sat down in the chair my father had just vacated and folded my hands neatly in my lap. "You were going to tell me how you rescued Papa." I sounded prim and remote even to my own ears.

He gave me a long look and I couldn't hold his gaze, I looked down at my hands.

"I'll spare you the details. We were given a small detachment, government sanctioned, with just one purpose, to see your father safely back to England. We constructed a plan involving a deal of diplomacy and we were given permission to use some ugly brute force if necessary. Diplomacy was necessary at first to find out what had actually happened to your father once Gilles had told us of his doubts. He heard rumours that your father had been removed to a notorious prison inland, having been captured while on a mission to estimate French military and naval strength and activities on the coast. We had to find out where he was being held and with diplomatic strategies get as close as we could to him before resorting to more violent methods. Gilles was very helpful in that department and, with some guile and patience, we closed in on our objective. This took some weeks and in the end was not enough. I won't bore you with the details, but brute force was eventually unavoidable and was followed by a night-time run for the coast and — as you can see, by the skin of our teeth, we survived. Of course, we first had to take your father to have an audience with Newcastle's aides, for he had pertinent information to share. Then, as soon as we could, we sailed for Plymouth." He sat down on the window seat and stretched out his booted legs. "I hardly need to tell you that your father has been through a terrible ordeal, he will need time to fully recover. He was extraordinarily brave. It obviously runs in the family."

I was staring hard at my hands, knotted so tightly, the knuckles white. "Thank you," I said simply. "It means everything to me."

"I'd do it again tomorrow — if you asked."

I said nothing.

"By the bye, I know you will be happy to hear that Letitia Tregallas is safely with her sister and her seven nieces in York and your friend Patience is recovering in a Quaker retreat — when she is finally well enough her husband wishes her to return to him. Squire Tregallas has been arrested for his part in the wrecking — in which he was the leading light and due to Harry's very comprehensive confession he has also been found guilty of helping Hester Jarrett with the poisoning of Nell Pezzack and blackmailing your aunt."

I nodded, not trusting my voice.

He gave me a dark glance, "I wasn't able to tell you that I was afraid your father believed Rebecca was my child — as did you, for a while. We were such good friends, it was hard to endure — knowing that he still believed that and not being able to disabuse him. He now knows the truth and has come to terms in his way, with the tragic consequences."

"I see. Is that why he left us without explanation?"

"I believe so. I blamed myself."

He stood up again and took a step towards me, "Martha —"

I jumped to my feet, "No — I — I am very tired. I shall go upstairs now. Thank you again, Captain Cavanagh," and I dashed out of the room.

* * *

Once safely in my bedchamber, I threw myself on my bed and wept. I cried for my father's return, for my mother's reckless nature, for the joy of having Rebecca in my life but mainly for myself because I knew I was being stubborn and childish. There was such a hollow ache deep inside that I feared could never be assuaged, a longing for someone who was now lost to me forever. I could only look forward to a lifetime of regret and emptiness.

Eleanor came quietly into the room. I felt the bed give as she sat down beside me. She gently stroked my back and let me cry.

Gradually, the hiccoughing sobs lessened, and I drew a shuddering breath. After a while I was able to sit up and Eleanor held on to my hand, anchoring me.

"I cannot advise you in this, Martha. I have made some very odd choices myself, as you know. I am in no position to tell you how to live your life but — I will say that in order to find my happiness I had to learn to forgive. Lucius is a far from perfect human being and I have no doubt that he will run me ragged in the future. I just know I'd rather be with him than without him. He has proposed, by the bye."

I sniffled, "Oh, Eleanor! That is wonderful! *Is* it wonderful? Did you accept?"

A beatific smile lit up her face, "Of course. We will marry in the summer. I want you to be as happy as I am, Martha."

"I don't know *how*!" I wailed.

"Yes, you do. Stop punishing yourself and him - it's utterly nonsensical." She got up, kissed my cheek and declared that I finally had a chance to sort everything out and that she was going to bed.

I sat on the edge of my bed, fully dressed, thinking about what she had said.

* * *

I was still sitting there half an hour later when I heard tired footsteps on the stairs. I tensed as they came past my door. They paused. I held my breath. He moved away, along the corridor.

I waited for my heart to stop skipping beats and then removed my shoes and stockings and tiptoed barefoot along the corridor, past Eleanor's and Sarah and Aubrey's rooms and up the second staircase to his bedchamber.

I took a deep breath and entered without knocking. The room was lit by a few candles and the red glow from the fire. He was sitting sprawled in a chair beside the hearth, in just shirt and breeches, his long legs stretched out in front of him, his chin sunk into his cravat. I stood with my back to the door, uncertain and afraid.

* * *

Rain was rattling hard against the windowpanes like gravel being thrown and the wind was whistling in the eaves. It felt like we were in a ship at sea.

"What is it Martha?", he asked softly, not looking up.

"I wanted to ask you something."

"I'm listening."

I stayed by the door.

"The little ink portrait of my mother — I saw it — in your notebook — "

He slowly stood up and turned to face me, "Ah, my notebook. I wondered. You seemed so *very* agitated." A crooked smile twisted the corner of his mouth, "The portrait? You didn't recognise it. It was of you. The night I found you on the beach."

"*Me?* But it was of — "

"A beautiful woman. You."

I felt the colour creeping up my neck and into my face. I put my hands up to cover it.

"You looked like a stranded mermaid. I've never seen anything so lovely — or so cross." He moved a little closer. "Jeckie thinks you're a goddess." He raised an eyebrow, "I have to agree with him - hence the gown."

"It was too beautiful — it made me feel invulnerable. *And* you paid off the Polgrey debts! I fear you must be a little mad."

"Possibly."

"Are you *very* rich?"

"Very."

"And somehow you found me in that awful place. I had given up hope, I think."

"I *never* gave up hope. I was going to find you, come what may or die trying. Those were bleak days. When we finally found you and you were — thank God, alive — " He rubbed a hand over his eyes. "I think — Jeckie may have cried a little. He was quite ferocious with his dagger, threatening to gut the proprietor like a fish! Colquite and Riordan were there too, brandishing pistols — they seem oddly devoted to you. And then, afterwards, at the inn — I was just so relieved that you were safe — I may have overstepped — in hindsight I realise I should probably have provided a female companion for you but I'm afraid I wasn't thinking clearly — in the heat of the moment." He shot me a fathomless glance, "Although — I don't believe you objected to your inexperienced handmaiden *too* much."

The damned blush flamed again but I looked him directly in the eye. "If you recall, sir, I was a trifle unhinged at the time and therefore not accountable for my actions."

He chuckled, "If you say so."

"And what about that dreadful Mary Yates — ?"

His lips thinned slightly, "She was nothing to me. When I realised you had shot her — I could only think of how to keep you from being arrested, had she inconveniently died."

"I thought you were overly concerned with her well-being. It was exasperating."

"Was it? I wonder why?" That eyebrow again.

"Possibly because she tried to kill Solomon," I snapped.

His eyes narrowed, "Is that so? Nothing else?"

"No," I said, without much conviction, "I really didn't like you very much."

"Ah — and there we have it. The crux of the matter. Your affections were engaged elsewhere, no?"

"I'm sure I have no idea what you mean."

A little closer, "I think you do — Linnet," he murmured.

Tears started to my eyes and I turned away to face the door, leaning my forehead on it, "No, *please* — don't! I cannot bear it."

His shirt sleeve grazed my gown, but he didn't touch me.

"But he and I are one and the same," he said.

"I miss him so!"

"Confound it, Linnet, I am here and always will be," he said without the brogue and in Sir Montagu's soft, elegant tones.

I shuddered with longing and he moved so close I could feel the heat from his body. He put a hand on either side of me, against the door, trapping me. I turned to face him, within the circle of his arms, looking up into the shadowed eyes above me and bit my lip.

"Linnet." he whispered huskily.

I put my arms about his waist and pulled him towards me.

"This is not at all sensible, Miss Pentreath."

"I don't care." I buried my face in his neck. "Sandalwood." I said, with a shaky sigh.

"Ah, yes, I had not thought of that. A sandalwood clothes press. An unfortunate oversight."

"I found it very confusing. And also, when you accidentally mentioned my being unwell on the boat — " I tipped my head back and pulled him even closer, pressing myself against his hips.

He let out a low groan and suddenly he was lifting me and holding me up against the door and his mouth was on mine and I'd wrapped my arms about his neck, and I could barely breathe for sheer ridiculous happiness. His lips were travelling down my neck, making me shiver and then I was wriggling to be free. He released me immediately and stepped away, his breathing ragged.

I grinned up at him and turned my back. "My skirts! Undo them, at once."

He took another step away from me.

I frowned over my shoulder. "Where are you going?"

"No, I will not allow it. You're not thinkin' clearly. Keep away from me."

I pouted coquettishly and began to undo the ties on my skirts.

"Don't, Linnet. Egad. Stop. You don't know what you're doin'."

"Sir Montagu, I can assure you, I know *exactly* what I'm doing. I must admit I had no idea you were such a Puritan."

"And I had no idea you were such a wanton, madam! To think I was going to ask your father for your hand tomorrow."

I stopped.

"My hand!"

"Of course. How can you doubt it? 'Tis very clear that I must make an honest woman of you before it's entirely too late to redeem you."

"But you haven't asked *me!*"

He laughed, "I have the utmost confidence in your answer, m'dear. After the Masquerade, I had no doubt about the warmth of your — er — feelings."

"Oh, that's most unchivalrous of you to mention it. I was wearing that gown. I was in disguise."

"My love, I would recognise you anywhere."

"*What* did you call me?"

"My love. I love you to distraction, y'know. Have since the first moment I saw you at The Manor looking so frightened yet determined not to show it."

"Oh, well, in that case, sir, I *will* marry you, but I feel obliged to warn you that I am only marrying you for your library."

His eyes darkened dangerously, and he pulled me against him. My skirts slid unnoticed to the floor.

"Oh, by Jupiter! I'll be Lady Fitzroy! How delightfully absurd!"

He pressed his lips hard against mine to stop me talking, his long fingers unlacing my bodice and deftly removing my shift.

"Aunt Louisa is going to be absolutely *furious!*"

Historical Romance
by Caroline Elkington

Set in the years shown

A Very Civil War (1645)
Dark Lantern (1755)
The House on the Hill (1765)
Three Sisters (1772)
The Widow (1782)
Out of the Shadows (1792)

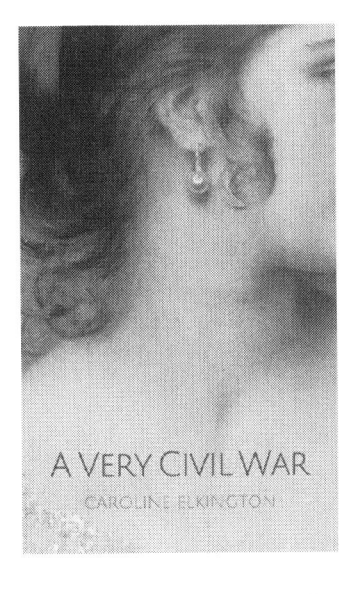

A VERY CIVIL WAR
1645

Con's life in the small Cotswold village, where she spent an idyllic childhood, is nothing out of the ordinary, which is good because she likes ordinary. She likes safe.

Her three boisterous nephews have come to stay for the summer holidays, and she's determined to show them that life in the countryside can be fun — she has no idea just how exciting it's about to get.

Whilst out exploring with them in the fields near the village, they find themselves face to face with a Roundhead colonel from the English Civil Wars and, due to some glitching twenty-first century technology, Con is transported back to 1645 and into a world she only recognises from books and historical dramas on television and finds hard to understand. She reluctantly falls for the gruff officer, who is recovering from injuries sustained in recent hostilities with Royalists but must battle archaic attitudes and unexpected violence in order to survive.

With no way of getting back to her family and her nice secure real life and unable to reveal who she really is, for fear of being thought a witch, she struggles to acclimatise to her new life and must fight her growing feelings for Colonel Sir Lucas Deverell and deal with the daily problems of life in the seventeenth century and the encroaching war. When she intervenes to save a dying man, suspicions are raised and she begins to fear for her life, with enemies on all sides.

Constance Harcourt discovers a love that crosses centuries and all barriers, but which could potentially end in heartbreak. Can the power of True Love overcome the power of the Universe?

This is a time-slip story filled with passionate romance, the very real threat of persecution and war, the charm of the Cotswolds and touches of Beauty and the Beast.

Dark Lantern
1755

An unexpected funeral, a new life with unwelcoming relations and a mysterious stranger who is destined to change her life forever. Martha Pentreath has been thrust into a bewildering and perilous adventure.

Set in 1755, on the wild coast between Cornwall and Devon, this swashbuckling tale of high society and secretive seafarers follows Martha as she valiantly juggles her conflicting roles, one moment hard at work in the kitchens of Polgrey Hall and the next elbow to elbow with the local gentry.

Then as dragoons scour the coast for smugglers, she finds herself beholden to the captain of a lugger tellingly built for speed. Unsure whom to trust, Martha soon realises that everything she thought she knew was a lie and people are not what they seem.

With undercurrents of The Scarlet Pimpernel, Cinderella and Jamaica Inn, this is a story of windswept cliffs, wreckers, betrayal, secrets, murder and passionate romance.

Martha fights back against those who would relish her downfall and discovers the shocking truth about her own family. But she will find loyalty and friendship and a love that will surprise her but also bring her heartache.

THE HOUSE on the HILL
1765

After falling on hard times due to a family scandal, Henrietta Swift lives with her grandfather in a dilapidated farmhouse and is quite content to live without luxury or even basic comforts.

However, she's being watched.

Someone has plans for her and despite suffering misgivings she has no real choice but to accept their surprising proposition in order to give her beloved grandfather a better life.

It leads her to Galdre Knap, a darkly mysterious house, where her enigmatic employer, Torquhil Guivre, requires a companion for his seriously ill sister, Eirwen, who is being brought home to convalesce.

With her habitual optimism, Henrietta believes all will be well — until the other-worldly Eirwen arrives in a snowstorm. The house then begins to reveal its long-buried secrets and Henrietta must battle to save those she loves from the sinister forces that threaten their safety and her happiness.

In the process, she unexpectedly finds true love and discovers that the world is filled with real magic and that she is capable of far more than she ever thought possible.

Here be Dragons and Enchantment and Happy Ever Afters.

Three Sisters
1772

The prim and proper Augusta Pennington has taken over the management of a failing Ladies' Seminary with her two sisters, grumpy Flora and wild Pandora. Their elderly aunts, Ida and Euphemia Beauchamp, can no longer run the school and have been forced to hand over the reins. They are losing pupils, as they lag the fashions in female education, and are struggling financially.

Their scandalous and irascible neighbour, Sir Marcus Denby, is reluctantly drawn into their ventures by the younger sister, Pandora, who tumbles from one scrape into another, without any concern for her safety or her family's reputation.

With the help of Quince, a delinquent hound, Pandora befriends Sir Marcus's estranged daughter, Imogen, who has been much neglected by her beautiful but venomous mother.

Augusta, initially repelled by Sir Marcus's notoriety, tries desperately to resist the growing attraction between them. It takes a series of mishaps and the arrival of some unwanted guests to finally make Augusta understand that not everything is as it seems and love really can conquer all.

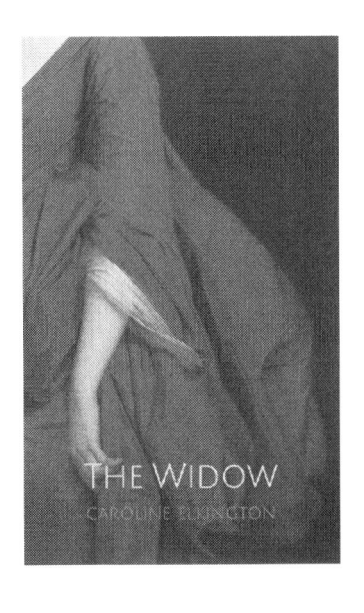

THE WIDOW
1782

Nathaniel Heywood arrived at Winterborne Place with no intention of remaining there for longer than it took to conclude a business proposition on behalf of his impulsive friend Emery Talmarch.

Impecunious, cynical and world-weary, he is reluctant to shoulder any kind of responsibility. Nathaniel was just looking for an easy way to make some money to save Emery from debtor's prison and possibly worse. He had no idea that he would be offered such an outrageous proposal by his host, Lord Winterborne, and find himself swiftly drawn into a web of intrigue and danger. He wants nothing more than to escape and be trouble-free again.

Above anything else he wanted his freedom.

And then he meets Grace.

OUT of the SHADOWS
1792

In this deeply romantic thriller, an inebriated and perhaps foolhardy visit to London's Bartholomew Fair begins with an eye to some light-hearted entertainment and ends with a tragic accident.

Theo Rokewode and his close friends find themselves unexpectedly encumbered with two young girls in desperate need of rescue. As a result, their usually ordered lives are turned upside down as danger stalks the girls into the hallowed halls of refined Georgian London and beyond to Rokewode Abbey in Gloucestershire.

Sephie and Biddy are hugely relieved to be rescued from the brutal life they had been forced to endure but know that they are still not truly safe. Only they know what could be coming and as Sephie loses her heart to Theo, she dreads the truth about her past being revealed and determines to somehow repay her new-found friends for their gallantry and unquestioning hospitality, but vows to leave before the man she loves so desperately sees her for what she really is.

Her carefully laid plans bring both delight and disaster as her past finally catches up with her and mayhem ensues, as Theo, his eccentric friends and family valiantly attempt to put the lid back on the Pandora's Box they'd unwittingly opened that fateful night at the fair.

About Caroline Elkington

When not writing novels, Caroline's reading them - every few days a knock on the door brings more. She has always preferred the feel — and smell — of a real book.

She began reading out of boredom as she was tucked up in bed by her mother, herself an avid reader, at a ridiculously early hour.

In the winter months she read by moving her book sideways back and forth to catch a slither of light that shone through the crack between the hinges of her bedroom door.

Fast forward sixty years and she's someone who knows what she wants from a book: to be immersed in history (preferably Georgian), to be captivated by a romantic hero, to be thrilled by the story, and to feel uplifted at the end.

After a long career that began with fashion design and morphed into painting ornately costumed portraits and teaching art, she has a strong eye for the kind of detail that draws the reader into a scene.

Review This Novel and See More by Caroline

Point your phone's camera at the code.
A banner will appear on your screen.
Tap it to see Caroline's novels on Amazon.

Printed in Great Britain
by Amazon